ARCTIC DRIFT

ARCTIC DRIFT

CLIVE CUSSLER
AND
DIRK CUSSLER

WHEELER
WINDSOR
PARAGON

This Large Print edition is published by Thorndike Press, Waterville, Maine USA and by BBC Audiobooks Ltd, Bath, England

Copyright © 2008 by Sandecker, RLLLP.

The moral right of the author has been asserted.

Maps and illustrations by Roland Dahlquist.

Thorndike Press, a part of Gale, Cengage Learning.

Thorndike Press® Large Print Biography.

The text of this Large Print edition is unabridged.

Other aspects of the book may vary from the original edition.

Set in 16 pt. Plantin.

Printed on permanent paper.

LIBRARY OF CONGRESS CATALOGING-IN-PUBLICATION DATA

Cussler, Clive.
    Artic drift / by Clive Cussler and Dirk Cussler.
     p. cm.
    ISBN-13: 978-1-59722-875-6 (hardcover : alk. paper)
    ISBN-10: 1-59722-875-3 (hardcover : alk. paper)
    1. Pitt, Dirk (Fictitious character) — Fiction. 2. Marine biologists
    — Fiction. 3. Global warming — Fiction. 4. Northwest Passage
    — Fiction. 5. Arctic regions — Fiction. 6. Large type books.
    I. Cussler, Dirk. II. Title.
    PS3553.U75A89 2008
    813'.54—dc22

BRITISH LIBRARY CATALOGUING-IN-PUBLICATION DATA AVAILABLE

Published in the U.S. in 2008 by arrangement with G. P. Putnam's Sons, a member of Penguin Group (USA) Inc.

Published in the U.K. in 2009 by arrangement with Penguin Books Ltd.

U.K. Hardcover: 978 1 408 42839 9 (Windsor Large Print)

U.K. Softcover: 978 1 408 42840 5 (Paragon Large Print)

Printed in the United States of America
1 2 3 4 5 6 7 12 11 10 09 08

In memory of Leigh Hunt.

And yes, there really was a Leigh Hunt.

A dear friend, bon vivant, wit, and madcap
Don Juan who had a way with women
that made him the envy of every man in town.

I killed him off in the prologues of ten Dirk
Pitt books. He always wanted to play a bigger
role in the stories but didn't complain because
he enjoyed the fame.

So long, old pal, you are sorely missed.

■ ■ ■ ■

PROLOGUE
PASSAGE TO DEATH

■ ■ ■ ■

ABANDONING THE SHIPS

APRIL 1848
VICTORIA STRAIT
THE ARCTIC OCEAN

The cry rattled through the ship like the howl of a wounded jungle beast, a mournful wail that sounded like a plea for death. The moan incited a second voice, and then a third, until a ghoulish chorus echoed through the darkness. When the morbid cries ran their course, a few moments of uneasy silence prevailed until the tortured soul initiated the sequence again. A few sequestered crewmen, those with their senses still intact, listened to the sounds while praying that their own death would arrive more easily.

In his cabin, Commander James Fitzjames listened as he squeezed a clump of silver rock in his hand. Holding the cold shiny mineral to his eye, he swore at its luster. Whatever the composite was, it seemed to have cursed his ship. Even before it had been brought aboard, the mineral carried with it an essence of death. Two crewmen in a whaleboat had fallen overboard while transporting the first sample rocks, quickly freezing to death in the icy Arctic waters. Another sailor had died in a knife fight, after trying to barter some of the rocks for tobacco with a demented carpenter's mate. Now in the last few weeks, more than half his crew had gone slowly and inexorably mad. The winter confinement was no doubt to blame, he mused, but the rocks somehow played a role as well.

His thoughts were interrupted by a harsh banging on the cabin door. Conserving the energy needed to stand and answer, he simply responded with a raspy, "Yes?"

The door swung open to reveal a short man in a soiled sweater, his ruddy face lean and dirty.

"Cap'n, one or two of 'em are trying to breach the barricade again," the ship's quartermaster stated in a thick Scottish accent.

"Call Lieutenant Fairholme," Fitzjames replied, rising slowly to his feet. "Have him assemble the men."

Fitzjames tossed the rock onto his bunk and followed the quartermaster out the door. They stepped down a dark and musty passageway, illuminated by a few small candle lanterns. Passing the main hatchway, the quartermaster disappeared as Fitzjames continued forward. He soon stopped at the base of a tall pile of debris that blocked his path. A mass of barrels, crates, and casks had been strategically wedged into the passageway, piled to the overhead deck and creating a temporary barricade to the forward compartments. Somewhere on the opposite side of the mound, the sound of shifting crates and human grunts resonated through the mass.

"They're at it again, sir," spoke a sleepy-eyed marine who stood watch over the pile with a Brown Bess musket. Barely nineteen, the guard had a dirty growth of beard that sprouted off his jaw like a patch of briar.

"We'll be leaving the ship to them soon enough," Fitzjames replied in a tired voice.

Behind them a wooden ladder creaked as three men climbed up the main hatchway from the orlop deck below. A cold blast of frigid air surged through the passageway until one of the men tugged a canvas hatch cover in place, sealing it shut. A gaunt man in a heavy wool officer's jacket emerged from the shadows and addressed Fitzjames.

"Sir, the arms locker is still secure," Lieutenant Fairholme reported, a frozen cloud of vapor rising from his mouth as he spoke. "Quartermaster McDonald is assembling the men in the officers' Great Cabin." Holding up a small percussion-cap pistol, he added, "We retrieved three weapons for ourselves."

Fitzjames nodded as he surveyed the other two men, haggard-looking Royal Marines

11

who each clutched a musket.

"Thank you, Lieutenant. There shall be no firing except by direct order," the commander said quietly.

A shrill cry erupted from behind the barrier, followed by a loud clanging of pots and pans. The sounds were becoming more manic, Fitzjames thought. Whatever abominations were taking place on the other side of the barricade, he could only imagine.

"They're turning increasingly violent," the lieutenant said in a hushed tone.

Fitzjames nodded grimly. Subduing a crew gone mad was a prospect he could never have imagined when he first signed on for the Arctic Discovery Service. A bright and affable man, he had quickly risen through the ranks of the Royal Navy, attaining command of a sloop of war by age thirty. Now thirty-six and in a fight for survival, the officer once referred to as "the best-looking man in the Navy" faced his toughest ordeal.

Perhaps it was no surprise that part of the crew had become deranged. Surviving an Arctic winter aboard an icebound ship was a frightful challenge. Bound for months in darkness and unrelenting cold, the men were trapped in the cramped confines of the ship's lower deck. There they battled rats, claustrophobia, and isolation, in addition to the physical ravages of scurvy and frostbite. Passing a single winter was difficult enough, but

Fitzjames's crew was coming off a third consecutive Arctic winter, their ills compounded by short rations of food and fuel. The death of their expedition leader, Sir John Franklin, earlier only added to the fading sense of optimism.

Yet Fitzjames knew there was something more sinister at work. When a bosun's mate tore off his clothes, climbed topside, and ran screaming across the ice floes, it could have been marked down as a single case of dementia. But when three-fourths of the crew began yelling in their sleep, staggering around listlessly, mumbling in confused speech patterns, and hallucinating, there was clearly something else at play. When the behaviors gradually turned violent, Fitzjames had the afflicted quietly moved to the forward deck and sequestered.

"It's something on the ship driving them mad," Fairholme said quietly, as if reading Fitzjames's mind.

Fitzjames started to nod in reply when a small crate came hurtling off the upper reaches of the barrier, nearly striking him in the head. The pale face of an emaciated man burst through the opening, his eyes glowing red under the flickering candlelight. He quickly squeezed himself through the opening and then tumbled down the face of the barrier. As the man staggered to his feet, Fitzjames recognized him as one of the stokers for the ship's coal-fired steam engine. The stoker was shirtless despite the freezing temperatures inside the ship, and in his hand he wielded a heavy butcher knife taken from the ship's galley.

"Where be the lambs for slaughter?" he cried, holding up the knife.

Before he could start slashing, one of the Royal Marines countered with a musket stock, striking the stoker on the side of the face. The knife clanged against a crate as the man crumpled to the deck, a trickle of blood running down his face.

Fitzjames turned from the unconscious stoker to the crewmen around him. Tired, haggard, and gaunt from an inadequate diet, they all looked to him for direction.

"We abandon ship at once. There is still more than an hour of daylight left. We will make for the *Terror*. Lieutenant, bring the cold-weather gear up to the Great Cabin."

"How many sledges shall I prepare?"

"None. Pack what provisions each man can carry but no extra equipment."

"Yes, sir," Fairholme replied, taking two men with him and disappearing down the main hatch. Buried in the ship's hold were the parkas, boots, and gloves worn by the crew when working on deck or while exploring away from the ship on sledging parties. Fairholme and his men quickly hauled up sets of foul-weather gear and dragged them to the

14

large officers' lounge at the stern of the ship.

Fitzjames made his way to his stateroom, retrieving a compass, a gold watch, and some letters written to his family. He opened the ship's log to the last entry and wrote a final notation in a shaky hand, then squeezed his eyes shut in defeat as he closed the leather-bound book. Tradition would dictate that he take the logbook with him, but instead he locked it in his desk atop a portfolio of daguerreotypes.

Eleven crewmen, the sane remnants of the ship's original complement of sixty-eight men, were waiting for him in the Great Cabin. The captain slipped into a parka and boots alongside his crew, then led them up the main hatchway. Shoving aside the top hatch, they climbed onto the main deck and into the elements. It was like stepping through the gates of a frozen hell.

From the dark, dank interior of the ship, they entered a blistering world of bone white. Howling winds hurled a trillion specks of crystalline ice at the men, peppering their bodies with the force of a hundred-degrees-below-zero windchill. The sky could not be distinguished from the ground, nor up from down, in the dizzying vortex of white. Fighting the gusts, Fitzjames felt his way across the snowbound deck and down a stepladder to the frozen ice pack below.

Unseen a half mile away, the expedition's sister ship, HMS *Terror,* sat locked in the same

15

ice sheet. But the relentless winds reduced visibility to just a few yards. If they should miss locating the *Terror* in the ravaging winds, they would wander around the ice pack and die. Wooden marker posts had been planted every hundred feet between the two ships for just such a contingency, but the blinding conditions made finding the next marker post a deadly challenge.

Fitzjames pulled out his compass and took a bearing at twelve degrees, which he knew to be the direction of the *Terror:* The sister ship was actually due east of his position, but her nearness to the magnetic north pole produced a deviated compass reading. Silently praying that the ice pack had not materially moved since the last bearings were taken, he hunched over the compass and began trudging across the ice in the targeted direction. A rope line was passed back to all the crewmen, and the party proceeded across the ice field like a giant centipede.

The young commander shuffled along, head down and eyes glued to the compass, as the frigid wind and blowing snow stung his face. Counting a hundred paces, he stopped and peered about. With an initial sense of relief, he spotted the first marker post through the cottony swirls. Moving alongside the post, he took another bearing and proceeded to the next marker. The string of men leapfrogged from marker to marker, clambering over uneven mounds of snow that often rose thirty or forty feet high. Fitzjames focused all his energy on the journey, shaking off the disappointment of abandoning his ship to a contingent of madmen. Deep down, he knew it was a matter of survival. After three years in the Arctic, nothing else now mattered.

Then a deep boom shook his hopes. The sound was deafening, even over the howling winds. It sounded like the report of a large cannon, but the captain knew better. It was the ice beneath his feet, layered in massive sheets that moved in a rhythmic cycle of contraction and expansion.

Since the two expedition ships had become trapped in the ice in September 1846, they had been propelled over twenty miles, pushed by the massive blanket of ice called the Beaufort ice stream. An unusually frigid summer kept them icebound through 1847, while the current year's spring thaw had materialized only briefly. The ravages of another cold spell again made it doubtful that the ships would break free over the coming summer. In the meantime, a shift in the ice could be fatal, crushing a stout wooden ship like it was a box of matches. In another sixty-seven years, Ernest Shackleton would watch helplessly as his ship the *Endurance* was crushed by an expanding ice pack in the Antarctic.

With his heart racing, Fitzjames increased his pace as another thunderous crack echoed in the distance. The rope in his hands grew taut as the men behind struggled to keep up, but he refused to slow. Reaching what he knew was the last marker pole, he squinted into the tempest. Through the blasting swirls of white, he caught a brief glimpse of a dark object ahead.

"She's just before us," he shouted to the men behind him. "Step lively, we're nearly there."

Moving as one, the group surged toward the target. Climbing over a rugged mound of ice, they at last saw the *Terror* before them. At one hundred and two feet, the vessel was nearly identical in size and appearance to their own ship, down to the black-painted hull with a wide gold band. The *Terror* barely resembled a ship now, however, with its sails and yardarms stowed away, and a large canvas awning covering her stern deck. Snow had been shoveled up in mounds nearly to the rails for insulation, while the mast and rigging were coated in a thick layer of ice. The stout bomb ship, as she was originally designated, now looked more like a giant spilt carton of milk.

Fitzjames boarded the ship, where he was surprised to see several crewmen scurrying about the ice-covered deck. A midshipman approached and led Fitzjames and his men down the main hatch and into the galley. A steward passed around shots of brandy while the men shook the ice from their clothes and warmed their hands by the cookstove. Savoring the liquor as it warmed his belly, the captain noticed a beehive of activity in the dim confines, with crewmen shouting and shoving stores about the main passageway. Like his own men, the crew of the *Terror* were frightful souls to look at. Pallid and emaciated, most of the men fought the advanced ravages of scurvy. Fitzjames had already lost two of his own teeth to the disease, a vitamin C deficiency that causes spongy gums and bleeding scalp. Though casks of lemon juice had been carried aboard and rationed regularly to all the crew, the juice had lost its efficacy over time. Combined with a shortage of fresh meat, the disease had left no man untouched. And as the sailors all knew, left unchecked, scurvy could eventually prove fatal.

The captain of the *Terror* presently appeared, a tough Irishman named Francis Crozier. An Arctic veteran, Crozier had spent the better part of his life at sea. Like many before him, he had been drawn to the search for a passage between the Atlantic and the Pacific through the unexplored regions of the Arctic. The discovery of the Northwest Passage was perhaps the last great feat of seaborne exploration left to conquer. Dozens had tried and failed, but this expedition was different. Armed with two Arctic-ready ships under the command of an enigmatic leader in Sir John Franklin, success had been all but guaranteed. But Franklin had died the year before, after attempting a dash for the North American coastline too late in the summer. Unprotected in the open sea, the ships became trapped when the ice closed in around them. The strong-willed Crozier was determined to lead his remaining men to safety and salvage glory from the failure that was lying before them.

"You've abandoned the *Erebus*?" he asked Fitzjames pointedly.

The younger captain nodded in reply. "The remaining crew members have gone out of their heads."

"I received your earlier message detailing the troubles. Most peculiar. I've had one or two men lose their wits for a time but have not experienced such a mass breakdown."

"It is damned perplexing," Fitzjames replied with obvious discomfort. "I am just thankful to be off that lunatic asylum."

"They are dead men now," Crozier muttered. "And we might be as well, soon enough."

"The pack ice. It's fracturing."

Crozier nodded. Pressure points in the ice pack ruptured frequently from the underlying movements. Though most of the fracturing occurred in the fall and early winter as the open seas initially froze, the spring pack was also witness to dangerous thaws and convulsions.

"The hull timbers are groaning in protest," Crozier said. "It's right upon us, I'm afraid. I've ordered the bulk of our food stores moved onto the ice and the remaining boats put off. Looks like we are destined to give up both ships earlier than planned," he added with dread. "I just pray the storm blows out before we have to vacate in earnest."

After sharing a measured meal of tinned mutton and parsnips, Fitzjames and his men joined the *Terror*'s crew in offloading provisions onto the ice pack. The thunderous convulsions seemed to lessen in frequency, though they still bellowed over the blasting winds. Inside the *Terror,* the men listened to the unnerving creaks and groans of the ship's wooden timbers straining against the shifting ice. When the last of the crates was placed on the ice, the men huddled in the murky interior and waited for nature to deal its hand.

For forty-eight hours, they anxiously listened to the fickle ice, praying that the ship would be spared. But it was not to be. The deathblow came quickly, striking with a sudden rupture that came without warning. The stout ship was pitched up and onto its side before a section of its hull burst like a balloon. Only two men were injured, but the destruction was beyond any hope of repair. In an instant, the *Terror* had been consigned to a watery grave, only the date of her interment left to be settled.

Crozier evacuated the crew and loaded provisions into three of the remaining lifeboats, each affixed with runners to help navigate the ice. With foresight, Crozier and Fitzjames had already hauled several boats topped with provisions to the nearest landfall during the past nine months. The cache on King William Land would be a welcome asset to the homeless crew. But thirty miles of rugged ice separated the weary crew from land and the stockpile.

"We could retake the *Erebus,*" Fitzjames suggested, peering at the masts of his former ship rising above the jagged crests of white.

"The men are too spent to fight each other and the elements," Crozier replied. "She'll either find her way to the bottom like the *Terror* or spend another wretched summer icebound, I have no doubt."

"God have mercy on their souls," Fitzjames muttered under his breath as he took a final gaze at the distant vessel.

With teams of eight men harnessed to the heavy lifeboats like mules to a plow, they trudged over the uneven ice floe toward land. Mercifully, the winds settled, while the temperature climbed to near zero. But the exertions required of the starved and frozen crewmen began to break the body and the spirit of every man.

Tugging and shoving the burdensome loads, they reached the pebble-strewn island after five torturous days. King William Land, known today as King William Island, could hardly have been a less hospitable place. A low, windswept landmass the size of Connecticut, its ecosystem supported a bare minimum of plant and animal life. Even the indigenous Inuit avoided the island, recognizing it as a poor hunting ground for the food staples of caribou and seal.

None of this was known by Crozier and his men. Only their own exploratory sledge parties would have told them that the land was even an island, disputing the common geographic belief of 1845 that it was a finger of the North American continent. Crozier likely knew that, and one other thing. From where he stood on the northwest tip of King William Land, he recognized that he was nearly a thousand miles from the nearest civilization. A meager Hudson's Bay Company trading settlement located far to the south on the banks of the Great Fish River offered the best hope of rescue. But open water between the southern tip of King William Land and the mouth of that river, some one hundred and fifty miles away, meant that they had to keep dragging the cursed boats with them across the ice.

Crozier rested the crew a few days at the stockpile, allowing a temporary reward of full rations to boost their strength for the arduous journey ahead. Then he could wait no longer. Every day would count in the race to the Hudson Bay settlement before the autumn snows began to fall. The seasoned captain had no illusions that the full crew could make it that far or anywhere close. But with luck, a few of the heartiest men might make it in time to send a relief party to the others. It was their only chance.

Once again hauling the boats foot by foot, they found the shoreline ice less imposing. But the bitter reality quickly set in that they were on a death march. The physical rigors of unending exertion in the biting cold were too much for the malnurished body to bear. The worst agony, perhaps more than frostbite, was the sense of unquenchable thirst. Since their portable gas stoves mostly depleted of fuel, there was no efficient way to produce fresh water from the ice. Men desperately stuffed snow in their mouths to melt a few drops, then shivered with cold. Like a caravan crossing the Sahara, they fought the vestiges of dehydration along with the other ailments. Day by day and one by one, men began to wither and die as the contingent marched south. Shallow graves were dug at first, but then the dead were left on the ice as all energy was conserved for the migration.

Cresting a small snow-covered ridge, Fitzjames held up his hand and stopped in his tracks. Two sledge crews of eight men apiece staggered to a halt behind him, letting loose the harness ropes attached to a wood-planked pinnace. The heavy wooden boat, packed with food and gear, weighed over two thousand pounds. Transporting it was like dragging a rhinoceros across the ice. All of the men fell to their knees to rest, sucking deep breaths of icy air into their starved lungs.

The sky was clear, showering the landscape with bright sunlight that reflected off the snow in a blinding dazzle. Fitzjames slipped off a pair of wire-mesh snow goggles and walked from man to man, offering words of encouragement while checking their extremities for frostbite. He was nearly through the second crew when one of the men shouted.

"Sir, it's the *Erebus*! She's free of the ice pack."

Fitzjames turned to see one of the seamen pointing toward the horizon. The man, a yeoman's mate, slipped out of his harness and began scampering toward the shoreline and onto the ice pack.

"Strickland! Stand where you are!" Fitzjames ordered.

But the command fell on deaf ears. The seaman slowed not a step, stumbling and careening over the uneven ice floe toward a dark smudge on the horizon. Fitzjames adjusted his gaze in the same direction and felt his jaw drop. Three leagues distant, the black hull and upright masts of a large sailing ship were clearly visible. It could be no vessel but the *Erebus*.

Fitzjames stared for several seconds, barely breathing. Strickland was right. The ship was moving, appearing to drift clear of the ice pack.

The startled commander stepped to the pinnace and rummaged under a bench seat until locating a folding telescope. Training the glass on the vessel, he readily identified his former command. She looked like a ghost ship, though, with sails furled and her decks empty. He idly wondered if the crazed men below even knew they were adrift. His excitement at seeing the vessel was tempered when he studied the surface area around the ship. It was unbroken ice.

"She's still locked in the pack ice," he muttered, noting that the ship was moving stern first. The *Erebus* was in fact encased in a ten-mile-long sheet of ice that had splintered from the frozen sea and was drifting south. Her survival prospects had improved slightly, but she still faced the risk of pulverization from rupturing ice.

Fitzjames let out a sigh, then turned to two of his fittest crewmen.

"Reed, Sullivan, go retrieve Seaman Strickland at once," he barked.

The two men rose and charged after Strickland, who had now reached the ice pack and was disappearing over a large hummock. Fitzjames peered again at the ship, searching for damage to the hull or signs of life above deck. But the distance was too great to observe any detail. His thoughts turned to the expedition's commander, Franklin, whose body lay packed in ice in the depths of the hold. Maybe the old bird will yet get buried in England, Fitzjames mused, knowing that his own prospects of making it home, dead or alive, were looking quite thin.

A half hour passed before Reed and Sullivan returned to the boat. Fitzjames noticed that both men stared at the ground, while one of them clutched a scarf that Strickland had been wearing around his face and neck.

"Where is he?" the commander asked.

"He broke through a snow-covered lead in the pack ice," replied Sullivan, a ship's rigger with plaintive blue eyes. "We tried to pull him out, but he went under before we could get a good grip on him." He held up the frozen-stiff scarf, showing all they had been able to grasp.

It was no matter, Fitzjames thought. Had they pulled him out, he would have likely died before they could have got him into dry clothes anyway. Strickland was actually lucky. At least he got to die quickly.

Shaking the image from his mind, Fitzjames shouted harshly to the somber crew, "Back in the harnesses. Let's get the sledge moving," dismissing the loss without another word.

The days passed with growing strain as the men trudged south. Gradually, the crewmen broke into separate parties, divided by their physical stamina. Crozier and a small party from the *Terror* blazed a path down the coastline ten miles ahead of everyone else. Fitzjames followed next but was tailed several miles behind by three or four groups of stragglers, the weakest and sickest who could not keep pace and for all practical purposes were already dead. Fitzjames had lost three men of his own, forging ahead with only thirteen to haul the heavy load.

Light winds and moderate temperatures had given the men hope for escape. But a late-spring blizzard turned their fortunes. Like an approaching veil of death, a black line of clouds appeared to the west and rolled in with a fury. Blistering winds blasted across the ice pack, pounding the low island without mercy. Buffeted by the winds and unable to see, Fitzjames had no choice but to turn the boat turtle and seek refuge beneath its wood-planked hull. For four days, the winds pounded them like a mallet. Imprisoned in their shell with scant food and no source of heat but their bodies, the emaciated men slowly began to succumb.

Like the rest of his men, Fitzjames drifted in and out of consciousness as his bodily functions slowly shut down. When the end was near, an odd burst of energy surged through him, driven perhaps by a dying curiosity. Climbing over the bodies of his comrades, he slipped under the gunwale and pulled himself upright against the exterior hull. A brief respite in the gale winds let him stand unmolested in the elements as the fading light of dusk approached. Peering over the ice, he forced himself to look one more time.

She was still there. A dark projectile scratching the horizon, the *Erebus* loomed, creeping with the ice like a black wraith.

"What mystery hath thou?" he cried, though the final words left his parched lips in barely a whisper. With its glistening eyes locked on the horizon, Fitzjames's dead body wilted against the pinnace.

Across the ice, the *Erebus* silently sailed on, an ice-encrusted tomb. Like her crew, she would eventually fall victim to the harsh Arctic environment, a last vestige of Franklin's quest to navigate the Northwest Passage. With her disappearance, the saga of Fitzjames's mad crew would be obscured from history. But unbeknownst to her commander, the ship held a greater mystery, one that over a century later would impact man's very survival on the planet.

■ ■ ■ ■

PART I
DEVIL'S BREATH

■ ■ ■ ■

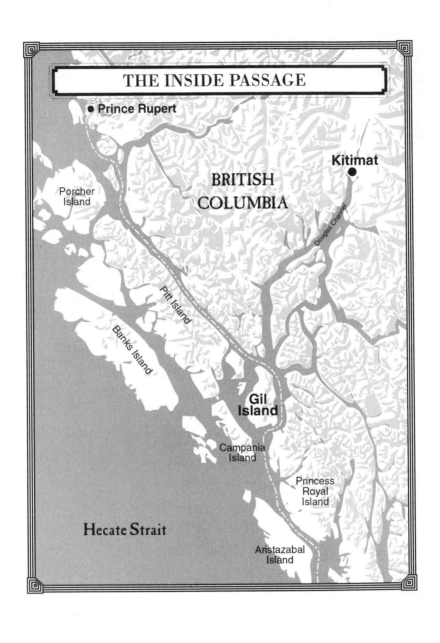

1

The sixty-foot steel-hulled trawler was what all commercial fishing boats ought to look like but seldom did. Her nets were stowed neatly on their rollers, the deck was free of clutter. The boat's hull and topside were absent of rust and grime, while a fresh coat of paint covered the most weathered areas. Even the boat's worn dock fenders had been regularly scrubbed of grit. While not the most profitable fishing boat plying the northern waters of British Columbia, the *Ventura* was easily the best maintained.

Her shipshape appearance reflected the character of her owner, a meticulous and hardworking man named Steve Miller. Like his boat, Miller didn't fit the bill of the average independent fisherman. A trauma doctor who'd grown tired of patching up mangled auto accident victims in Indianapolis, he'd returned to the small Pacific Northwest town of his youth to try something different. Possessing a secure bank account and a love of the water, commercial fishing had seemed the perfect fit. Steering the boat through an early morning drizzle now, he wore his happiness in the form of a wide grin.

A young man with shaggy black hair poked his head into the wheelhouse and called to Miller.

"Where they biting today, skipper?" he asked.

Miller gazed out the forward window, then poked his nose up and sniffed the air.

"Well, Bucky, I'd say the west coast of Gil Island, without a doubt," he grinned, taking the bait. "Better grab some shut-eye now, as we'll be reeling them in soon enough."

"Sure, boss. Like, a whole twenty minutes?"

"I'd say closer to eighteen." He smiled, gazing at a nearby nautical chart. He cinched the wheel a few degrees, aiming the bow toward a narrow slot dividing two green landmasses ahead of them. They were cutting across the Inside Passage, a ribbon of protected sea that stretched from Vancouver to Juneau. Sheltered by dozens of pine-covered islands, the winding waterway inspired comparisons to the scenic fjords of Norway.

Only the occasional commercial or tourist

fishing boat, casting its lines for salmon or halibut, was found dodging the Alaska-bound cruise ship traffic. Like most independent fishermen, Miller chased after the more valuable sockeye salmon, utilizing purse seine nets to capture the fish near inlets and in ocean waters. He was content to break even with his catches, knowing few got rich fishing in these parts. Yet despite his limited experience, he still managed a small profit due to his planning and enthusiasm. Sipping a mug of coffee, he glanced at a flush-mounted radar screen. Spotting two vessels several miles to the north, he let go of the wheel and walked outside the pilothouse to inspect his nets for the third time that day. Satisfied there were no holes in the mesh, he climbed back to the bridge.

Bucky was standing by the rail, forgoing his bunk for a cigarette instead. Puffing on a Marlboro, he nodded at Miller, then looked up at the sky. An ever-present blanket of gray clouds floated in an airy mass yet appeared too light to dispense more than a light drizzle. Bucky peered across Hecate Strait at the green islands that bound it to the west. Ahead off the port bow, he noticed an unusually thick cloud rolling along the water's surface. Fog was a common companion in these waters, but there was something peculiar about this formation. The color was a brighter white than that of a normal fogbank, its billows heavier. Taking a long drag on his cigarette, Bucky exhaled deeply, then walked to the wheelhouse.

Miller had already taken note of the white cloud and had a pair of binoculars trained on the mist.

"You seen it too, boss? Kind of a funky-looking cloud, ain't it?" Bucky drawled.

"It is. I don't see any other vessels around that could have discharged it," Miller replied, scanning the horizon. "Might be some sort of smoke or exhaust that drifted over from Gil."

"Yep, maybe somebody's fish smoker blew," the deckhand replied, his crooked teeth in a wide grin.

Miller set down the binoculars and grabbed the wheel. Their path around Gil Island led directly through the center of the cloud. Miller rapped his knuckles on the worn wooden wheel in uneasiness, but he made no effort to alter course.

As the boat approached the cloud's periphery, Miller stared at the water and crinkled his brow. The color of the water changed visibly, from green to brown to copper-red. A number of dead salmon appeared in the crimson broth, their silver bellies pointing skyward. Then the fishing boat chugged into the haze.

The men in the wheelhouse immediately felt a change in temperature, as if a cold, wet blanket had been thrown over them. Miller

36

felt a dampness in his throat while tasting a strong acidic flavor. A tingling sensation rippled through his head, and he felt a sudden tightening in his chest. When he sucked in a breath of air, his legs buckled, and stars began to appear before his eyes. His pain was diverted when the second deckhand burst into the cabin with a shriek.

"Captain . . . I'm suffocating," gasped the man, a ruddy-faced fellow with long sideburns. The man's eyes bulged from his head, and his face was tinted a dark shade of blue. Miller took a step toward him, but the man fell to the deck unconscious.

The cabin started to spin before Miller's eyes as he made a desperate lunge for the boat's radio. In a blur, he noticed Bucky sprawled flat on the deck. With his chest constricting tightly, Miller grasped at the radio, scooping up the transmitter while knocking over some charts and pencils. Pulling the transmitter to his mouth, he tried to call a Mayday, but the words refused to leave his lips. Falling to his knees, he felt like his entire body was being crushed on an anvil. The constriction tightened as blackness slowly crept over his vision. He fought to stay conscious but felt himself slipping into the void. Miller struggled desperately, then let out a final deep gasp as the icy hand of death beckoned him to let go.

2

"Catch is aboard," Summer Pitt shouted toward the wheelhouse. "Take us to the next magic spot."

The tall, lithe oceanographer stood on the open stern deck of the research boat, dressed in a turquoise rain jacket. In her hands, she reeled in a polypropylene line wrapped around the spool of a mock fishing pole. The line stretched to the end of a guided rod where her prize catch dangled in the breeze. It wasn't a fish but a gray plastic tube called a Niskin bottle, which allowed seawater samples to be collected at depth. Summer carefully grabbed the bottle and stepped toward the pilothouse as the inboard motors suddenly revved loudly beneath the deck. The abrupt propulsion nearly threw her off her feet as the workboat leaped forward.

"Easy on the acceleration," she yelled, finally making her way into the cabin.

Seated behind the wheel, her brother turned and chuckled.

"Just wanted to keep you on your toes," Dirk Pitt replied. "That was a remarkable imitation of a drunken ballerina, I might add."

The comment only infuriated Summer more. Then she saw the humor in it all and just as quickly laughed it off.

"Don't be surprised to find a bucket of wet clams in your bunk tonight," she said.

"As long as they're steamed with Cajun sauce first," he replied. Dirk eased the throttle back to a more stable speed, then eyed a digital navigation chart on a nearby monitor.

"That was sample 17-F, by the way," he said.

Summer poured the water sample into a clear vial and wrote down the designation on a preprinted label. She then placed the vial in a foam-lined case that contained a dozen other samples of seawater. What had started as a simple study of plankton health along the south Alaska coastline had grown in scope when the Canadian Fisheries and Oceans Department had gotten wind of their project and asked if they could continue their assessment down to Vancouver. Besides cruise ships, the Inside Passage also was an important migratory route for humpbacks, grays, and other whales that attracted the attention of marine biologists. The microscopic plankton was a key to the aquatic food chain as it attracted krill, a primary food source for baleen whales. Dirk and Summer realized the importance of obtaining a complete ecological snapshot of the region and had obtained approval to expand the research project from their bosses at the National Underwater and Marine Agency.

"How far to the next collection point?" Summer asked, taking a seat on a wooden stool and watching the waves roll by.

Dirk peered at the computer monitor again, locating a small black triangle at the top of the screen. A HYPACK software program marked the previous collection sites and plotted a route to the next sample target.

"We have about eight miles to go. Plenty of time for a bite before we get there." He kicked open a cooler and pulled out a ham sandwich and a root beer, then tweaked the wheel to keep the boat on track.

The forty-five-foot aluminum workboat skimmed over the flat waters of the passage like a dart. Painted turquoise blue like all National Underwater and Marine Agency research vessels, it was fitted with cold-water dive gear, marine survey equipment, and even a tiny ROV for underwater videotaping. Creature comforts were minimal, but the boat was the perfect platform for performing coastal research studies.

Dirk swung the wheel to starboard, giving wide berth to a gleaming white Princess Lines cruise ship headed in the opposite direction. A handful of topside tourists waved heartily in their direction, whom Dirk obliged by waggling his arm out a side window.

"Seems like one goes by every hour," Summer remarked.

"More than thirty vessels run the passage in the summer months, so it does seem like the Jersey Turnpike."

"You've never even laid eyes on the Jersey Turnpike."

Dirk shook his head. "Fine. Then it seems like Interstate H-1 in Honolulu at rush hour."

The siblings had grown up in Hawaii, where they developed a passion for the sea. Their single mother fostered an early interest in marine biology and encouraged both children to learn to dive at a young age. Fraternal twins who were both athletic and adventurous, Dirk and Summer spent much of their youth on or near the water. Their interest continued into college, where both studied ocean sciences. They somehow ended on opposite coasts, Summer obtaining an advanced degree from Scripps Institute while Dirk garnered a graduate degree in marine engineering from New York Maritime College.

It was on their mother's deathbed that they first learned the identity of their father, who ran the National Underwater and Marine Agency and shared the same name as Dirk. An emotional reunion led to a close relationship with the man they had never known. They now found themselves working under his tutelage in the special projects department of NUMA. It was a dream job, enabling them to travel the world together, studying the oceans and solving some of the never-ending mysteries of the deep.

Dirk kept the throttle down as they passed a fishing boat headed north, then pulled up a quarter mile later. As the boat approached the designated target, he killed the engines and drifted over the position. Summer walked to the stern and rigged her fishing line with an empty vial as a pair of Dall's porpoises broke the surface nearby and eyed the boat with curiosity.

"Watch out for Flipper when you cast that thing," Dirk said, walking onto the deck. "Beaning a porpoise brings bad karma."

"How about beaning your brother?"

"Much, much worse." He smiled as the marine mammals ducked under the surface. He scanned the surrounding waters, waiting for them to resurface, when he noticed the fishing boat again. She had gradually changed course and was now turning south. Dirk noted that it sailed on a circular course and would soon bear down on his own craft.

"You better make it quick, Summer. I don't think this guy is watching where he's going."

Summer glanced at the approaching boat, then tossed the water vial over the side. The weighted apparatus quickly sank into the murk as a dozen feet of loose line was let out. When the line drew taut, Summer jerked it, causing the inverted vial to flip over and fill with subsurface water. Reeling in the line, she looked toward the fishing boat. It continued to turn in a lazy arc barely a hundred feet away, its bow easing toward the NUMA vessel.

Dirk had already returned to the wheelhouse and hit a button on the cowl. A honking blast erupted from a pair of trumpeted air horns mounted on the bow. The loud bellow echoed across the water but incited no reaction from the fishing boat. It continued to turn lazily toward a rendezvous with the research boat.

Dirk quickly fired up the engine and shoved the throttle forward as Summer finished pulling in the water sample. With a quick surge, the boat knifed to port a few yards, then slowed as the fishing boat edged by just a few feet away.

"Doesn't look like anyone is on the bridge," Summer shouted. She saw Dirk hang up the radio transmitter.

"I get no reply on the radio," he confirmed with a nod. "Summer, come take the wheel."

Summer rushed into the cabin and stowed the water sample, then slid into the pilot's seat.

"You want to get aboard?" she asked, gauging her brother's intent.

"Yes. See if you can match speed with her, then bring us alongside."

Summer chased after the fishing boat, following in its wake, before pulling up along-side. She could tell that the fishing boat was traveling in ever-widening circles, then looked in alarm at its projected path. A widening arc along with a peaking flood tide was driving it in a loop toward Gil Island. In just a few minutes, the boat would reach the fringe of the island and rip its hull out on the rocky shoreline.

"Better act quick," she yelled to her brother. "She'll be on the rocks in no time."

Dirk nodded and motioned with his hand to bring the boat closer. He had scrambled onto the bow and hunched with his feet over the low side railing. Summer held steady for a moment, getting a feel for the other boat's speed and turning radius, then inched closer. When she pulled within two feet of the other boat, Dirk leaped, landing on the deck beside a net roller. Summer instantly pulled away, then followed the fishing boat a few yards behind.

Scrambling past the nets, Dirk headed straight for the fishing boat's wheelhouse, where he found a scene of horror. Three men were sprawled on the deck, a look of agony etched on their faces. One of the men stared through open, glassy eyes and oddly clutched a pencil with a frozen hand. Dirk could tell by their gray pallor that the men were dead, but he quickly checked for pulses all the same. He noted curiously that the bodies were un-

44

marked, with no visible blood or open wounds. Finding no signs of life, he grimly took the wheel and straightened the boat's course, calling Summer over the radio to follow him. Shaking off a chill, he anxiously piloted the vessel toward the nearest port, silently wondering what had killed the men lying dead at his feet.

3

The White House security guard stood at the Pennsylvania Avenue entrance and stared in puzzlement at the man approaching on the sidewalk. He was short yet walked with a bold stride, his chest out and chin up, with an air of command. With fire-red hair and matching goatee, he reminded the guard of a bantam rooster stalking the henhouse. But it wasn't his appearance or demeanor that most caught the guard's attention. Rather, it was the large unlit stogie that protruded from the man's lips.

"Charlie . . . isn't that the VP?" he asked his companion in the guard box. But his fellow agent was on the telephone and didn't hear him. By now, the man had approached the small entryway alongside the guardhouse.

"Good evening," he said in a gritty voice. "I have an eight o'clock appointment with the President."

"May I see your credentials, sir?" the guard asked nervously.

"I don't carry that nonsense around," the man replied gruffly. He stopped and took the cigar out of his mouth. "The name's Sandecker."

"Yes, sir. But I still need your credentials, sir," the guard replied, his face turning bright red.

Sandecker squinted at the guard, then softened. "I understand that you are just doing your job, son. Why don't you call Chief of Staff Meade and tell him I'm at the gate?"

Before the disheveled guard could respond, his partner stuck his head out of the guard box.

"Good evening, Mr. Vice President. Another late meeting with the President?" he asked.

"Good evening, Charlie," Sandecker replied. "Yes, I'm afraid this is the only time we can talk without interruption."

"Why don't you go on in," Charlie said.

Sandecker took a step, then stopped. "See you've got a new man on the job," he said, turning to the numb guard who had stopped him. The Vice President then reached out and shook hands with the man.

"Keep up the good work, son," he said, then turned and ambled up the drive to the White House.

Though he had spent the better part of his career in the nation's capital, James Sandecker was never one for official Washington protocol. A retired admiral, Sandecker was well known within the Beltway for the blunt manner in which he had administered the National Underwater and Marine Agency for many years. He'd been startled when the President asked him to replace his elected running mate, who had died in office. Though he lacked a political bone in his body, Sandecker knew he could be a stronger proponent for the environment and the oceans that he loved and so had readily accepted the offer.

As Vice President, Sandecker tried his best to shun the trappings that came with the office. He continually frustrated his Secret Service contingent by ditching them at will. A physical-fitness fanatic, he was often seen out jogging solo along the Mall. He worked out of an office in the Eisenhower Executive Office Building rather than utilizing a similar space in the West Wing, preferring to avoid the political haze that enveloped all White House administrations. Even in poor weather he would stroll down Pennsylvania Avenue for meetings in the White House, preferring a dose of fresh air to the underground tunnel that connected the two buildings. In good weather, he was even known to hike up to Capitol Hill for congressional meetings, tiring the Secret Service agents assigned to keep up with him.

Passing through another security checkpoint at the entrance to the West Wing, Sandecker was escorted by a White House staffer to the Oval Office. Shown through the northwest doorway, he crossed the blue-carpeted room alone and took a seat across from the President at his desk. It wasn't until he was seated that he took a good look at the President and nearly winced.

President Garner Ward was a mess. The populist independent from Montana, who bore a passing resemblance in character and appearance to Teddy Roosevelt, looked like he hadn't slept in a week. Puffy sandbags of flesh protruded beneath his blotchy red eyes while his facial skin appeared sullen and gray. He stared at Sandecker with a grim demeanor that was uncharacteristic of the normally jocular Chief Executive.

"Garner, you've been burning the midnight oil a bit too much," Sandecker said in a concerned tone.

"Can't be helped," the President replied in a weary voice. "We're in a helluva state at the moment."

"I saw the news that the price of gasoline has hit ten dollars a gallon. This latest oil shock is hitting quite hard."

The country was facing yet another unexpected spike in oil prices. Iran had recently halted all oil exports in response to Western sanctions, while labor strikes in Nigeria had reduced African oil exports to nearly zero. Worse for the U.S. was the suspension of oil exports from Venezuela, orchestrated by the country's volatile President. The price of gasoline and fuel oil quickly skyrocketed while shortages erupted nationwide.

"We haven't seen the worst of it," the President replied. He slid a letter across his desk for Sandecker to read.

"It's from the Canadian Prime Minister," Ward continued. "Because of legislation passed by Parliament that drastically curtails greenhouse gas emissions, the Canadian government is forcing closure of most of the Athabasca oil sands operations. The Prime Minister regrets to inform us that all associated oil exports to the U.S. will be halted until they can solve the carbon emission problem."

Sandecker read the letter and slowly shook his head. "Those sands account for nearly fifteen percent of our imported oil. That'll be a crushing blow to the economy."

The recent price surge had already been felt hard across the country. Hundreds of people in the Northeast had died during a winter cold snap when fuel oil stocks ran dry. Airlines, trucking companies, and related transport businesses were driven toward bankruptcy, while hundreds of thousands of workers in other industries had already been laid off. The entire economy seemed on the brink of collapse, while public outrage swelled at a government that could do little to alter the forces of supply and demand.

"There's no sense in getting angry at the Canadians," the President said. "Shutting down Athabasca is a rather noble gesture, in light of the accelerated global-warming figures we keep seeing."

Sandecker nodded. "I just received a National Underwater and Marine Agency report on ocean temperatures. The seas are warming much faster than previously predicted, while rising at the same pace. There seems to be no stopping the melting of the polar ice caps. The rise in sea level is going to create a global upheaval that we can't even imagine."

"As if we don't have enough problems," the President muttered. "And not only that, we're also facing potentially devastating economic repercussions. The global anti-coal campaign is gaining real support. A lot of countries are considering the proposed boycott of American and Chinese goods unless we give up burning coal."

"The problem is," Sandecker noted, "coal-fired power plants are the largest single source of greenhouse gas emissions — but they also provide half of our electricity. And we have the largest coal reserves in the world. It's a painful dilemma."

"I'm not sure that our nation could survive economically if an international boycott gained momentum," the President replied in a low voice. The exhausted Chief Executive leaned back in his chair and rubbed his eyes.

"I fear we are at a tipping point, Jim, in terms of both the economy and the environment. Disaster awaits if we don't take the right steps."

The pressures of the situation were building, and Sandecker could see that they were clearly taking a toll on the President's health. "We're in for some tough choices," Sandecker replied. Taking pity on a man he considered a close friend, he added, "You can't solve it all yourself, Garner."

An angry fire suddenly lit in the President's tired eyes. "Maybe I can't. But I shouldn't have to try. We've seen this coming for a decade or more yet nobody had the will to act. Prior administrations spent their time propping up the oil companies while throwing peanuts at renewable-energy research. The same goes for global warming. Congress was too busy protecting the coal industry to see that they were setting the planet up for destruction. Everyone knew that our economic reliance on foreign oil would someday come to haunt us, and now that day has arrived."

"There's no debating the shortsightedness of our predecessors," Sandecker agreed. "Washington has never been a town known for its courage. But we owe it to the American people to do what we can to right the wrongs of the past."

"The American people," the President replied with anguish. "What am I supposed to tell them now? Sorry, we had our head in the sand? Sorry, we're now facing rampant fuel shortages, hyperinflation, staggering unemployment, and an economic depression? And, sorry, the rest of the world wants us to stop burning coal, so the lights are going out, too?"

The President slumped in his chair, staring at the wall in a lost gaze.

"I can't offer them a miracle," he said.

A long silence lingered over the office before Sandecker responded in a low tone. "You don't need to offer a miracle, just a sharing of the pain. It will be a tough pill to swallow, but we'll have to take a stand and redirect our energy use away from oil. The public is resilient when it counts. Lay it on the line, Garner, and they will stand with us and accept the sacrifices to come."

"Perhaps," the President replied in a defeated tone. "But will they stand with us when they figure out that it may be too late?"

4

Elizabeth Finlay stepped to the bedroom window and glanced at the sky. A light drizzle beat down, as it had for most of the day, and showed no signs of letting up. She turned and gazed at the waters of Victoria Harbor, which lapped at a stone seawall behind her house. The harbor waters appeared calm, broken by a sprinkling of whitecaps kicked up by the light breeze. It was about as good a spring sailing day as it got in the Pacific Northwest, she thought.

Pulling on a thick sweater and a weathered yellow rain slicker, she padded down the stairs of her expansive shoreline home. Built by her late husband in the 1990s, it featured a honeycomb of broad glass windows, which captured a dramatic view of downtown Victoria across the harbor. T. J. Finlay had planned it that way, as a constant reminder of the city he loved. A larger-than-life character, Finlay had dominated the local political scene. An heir to the Canadian Pacific Railway fortune, he had entered politics at an early age, becoming a popular and long-standing MP for greater Victoria. He had died unexpectedly of a heart attack but would have been delighted to know that his wife of thirty-five years had easily won election to his seat in Parliament.

A delicate yet adventurous woman, Elizabeth Finlay came from a long line of Canadian settlers and was fiercely proud of her heritage. She was troubled by what she saw as unjust external influences on Canada and was a vocal critic for tougher immigration standards and tighter restrictions on foreign ownership and investment. While ruffling feathers in the business community, she was widely admired for her courage, bluntness, and honesty.

Stepping out a back door, she made her way across a manicured lawn and down a flight of steps to a heavy wooden dock that marched into the bay. A happy black Lab followed at her heels, wagging its tail in tireless bliss. Moored at the dock was a sleek sixty-five-foot offshore motor yacht. Though nearly twenty years old, it sparkled like new, the product of impeccable care. Opposite the yacht was a small wooden Wayfarer sailboat of sixteen feet, emblazoned with a bright yellow hull. Like the yacht, the vintage racing sailboat was kept looking new with polished brightwork and fresh lines and sails.

At the sound of her footsteps across the wooden slats, a thin gray-haired man stepped off the yacht and greeted Finlay.

"Good morning, Mrs. Finlay. Do you wish to take out the *Columbia Empress*?" he asked, motioning toward the yacht.

"No, Edward, I'm up for a sail today. It's a better way to clear my head of Ottawa politics."

"An excellent proposition," he replied, helping her and the dog into the sailboat. Untying the bow and stern lines, he shoved the boat away from the dock as Finlay raised the mainsail.

"Watch out for freighters," the caretaker said. "Traffic seems a bit lively today."

"Thank you, Edward. I shall be back by lunchtime."

The breeze quickly filled the mainsail, and Finlay was able to maneuver into the harbor without use of the outboard motor. As the harbor opened up before her, she tacked to the southeast, maneuvering past a Seattle-bound ferry. Seated in the small cockpit, she clipped on a safety harness, then took in the view around her. The quaint shore of Victoria Island receded on her left, its gabled, turn-of-the-century structures resembling a row of dollhouses. In the distance ahead, a steady stream of freighters rolled in along the Juan de Fuca Strait, splitting their forces between Vancouver and Seattle. A few other hardy sailboats and fishing boats dotted the sound, but the open expanse of water left a wide berth to the other vessels. Finlay watched as a small runabout roared past, its lone occupant tossing her a friendly wave before plowing on ahead of her.

She sat back and soaked in the salt air, turning up her collar to the damp sea spray. She sailed toward a small group of islands east of Victoria, letting the Wayfarer run free while her mind did likewise. Twenty years before, she and T.J. had sailed across the Pacific on a much larger boat. Crossing remote stretches of ocean, she found that the solitude gave her a sense of comfort. She always considered the sailboat to be a remarkably therapeutic device. Just a few minutes on the water purged away the daily stresses while calming her emotions. She often joked that the country needed more sailboats and fewer psychologists.

The small boat skimmed through quietly building swells as Finlay crossed the open bay. Approaching Discovery Island, she tacked to the southeast, breezing into a sheltered cove on the green island that stretched only a mile long. A pod of orcas broke the surface nearby, and Finlay chased after them for several minutes until they disappeared under the surface. Tacking again back toward the island, she saw that the nearby waters were clear of other vessels, save for the runabout that had passed earlier. The powerboat seemed to be running in large circles ahead of her. Finlay shook her head in loathing at the disruptive noise from its large outboard motor.

The runabout suddenly stopped a short distance ahead of her, and Finlay could see the occupant fidgeting with a fishing pole. She shifted the rudder and tacked to her port, intending to pass offshore. Skirting by a few yards away, she was startled to hear a loud splash followed by a cry for help.

Finlay looked to see the man flailing his arms wildly in the water, a sure sign that he didn't know how to swim. He appeared to be weighed down by a heavy jacket and plunged under the water for a moment before struggling back to the surface. Finlay cut the tiller sharply, catching a quick burst of wind in the mainsail that shoved the boat toward the stricken man. Drawing closer, she quickly dropped the sails and drifted the last few yards, steering the sailboat alongside the flailing man.

Finlay could see that he was a hefty man, with short hair and a weathered face. Despite his panicked motions, the man looked at his rescuer with penetrating eyes that showed a complete lack of fear. He turned and gave an annoyed look at the black Lab, who stood at the sailboat's rail barking incessantly.

Finlay knew enough not to try and struggle with a drowning victim, so she scanned the deck for a boat hook. Not finding it, she quickly coiled up the sailboat's stern line and expertly tossed it to the man. He managed to loop an arm around the rope before slipping once more underwater. With a leg braced against the gunwale, Finlay pulled on the line, heaving the deadweight toward her. A few feet off the stern, the man popped to the surface, wheezing and sputtering for air.

"Take it easy," Finlay assured the man in a comforting voice. "You're going to be all right." She pulled him closer, then tied off the line on a cleat.

The man regained his composure and pulled himself to the stern while breathing heavily.

"Can you help me aboard?" he rasped, extending an arm skyward.

Finlay instinctively reached down and grabbed the man's thick hand. Before she could brace herself to pull, she felt herself roughly tugged toward the water. The man had gripped her wrist and flung himself backward, pushing off the sailboat's stern with his feet. Taken off balance, the slight older woman flew over the railing and struck the water headfirst.

Elizabeth Finlay's surprise at being pulled over the rail was surpassed by the shock of immersion in the frigid waters. She gasped at the cold, then regained her bearings and kicked to the surface. Only she couldn't get there.

The drowning man had let go of her wrist but now gripped her about the arm above the elbow. To Finlay's horror, she found herself being dragged deeper under the water. Only her safety harness, stretched to its full extension, kept her from descending farther into the depths. Caught in the middle of a lethal tug-of-war, she looked through a churning veil of bubbles at her underwater assailant. She was shocked to see that he had a dive regulator in his mouth spewing a stream of exhaust bubbles. Writhing to break free of his grasp, she pushed against him and felt a spongy layer beneath his clothes.

A dry suit. The horror of it all suddenly set in. He was trying to kill her.

Fear and panic preceded a surge of adrenaline, and the tough little woman kicked and flailed for all she was worth. A swinging elbow connected with the man's face, knocking the regulator from his mouth. He momentarily let go of her arm, and she made a desperate kick for the surface. But his other hand reached out and clutched her ankle just before her head broke the water, and her fate was sealed.

Finlay struggled desperately for another minute, her lungs screaming for relief, before a shroud of darkness clouded her vision. Amidst the terror, she curiously fretted about the safety of her pet Lab, whose muffled bark could be detected underwater. Slowly the struggle eased as the oxygen flow to her brain ceased. Unable to hold her breath any longer, she involuntarily gasped for air, filling her lungs with cold salt water. With a spastic choke and a final flail of the arms, Elizabeth Finlay collapsed.

Her assailant held her limp body underwater for another two minutes, then cautiously surfaced alongside the sailboat. Seeing no other vessels about, he swam to the runabout and hoisted himself over the side. He pulled off a loose overcoat, revealing a dive tank and weight belt that he quickly unbuckled. Stripping out of the dry suit, he threw on some dry clothes, started the outboard, and quickly sped past the sailboat. On board the dinghy, the black Lab barked morosely as it eyed its owner drifting lifelessly off the stern.

The man gazed at the dog without pity, then turned from the scene of death and calmly cruised toward Victoria.

5

The *Ventura*'s arrival at its home port of Kitimat created an immediate stir. Most of the hamlet's eleven thousand residents knew the dead fishermen as neighbors, friends, or acquaintances. It was only minutes after Dirk docked the boat at the Royal Canadian Mounted Police wharf that word leaked out to the local townspeople. Family and friends quickly assembled on the dock until being pushed behind a temporary barricade erected by a bull-sized Mountie.

Tying up the NUMA research boat just astern, Summer joined her brother, attracting curious gazes from the nearby onlookers. A hospital van was backed down the dock and the three bodies loaded aboard on covered stretchers. In a dingy bait shack a few feet away, Dirk and Summer chronicled their morbid discovery.

"All three were dead when you went aboard?"

The monotonous tone of the questioner's

voice matched his face. Kitimat's police chief peered at Dirk and Summer with unblinking gray eyes that glared over a small nose and an expressionless mouth. Dirk had immediately pegged the inspector as a frustrated lawman trapped in a job too small for his ambitions.

"Yes," Dirk replied. "First thing I did was check for a pulse, but it was evident by their color and skin temperature that they had died at least a short while before I got aboard."

"Did you move the bodies?"

"No. I just covered them up with some blankets when we got close to port. They looked to me like they died where they fell."

The chief nodded blankly. "Did you hear any distress calls on the radio beforehand? And were there any other vessels in the area?"

"We heard no calls on the radio," Summer replied.

"The only other vessel I noted was a cruise ship sailing down the passage. She was several miles to the north of us when we found the *Ventura*," Dirk added.

The chief stared at them for an awkward minute, then closed a small notebook he had been scribbling in. "What do you think happened?" he asked, arching brows finally cracking his stone face.

"I'll leave that for the pathologists to determine," Dirk said, "though if you forced me to guess, I'd say carbon monoxide poisoning. Maybe an exhaust leak under the wheelhouse allowed gases to accumulate inside."

"They were all found together in the bridge, so it might figure," the chief nodded. "You don't feel any ill effects?"

"I'm fine. Opened all the windows, just to be safe."

"Anything else you can tell me that might be of help?"

Dirk looked up for a moment then nodded. "There's the odd message on the footwell."

The chief's brows arched again. "Show me."

Dirk led him and Summer onto the *Ventura* and into the bridge. Standing near the wheel, he poked a toe toward the helm. The chief dropped to his knees for a closer look, disturbed that he had missed something during his initial crime scene investigation. A faint penciled inscription was scribbled on the face of the helm, just a few inches above the deck. It was a spot where a prone man dying on the deck might try to leave a last message.

The inspector pulled out a flashlight and aimed it at the inscription. In a shaky hand was spelled the word CHOKE D, with a small gap in front of the D. The chief reached over and picked up a yellow pencil that had rolled against the bulkhead.

"The writing was in reach of the captain's

body," Dirk said. "Maybe he fell quickly and couldn't reach the radio."

The chief grunted, still upset he had missed it earlier. "Doesn't mean much. Might have already been there." He turned and stared at Dirk and Summer. "What is your business in Hecate Strait?" he asked.

"We are with the National Underwater and Marine Agency, conducting a study of phytoplankton health along the Inside Passage," Summer explained. "We are sampling the waters between Juneau and Vancouver, at the request of the Canadian Fisheries Department."

The inspector looked at the NUMA boat, then nodded. "I'm going to have to ask you people to stay here in Kitimat for a day or two until the preliminary investigation is complete. You can keep your boat tied up here; this is a municipal dock. There's a motel just a block or two up the road, if you need it. Why don't you plan on coming by my office tomorrow afternoon around three? I'll send a car to pick you up."

"Glad to be of help," Dirk replied drily, slightly annoyed at their being treated as potential suspects.

The interview complete, Dirk and Summer jumped to the dock and started walking back to their boat. They looked up as a fiberglass workboat nearly identical to their own came roaring toward the dock. The pilot brought it in way too fast, the bow kissing the dock hard just seconds after the engines had been cut. A tall man in a flannel shirt burst from the wheelhouse, grabbed a bow line, and leaped to the dock. Quickly tying the line behind the NUMA boat, he stomped along the pier, his boots pounding the wooden planks. Summer noted his rugged features and shaggy hair as he approached but sensed a measure of grace in his wide, dark eyes.

"Are you the folks who found the *Ventura*?" he asked, giving Dirk and Summer a hard stare. The voice was refined and articulate, which seemed to Summer an odd contrast to the man's appearance.

"Yes," Dirk replied. "I brought her in to port."

The man nodded briskly, then stormed down the dock, catching the police inspector as he stepped ashore. Summer watched as the man engaged the Mountie in an animated conversation, their voices elevating to a high pitch.

"Can't say we've had the warmest of welcomes," Dirk muttered, climbing into the NUMA vessel. "Does everybody here have the demeanor of a grizzly bear?"

"Guess we brought too much drama to sleepy little Kitimat," Summer replied.

Securing their boat and retrieving their water samples, they headed into the north-woods town, finding it not so sleepy after all. A miniboom was taking place in Kitimat, an outgrowth of the deepwater port facility located southwest of downtown. International industry had quietly taken notice of the shipping capabilities and was turning the town into the busiest Canadian port north of Vancouver. A longtime Alcon Aluminum smelter had recently undergone a billion-dollar expansion, while logging operations and tourism continued to grow.

Locating a shipping office, they overnighted their water samples to a NUMA lab facility in Seattle, then grabbed a late dinner. Walking back to their motel, they took a detour to the dock to retrieve a few items from the boat. Standing on the bridge, Summer found herself staring at the *Ventura,* moored in front of them. The police had finished their investigation and the boat sat empty, a silent blanket of morbidity hanging over it. Dirk stepped up from belowdecks, noticing his sister's concentration.

"Can't do anything to bring them back," he said. "It's been a long day. Let's head to the motel and turn in."

"Just thinking about that message on the footwell and what the captain was trying to say. I wonder if it was a warning of some sort."

"They died quickly. We don't even know if it was a last message."

Summer thought about the inscription again

and shook her head. It meant something more than it appeared to, of that much she was certain. Beyond that, she had no clue. Somehow, she told herself, she would figure it out.

6

The restaurant's decor would never be featured in *Architectural Digest,* Dirk thought, but the smoked salmon and eggs certainly rated five stars. He grinned at the moose head protruding above Summer as he swallowed another bite of breakfast. The moose was only one of a dozen stuffed animal heads mounted on the wall. Each seemed to be staring at Summer through hard glassy eyes.

"All this roadkill is enough to make a person turn vegan," Summer grimaced, shaking her head at the bared snout of a grizzly bear.

"Kitimat's taxidermist must be the richest guy in town," Dirk replied.

"Probably owns the motel."

She sipped at a cup of coffee as the door to the café opened and a tall man entered the restaurant. He strode directly to their table as Dirk and Summer recognized him as the agitated man they'd encountered on the dock the day before.

"May I please join you?" he asked in a non-threatening manner.

"Please do," Dirk said, pushing out a chair. He stuck his hand out at the stranger. "I'm Dirk Pitt. This is my sister, Summer."

The man's brow rose a fraction as he gazed at Summer.

"Glad to know you," he replied, shaking hands. "My name is Trevor Miller. My older brother, Steve, was captain of the *Ventura*."

"We're sorry for what happened yesterday," Summer replied. She could tell by the look in the man's eyes that he was deeply shaken by the loss of his brother.

"He was a good man," Trevor said, his gaze turning distant. He then looked at Summer and offered a sheepish grin. "My apologies for the gruff behavior yesterday. I had just received word of my brother's death over the marine radio and was a little upset and confused."

"A natural reaction," Summer said. "I think we were all a little confused."

Trevor inquired about their involvement, and Summer told of their discovery of the fishing boat while surveying the Hecate Strait.

"Your brother fished these waters for some time?" Dirk asked.

"No, only two or three years. He was actually a doctor who sold his practice and turned to fishing out of passion. Did pretty well at it, too, despite all the restrictions placed on commercial fishing these days to protect the stocks."

"Seems like an odd career transition," Summer remarked.

"We grew up on the water. Our father was an engineer for the local mining company and an avid fisherman. We traveled around a lot but always had a boat. Steve would be on the water every chance he got. He even crewed on a trawler in high school."

"He sure kept a smart boat," Dirk said. "I've never seen such an immaculate fishing boat."

"The *Ventura* was the pride of the Northwest, he used to joke. Steve was a bit of a perfectionist. He always kept his boat spotless and his equipment maintained in the highest order. That's what makes everything so troubling." He gazed out the window, a faraway look in his eyes. Then he turned to Dirk and asked quietly, "They were dead when you found them?"

"I'm afraid so. The boat was circling haphazardly with no one at the helm when we first spotted it."

"The *Ventura* would have piled onto the rocks of Gil Island if Dirk hadn't jumped aboard," Summer added.

"I'm glad you did," Trevor said. "The autopsies revealed that the men died of asphyxiation. The police are certain that carbon monoxide poisoning was the cause. Yet I went all over the *Ventura* and could find no evidence of an exhaust leak."

"The engine is well astern of the wheelhouse, which makes it perplexing. Perhaps there is no leak and it was just an odd mix of wind and running conditions that allowed the exhaust fumes to accumulate in the cabin," Dirk suggested. "It does seem odd that the three men succumbed so quickly."

"It might not be that unusual," Summer said. "There was a mystery several years ago when a high number of drowning deaths began plaguing houseboat vacationers on Lake Powell. They finally discovered that exhaust fumes were accumulating off the stern of the houseboats and incapacitating swimmers in the water."

"Steve was such a cautious man," Miller noted.

"It's not difficult to be overcome by an unseen killer," Dirk said.

The discussion was taking a toll on Trevor, and he paled from the strain. Summer poured him a cup of coffee and tried to move the conversation elsewhere.

"If there is anything we can do to help, please ask," she said, her soft gray eyes showing genuine concern.

"Thank you for trying to help my brother and his crew, and for saving the *Ventura*. My family is grateful." Trevor hesitated, then added, "There is one favor I would like to ask you. I wonder if you would consider taking me to the site where you found them."

"It's over fifty miles from here," Dirk said.

"We can take my boat. She cruises at twenty-five knots. I'd just like to see where he was at the time."

Summer glanced at a clock mounted beneath a sneering mountain lion. "We don't have to meet with the police inspector until three o'clock," she said to her brother. "We might be able to make a quick run out and back."

"I need to check out the ROV and see if we get anything back from the Seattle lab," Dirk replied. "How about you go with Mr. Miller, and I'll handle the inspector in case you're late getting back."

"Call me Trevor. And I'll have her back on time," Trevor said, smiling at Summer as if he were asking her father's permission to take her out. She was surprised to feel a slight blush cross her cheeks.

"Save me a seat under the hot interrogation light," she said to Dirk, rising from her chair. "I'll see you at three."

7

Trevor helped Summer aboard his boat, then quickly cast off the lines. As the workboat edged away from the dock, she leaned over the side and noted a NATURAL RESOURCES CANADA logo painted on the hull. When the boat had safely slipped past the port dockage and was speeding down Douglas Channel, Summer walked into the cabin and sat on a bench near the pilot's seat.

"What do you do for the Natural Resources Department?" she asked.

"Coastal ecologist for the department's Forestry Service," he replied, steering around a logging ship chugging down the center of the channel. "I work mostly with industrial concerns in the northern British Columbia coastal region. I have been fortunate to base out of Kitimat, since the ongoing port expansion provides plenty of activity." He turned to Summer and smiled. "Tame stuff compared to what you and your brother do for NUMA, I'm sure."

"Collecting plankton samples along the Inside Passage isn't too wild and crazy," she replied.

"I would be interested in seeing your results. We've had reports of concentrated marine mortality in a few areas around here, though I've never been able to successfully document the occurrences."

"Be only too happy to work with a fellow disciple of the deep," she laughed.

The boat snaked through the winding channel at high speed, gliding easily over the calm water. Green fingers of land laden with thick pines jutted into the sound, a series of scenic obstacles. Following their progress on a navigation chart, Summer instructed Trevor to slow as they entered the main cross channel of Hecate Strait. A brief rain shower pelted them for a few minutes, leaving them in a gray gloom. As they approached Gil Island, the rain lifted, increasing visibility to a mile or two. Looking from the radar to the horizon, Summer could see that there were no other vessels around them.

"Here, let me steer," Summer said, standing and putting a hand on the wheel. Trevor gave her a reluctant look, then stood and stepped aside. Summer angled the boat toward the island, then slowed and swung north.

"We were situated about here when we noticed the *Ventura* running from the northwest, a mile or so off. She made a lazy turn, gradually coming up on our beam. Would have struck us if we hadn't jumped off her path."

Trevor stared out the window, trying to visualize the scene.

"I had just taken a water sample. We saw no one at the helm, and a radio call went unanswered. I brought us alongside, and Dirk was able to jump aboard. That's when he found your brother," she said, her voice trailing off.

Trevor nodded, then walked to the stern deck and gazed across the water. A light drizzle began to fall, streaming his face with moisture. Summer left him alone with his thoughts for several minutes, then approached quietly and grabbed his hand.

"I'm sorry about your brother," she said softly.

He squeezed her hand but continued staring off in the distance. His eyes suddenly sharpened as he focused on something nearby. A white cloud had materialized on the water a few dozen yards off the bow. The vapor grew rapidly until it encroached upon the boat.

"Awfully white for a fogbank," Summer said with a curious look. She noted that the air took on a pungent odor as the mist drew closer.

The cloud had billowed to the tip of the bow when the light drizzle overhead suddenly thickened into a downpour. Trevor and Summer ducked into the wheelhouse as a deluge of rainwater pelted the boat. Through the window, they watched the approaching white cloud disappear under the gray canopy of falling water.

"That was odd," Summer remarked as Trevor fired up the motor. He aimed the boat toward Kitimat, applying a heavy throttle, as he noticed a scattering of dead fish whir by in the water.

"Devil's Breath," he said quietly.

"Devil's what?"

"Devil's Breath," he repeated, turning a troubled eye toward Summer. "A local native Haisla was fishing in this area a few weeks ago and washed up dead on one of the islands. The authorities said he drowned, possibly run over by a vessel that didn't see him in the fog. Maybe he had a heart attack, I don't really know." The rain outside had let up, but Trevor kept his eyes on the boat's path ahead.

"Go on," Summer prodded after a lengthy pause.

"I never thought much about it. But a few days ago, my brother recovered the man's skiff while fishing out here and asked me to return it to the family. The man had lived in Kitamaat Village, a Haisla settlement. I had done some water studies for the village, so I was friendly with a number of residents. When I met with the family, the deceased man's uncle kept crying that Devil's Breath had killed him."

"What did he mean?"

"He said that the devil had decided his time had come and cast down a cold white breath of death that killed him and everything around him."

"The reported fish and marine life kills?"

Trevor turned and gave Summer a half grin. "I'm pretty sure the old guy was drunk when he told me that. The Haisla have no shortage of supernatural deeds in their storytelling."

"It does sound like an old wives' tale," Summer agreed.

But her words didn't stop a sudden chill from tingling up her spine. The rest of the journey was made in silence, as they both contemplated the strange words of the Haisla native and how it fit with the things they had seen.

They were within a few miles of Kitimat when an executive helicopter whisked across their bow low overhead. The chopper angled toward a protruding chunk of land on the north bank, where an industrial facility was nestled in the trees. A wooden pier stretched into the sound, berthing several small boats and a large luxury yacht. On an adjacent grass clearing was pitched a large white party tent.

"Private hunting lodge for the rich and famous?" Summer asked with a tilt of her head.

"Nothing that glamorous. It's actually a prototype carbon sequestration plant, built by Terra Green Industries. I was involved in some of the site approval and inspection work as it was being built."

"I'm familiar with the concept of carbon sequestration. Collecting and liquefying industrial carbon dioxide gases and pumping them deep into the earth or beneath the ocean floor. Seems like an expensive way to keep pollutants out of the atmosphere."

"The new greenhouse gas emission limits make it a hot technology. The clampdown on industrial carbon dioxide releases in Canada is especially stringent. Companies can now trade carbon credits, but the cost is much higher than many had anticipated. Mining and power companies are particularly desperate to find lower-cost alternatives. Goyette expects to make a lot of money from his sequestration technology if he is allowed to expand the process."

"Mitchell Goyette, the environmental magnate?"

"Yes, he's the owner of Terra Green. Goyette is something of a cultural hero to many Canadians. He's built dams, wind farms, and solar panel fields all over the country while touting hydrogen fuel technologies."

"I'm familiar with his call for offshore wind farms along the Atlantic seaboard to produce clean energy. I have to tell you, that doesn't exactly look like a hydrogen-powered yacht," Summer said, pointing toward the Italian-built luxury vessel.

"No, he doesn't live the self-deprived life of a true greenie. He's become a billionaire off the environmental movement, yet nobody holds it against him. Some people say that he doesn't even believe in the movement, that it's just a means for him to make money."

"Apparently he has succeeded," she said, still eyeing the yacht. "Why did he build a sequestration facility here?"

"In a word, Athabasca. The oil sands of Athabasca, Alberta, require a tremendous amount of energy to refine into crude oil. A by-product of the process is carbon dioxide, apparently in large quantities. The new greenhouse gas agreement will shut down the refinery operations unless they can find a way around their CO_2 problem. Enter Mitchell Goyette. The oil companies were already building a small pipeline from the oil fields to Kitimat. Goyette convinced them to build an extra pipeline to run liquefied carbon dioxide."

"We noticed a pair of small oil tankers in the channel," Summer said.

"We fought the pipelines hard for fear of oil spills, but the commerce powers won out. Goyette, meanwhile, convinced the government that a coastal location was key for his facility, and even received a land grant from

80

the Natural Resources Department."

"A shame it ended up in such a pristine location."

"There was a lot of dissent in the department, but the natural resources minister ultimately signed off on it. In fact, I'm told he is one of the guests visiting the official grand opening today."

"And you didn't make the cut?" Summer asked.

"My invitation must have gotten lost in the mail. No, wait, the dog ate it." He laughed. It was the first time Summer had caught Trevor in a light moment, and she observed a sudden warmth in his eyes.

They sped on into Kitimat, Trevor easing the boat to berth behind the docked NUMA vessel. Dirk could be seen inside the research vessel's cabin, typing on a laptop computer. He closed the computer and stepped out with a morose look on his face as Summer and Trevor tied up the other vessel, then walked alongside.

"Back before three, with room to spare," Summer greeted, eyeing her wristwatch.

"I think the police chief's visit is the least of our worries," Dirk replied. "I just downloaded the lab results from the water samples we sent to Seattle yesterday."

"Why so glum?"

Dirk handed the printout to Summer, then gazed across the waters of the sound. "The pristine-looking waters lying off Kitimat are threatening to kill anything that swims through them."

8

Mitchell Goyette drained the glass of Krug Clos du Mesnil champagne with a smug look of satisfaction. He placed the empty crystal flute on a cocktail table just as the wash from the helicopter's rotor rippled the tent overhead.

"Excuse me, gentlemen," he said in a deep voice. "That would be the Prime Minister." Extricating himself from a small group of province politicians, Goyette exited the tent and strode toward a nearby landing pad.

A large and imposing man, Goyette had a polished demeanor that bordered on slick. With wide eyes, greased-back hair, and a permanent grin, he had the look of a wild boar. Yet he moved in a fluid, almost graceful manner that belied his simmering arrogance. It was the conceit of a man who had amassed his wealth through shrewdness, deceit, and intimidation.

Though not the product of a rags-to-riches story, Goyette had parlayed a family land inheritance into a small fortune when a power company solicited a portion of the site for a proposed hydroelectric project. Goyette astutely negotiated a percentage of the power revenues for use of the land, correctly predicting the insatiable power demands of a booming Vancouver. He leveraged one investment after another, acquiring mineral and logging rights, thermal power resources, and his own hydroelectric plants. A powerful publicity campaign carefully focused on his alternative energy holdings and painted him as a man of the people in order to increase his negotiating strength with the government powers. With his assets privately held, few knew of his major holdings in gas, coal, and oil properties, and the complete hypocrisy of his carefully cultivated image.

Goyette watched as the Sikorsky S-76 hovered briefly, then touched its wheels down onto a wide circular landing pad. The twin engines were shut down, then the copilot climbed out and opened the side passenger door. A short man with shiny silver hair stepped out and held his head low under the swirling rotor blades, as two aides followed him close behind.

"Mr. Prime Minister, welcome to Kitimat and our new Terra Green facility," Goyette greeted with an extrawide smile. "How was your flight?"

"That's one plush bird. I'm just glad the

rain let up so we could enjoy the view." The Canadian Prime Minister, a polished man in his own right named Barrett, reached over and shook Goyette's hand. "Good to see you again, Mitch. And thanks for the lift. I didn't realize that you were also abducting one of my own cabinet members."

He motioned toward a droopy-eyed man with a receding hairline who stepped off the chopper and approached the group.

"Natural Resources Minister Jameson was instrumental in approving our facility here," Goyette beamed. "Welcome to the finished product," he added, turning to Jameson.

The resources minister didn't return the exuberance. With a forced grin, he replied, "I'm happy to see the facility operational."

"The first of many, with your help," Goyette said, winking at the Prime Minister.

"Yes, your firm's capital planning director tells us that you already have a site under development in New Brunswick." Barrett pointed back toward the helicopter.

"My capital planning director?" Goyette asked in a confused tone. He followed the Prime Minister's gaze and turned toward the helicopter. Another man exited the side door and stretched his arms skyward. He crinkled his dark eyes at a fleeting burst of sunlight, then ran a hand through his short-cropped hair. The tailored blue suit he wore failed to hide his muscular build but passed the mark for corporate executive attire. Goyette had to fight to keep his jaw from dropping as the man approached.

"Mr. Goyette" — he grinned with a self-confident smile — "I have the papers on our Vancouver property divestiture for your signature." He tapped a leather satchel held under one arm for effect.

"Excellent," Goyette snorted, regaining his composure at the sight of his hired hit man strolling off his private helicopter. "Why don't you wait in the plant manager's office, and we'll attend to it shortly."

Goyette turned and hurriedly escorted the Prime Minister into the white tent. Wine and hors d'oeuvres were served to the accompaniment of a string quartet before Goyette led the dignitaries to the entrance of the sequestration facility. A droll-faced engineer identified as the plant manager took charge of the group and led them on a short tour. They walked through two large pump stations, then moved outside, where the plant manager pointed out several mammoth holding tanks that were partially concealed in the surrounding pines.

"The carbon dioxide is pumped as a liquid from Alberta and received into the holding tanks," the manager explained. "It is then pumped under pressure into the ground beneath us. An eight-hundred-meter well was dug here, driving through a thick layer of caprock until reaching a porous sedimentary formation filled with brine. It is the ideal geology to hold CO_2 and virtually impervious to surface leakage."

"What would happen if an earthquake should strike here?" the Prime Minister asked.

"We are at least thirty miles from the nearest known fault line, so the odds of a large quake occurring here are quite remote. And at the depths we are storing the product, there is virtually no chance of an accidental release from a geological event."

"And exactly how much of the Athabasca refineries' carbon dioxide output are we sequestering here?"

"Just a fraction, I'm afraid. We'll need many more facilities to absorb the full output from the oil sand fields and allow them to operate at peak production again."

Goyette capitalized on the line of questioning to insert a sales pitch. "As you know, Alberta oil production has had to face serious cutbacks because of the tighter carbon emission mandate. The situation is equally dire for the coal-fired power plants back east. The economic impact to the country will be enormous. But you are standing at the heart of the solution. We've already scouted more locations in the region that are suitable for sequestration facilities. All we need is your help to move forward."

"Perhaps, but I'm not sure I like the idea of British Columbia's coastline being a receptacle for Alberta's industrial pollution," the Prime Minister said drily. A product of Vancouver, he still had a homegrown pride in his native province.

"Don't forget the tax that British Columbia imposes for each metric ton of carbon transferred across its border, a fraction of which goes back to the federal coffers. The fact is, it is a safe moneymaking play for the province. Plus, you may have noticed our dock facility." Goyette pointed to a huge covered building across the grounds that sat adjacent to a small inlet. "We have a five-hundred-foot covered dock capable of accommodating tanker ships that can carry liquid CO_2. We're already receiving shipments and intend to show that we can process carbon waste from Vancouver industry, as well as logging and mining businesses up and down the coast. Allow us to build similar facilities across the country and we'll be able to manage a large portion of our national carbon quotas. And with excess capacity built into the new coastal facilities, we can even bury American and Chinese carbon at a nice profit."

The politician's eyes glimmered at the prospect of additional revenues flowing to the government's ledgers.

"The technology, it is perfectly safe?" he asked.

"We're not talking nuclear waste here, sir. This facility was built as a prototype and has been operating flawlessly for several weeks now. Mr. Prime Minister, it is a no-lose proposition. I build and operate the plants, and ensure their safety. The government just gives me the go-ahead and receives a cut off the top."

"And there is plenty left for you?"

"I'll get by," Goyette replied, roaring like a hyena. "All I need is the continued site and pipeline approvals from you and the resources minister. And that won't be a problem, will it, Minister Jameson?"

Jameson looked at Goyette with a beaten subservience. "I should think there is little to interrupt our trusting relationship," he replied.

"Very well," Barrett said. "Send me your draft proposals and I'll run it past my advisers. Now, where's some more of that fine champagne?"

As the group made their way back to the refreshment tent, Goyette quietly pulled the resources minster aside.

"I trust you received delivery of the BMW?" Goyette asked with a sharklike grin.

"A generous gift that my wife is quite ecstatic about. I would prefer, however, that future compensations remain less conspicuous."

"Not to worry. The contribution to your off-shore trust account has already been made."

Jameson ignored the comment. "What is

this nonsense about building new facilities along the coast? We both know the geology here is marginal, at best. Your so-called aquifer at this site will reach capacity in just a matter of months."

"This site will run indefinitely," Goyette lectured. "We have solved the capacity issue. And as long as you send me the same geological assessment team as before, there will be no problem with our coastal expansion plans. The chief geologist was quite amenable to revising his conclusions for a rather nominal price." He grinned.

Jameson grimaced at the knowledge that corruption flourished within the department well beyond his own dirty hands. He could never recall the exact day that he woke up and realized that Goyette had owned him. It was several years past. The two had met at a hockey game, when Jameson was making his first bid for a seat in Parliament. In Goyette, he had seemingly found a wealthy benefactor who shared a progressive vision for the country. The political campaign contributions grew as Jameson's career advanced, and somewhere along the way he had foolishly crossed the line. Campaign contributions progressed to jet rides and free vacations, ultimately leading to outright cash bribes. With ambition in his heart and a wife and four children to support on a civil servant's salary, he blindly took the cash, convincing himself that the policies he promoted for Goyette were just. It wasn't until he was appointed natural resources minister that he saw the other side of Goyette. The public perception of him as an environmental prophet was just a cleverly designed façade, he came to learn, disguising Goyette's true nature as a money-hungry megalomaniac. For every wind farm he developed with public fanfare, there were a half dozen coal mines he operated, his actual ownership buried in a laundry list of corporate subsidies. Phony mining claims, forged environmental impact statements, and outright federal grants to Goyette's holdings were all jury-rigged by the minister. In return, the bribes had been steady and generous. Jameson had been able to purchase an elegant house in the upscale Ottawa neighborhood of Rockcliffe Park and accumulate more than enough cash in the bank to send his kids to the finest schools. Yet he had never intended for things to slip so far, and he knew there was nothing he could do to escape.

"I don't know how much more of this I can support," he told Goyette in a tired voice.

"You will support as much as I need," Goyette hissed, his eyes quickly turning ice cold. "Unless you wish to spend the rest of your days at Kingston Penitentiary."

Jameson physically wilted, accepting the reality with a weak nod.

Confident in Jameson's indenture, Goyette,

features softened, waved an arm toward the tent.

"Come, cheer up now," he said. "Let us join the Prime Minister and drink a toast to the riches he is about to bestow upon us."

9

Clay Zak had his feet up on the plant manager's desk while casually perusing a book on frontier history. He glanced out a picture window as the thumping from the departing helicopter rattled the glass panes. Goyette entered the room a few seconds later, a suppressed look of annoyance on his face.

"Well, well, my capital planning director," Goyette remarked, "looks like you missed your flight out."

"It was rather a cramped ride," Zak replied, placing the book into his satchel. "Quite stuffy, as a matter of fact, with all those politicians aboard. You should really get a Eurocopter EC-155. A much faster ride. You wouldn't have to spend as much time trapped conversing with those prostitutes. By the way, that natural resources minister? He really doesn't like you."

Goyette ignored the remarks and slid into a leather chair facing the desk. "The PM was just notified of Elizabeth Finlay's death. It was reported as a boating accident."

"Yes, she fell overboard and drowned. You'd think a woman of her means would know how to swim," he smiled.

"You kept things tidy?" Goyette asked in a hushed voice.

A pained look crossed Zak's face. "You know that is why I don't come cheap. Unless her dog can talk, there will be no reason to suspect it was anything but a tragic accident."

Zak leaned back in his chair and gazed up at the ceiling. "As Elizabeth Finlay goes, so goes the movement to halt natural gas and oil exports to China." He then leaned forward and prodded Goyette. "Exactly how much would that bit of legislature have cost your Melville gas field operation?"

Goyette stared into the killer's eyes but saw nothing illuminating. The man's weathered, slightly longish face showed no emotion. It was the perfect poker face. The dark eyes offered no window to his soul, if he even had one, Goyette thought. Hiring a mercenary was playing with fire, but Zak was clearly a tactful professional. And the dividends were proving to be enormous.

"It is not an inconsequential amount," he finally replied.

"Which brings us to my compensation."

"You will be paid as agreed. Half now, half after the investigation is closed. The funds will be wired to your Cayman Islands account, as before."

"The first stop of many." Zak smiled. "It might be time for me to check in on my little nest egg and enjoy a few weeks of R and R in the sunny Caribbean."

"I think vacating Canadian soil for a short time would be a good idea." Goyette hesitated, not sure whether to keep rolling the dice. The man did nice work, he had to admit, and always covered his tracks. "I've got another project for you," he finally proposed. "Small job. It's in the States. And no body work required."

"Name your tune," Zak said. He had yet to turn down a request. As much as he thought Goyette a cretin, he had to admit that the man paid well. Extremely well.

Goyette handed him a folder. "You can read it on the next flight out of here. There's a driver at the gate who will take you to the airport."

"Flying commercial? You may have to get a new capital planning director if this keeps up."

Zak rose and strode out of the office like an emperor, leaving Goyette sitting there shaking his head.

10

Lisa Lane rubbed her tired eyes and again scanned the periodic table of elements, the same standard chemistry chart posted in most every high school science class across the land. The research biochemist had long ago memorized the table of known elements and could probably recite it backward if given the challenge. Now she gazed at the chart hoping for inspiration, something that would trigger a new idea.

She was searching for a durable catalyst that would separate an oxygen molecule from a carbon molecule. Scanning the periodic table, her eyes stopped at the forty-fifth element, rhodium, symbol Rh. Lane's computer modeling kept pointing to a metal compound as a likely catalyst. Rhodium had proved to be the best she had found so far, but it was totally inefficient, in addition to being a horribly expensive precious metal. Her project at the George Washington University Environmental Research and Technology Lab had been called "blue sky research," and maybe it would stay that way. Yet the potential benefits of a breakthrough were too enormous to overlook. There had to be an answer.

Staring at the square denoting rhodium, she noticed the preceding element had a similar symbol, Ru. Absently twisting a lock of her long brown hair, she said the name aloud: "Ruthenium." A transitional metal of the platinum family, it was an element that she had not yet been able to test.

"Bob," she called to a wiry man in a lab coat seated at a nearby computer, "did we ever receive that sample of ruthenium that I requested?"

Bob Hamilton turned from the computer and rolled his eyes. "Ruthenium. The stuff is harder to obtain than a day off. I must have contacted twenty suppliers, and none of them stocked it. I was finally referred to a geology lab in Ontario that had a limited amount. It cost even more than your rhodium sample, so I only ordered two ounces. Let me check the stockroom to see if it came in yet."

He walked out of the lab and down a hall to a small storeroom where special materials were kept under lock and key. A graduate assistant behind a caged window retrieved a small box and slid it across the counter. Returning to the lab, Bob set the container on Lisa's desk.

"You're in luck. The sample arrived yesterday."

Lisa opened the box to find several tiny slivers of a lusterless metal housed in a plastic container. She selected one of the samples and placed it onto a slide, then examined it under a microscope. The tiny sliver resembled a furry snowball under magnification. Measuring the mass of the sample, she placed it in the sealed compartment of a large gray housing that was attached to a mass spectrometer. No less than four computers and several pressurized gas tanks were affixed to the device. Lisa sat down at one of the keyboards and typed in a string of software commands, which initiated a test program.

"Is that the one that's going to be your ticket to the Nobel Prize?" Bob asked.

"I'd settle for a ticket to a Redskins game if it works."

Glancing at a wall clock, she asked, "Want to go grab some lunch? I won't be able to get any preliminary results for at least an hour or so."

"I'm there," Bob replied, slipping off his lab coat and racing her to the door.

After a turkey sandwich in the cafeteria, Lisa returned to her tiny office at the back of the lab. A minute later, Bob ducked his head around the door, his eyes opened wide in bewilderment.

"Lisa, you better come take a look at this,"

he stammered.

Lisa quickly followed him into the lab, her heart skipping a beat as she saw Bob approach the spectrometer. He pointed to one of the computer monitors, which showed a string of numbers rushing down the screen beside a fluctuating bar graph.

"You forgot to remove the rhodium sample before you initiated the new test. But look at the results. The oxalate count is off the charts," he said quietly.

Lisa looked at the monitor and trembled. Inside the spectrometer, a detector system was tabulating the molecular outcome of the forced chemical reaction. The ruthenium catalyst was successfully breaking the carbon dioxide bond, causing the particles to recombine into a two-carbon compound called an oxalate. Unlike her earlier catalysts, the ruthenium/rhodium combination created no material waste by-product. She had stumbled upon a result that scientists around the world had been seeking.

"I can hardly believe it," Bob muttered. "The catalytic reaction is dead-on."

Lisa felt light-headed and dropped into a chair. She checked and rechecked the output, searching for an error but finding none. She finally allowed herself to accept the probability that she had hit pay dirt.

"I've got to tell Maxwell," she said. Dr. Horace Maxwell was director of the GWU Environmental Research and Technology Lab.

"Maxwell? Are you crazy? He's testifying before Congress in two days."

"I know. I'm supposed to accompany him to the Hill."

"Now, there's a suicide mission," Bob said, shaking his head. "If you tell him now, he's liable to bring it up in testimony in order to obtain more funding for the lab."

"Would that be such a bad thing?"

"It would if the results can't be duplicated. One lab test doesn't solve the mysteries of the universe. Let's rerun things and fully document every step before going to Maxwell. At least wait until after he testifies," Bob urged.

"I suppose you're right. We can duplicate the experiment under different scenarios just to be sure. The only limitation is our supply of ruthenium."

"That, I'm sure, will be the least of our problems," Bob said with a hint of prophecy.

11

The Air Canada jet skimmed high over Ontario, the landscape below appearing like a green patchwork comforter from the tiny first-class windows. Clay Zak was oblivious to the view, focusing instead on the shapely legs of a young flight attendant pushing a drinks cart. She caught his stare and brought over a martini in a plastic cup.

"Last one I can serve you," she said with a perky smile. "We'll be landing in Toronto shortly."

"I'll savor it all the more," he replied with a leer.

Dressed in the traveling businessman's uniform of khaki slacks and a blue blazer, he looked like just another sales manager headed to an off-site conference. The reality was quite different.

The only child of an alcoholic single mother, he'd grown up in a ragtag section of Sudbury, Ontario, with little guidance. At fifteen, he'd dropped out of school to work in the nearby nickel mines, developing the physical strength that he still retained twenty years later. His life as a miner was short-lived, however, when he committed his first murder, driving a pickax into the ear of a fellow miner who'd taunted his family lineage.

Fleeing Ontario, he assumed a new identity in Vancouver and drifted into the drug trade. His strength and toughness were put to use as an enforcer for a major local methamphet-amine trafficker named "The Swede." The money came easily, but Zak treated it with an unusual intelligence. A self-taught man, he read voraciously, and judiciously studied busi-ness and finance. Rather than blowing his ill-gotten gains on tawdry women and flashy cars like his cohorts did, he shrewdly invested in stocks and real estate. His lucrative drug career, however, was cut short in an ambush.

It wasn't the police but a Hong Kong sup-plier looking to expand his control of the mar-ket. The Swede and his escorts were gunned down during a nighttime deal in Vancouver's rambling Stanley Park. Zak managed to duck the fire and disappear unscathed into a maze of hedges.

He bided his time before taking revenge, spending weeks staking out a luxury yacht leased by the Chinese syndicate. Setting off a timed explosive charge, using knowledge gleaned from his days in the nickel mines, he blew up the boat with all of the Hong Kong associates aboard. Watching from a small speedboat as the fireball erupted, he saw a man on an adjacent yacht get thrown into the water by the concussion. Realizing the authorities would spend little time investigating the death of a known drug dealer but might expand the dragnet if a wealthy socialite was an added victim, he sped over and fished the unconscious man out of the water.

When a sputtering Mitchell Goyette came to, his gratitude was uncharacteristically effusive.

"You saved my life," he coughed. "I will reward you for that."

"Give me a job instead," Zak said.

Zak enjoyed a huge laugh when he reminded Goyette of the whole story years later. Even Goyette conceded the humor in it. By then, the mogul had come to admire the subversive talents of the former miner, employing him as a high-level enforcer once again. But Goyette knew Zak's loyalty was based solely on cash, and he always kept a wary eye on him. For his part, Zak enjoyed being the lone wolf. He had influence with Goyette, and while he enjoyed the compensation he also enjoyed tweaking his rich and powerful employer.

The plane landed at Toronto's Lester B. Pearson International Airport a few minutes ahead of schedule. Shaking off the effects of the in-flight martinis, Zak stepped out of the first-class compartment and headed to the rental-car counter while waiting for his bags to be unloaded. Taking the keys to a beige four-door sedan, he drove south, skirting the western shoreline of Lake Ontario. Cruising the lakefront expressway for another seventy miles, he exited at a sign reading NIAGARA. A mile below the famous falls, he crossed the Rainbow Bridge and entered the state of New York, handing the immigration officer a phony Canadian passport.

Turning past the falls, it was just a short drive south to Buffalo. He found the city airport in plenty of time to catch a half-empty 767 to Washington, D.C., flying under yet another assumed name, this time with a phony American identification. Dusk had fallen as the jet crossed over the Potomac River on its final approach to Reagan National Airport. It was Zak's first time in the nation's capital, and he duly stared at the city's monuments from the back of a cab. Watching the blinking red lights atop the Washington Monument, he idly wondered if George would have deemed the towering obelisk an absurdity.

Checking in at the Mayflower Hotel, he perused the file that Goyette had given him, then rode the elevator down to the wood-paneled Town & Country Lounge on the lobby floor. Finding a quiet corner booth, he ordered a martini and checked his watch. At a quarter past seven, a thin man with an unkempt beard approached the table.

"Mr. Jones?" he asked, eyeing Zak nervously. Zak gave the man a weak smile.

"Yes. Please sit down," Zak replied.

"I'm Hamilton. Bob Hamilton, from the GWU Environmental Research and Technology Lab," the man said quietly. He stared at Zak with trepidation, then took a deep breath and slid tentatively into the booth.

12

A miracle of sorts arrived on the President's desk shortly after his meeting with Sandecker. It was another letter from the Canadian Prime Minister, offering a potential solution to the growing crisis. A major natural gas field had quietly been discovered last year, the Prime Minister wrote, in a remote section of the Canadian Arctic. Preliminary explorations indicated that the site, located in Viscount Melville Sound, could prove to be one of the richest reserves of natural gas in the world. The privately held firm that made the discovery already had a fleet of tanker ships on line to transport the gas to America.

It was just the tonic the President was seeking to help boost his broader objectives. A major purchase agreement was quickly put in place to get the gas flowing. Though market price was exceeded, the company promised to provide all the gas it could deliver. Or so guaranteed the CEO of the private exploration firm, one Mitchell Goyette.

Ignoring the pleas from his economic and political advisers that he was being too brash, the President quickly acted on the news. In a nationally televised address from the Oval Office, he outlined his ambitious plans to the public.

"My fellow Americans, we are living in a moment of great peril," he said into the cameras, his normally upbeat mood masked by solemnity. "Our daily lives are imperiled by a crisis of energy while our very future existence is threatened by a crisis of the environment. Our dependency on foreign oil has created damaging economic consequences that we all feel while promoting the emission of dangerous greenhouse gases. Troubling new evidence continues to show that we are losing the battle against global warming. For our own security, and for the safety of the entire world, I am hereby directing that the United States achieve a national goal of carbon neutrality by the year 2020. While some may call this objective drastic or even impossible to attain, we have no other choice. I call tonight for a crash research effort by private industry, academic institutions, and our own government agencies to solve our energy needs through alternative fuels and renewable sources. Oil cannot and will not be the fuel that powers our future economy. A funding package will be presented to Congress shortly, outlining our specific investments in new research and technology.

"With the proper resources and a determined will, I am confident that we can reach this goal together. Nevertheless, we must make sacrifices today to cut our emissions and reduce our reliance on oil, which continues to choke our economy. Due to the recent availability of natural gas supplies, I am directing that all of our domestic coal and oil-fired power plants be converted to natural gas within two years. I am pleased to announce tonight that President Zhen of China has agreed to impose similar mandates in his country. In addition, I will be presenting plans shortly for our nation's automakers to accelerate the production of natural-gas- and hybrid-electric-powered vehicles, which I hope will be adopted at the international level.

"We are facing difficult times, but with your support we can reach a more secure tomorrow. Thank you."

As the cameras turned off, the President's chief of staff, a short, balding man named Charles Meade, approached Ward.

"Excellent job, sir. I believe it was an effective speech, and it ought to pacify the anti-coal fanatics and their proposed boycott."

"Thanks, Charlie, I believe you are right,"

the President said. "It was quite effective. Effective, that is, at eliminating any chance of my being reelected," he added with a twisted grin.

13

Room 2318 of the Rayburn House Office Building was uncharacteristically packed with reporters and spectators. Open hearings of the House Subcommittee on Energy and the Environment seldom drew more than a handful of onlookers. But in light of the President's mandate on greenhouse gas emissions, the resulting media firestorm brought a flurry of attention to the subcommittee and its previously scheduled hearing. Its topic: the status of new technologies to aid the battle against global warming.

The assembled crowd slowly hushed as an anteroom door opened and eighteen members of Congress filed to their respective seats on the dais. The last member to enter was an attractive woman with cinnamon-colored hair. She was dressed in a deep purple Prada jacket and skirt, which nearly matched the hue of her violet eyes.

Loren Smith, devoted congresswoman from Colorado's Seventh District, had never traded away her femininity since arriving at the blue-suited halls of Congress years before. Even in her forties, she still made a smart and stylish appearance, but her colleagues had learned long ago that Loren's beauty and fashion sense did nothing to lessen her skill and intelligence in the political arena.

Walking gracefully to the center of the dais, she took her seat next to a plump, white-haired congressman from Georgia who chaired the committee.

"Ah call this hearing to order," he brayed with a thick accent. "Given the public interest in our topic, Ah will forgo opening remarks today and invite our first speaker to testify." He turned and gave a quick wink to Loren, who smiled in return. Longtime colleagues and friends despite sitting on different sides of the aisle, they were among a rare minority of House members who shunned partisan grandstanding in order to focus on the good of the country.

A succession of industry and academic leaders took turns testifying on the latest advances in energy alternatives that emitted zero carbon. While offering up sunny long-term prospects, every speaker wavered when pressed by the committee to provide an immediate technological solution.

"Volume production of hydrogen hasn't been perfected yet," testified one expert. "Even if every man, woman, and child in the country had a hydrogen fuel cell car, there wouldn't be enough hydrogen available to power a fraction of them."

"How far off are we?" asked a representative from Missouri.

"Probably ten years," the witness replied. A ripple of murmurs quickly spread across the gallery. The story was the same from each spokesperson. Advances in technology and product improvements were hitting the marketplace, but the progress was being made in baby steps, not leaps and bounds. There was no imminent breakthrough that would satisfy the President's mandate and save the country, and the world, from the physical and economic devastation of accelerated global warming.

The final speaker was a short bespectacled man who headed up the GWU Environmental Research and Technology Lab in suburban Maryland. Loren leaned forward and smiled as she recognized Lisa Lane taking a seat next to Dr. Horace Maxwell. After the lab director made a preliminary statement, Loren jumped in with the initial questioning.

"Dr. Maxwell, your lab is at the forefront of alternate fuels research. Can you tell us what technological advances we might expect from your work in the near term?"

Maxwell nodded before speaking in a hen-like voice. "We have several outstanding research programs in solar energy, biofuels, and hydrogen synthesis. But in answer to your question, I'm afraid we have no imminent product development that will satisfy the President's tough new mandate."

Loren noticed Lisa bite her lip at Maxwell's last remark. The rest of the House panel took over and grilled Maxwell for another hour, but it was clear there was to be no noteworthy revelation. The President had gone out on a limb to challenge the brightest minds of industry and academia to solve the energy problem, but he was clearly striking out.

As the hearing was adjourned and the reporters rushed out of the chamber to file their stories, Loren stepped down and thanked Dr. Maxwell for his testimony, then greeted Lisa.

"Hi, roomie." She smiled, giving a hug to her old college roommate. "I thought you were still at Brookhaven National Laboratory in New York."

"No, I left a few months ago to join Dr. Maxwell's program. He had more funds for blue sky research." She grinned. "I've been meaning to call you since I moved back to Washington, but I've just been swamped."

"I can sympathize. With the President's speech, the work at your lab has suddenly become very important."

Lisa's face turned solemn, and she moved closer to Loren. "I really would like to talk to you about my own research," she said in a low voice.

"Would dinner tonight work? My husband is picking me up in half an hour. We'd love to have you join us."

Lisa thought for a moment. "I'd like that. Let me tell Dr. Maxwell that I'll make my own way home tonight. Your husband won't mind driving?"

Loren laughed. "Taking a pretty girl for a ride is one of his favorite pastimes."

Loren and Lisa stood on the north steps of the Rayburn Building as a string of limos and Mercedes sedans rolled through the dignitary lane, picking up the wealthier members of Congress and their ever-hovering lobbyists. Lisa was distracted by the appearance of the House Majority Leader and almost missed seeing a rakish antique convertible come barreling to the curb, nearly creasing her thigh with its high-turned fender. She stared wide-eyed as a rugged-looking man with ebony hair and sparkling green eyes hopped out of the car and grabbed Loren in a tight embrace, then kissed her passionately.

"Lisa," Loren said, pushing the man away with a tinge of embarrassment, "this is my husband, Dirk Pitt."

Pitt saw the look of surprise in Lisa's eyes and smiled warmly as he shook her hand. "Don't worry," he laughed, "I only maul pretty women if they're members of Congress."

Lisa felt herself blush slightly. She saw an

114

adventuresome glow in his eyes, tempered by a warm soul.

"I invited Lisa to join us for dinner," Loren explained.

"Glad for you to come. I just hope you don't mind a little wind," Pitt said, nodding toward the car.

"That's some set of wheels," Lisa stammered. "What is it?"

"A 1932 Auburn Speedster. I just finished rebuilding the brakes last night and thought it would be fun to take her out."

Lisa gazed at the sleek car, painted in dual shades of cream and blue. The open cockpit offered cramped seating for two, and there was no backseat. Instead, the bodywork behind the driver's compartment flared to a triangular point at the rear bumper, in the classic boattail shape.

"I don't think there's room for all of us," she lamented.

"There is if somebody doesn't mind riding in back," Pitt replied. He walked over and pushed down on the flush topside surface of the boattail. A hideaway seat folded back, revealing a one-passenger compartment.

"Oh my, I've always wanted to ride in a rumble seat," Lisa said. Without hesitation, she climbed onto a foot bracket and hopped into the compartment.

"My grandfather used to tell me how he rode in the rumble seat of his father's Packard during the Depression," she explained.

"No better way to see the world," Pitt joked, winking at her before helping Loren into the front seat.

They loped through rush hour traffic along the Mall and across the George Mason Bridge before heading south into Virginia. As the city monuments grew smaller behind them, the traffic lightened and Pitt mashed down on the accelerator. With a smooth and powerful twelve-cylinder engine under the hood, the sleek Auburn quickly sprinted past the speed limit. As the car accelerated, Lisa grinned and waved like a little girl at the passing traffic, enjoying the wind as it rustled through her hair. Up front, Loren placed a hand on Pitt's knee and smiled at her husband, who always seemed to find a touch of adventure wherever he went.

Pitt drove past Mount Vernon, then exited the main highway. At a small crossroad, he turned down a dirt road that meandered through the trees until ending at a small restaurant facing the Potomac River. Pitt parked the Auburn and turned off the motor as the heavy scent of Old Bay Seasoning filled the air.

"Best spiced crabs in the territory," Pitt promised.

The restaurant was an old riverside home converted to a café, plainly decorated but with a cozy atmosphere. They were seated at a table overlooking the Potomac as a crowd of locals began filtering in.

"Loren tells me you are a research chemist at GWU," Pitt said to Lisa, after ordering a round of beers and crab.

"Yes, I'm part of an environmental studies group looking at the global-warming problem," she replied.

"If you ever get bored, NUMA can put you to work on some cutting-edge undersea research," he offered with a smile. "We have a large team studying the effects of ocean warming and higher acidity levels. I just had a project review with a team studying carbon saturation in the oceans and possible means of boosting carbon absorption in deep water."

"With all the focus on the atmosphere, I'm glad to see someone is paying attention to the oceans as well. It sounds like there might be some parallels with my research. I'm working on a project related to airborne carbon reduction. I'd love to see the results of your team's work."

"It's just a preliminary report, but you might find it useful. I'll send a copy to you. Or better yet, I'll drop it off to you in the morning. I have an appearance to make on the Hill myself," he added, rolling his eyes at Loren.

"All executive agencies must justify their annual budgets," Loren replied. "Especially those run by renegade pirates."

She laughed and gave Pitt a hug, then turned

to her friend. "Lisa, you seemed anxious after the hearing today to discuss your research work. Tell me more about it."

Lisa took a large swallow from her beer, then looked at Loren with trusting eyes.

"I haven't spoken of this to anyone besides my lab assistant, but I believe we have hit upon a profound discovery." She spoke in a quiet voice, as if afraid the neighboring diners might hear.

"Go on," Loren urged, drawn close by Lisa's demeanor.

"My research involves molecular manipulation of hydrocarbons. We've discovered an important catalyst that I believe will allow for artificial photosynthesis on a mass scale."

"Do you mean like in plants? Converting light into energy?"

"Yes, you remember your botany. But just to make sure . . . Take that plant over there," she said, pointing to a large Boston fern dangling in a planter by the window. "It captures light energy from the sun, water from the soil, and carbon dioxide from the air to produce carbohydrates, the fuel source for it to grow. Its only waste product is oxygen, which allows the rest of us to survive. That's the basic cycle of photosynthesis."

"Yet the actual process is so complicated, scientists have been unable to duplicate it," Pitt said with growing interest.

Lisa sat quietly as the waitress appeared

and unrolled a sheet of brown butcher paper on the table, then dumped a small mountain of steamed blue crabs in front of them. When they each began attacking a spiced crab with a wood mallet, she continued.

"You're correct in the general sense. Elements of photosynthesis have been successfully duplicated, but none with anywhere near the efficiency seen in nature. The complexity is very real. That's why the hundreds of scientists around the world working on artificial photosynthesis typically focus on a single component of the process."

"Yourself included?" Loren asked.

"Myself included. The research at our lab has focused on the ability of plants to break down water molecules into their individual elements. If we can duplicate the process efficiently, and we'll get there someday, then we'll have an unlimited source of cheap hydrogen fuel at our disposal."

"Your breakthrough is in another direction?" Loren asked.

"My focus has been on a reaction called Photosystem I, and the breakdown of carbon dioxide that occurs in the process."

"What are the primary challenges?" Pitt asked.

Lisa tore into a second crab, sucking the meat out of a hind claw.

"These are delicious, by the way. The basic problem has been in developing an efficient means of triggering a chemical breakdown. Chlorophyll plays that role in nature, but it decomposes too quickly in the lab. The trick I pursued was to find an artificial catalyst that could break down carbon dioxide molecules."

Lisa set down her food, then spoke in a low voice again. "That's where I came up with a solution. Blundered upon it, actually. I left a rhodium sample in the test chamber by mistake and added to it another element called ruthenium. When combined with a light charge, the reaction was an immediate dimerization of the CO_2 molecules into oxalate."

Loren wiped the crab juice off her hands and took a sip of beer. "All of this chemistry is starting to make my head spin," she complained.

"You sure it's not the beer and the Bay Seasoning?" Pitt asked with a grin.

"I'm sorry," Lisa said. "Most of my friends are biochemists, so I sometimes forget to take off my verbal lab coat."

"Loren has a much better head for public policy than for science," Pitt kidded. "You were mentioning the outcome of your experiment?"

"In other words, the catalytic reaction converted the carbon dioxide into a simple compound. With further processing, we can get to a carbon-based fuel, such as ethanol. But the critical reaction was the actual breakdown of the carbon dioxide."

The pile of crabs had been transformed into a mass of broken claws and empty shells. The middle-aged waitress deftly cleared away the mess and returned a short time later with coffee and key lime pie for the table.

"Forgive me, but I'm not sure I understand what you are saying," Loren said between bites.

Lisa gazed out the window at some twinkling lights on the far side of the river.

"I'm quite certain that the application of my catalyst can be used to construct a high-output artificial-photosynthesis device."

"Could it be expanded to industrial proportions?" Pitt asked.

Lisa nodded with a humble look. "I'm sure of it. All that is needed is some light, rhodium, and ruthenium to make it tick."

Loren shook her head. "So what you're saying is that we'll be able to construct a facility that can filter carbon dioxide into a harmless substance? And the process can be applied to power plants and other industrial polluters?"

"Yes, that's the prospect. But even more than that."

"What do you mean?"

"*Hundreds* of facilities could be built. In terms of carbon reduction, it'd be like putting a pine forest in a box."

"So you're talking about actually reducing

the existing levels of carbon dioxide in the atmosphere," Pitt stated.

Lisa nodded again, her lips pursed tight.

Loren grabbed Lisa's hand and squeezed it hard. "Then . . . you've found a genuine solution to global warming." The words came out in a whisper.

Lisa looked sheepishly at her pie and nodded. "The process is sound. There's still work ahead, but I see no reason why we can't have a large-scale artificial-photosynthesis facility designed and built in a matter of months. All it will take is money and political support," she said, looking at Loren.

Loren was too startled to eat her dessert. "But the hearings today," she said. "Why didn't Dr. Maxwell mention it?"

Lisa stared up at the fern. "I haven't told him yet," she replied quietly. "I only just made the discovery a few days ago. To be honest, I was a little overwhelmed at the findings. My research assistant convinced me not to tell Dr. Maxwell before the hearings, until we were sure about the results. We were both afraid of the potential media frenzy."

"You would have been right about that," Pitt agreed.

"So do you still have doubts about the results?" Loren asked.

Lisa shook her head. "We've duplicated the results at least a dozen times, consistently. There is no question in my mind that the catalyst works."

"Then it is time to act," Loren urged. "Brief Maxwell tomorrow, and I'll follow up with an innocuous hearing question. Then I'll try and get us in to see the President."

"The President?" Lisa blushed.

"Absolutely. We'll need an Executive Order to put a crash production program into place until an emergency funding bill can be authorized. The President clearly understands the carbon problem. If the solution is within our grasp, I'm sure he will act immediately."

Lisa fell silent, overcome by the ramifications. Finally, she nodded her head.

"You are right, of course. I'll do it. Tomorrow."

Pitt paid the bill, and the trio drifted out to the car. They drove home in relative silence, their thoughts absorbed with the magnitude of Lisa's discovery. When Pitt pulled up in front of Lisa's town house in Alexandria, Loren jumped out and gave her old friend a hug.

"I'm so proud of what you've done," she said. "We used to joke about changing the world. Now you really have." She smiled.

"Thanks for giving me the courage to go forward," Lisa replied. "Good night, Dirk," she said, waving at Pitt.

"Don't forget. I'll see you in the morning with the ocean carbon report."

After Loren climbed back into the car, Pitt

slid the gearshift into first and sped down the street.

"Georgetown or the hangar?" he asked Loren.

She snuggled close to him. "The hangar tonight."

Pitt smiled as he steered the Auburn toward Reagan National Airport. Though married, they still kept separate residences. Loren maintained a fashionable town house in Georgetown but spent most of her time at Pitt's eclectic home.

Reaching the grounds of the airport, he drove down a dusty side road toward a dark, vacant section of the field. Passing through an electric gate, he pulled up in front of a dimly lit hangar that looked as if it had been collecting dust for several decades. Pitt pressed the security code on a wireless transmitter and watched as a side door to the hangar slid open. A bank of overhead lights popped on, revealing a glistening interior that resembled a transportation museum. Dozens of brightly polished antique cars were neatly aligned in the center of the building. Along one wall, a majestic Pullman railroad car sat parked on a set of steel tracks embedded in the floor. A rusty bathtub with an ancient outboard motor bolted to the side and a weathered and dilapidated semi-inflatable boat sat incongruously nearby. As Pitt pulled into the hangar, the Auburn's headlights flashed on a pair of aircraft parked at the back of the building. One was an old Ford Tri-Motor and the other a sleek World War II Messerschmitt ME-162 jet. The planes, like many of the cars in the collection, were relics of past adventures. Even the bathtub and raft told a tale of peril and lost love that Pitt retained as sentimental reminders of life's frailty.

Pitt parked the Auburn next to a 1921 Rolls-Royce Silver Ghost that was undergoing restoration and turned off the motor. As the garage door closed behind them, Loren turned to Pitt and asked, "What would my constituents think if they knew I was living in an abandoned aircraft hangar?"

"They'd probably feel pity for you and increase their campaign donations," Pitt replied with a laugh.

He took her hand and led her up a spiral staircase to a loft apartment in one corner of the building. Loren had exerted her marriage rights and coerced Pitt to remodel the kitchen and add an extra room to the apartment, which she used as an exercise area and office. But she knew better than to touch the brass portholes, ship paintings, and other nautical artifacts that gave the residence a decidedly masculine tone.

"Do you really think Lisa's discovery will be able to reverse global warming?" Loren asked, pouring two glasses of pinot noir from a bottle labeled Sea Smoke Botella.

"Given enough resources, there seems no reason to think that it can't happen. Of course, going from the lab to real world production is always more problematic than people think. But if a working design already exists, then the hard part is done."

Loren walked across the room and handed Pitt a glass. "Once the bombshell hits, it's going to get pretty hectic," she said, already dreading the demands on her time.

Pitt hooked an arm around her waist and drew her tight to him. "That's all right," he smiled with a yearning grin. "We've still got tonight before the wolves start howling."

14

After dropping Loren at the airport Metro-rail station for a subway ride to the Hill, Pitt drove to the NUMA headquarters building, a tall glass structure that hugged the bank of the Potomac River. Collecting a copy of the research study on ocean carbon absorption, he returned to the Auburn and drove into D.C., turning northwest up Massachusetts Avenue. It was a beautiful spring day in the capital city. The oppressive heat and humidity of summer, when all were reminded that the city was built on a swamp, was still weeks away. The warm morning still felt comfortable driving in a convertible. Though he knew he should have left it safely tucked away in his hangar, Pitt couldn't resist driving the topless Auburn one more time. The old car was remarkably nimble, and most of the surrounding traffic gave him plenty of leeway as they gawked at the sleek lines of the antique.

Pitt was every bit the anachronism he appeared to the passersby. His love of old planes and cars ran deep, as if he had grown up with the aged machines in another lifetime. The attraction nearly matched the draw of the sea and the mysteries that came with exploring the deep. A gnawing sense of restlessness swirled within him, always fueling the wanderlust. Perhaps it was his sense of history that set him apart, allowing him to solve the problems of the modern world by finding answers in the past.

Pitt located the GWU Environmental Research and Technology Lab on a quiet side street off Rock Creek Park, not far from the Lebanese embassy. He happened upon a parking spot in front of the three-story brick building and walked to the entrance with the ocean study tucked under his arm. The lobby guard signed him in with a visitor's badge, then gave him directions to Lisa's office on the second floor.

Pitt took the elevator, waiting first for a janitor in a gray jumpsuit to push a trash cart out of the lift. A broad-shouldered man with dark eyes, the janitor gave Pitt a penetrating gaze before smiling good-naturedly as he passed by. Pitt pushed the button for the second floor and stood patiently as the cables pulled the elevator compartment skyward. He heard a muffled *ding* as the elevator approached the second floor, but before the doors slid open a massive concussion slammed him to the floor.

The detonation was centered over a hundred feet away, yet it shook the entire building like an earthquake. Pitt felt the elevator rattle and sway before the power failed and the compartment turned black. Rubbing a knot on the back of his head, he gingerly pulled himself to his feet and groped for the control panel. None of the buttons triggered a response. Sliding his hands along the door, he pressed his fingertips into the center seam and wedged open the inner doors. A few inches beyond, the outer doors to the second story rose a foot above the floor of the elevator. Pitt reached over and forced open the outer doors and climbed up onto the second-floor landing, stepping into a scene of chaos.

An emergency alarm blared with a deafening din, drowning out numerous shouting voices. A thick cloud of dust hung in the air, choking the breath for several minutes. Through the smoky haze, Pitt saw a crowd of people fighting their way down a nearby stairwell. The damage appeared most severe along a main corridor that stretched in front of him. The explosion had not been powerful enough to structurally damage the building but had blown out scores of windows and several interior walls. Looking past the immediate congestion, Pitt grimly realized that Lisa's lab was near the heart of the blast.

He made his way down the hallway, giving way to a group of coughing scientists caked in dust. The ground crunched underfoot as he passed the shattered remains of a hallway window. A pale-looking woman staggered out of an office with a bleeding hand, and Pitt stopped and helped her wrap a scarf around the wound.

"Which one is Lisa Lane's office?" he asked.

The woman pointed toward a gaping hole on the left side of the corridor, then shuffled off to the stairwell.

Pitt approached the jagged hole where a doorway had stood and stepped into the bay. A thick cloud of white smoke still hung in the air, slowly drifting out the shattered remains of a picture window that faced the street. Through the vacant window, he could hear the sirens of approaching fire rescue vehicles.

The lab itself was a jumbled mass of smoldering electronics and debris. Pitt noted an old Bunsen burner embedded into a side wall from the force of the blast. The smoking remains and punctured walls confirmed what he had feared. Lisa's lab had indeed been the epicenter of the explosion. The walls still stood and the furnishings had not been obliterated, so it was clearly not a completely debilitating blast. Pitt guessed there would be no fatalities in the rest of the building. But any occupants of the lab were probably not so lucky.

Pitt quickly scoured the room, calling out Lisa's name as he picked through the debris.

He nearly missed her, just catching sight of a dust-covered shoe protruding beneath a fallen cabinet door. He quickly pulled the cabinet aside to reveal Lisa lying in a crumpled heap. Her lower left leg was twisted at an unnatural angle, and her blouse was soaked in blood. But her listless eyes turned and gazed up at Pitt, then blinked in acknowledgment.

"Didn't they teach you to stay away from chemical experiments that go boom?" Pitt said with a forced smile.

He ran his hand along her blood-wet shoulder until finding a large sliver of glass jutting from her blouse. It appeared loose, so he yanked it out with a quick tug, then applied pressure with the palm of his hand to the stem the bleeding. Lisa grimaced briefly, then passed out.

Pitt held still and checked her pulse with his free hand until a fireman entered the room wielding an ax.

"I need a paramedic here," Pitt shouted.

The fireman gave Pitt a surprised look, then called on his radio. A paramedic team arrived minutes later and quickly attended to her injuries. Pitt followed as they placed her on a stretcher and carried her down to a waiting ambulance.

"Her pulse is low, but I think she'll make it," one of the emergency workers told Pitt before the vehicle roared off to Georgetown University Hospital.

Threading his way through a horde of emergency workers and onlookers, Pitt was suddenly grabbed by a young paramedic.

"Sir, you better sit down and let me take a look at that," the young man said excitedly, nodding at Pitt's arm. Pitt looked down to see that his sleeve was soaked red.

"No worries," he shrugged. "It's not my blood."

He made his way to the curb, then stopped in dismay. The Auburn sat covered in a blanket of shattered glass. Dings and scratches pockmarked the car from nose to tail. A piece of file cabinetry was mashed into the grille, spawning a growing pool of radiator fluid beneath the car. Inside, a chunk of flying building mortar had carved through the leather seats. Pitt looked up and shook his head as he realized that he'd unknowingly parked right beneath Lisa's office.

Sitting on the running board and collecting himself, he observed the scene of chaos around him. Sirens blared as dozens of disheveled lab workers wandered around in a daze. Smoke still rose from the building, though fire had thankfully not materialized. Taking it all in, Pitt somehow had an odd sense that the explosion was no accident. Rising to his feet, he thought of Lisa as he gazed at the damaged Auburn, then felt a pang of anger gradually swell from within.

Standing behind a row of hedges across the street, Clay Zak watched the mayhem with idle satisfaction. After Lisa's ambulance roared away and the smoke began to clear, he walked several blocks down a side alley to his parked rental car. Unzipping a gray jumpsuit, he tossed it into a nearby trash can, then climbed into the car and cautiously drove to Reagan National Airport.

15

A low mist hung over the still waters surrounding Kitimat as the first gray swaths of dawn streaked the eastern sky. A distant rumble of a truck rolling through the streets of the town drifted over the water, breaking the early-morning silence.

In the cabin of the NUMA workboat, Dirk set down a mug of hot coffee and started the boat's engine. The inboard diesel sprang immediately to life, murmuring quietly in the damp air. Dirk glanced out the cockpit window, spying a tall figure approaching on the dock.

"Your suitor has arrived right on time," Dirk said aloud.

Summer climbed up from the berths below and gave her brother a scornful look, then stepped onto the stern deck. Trevor Miller walked up with a heavy case under one arm.

"Good morning," Summer greeted. "You were successful?"

Trevor handed the case to Summer, then

stepped aboard. He gave Summer an admiring look, then nodded.

"A lucky stroke for us that the municipality of Kitimat has its own Olympic-sized swimming pool. The pool maintenance director willfully parted with his water quality analyzer in exchange for a case of beer."

"The price of science," Dirk said, poking his head out the wheelhouse door.

"The results obviously won't be on a par with NUMA's computer analysis, but it will allow us to at least measure the pH levels."

"That will give us a ballpark gauge. If we find a low pH level, then we know that the acidity has increased. And an increase in acidity can occur from elevated amounts of carbon dioxide in the seawater," Summer said.

Summer opened the case, finding a commercial-grade portable water analyzer along with numerous plastic vials. "The important thing is to replicate the high acidity readings identified by the lab. This ought to do the job for us."

The results of the Seattle lab test had been shocking. The pH levels in several water samples taken near the mouth of the Douglas Channel were three hundred times lower than base levels taken elsewhere along the Inside Passage. Most disturbing was the final sample taken, just minutes before the *Ventura* nearly ran into the NUMA boat. The test results showed extreme acidity not far removed from the caustic levels of battery acid.

"Thanks for sticking around," Trevor said, as Summer cast off the lines and Dirk powered the boat into the passage. "This certainly appears to be just a local problem."

"The waters know no international boundaries. If there is an environmental impact occurring, then we have a responsibility to investigate," Dirk replied.

Summer looked into Trevor's eyes and could see the concern ran much deeper. Left unspoken was the potential connection to the death of his brother.

"We met with the police inspector yesterday," Summer said quietly. "He had nothing more to add about your brother's death."

"Yes," Trevor replied, his voice turning cold. "He's closed the case, reporting the deaths as accidental. Claims an accumulation of exhaust gases likely collected in the wheelhouse and killed everyone. Of course, there's no evidence for that . . ." he said, his voice trailing off.

Summer thought of the strange cloud they had seen on the water, and the eerie Haisla tale of Devil's Breath. "I don't believe it either," she said.

"I don't know what the truth is. Maybe that will help tell us," he said, staring at the water sample kit.

Dirk piloted the boat at top speed for over two hours until they reached the Hecate

Strait. Tracking the navigation system, he cut the engine when they reached the GPS coordinates where the last water sample had been taken. Summer dropped a Niskin bottle over the side and scooped up a vial of seawater, then inserted a probe from the water analyzer.

"The pH reading is about 6.4. Not nearly the extreme we found two days ago, but still well below normal seawater levels."

"Low enough to create havoc with the phytoplankton, which will ultimately sound a death knell up the food chain," Dirk noted.

Summer gazed at the serene beauty of Gil Island and the surrounding passage inlets, then shook her head. "Hard to figure what could be causing the high acidity levels in such a pristine area," she said.

"Maybe a passing freighter with a leaky bilge or one that outright dumped some toxic waste," Dirk posed.

Trevor shook his head. "It's not very likely here. Commercial traffic generally runs on the other side of Gil Island. Typically, the only traffic through here is fishing boats and ferryboats. And of course the occasional Alaskan cruise ship."

"Then we've got to expand our sampling until we can pinpoint the source," Summer said, labeling the specimen and preparing the Niskin bottle for another drop.

For the next several hours, Dirk steered the

boat in ever-widening circles, while Summer and Trevor took dozens of water samples. To their chagrin, none of the samples approached the low pH levels reported by the Seattle lab. Letting the boat drift as they took a late-afternoon lunch, Dirk printed out a chart and showed it to the others.

"We've run a series of circles extending to an eight-mile radius from our initial sample. As it turns out, that was our peak reading. Everything south of there showed normal pH levels. But north of that point, it is a different story. We're picking up reduced pH levels in a rough cone shape."

"Flowing with the prevailing currents," Trevor noted. "It might well have been a one-time spill of pollutants."

"Perhaps it's a natural phenomenon," Summer suggested. "An underwater volcanic mineral that is creating a high acidity."

"Now that we know where to look, we'll be able to find the answer," Dirk said.

"I don't understand," Trevor replied with a blank look.

"NUMA technology to the rescue," Summer replied. "We've got side-scan sonar and an ROV aboard. If there is something on the bottom, we'll be able to spot it one way or another."

"But that will have to wait for another day," Dirk said, noting the late hour. Restarting the motor, he nosed the research boat in the direction of Kitimat and accelerated to twenty-five knots. When they drew closer to Kitimat, Dirk let out a low whistle when he noticed an LNG tanker tucked under a covered dock off a small inlet.

"Can't believe they run one of those babies in and out of here," he said.

"She must be offloading at Mitchell Goyette's carbon sequestration facility," Summer replied. As she and Trevor explained to Dirk the function of the facility, he eased off the throttle and turned toward the docked tanker.

"What are you doing?" Summer asked.

"Carbon sequestration. Carbon dioxide and acidity go together like peanut butter and jelly — you said so yourself," he replied. "Maybe there's a connection with the tanker."

"The tanker is bringing in CO_2 to offload at the facility. An inbound ship could have had an accidental leakage in the passage," Trevor said. "Though that particular tanker must have come in last night or early this morning."

"Trevor's right," Summer added. "The tanker wasn't there yesterday, and we didn't see it in the channel before that." She studied the facility's pier, which stretched out into the channel, noticing that Goyette's luxury yacht and the other visiting boats had all disappeared.

"No harm in collecting a few samples to

make sure they're honest," Dirk countered.

Seconds later, a dark speedboat came roaring out of the covered dock and headed directly for the NUMA vessel. Dirk ignored the boat and held his course and speed.

"Somebody's awake," he muttered. "We're not even within a mile of the place. A tad touchy, aren't they?"

He watched as the speedboat veered off when it drew near, circling around in a loop before pulling alongside the research boat. There were three men seated aboard, dressed in innocuous brown security uniforms. But there was nothing innocuous about the Heckler & Koch HK416 assault rifles they each held across their laps.

"You are approaching private waters," barked one of the men through a bullhorn. "Turn away immediately." One of his partners, a stocky Inuit wearing a crew cut, waved his rifle toward the NUMA boat's wheelhouse for added emphasis.

"I just want to fish off the inlet," Dirk yelled back, pointing toward the waterway that led to the covered dock. "There's a deep hole off the mouth teeming with coho."

"No fishing," blared the voice through the bullhorn. Crew Cut stood up and pointed his rifle at Dirk for a moment, then motioned with his barrel to turn away. Dirk casually spun the wheel to starboard and pulled away, feigning ignorance of the threat on his life as he tossed a friendly wave at the speedboat. As the boat turned away, Summer nonchalantly leaned over the stern deck gunwale and scooped up a vial of water.

"What's with the heavy security?" Dirk asked Trevor, as they sped the last few miles to Kitimat.

"They claim they're trying to protect their proprietary technology, but who knows for sure? The company has shown signs of paranoia from the first day that they broke ground. They brought in their own team of construction workers to build it and have their own team of people to run it. They're mostly Tlingit, but not from around here. I've heard that not a single local resident has been hired for any phase of the operation. On top of that, the employees have their own housing on the grounds. They are never even seen in town."

"Have you been through the facility?"

"No," Trevor replied. "My involvement was upfront, with environmental impact statements and the like. I reviewed the plans and walked the site during construction, but was never invited back after they received all of their building approvals. I made several requests to make an on-site review after they went operational, but never got the backing from my higher-ups to press the issue."

"A powerful guy like Mitchell Goyette can incite a lot of fear in the right places," Dirk noted.

"You are exactly right. I heard rumors that his acquisition of the building site was accomplished by a great deal of coercion. His building and environmental approvals breezed through without a hiccup, which is nearly unheard-of around here. Somehow, somewhere, there were some skids greased."

Summer interrupted the conversation by entering the bridge with a vial of water held up in front of her. "Acidity level is normal, at least from a mile outside the facility."

"Too far off to tell us anything for sure," Trevor said, looking back at the facility with a contemplative gaze.

Dirk had his own deliberate look about him. He liked to play by the rules but had little tolerance for authoritarian bullying tactics. Summer liked to joke that he was a jovial Clark Kent, who always gave a handout to a beggar or held a door open for a woman. But if someone told him he couldn't do something, he was apt to turn into the Tasmanian Devil. The confrontation with the security boat rattled his sense of propriety and alerted his suspicions, while silently elevating his blood pressure a few millimeters. He waited until the boat was docked and Trevor waved good-bye, agreeing to meet for dinner in an hour. Then he turned to Summer.

"I'd like to take a closer look at that sequestration facility," he said.

Summer stared at the first lights of Kitimat shimmering on the water as twilight approached. Then she replied, answering in a way that Dirk least expected.

"You know, I think I would, too."

16

It was after six p.m. when Loren and Pitt arrived at Georgetown University Hospital and were allowed into Lisa Lane's room. Given her brush with death earlier in the day, she looked remarkably robust. A mammoth bandage covered her left shoulder, and her broken leg had been set in a cast and elevated. Beyond a pallor from loss of blood, she appeared fully lucid, and perked up at the sight of her visitors.

Loren rushed over and gave her a peck on the cheek while Pitt set a large vase of pink lilies next to the bed.

"Looks like the good folks of Georgetown patched you up nicely," Pitt observed with a grin.

"My dear, how are you feeling?" Loren asked, pulling a chair up alongside the bed.

"Pretty good, under the circumstances," Lisa replied with a forced smile. "The pain medication isn't quite keeping up with my throbbing leg, but the doctors tell me it will heal as good as new. Just remind me to cancel my aerobics class for the next few weeks."

She turned to Pitt with a serious look. "They've given me six units of red blood cells since I arrived. The doctor said I was lucky. I would have died from blood loss if you hadn't found me when you did. Thank you for saving my life."

Pitt winked at her. "You are much too important to lose now," he said, brushing off his actions.

"It was a miracle," Loren said. "Dirk told me how devastated the lab was. It is amazing that no one in the building was killed."

"Dr. Maxwell stopped by earlier. He promised to buy me a new lab." She smiled. "Though he was a little disappointed that I didn't know what happened."

"You don't know what caused the explosion?" Loren asked.

"No. I thought it came from a neighboring lab."

"From what I saw of the damage, it appeared that the blast was centered in the room where I found you," Pitt said.

"Yes, that's what Dr. Maxwell told me. I'm not sure he believed me when I told him that there was nothing in my lab that could have caused that large of an explosion."

"It was a pretty powerful bang," Pitt agreed.

Lisa nodded. "I've sat here and pictured every element and piece of equipment in that lab. All of the materials we have been working with are inert. We have a number of gas tanks for the experiments, but Dr. Maxwell indicated that they were all found intact. The equipment is basically benevolent. There was simply nothing volatile I can think of that would have caused such a thing."

"Don't blame yourself," Loren said. "Maybe it was something with the building, an old gas line or something."

They were interrupted by a stern-faced nurse who came in and propped up Lisa's bed, then slid a tray of dinner in front of her.

"Guess we better be on our way so that you can enjoy the hospital's epicurean delights," Pitt said.

"I'm sure it won't compare to last night's crabs," Lisa said, struggling to laugh. Then her face turned to a frown. "By the way, Dr. Maxwell mentioned that an old car parked in front of the building was severely damaged by the explosion. The Auburn?"

Pitt nodded with a hurt look. "Afraid so," he said. "But don't worry. Like you, she can be rebuilt to as good as new."

There was a knock on the door behind them, then a lean man with a ragged beard entered the room.

"Bob," Lisa greeted. "I'm glad you're here. Come meet my friends," she said, introducing Loren and Pitt to her lab assistant Bob Hamilton.

"I still can't believe you made it out without a scratch," Lisa kidded him.

"Lucky for me I was in the cafeteria having lunch when the lab went boom," he said, eyeing Loren and Pitt with uncertainty.

"A fortunate thing," Loren agreed. "Are you as stumped as Lisa by what happened?"

"Completely. There could have been a leak in one of our pressure canisters that somehow ignited, but I think it was something in the building. A freak accident, whatever the source, and now all of Lisa's research is destroyed."

"Is that true?" Pitt asked.

"All the computers were destroyed, which contained the research databases," Bob replied.

"We should be able to piece it together once I get back to the lab . . . if I still have a lab," Lisa said.

"I'll demand that the president of GWU ensure that it is safe before you step into that building again," Loren said.

She turned to Bob. "We were just leaving. Very nice to meet you, Bob." Then she leaned over and kissed Lisa again. "Take care, honey. I'll visit again tomorrow."

"What a terrible ordeal," Loren said to Pitt as they left the room and walked down the brightly lit hospital corridor to the elevator. "I'm so glad she is going to be all right."

When all she got from Pitt was a slight nod

in reply, she looked into his green eyes. They had a faraway look, one she had seen on many occasions, usually when Pitt was struggling to track down a lost shipwreck or decipher the mystery of some ancient documents.

"Where are you?" she finally prodded him.

"Lunch," he replied cryptically.

"Lunch?"

"What time do most people eat lunch?" he asked.

She looked at him oddly. "Eleven-thirty to one, I suppose, for whatever that is worth."

"I walked into the building just prior to the explosion. The time was ten-fifteen, and our friend Bob was already having lunch," he said with a skeptical tone. "And I'm pretty sure I saw him standing across the street looking like a spectator after the ambulance left with Lisa. He didn't seem to show much concern that his coworker might be dead."

"He was probably in a state of shock. You were probably in a state of shock, for that matter. And maybe he's one of those guys that goes to work at five in the morning, so he'd hungry for lunch by ten." She gave him a skeptical look. "You'll have to do better than that," she added, shaking her head.

"I suppose you are right," he said, grabbing her hand as they walked out of the hospital's front door. "Who am I to argue with a politician?"

17

Arthur Jameson was tidying up his mahogany desk when an aide knocked on the open door and walked in. The spacious but conservatively decorated office of the natural resources minister commanded an impressive view of Ottawa from its twenty-first-floor perch in the Sir William Logan Building, and the aide couldn't help but peek out the window as he approached the minister's desk. Seated in a high-back leather chair, Jameson peered from the aide to an antique grandfather clock that was ticking toward four o'clock. Hopes of escaping the bureaucracy early vanished with the aide's approaching footsteps.

"Yes, Steven," the minister said, welcoming the twenty-something aide who faintly resembled Jim Carrey. "What do you have to sour my weekend?"

"Don't worry, sir, no environmental disasters of note," the aide smiled. "Just a brief report from the Pacific Forestry Centre in British Columbia that I thought you should take a look at. One of our field ecologists has reported unusually high levels of acidity in the waters off Kitimat."

"Kitimat, you say?" the minister asked, suddenly stiffening.

"Yes. You were just there visiting a carbon waste facility, weren't you?"

Jameson nodded as he grabbed the file and quickly scanned the report. He visibly relaxed after studying a small map of the area. "The results were found some sixty miles from Kitimat, along the Inside Passage. There are no industrial facilities anywhere near that area. It was probably an error in the sampling. You know how we get false reports all the time," he said with a reassuring look. He calmly closed the file and slid it to the side of his desk without interest.

"Shouldn't we call the B.C. office and have them resample the water?"

Jameson exhaled slowly. "Yes, that would be the prudent thing to do," he said quietly. "Call them on Monday and request another test. No sense in getting excited unless they can duplicate the results."

The aide nodded in consent but stood rooted in front of the desk. Jameson gave him a fatherly look.

"Why don't you clear out of here, Steven? Go take that fiancée of yours out to dinner. I hear there's a great new bistro that just opened on the riverfront."

"You don't pay me enough to dine there," the aide grinned. "But I'll take you up on the early exit. Have a great weekend, sir, and I'll see you on Monday."

Jameson watched the aide leave his office and waited as the sound of his footsteps faded down the hallway. Then he grabbed the file and read through the report details. The acidity results didn't appear to have any correlation to Goyette's facility, but a feeling in Jameson's stomach told him otherwise. He was in too deep to get crossways with Goyette now, he thought, as the instinct for self-preservation took over. He picked up the telephone and quickly punched a number by memory, grinding his teeth in anxiety as the line rang three times. A woman's voice finally answered, her tone feminine but efficient.

"Terra Green Industries. May I help you?"

"Resources Minister Jameson," he replied brusquely. "Calling for Mitchell Goyette."

18

Dirk and Summer quietly shoved their boat away from the municipal dock and drifted into the harbor. When the current had pushed them out of view of the dock, Dirk started the engine and guided them slowly down the channel. The sky overhead had partially cleared, allowing a splash of starlight to strike the water as the midnight hour was consumed. The bellow from a bay-front honky-tonk provided the only competing sound as they motored slowly away from town.

Dirk kept the boat in the center of the channel, following the mast light of a distant troll boat heading out early in search of some prize coho salmon. Easing away from the lights of Kitimat, they sailed in darkness for several miles until navigating a wide bend in the channel. Ahead, the water glistened like polished chrome, reflecting the bright lights of the Terra Green sequestration plant.

As the boat moved downstream, Dirk could see that the facility grounds were dotted with brilliant overhead floodlights, which cast abstract shadows against the surrounding pines. Only the huge covered dock was kept muted by the spotlights, shading the presence of the LNG tanker that lay moored inside.

Summer retrieved a pair of night vision binoculars and scrutinized the shoreline as they cruised past at a benign distance.

"All quiet on the Western Front," she said. "I only got a quick glimpse under the big top but saw no signs of life around the dock or the ship."

"Security at this hour can't be more than a couple of goons in a box staring at some video camera feeds."

"Let's hope they're watching a wrestling match on TV instead, so we can grab our water samples and get out."

Dirk held the boat at a steady pace until they had traveled two miles past the facility. Safely lost from view behind several bends in the channel, he spun the wheel to starboard and brought the boat up tight along the shoreline, then cut the running lights. The patchy starlight provided enough visibility to distinguish the tree-lined bank, but he still eased off the throttle while keeping one eye glued to the depth readings on an Odom fathometer. Summer stood alongside, scanning for obstructions with the night vision binoculars and whispering course changes to her brother.

Moving barely over idle, they crept to within three-quarters of a mile of the Terra Green facility, staying out of direct view. A small cove provided the last point of concealment before the floodlights scorched the channel surface. Summer quietly released an anchor off the bow, then Dirk killed the engine. A slight whisper of wind through some nearby pines rattled an otherwise eerie nighttime silence. The wind shifted, bringing with it the whine of pumps and the humming of electrical generators from the nearby facility, the noise easily concealing their movements.

Dirk glanced at his Doxa dive watch before joining Summer in slipping into a dark-colored dry suit.

"We're approaching slack tide," he said quietly. "We'll have a little head current going in, but that will give us a push at our backs on the return swim."

He had calculated as such earlier in the evening, knowing that they didn't want to be fighting the current to return to the boat. Though it probably wouldn't have mattered. Both Dirk and Summer were excellent swimmers, often engaging in marathon ocean swims whenever they were near warm water.

Summer adjusted the straps on her BC, which held a single dive tank, then clipped on a small dive bag containing several empty vials. She waited until Dirk had his tank on before slipping on a pair of fins.

"A midnight swim in the great Pacific Northwest," she said, eyeing the stars overhead. "Almost sounds romantic."

"There is nothing romantic about a swim in forty-two-degree water," Dirk replied, then clamped a snorkel between his teeth.

With a quiet nod, they both slipped over the side and into the chilly black water. Adjusting their buoyancy, they took their bearings and began kicking their way out of the cove and toward the facility. They swam near the surface, their heads just breaking the water like a pair of a prowling alligators. Conserving their dive tanks, they used snorkels to breathe, sucking in the brisk night air through their silicone breathing tubes.

The current was slightly stronger than Dirk had anticipated, led by the runoff from the Kitimat River at the head of the channel. They easily overpowered the headwaters, but the extra exertion built up body heat. Despite the frigid water, Dirk could feel himself sweating inside the thermal dry suit.

A half mile from the plant, Dirk felt Summer tap his shoulder and turned to see her pointing toward the shore. In the shadows of a jagged ridge of pine trees, he could make out a boat moored close to land. It was darkened like their own vessel, and, in the dim night light, he was unable to ascertain its dimensions.

Dirk nodded at Summer and swam deeper

into the channel, putting a wide berth between them and the boat. They continued swimming at a measured pace until they closed within two hundred yards of the facility. Stopping to rest, Dirk tried to get a lay of the land beneath the blaring spotlights.

A large L-shaped building stretched across the grounds, its base next to the covered dock. The whine of pumps and generators emanated from the structure, which processed the liquid carbon dioxide. A separate windowed building adjacent to a helicopter pad stood a few yards away and appeared to contain offices. Dirk guessed that the housing accommodations for the workers were located up the road, in the direction of Kitimat. Off to his right, a sturdy pier jutted into the channel, hosting a single boat. It was the same dark speedboat that had chased them away earlier in the day.

Summer swam alongside, then reached down to her dive bag. Uncorking an empty vial, she collected a water sample while they drifted.

"I gathered two additional samples on the way in," she whispered. "If we can collect another one or two around the dock, then we should have the bases covered."

"Next stop," he replied. "Let's take it underwater from here."

Dirk took a bearing with a compass on his wrist, then slipped his regulator between his teeth and expelled a burst of air from his BC. Sinking a few feet below the surface, he gently began kicking toward the massive covered dock. The corrugated tin structure was relatively narrow, offering just a few feet of leeway for the ship occupying the lone berth. Yet the dock was well over a football field long, easily accommodating the ninety-meter tanker.

The luminescent dial of the compass was barely visible in the inky water as Dirk followed his set bearing. The water grew lighter from the shoreside lights as he approached the dock entrance. He continued swimming until the dark shape of the tanker's hull loomed before him. Slowly ascending, he broke the surface almost directly beneath the tanker's stern rail. He quickly scanned the nearby dock, finding it deserted at the late hour. Pulling his hood away from one ear, he listened for voices, but the drone of the pump house would have made a shout difficult to detect. Gently kicking away from the side of the ship, he tried to get a better look at the vessel.

Though a large ship from Dirk's perspective, she was tiny as far as LNG carriers go. Designed with a streamlined deck, she could carry twenty-five hundred cubic meters of liquefied natural gas in two horizontal metallic tanks belowdecks. Built for coastal transport duty, she was dwarfed by the large oceangoing carriers that could hold more than fifty times the amount of liquefied natural gas.

The ship was probably ten or twelve years old, Dirk gauged, showing wear at the seams but judiciously maintained. He didn't know what modifications had been made for the ship to carry liquid CO_2 but presumed they were minor. Though CO_2 was somewhat denser than LNG, it required less temperature and pressure extremes to reach a liquid state. He peered up at the name *Chichuyaa,* beaded in gold lettering across the stern, noting the home registry of Panama City painted in white lettering below.

A rise of bubbles rippled the water a few yards away, then Summer's head popped through the surface. She glanced at the ship and dock, then nodded at her brother as she pulled out a vial and collected a water sample. When she finished, Dirk pointed toward the bow and dropped back beneath the surface. Summer followed suit, tracking her brother as he swam forward. Following the dark outline of the tanker's hull, they swam down the length of the ship, quietly surfacing off the ship's bow. Dirk eyed the tanker's Plimsoll line a few feet overhead, noting that the vessel was just a foot or two shy of its fully loaded displacement.

Summer turned her attention to a series of overhead feeder tubes that dangled like thick tentacles over the ship from an adjacent dockside pumping station. Called "Chiksan arms," the large articulated pipes jimmied and swayed from the surge of the liquid CO_2 flowing through inside. Small wisps of white smoke spewed from the pump building roof, condensation from the cooled and pressurized gas. Summer reached down and retrieved the last empty vial from her dive bag, wondering whether the water around her was contaminated with pollutants as she took the final sample. Zipping the full vial into her dive bag, she kicked toward her brother, who had drifted near the dock.

As she approached, Dirk pointed toward the dock entrance and whispered, "Let's go."

Summer nodded and started to turn, then suddenly hesitated in the water. Her eyes fixated on the Chiksan arms above Dirk's head. With a quizzical look on her face, she raised a finger and pointed at the pipes far overhead. Dirk cocked his head and gazed up at the pipes for a minute but didn't notice anything amiss.

"What is it?" he whispered.

"There's something about the movement of the pipes," she replied, staring at the arms. "I think the carbon dioxide is being pumped onto the ship."

Dirk stared up at the wiggling arms. There was a rhythmic movement through the pipes, but it was hardly sufficient to tell which way the liquefied gas was flowing. He looked at his sister and nodded. Her occasional hunches or intuitions were usually right. It was enough for him to want to check it out.

"Do you think it means anything?" Summer asked, looking up at the ship's bow.

"Hard to say if it has any relevance," Dirk replied quietly. "It doesn't make any sense that they would be pumping CO_2 onto the ship. Maybe there is an LNG pipeline from Athabasca running through here."

"Trevor said there was only a small oil pipeline and the CO_2 line."

"Did you notice if the ship was sitting higher in the water this morning?"

"I couldn't say," Summer replied. "Though she ought to be a lot higher in the water now if she's been off-loading gas for any amount of time."

Dirk looked up at the hulking vessel. "What I know about LNG ships, and it ain't much, is that pumps on shore move the liquid onto the ships, and they have pumps on board to move it off at the destination. From the sound of it, the pump house on shore is clearly operating."

"That could be to pump the gas underground or into temporary storage tanks."

"True. But it is too noisy to tell if the shipboard pumps are running." He kicked a few yards over to the dock, then poked his head up and looked around. The dock and visible portions of the ship were still deserted. Dirk slipped off his tank and weight belt and hung them from a nearby cleat.

"You're not going aboard?" Summer whispered as if her brother were insane.

Dirk's white teeth flashed in a grin. "How else will we solve the mystery, my dear Watson?"

Summer knew that waiting in the water for her brother would be too nerve-racking, so she reluctantly hung her dive gear next to his and climbed onto the dock. Following him quietly toward the ship, she couldn't help muttering, "Thanks, Sherlock," under her breath.

19

The movement on the monitor was barely discernible. By all rights, the Aleut security guard should have missed it. A fortuitous glance at the bank of video monitors revealed a slight ripple in the water from one of the video feeds, aimed just astern of the tanker. The guard quickly hit a zoom button on the roof-mounted camera, catching sight of a dark object in the water seconds before it disappeared under the surface. Most likely a wayward harbor seal, the guard presumed, but it offered a good excuse to take a break from the dreary confines of the security station.

He reached for a radio and called the watch aboard the *Chichuyaa*.

"This is plant security. Video picked up an object in the water off your stern. I'm going to take the runabout alongside for a look."

"Roger, shore," replied a sleepy voice. "We'll keep the lights on for you."

The guard slipped on a jacket and grabbed a flashlight, then stopped in front of a gun cabinet. He eyed a black H&K assault rifle, then thought better of it, tucking a Glock automatic pistol into his holster instead.

"Best not to be shooting seals this time of night," he muttered to himself as he walked toward the pier.

The LNG carrier emitted a cacophony of mechanical sounds as the chilled gas flowed through the pipes stringing off its deck. Dirk knew there would be a few workers about monitoring the flow, but they were bound to be stationed in the bowels of the ship or at a control panel inside the pump house. Though the dockside area was dimly lit, the ship itself was brightly illuminated and rendered a high degree of exposure. Dirk figured they would need just a minute or two to slip on and determine if the ship's pumps were operating.

Slinking along the dock, they made their way to a main gangplank affixed amidships. Their sodden dry suits squished as they walked, but they made no effort to conceal the noise. The whir and throb of the nearby pump station was louder than ever and easily drowned out the sound of their movements. It also obscured the sound of an outboard motor chugging toward the covered dock.

The security guard ran the small boat into the dock facility without lights. He loitered about the stern undetected for several minutes, then cruised down the outboard side of the tanker. Passing the prow of the ship, he started to circle back when he caught sight of the dive gear hanging on the wharf. He quickly killed the engine and drifted to the dock, tying the boat up and then examining the equipment.

Summer saw him first, noticing a movement out of the corner of her eye as she turned to ascend the gangplank. Dirk had already taken a few steps up the ramp.

"We have company," she whispered, tilting her head in the guard's direction.

Dirk glanced quickly at the guard, who had his back turned to them. "Let's get aboard. We can lose him on the ship if he spots us."

Ducking low, he raced up the gangway taking long strides. Summer matched his pace a few steps behind. They were clearly visible from the guard's vantage, and they expected a shout from him to stop, but it never came. Instead, they zipped to the top of the ramp, escaping his scrutiny. But when Dirk was a step from the ship's open side rail, a faint shadow appeared on deck, followed by a dark blur. Too late, Dirk realized, the blur was a swinging truncheon aimed for the side of his face. He tried to duck in midstep but was unable to dodge the blow. The wooden club caught him with a stinging blow across the crown of his skull. His dry suit hood softened what would have otherwise been a lethal blow. A kaleidoscope of stars crossed his eyes as his knees turned to jelly. Off balance when the blow struck, he reeled sideways, his hip crushing against the gangplank's side rail. His momentum was all high, and his torso easily flipped over the side while his feet went skyward.

He caught a brief glimpse of Summer reaching for him, but her frantic hands slipped away. Her mouth opened in a brief scream, though he failed to hear her voice. In an instant, she was gone, as he tumbled into space.

The impact seemed to take forever in coming. When he finally collided with the water, it surprisingly induced no pain. There was just a cold smell of darkness before everything turned to black.

20

The shadow at the top of the ramp drifted into the light, revealing an ox of a man with a thick unkempt beard that brushed his chest. He stared at Summer through fiery eyes, his lips turning up in a slight grin as he waved the truncheon casually in her direction.

Summer froze on the gangplank, then subconsciously backpedaled as her eyes darted from the brute to the murky waters below. Dirk had struck the water hard, and he had yet to surface. She felt the ramp shake beneath her feet and turned to see the dock guard sprinting up behind her. The Aleut security guard was uniformed and clean-shaven, appearing to be a safer prospect than the heathen on the ship. Summer quickly took a step toward him.

"My brother is in the water. He's drowning," she yelled, rushing to move past the guard. He quickly pulled the Glock automatic pistol from a side holster and leveled it at Summer's thin midsection.

"You have trespassed on private property," he replied in a monotone voice that was short on mercy. "You shall be held in custody until company officials can be contacted in the morning."

"Let me take her into custody," the shipboard brute barked. "I'll show her some real trespassing." He laughed with a bellow, spraying a shower of spittle across his beard.

"This is a shore facility security matter, Johnson," the guard said, eyeing the ship's watchman with disdain.

"The engine died on our boat. We just came looking for help," Summer pleaded. "My brother . . ."

She looked over the side and cringed. The waters beneath the gangplank had turned flat, and there was no sign of Dirk.

The guard motioned with his gun for Summer to march down the ramp. Following behind, he turned over his shoulder and growled at Johnson.

"Fish that man out of the water, if you can find him. If he's still alive, then bring him to the guard station." He cut the man a sharp stare, then added, "For the sake of your own hide, you better hope he is still alive."

The ox grunted and begrudgingly strolled down the gangplank behind them. Marched along the dock, Summer tried in vain to spot Dirk in the water. Further pleas to the guard went unheeded. Walking beneath an overhead lamp, she saw a coldness in his eyes that gave her pause. While perhaps not a sadist like the ship's watch, he appeared more than capable of pulling the trigger on an uncooperative captive. A blow of disheartenment seemed to strike Summer, and she plodded forward with her head low, awash in helplessness. She suspected that Dirk had probably been unconscious when he hit the water. Several minutes had since elapsed, and she now choked on the bitter reality. He was gone, and there was nothing she could do about it.

Johnson reached the base of the gangplank and peered into the water. There was no sign of Dirk's body. The burly thug examined the edge of the dock but found no water marks indicating that he had pulled himself ashore. There was no way he could have swum the length of the ship without being seen. Somewhere under the surface, he knew, the man lay dead. The watch stared off the gangplank at the flat waters a last time, then ambled back onto the ship, cursing the shore guard.

Ten feet under the surface, Dirk was unconscious but far from dead. After the fall, he had fought to regain his senses, but he was hopelessly ensnarled in the blackness. For brief moments, he was able to break through the veil and seize vague notions of feeling. He sensed his body moving through the water without effort. Then something was wedged between his lips, followed by the sensation of a flowing garden hose jammed into his mouth. Soon the curtain returned, and he again drifted away into a calm darkness.

A pounding at his temple brought him back a second time. He felt a rap against his back and legs, then he felt like he was being stuffed into a closet. He heard a voice say his name, but the rest of the words were indecipherable. The voice vanished with the sound of receding footsteps. He tried with all his might to pry open an eyelid, but they were cemented shut. The pain in his head returned, growing fierce until a constellation of stars burst before his closed eyes. And then the lights and the sound and the pain blissfully departed once more.

21

Summer was led off the dock and past the long building housing the pumping station. The unexpected brutality against her brother had been a shock, but now she willed herself to suppress the difficult emotions and think logically. What was so important at the facility that it would warrant such behavior? Were they in fact pumping CO_2 onto the tanker? She glanced over her shoulder at the guard, who marched several paces behind with his pistol drawn. Even the hired guards acted like it was a top secret installation.

The drone of the pump machinery receded as they walked past the main building and across a small open area. Approaching the administration office and adjacent security station, Summer heard a rustling in some bushes to her left. Recalling the stuffed grizzly bear in the café, she quickly stepped right to veer away from the noise. The confused guard swung his gun hand after Summer while cocking his head toward the bushes. The rustling ceased as the guard stepped closer, then suddenly a figure rose from behind the bushes swinging his arm. The guard spun his gun to fire, but an object whipped out from the prowler's hand and struck him on the side of the face before he could shoot. Summer turned to see a dive belt, its lead weights strung to the end, clank to the ground. The guard had also dropped hard but managed to stagger to one knee. Stunned and bleeding, he slowly reaimed the pistol at the shadowy figure and squeezed the trigger.

Had the toe of Summer's foot not struck the guard's jaw, the bullet might have found its mark. But a hammering kick to his mouth forced the shot high and laid the man out. He slumped over unconscious, the gun slipping out of his hand.

"Those pretty legs are more dangerous than I suspected," spoke a familiar voice.

Summer looked toward the bushes to see Trevor Miller emerge with a crooked smile. Like Summer, he was clad in a dry suit, and appeared slightly out of breath.

"Trevor," she stammered, shocked at seeing him there. "Why are you here?"

"Same reason as you. Come on, let's get out of here." He picked up the guard's gun and flung it into the bushes, then grabbed her hand and began running toward the dock. Summer saw a light turn on in the building as she raced to keep up with Trevor.

They didn't stop until they reached the dock, rushing over to where the security boat was moored. Summer stopped and gazed down at the water as Trevor scooped up the nearby dive gear and tossed it in the boat.

"Dirk went in the water," Summer panted, pointing toward the gangplank.

"I know," Trevor replied. He nodded toward the boat, then stepped aside.

Sprawled across the stern bench, dazed and groggy, Dirk stared up at them through glassy eyes. With a laborious effort, he raised his head slightly and winked at his sister. Summer leaped into the boat and collapsed next to him in surprised relief.

"How did you make it out?" she asked, eyeing a trickle of dried blood along his temple.

Dirk weakly raised an arm and pointed at Trevor, who untied the lines and jumped into the boat.

"No time for platitudes, I'm afraid," Trevor said with a hurried smile. Starting the motor, he gunned the throttle and spun the small boat around the back side of the tanker and out the covered dock. Never looking back, he aimed the boat down the channel and pushed it to its top speed.

Summer tried to check Dirk's wound under the starlight, finding a large knot on the top of his skull that was still damp with blood. His dive hood had saved him from a deeper gouge to the skin, and perhaps a worse fate as well.

"Forgot to wear my hard hat," he mumbled, trying hard to focus his eyes on Summer.

"Your hard head is much too tough to break," she said, laughing aloud in an emotional release.

The boat plowed through the darkness, Trevor hugging the shoreline until suddenly easing off the throttle. The darkened boat Summer had spotted earlier loomed ahead, now recognizable as Trevor's Canadian Resources vessel. Trevor brought the outboard alongside and helped Dirk and Summer aboard, then let the security boat drift. He quickly pulled anchor and motored the research craft down the channel. When they were well out of sight of the facility, he crossed to the opposite side of the channel, then turned and crept back toward Kitimat at slow speed.

Cruising past the Terra Green facility, they witnessed several flashlight beams crisscrossing the grounds but noticed no obvious alarms. The boat slipped unseen into the Kitimat dock, and Trevor killed its motor and tied it off. On the stern deck, Dirk had begun to regain form, save for some dizziness and a pounding head. He shook Trevor's hand after the ecologist helped him ashore.

"Thanks for fishing me out. I would have had a long sleep underwater if not for you."

"Entirely good luck. I was swimming along the dock when I heard the small boat come

173

in. I was actually hiding in the water beneath the gangplank when the guard came ashore. I didn't even realize it was you until I recognized Summer's voice right before you went over the side. You hit the water just a few feet from me. When you didn't move, I immediately jammed my regulator in your mouth. The hard part was keeping us both submerged until we were out of view."

"Shame on a federal employee for trespassing on private property," Summer said with a grin.

"It's all your fault," Trevor replied. "You kept talking about the importance of the water samples, so I thought we needed to know if there was a link to the facility." He handed Summer a dive bag containing several small vials of water.

"Hope they match mine," Summer replied, showing her own samples. "Of course, I'll need to get our boat back to complete the analysis."

"Miller's taxi service is always open. I have a mining site inspection in the morning but can run you back down in the afternoon."

"That would be fine. Thanks, Trevor. Perhaps next time we should work a little closer together," Summer said with a beguiling smile.

Trevor's eyes twinkled at her words.

"I wouldn't want it any other way."

22

Scattered chunks of ice dotted the rolling waters of Lancaster Strait, appearing in the dusk like jagged marshmallows floating in a sea of hot chocolate. Against the dim background of Devon Island, a black behemoth crept along the horizon billowing a trail of dark smoke.

"Range twelve kilometers, sir. She's beating a path right across our bow." The helmsman, a red-haired ensign with jug ears, peered from a radarscope to the ship's captain and waited for a response.

Captain Dick Weber lowered a pair of binoculars without taking his gaze off the distant vessel.

"Keep us on intersect, at least until we obtain an identification," he replied without turning.

The helmsman twisted the ship's wheel a half turn, then resumed studying the radar screen. The eighty-foot Canadian Coast Guard patrol vessel plowed slowly through the dark Arctic waters toward the path of the oncoming vessel. Assigned to interdiction duty along the eastern approaches to the Northwest Passage, the *Harp* had been on station just a few days. Though the winter ice had continued the trend of breaking up early, this was the first commercial vessel the patrol craft had seen in the frosty waters this season. In another month or two, there would be a steady stream of massive tankers and containerships making the northerly transit accompanied by icebreakers.

Just a few years prior, the thought of policing traffic through the Northwest Passage would have been laughable. Since man's earliest forays into the Arctic, major sections of the annual winter pack ice remained frozen solid for all but a few summer days. Only a few hardy explorers and the occasional icebreaker dared fight their way through the blocked passage. But global warming had changed everything, and now the passage was navigable for months out of the year.

Scientists estimate that over forty thousand square miles of Arctic ice have receded in just the past thirty years. Much of the blame for the rapid melt off is due to the ice albedo-feedback effect. In its frozen state, Arctic ice will reflect up to ninety percent of incoming solar radiation. When melted, the resulting seawater will conversely absorb an equal amount of radiation, reflecting only about ten percent. This warming loop has ac-

176

counted for the fact that Arctic temperatures are climbing at double the global rate.

Watching the bow of his patrol boat slice through a small ice floe, Weber silently cursed what global climate change had done to him. Transferred from Quebec and comfortable sea duty along the Saint Lawrence River, he now found himself in command of a ship at one of the most remote locations on the planet. And his job, he thought, had been relegated to little more than that of a tollbooth operator.

Weber could hardly blame his superiors, though, for they were just following the mandate of Canada's saber-rattling Prime Minister. When historically frozen sections of the Northwest Passage began to melt clear, the Prime Minister was quick to act, affirming the passage as Canadian Internal Waters and authorizing funds for a deepwater Arctic port at Nanisivik. Promises to build a fleet of military icebreakers and establish new Arctic bases soon followed. Powerful lobbying by a shadowy interest group propelled the Parliament to support the Prime Minister by passing tough restrictions on foreign vessels transiting the passage.

By law, all non-Canadian-flagged ships seeking transit through the passage were now required to notify the Coast Guard of their planned route, pay a passage fee similar to that imposed at the Panama Canal, and be

177

accompanied by a Canadian commercial icebreaker through the more restrictive areas of the passage. A few countries, Russia, Denmark, and the United States among them, refuted Canada's claim and discouraged travel through the waters. But other developed nations gladly complied in the name of economics. Merchant ships connecting Europe with East Asia could trim thousands of miles off their shipping routes by avoiding the Panama Canal. The savings were even more dramatic for ships too large to pass through the canal that would otherwise have to sail around Cape Horn. With the potential to cut the shipping cost of an individual storage container by a thousand dollars, merchant fleets large and small were quick to eye the Arctic crossing as a lucrative commercial path.

As the ice melt off expanded more rapidly than scientists anticipated, the first few shipping companies had begun testing the frigid waters. Thick sheets of ice still clogged sections of the route for much of the year, but during the heat of summer the passage had regularly become ice-free. Powerful icebreakers aided the more ambitious merchant fleets that sought to run the passage from April through September. It was becoming all too evident that within a decade or two, the Northwest Passage would be a navigable waterway year-round.

Staring at the approaching black merchant

ship, Weber wished the whole passage would just freeze solid again. At least the presence of the ship broke up the monotony of staring at icebergs, he thought drily.

"Four kilometers and closing," the helmsman reported.

Weber turned to a lanky radioman wedged into a corner of the small bridge.

"Hopkins, request an identification and the nature of her cargo," he barked.

The radioman proceeded to call the ship, but all his queries were met with silence. He checked the radio, then transmitted several more times.

"She's not responding, sir," he finally replied with a perplexed look. His experience with passing vessels in the Arctic was that they were usually prone to excessive chitchat from the isolated crews.

"Keep trying," Weber ordered. "We're nearly close enough for a visual ID."

"Two kilometers off," the helmsman confirmed.

Weber retrained his binoculars and examined the vessel. She was a relatively small containership of no more than four hundred feet. She was by appearance a newer vessel but oddly showed only a few containers on her topside deck. Similar ships, he knew, often carried containers stacked six or seven layers high. Curious, he studied her Plimsoll line, noting the mark was several feet above the water. Moving his gaze vertically, he looked at a darkened bridge, then at a masthead behind the superstructure. He was startled to see the Stars and Stripes fluttering in the stiff breeze.

"She's American," he muttered. The nationality surprised him, as American ships had informally boycotted the passage at the urging of their government. Weber focused the glasses on the ship's bow, just making out the name ATLANTA in white lettering as the evening light began to fade.

"Her name is the *Atlanta*," he said to Hopkins. The radio operator nodded and tried hailing the ship by name, but there was still no response.

Weber hung the binoculars on a metal hook, then located a binder on the chart table and flipped it open, searching for the name *Atlanta* on a computer printout. All non-Canadian vessels making a transit of the Northwest Passage were required to file notification with the Coast Guard ninety-six hours in advance. Weber checked to see that his file had been updated by satellite link earlier in the day but still found no reference to the *Atlanta*.

"Bring us up on her port bow. Hopkins, tell them that they are crossing Canadian territorial waters and order her to stop for boarding and inspection."

While Hopkins transmitted the message, the helmsman adjusted the ship's heading, then glanced at the radar screen.

"The channel narrows ahead, sir," he reported. "Pack ice encroaching on our port beam approximately three kilometers ahead."

Weber nodded, his eyes still glued to the *Atlanta*. The merchant ship was moving at a surprisingly fast clip, over fifteen knots, he guessed. As the Coast Guard vessel edged closer, Weber again observed that the ship was riding high on the water. Why would a lightly laden ship be attempting the passage? he wondered.

"One kilometer to intercept," the helmsman said.

"Come right. Bring us to within a hundred meters," the captain ordered.

The black merchant ship was oblivious to the Coast Guard patrol craft, or so it seemed to the Canadians. Had they tracked the radar set more closely, they would have noticed that the American ship was both accelerating and subtly changing course.

"Why won't they respond?" muttered the helmsman, growing weary of Hopkins's unanswered radio calls.

"We'll get their attention now," Weber said. The captain walked to the console and pressed a button that activated the ship's marine air horn. Two long blasts bellowed from the horn, the deep bray echoing across the water. The blare drew the men on the bridge to silence as they awaited a response. Again, there was none.

There was little more Weber could do. Unlike in the United States, the Canadian Coast Guard was operated as a civilian organization. The *Harp*'s crew was not military trained, and the vessel carried no armament.

The helmsman eyed the radar screen and reported, "No reduction in speed. In fact, I think she's still accelerating. Sir, we're coming along the ice pack." Weber detected a sudden urgency in his voice. While focused on the merchant ship, the helmsman had neglected to track the hardened pack ice that now flanked their port side. To starboard, the steaming merchant ship rode just a dozen meters away and had drawn nearly even with the patrol craft.

Weber looked up at the high bridge of the *Atlanta* and wondered what kind of fool was in command of the ship. Then he noticed the bow of the freighter suddenly veer toward his own vessel and he quickly realized this was no game.

"Hard left rudder," he screamed.

The last thing anyone expected was for the merchant ship to turn into them, but in an instant the larger vessel was right on top of the *Harp*. Like a bug under the raised foot of an elephant, the patrol boat madly scrambled to escape a crushing blow. Frantically reacting to Weber's command, the helmsman jammed the wheel full over and prayed they would slip by the bigger ship. But the *Atlanta* was too close.

The side hull of the freighter slammed into the *Harp* with a deep thud. The point of impact came to the boat's stern, however, as the smaller vessel had nearly turned away. The blow knocked the *Harp* hard over, nearly capsizing her as a large wave rolled over the deck. In what felt like an eternity to the stricken crew, the Coast Guard craft gradually rolled back upright as it fell away from the bristling sides of the merchant ship. Their peril was not over, however. Unknown to the crew, the collision had torn off the vessel's rudder. With its propeller still spinning madly, the patrol boat surged straight into the nearby ice pack. The *Harp* drove several feet into the thick ice before grounding to a sudden halt, flinging the ship's crew forward.

On the bridge, Weber picked himself up off the deck and helped shut down the vessel's engine, then quickly assessed the health of his ship and crew. An assortment of cuts and bruises was the worst of the personal injuries, but the patrol boat fared less well. In addition to the lost rudder, the ship's crumpled bow had compromised the outer hull. The *Harp* would remain embedded in the ice for four days before a tow could arrive to take the ship to port for repairs.

Wiping away a trickle of blood from a gash on his cheek, Weber stepped to the bridge wing and peered to the west. He saw the running lights of the merchant ship for just a second before the big ship disappeared into a gloomy dark fogbank that stretched across the horizon. Watching as the ship disappeared, Weber shook his head.

"You brazen bastard," he muttered. "You'll pay for this."

Weber's words would prove to ring hollow. A fast-moving storm front south of Baffin Island grounded the Canadian Air Command CP-140 Aurora reconnaissance plane called in by the Coast Guard. When the aircraft finally lifted off from its base in Greenwood, Nova Scotia, and arrived over Lancaster Strait, more than six hours had elapsed. Farther west, a Navy icebreaker and another Coast Guard cutter blocked the passage off Prince of Wales Island, waiting for the belligerent freighter to arrive. But the large black ship never appeared.

The Canadian Coast Guard and Air Force scoured the navigable seas around Lancaster Strait for three days in search of the rogue vessel. Every available route west was scrutinized several times over. Yet the American merchant ship was nowhere to be seen. Baffled, the Canadian forces quietly called off the search, leaving Weber and his crew to wonder how the strange ship had somehow disappeared into the Arctic ice.

23

Dr. Kevin Bue peered at the blackening sky to the west and grimaced. Only hours earlier, the sun had shone brightly and the air was still while the mercury in the thermometer tickled twenty degrees Fahrenheit. But then the barometer had dropped like a stone in a well, accompanied by a gradual building of the westerly winds. A quarter of a mile away, the gray waters of the Arctic now rolled in deep swells that burst against the ragged edge of the ice pack with billowing fountains of spray.

Tugging the hood of his parka tighter, he turned away from the stinging winds and surveyed his home of the last few weeks. Ice Research Lab 7 wouldn't rate many stars in the *Mobil Travel Guide* for luxury or comfort. A half dozen prefabricated buildings made up the camp, huddled in a semicircle with their entrances facing south. Three tiny bunk-houses were jammed together on one side next to the largest building, a combination galley, mess hall, and meeting area. A squat structure just opposite housed a joint lab and radio room, while a snow-covered storage shed rounded out the camp at the far end.

The research lab was one of several Canadian Fisheries and Oceans Department temporary ice camps established as floating research labs to track and study the movements of the Arctic ice pack. Since the time Ice Research Lab 7 had been set up a year earlier, the camp had moved nearly two hundred miles, riding a mammoth sheet of polar ice south across the Beaufort Sea. Now positioned one hundred and fifty miles from the North American coastline, the camp sat on the edge of the ice shelf almost due north of the Yukon Territory. The camp faced a short life, however. The approaching summer meant the breakup of the pack ice where the camp now found itself. Daily measurements of the ice beneath their feet revealed a steady melting already, which had reduced the pack thickness from three feet to fourteen inches. Bue figured they had maybe two more weeks before he and his four-man team would be forced to disassemble the camp and wait for evacuation by Twin Otter ski-plane.

The Arctic oceanographer trudged through ankle-deep snow toward the radio shack. Over the blowing rustle of ice particles bounding across the ground, he heard the whine of a diesel engine revving up and down. Looking past the camp's structures, he spotted a yellow front-end track loader racing back and forth, its blunt blade piling up high mounds of drifted snow. The plow was keeping clear a five-hundred-foot ice runway that stretched along the back of the camp. The crude landing strip was the camp's lifeline, allowing Twin Otters to bring in food and supplies on a weekly basis. Bue made sure that the makeshift runway was kept clear at all times.

Ignoring the roving track loader, Bue entered the joint lab and radio hut, shaking the snow off his feet in an inner doorway before entering the main structure. Making his way past several cramped bays full of scientific journals and equipment, he turned into the closet-sized cubby that housed the satellite radio station. A wild-eyed man with sandy hair and a mirthful grin looked up from the radio set. Scott Case was a brilliant physicist who specialized in studying solar radiation at the poles. Like everyone else in the camp, Case wore multiple hats, including that of chief communications operator.

"Atmospherics are playing havoc with our radio signals again," he said to Bue. "Satellite reception is nil, and our ground transmitter is little better."

"I'm sure the approaching storm isn't helping matters any," Bue replied. "Does Tuktoyaktuk even know that we are trying to hail them?"

Case shook his head. "Can't tell for sure, but I've detected no callbacks."

The sound of the track loader shoving a load of ice just outside the structure echoed off the thin walls.

"You keeping the field clean just in case?" he asked Bue.

"Tuktoyaktuk has us scheduled for a supply drop later today. They may not know that we'll be in the middle of a gale-force blizzard in about an hour. Keep trying, Scott. See if you can wave off the flight for today, for the safety of the pilots."

Before Case could transmit again, the radio suddenly cackled. An authoritative voice backed by static interference blared through the speaker.

"Ice Research Lab 7, Ice Research Lab 7, this is NUMA research vessel *Narwhal*. Do you read, over?"

Bue beat Case to the transmitter and replied quickly. "*Narwhal,* this is Dr. Kevin Bue of Ice Research Lab 7. Go ahead, please."

"Dr. Bue, we're not trying to eavesdrop, but we've heard your repeated calls to the Coast Guard station at Tuktoyaktuk, and we've picked up a few unanswered calls back from Tuktoyaktuk. It sounds like the weather is keeping you two from connecting. Can we assist in relaying a message for you?"

"We'd be most grateful." Bue had the American ship forward a message to Tuktoyaktuk to delay sending the supply plane for twenty-four hours on account of the poor weather. A few minutes later, the *Narwhal* radioed a confirmation back from Tuktoyaktuk.

"Our sincere thanks," Bue radioed. "That will save some poor flyboy a rough trip."

"Don't mention it. Where's your camp located, by the way?"

Bue transmitted the latest position of the floating camp, and the vessel responded in kind.

"Are you boys in good shape to ride out the approaching storm? Looks to be a mean one," the *Narwhal* radioed.

"We've managed everything the Good Witch of the North has thrown at us so far, but thanks all the same," Bue replied.

"Farewell, Ice Lab 7. *Narwhal* out."

Bue set down the transmitter with a look of relief.

"Who says the Americans don't belong in the Arctic after all?" he said to Case, then slipped on his parka and left the building.

Thirty-five miles to the southwest, Captain Bill Stenseth examined a local meteorological forecast with studious concern. An imposing man with Scandinavian features and the build of an NFL linebacker, Stenseth had weathered storms in every ocean of the world. Yet facing a sudden blow in the ice-studded Arctic still made the veteran captain of the

Narwhal nervous.

"The winds seem to be ratcheting up a bit in the latest forecast," he said without looking up from the document. "I think we're in for a pretty good gale. Wouldn't want to be those poor saps hunkered down on the ice," he added, pointing toward the radio.

Standing beside Stenseth on the ship's bridge, Rudi Gunn suppressed a pained grin. Sailing through the teeth of a powerful Arctic storm was going to be anything but pleasant. He would gladly trade places with the ice camp members, who would likely sit out the storm in a warm hut playing pinochle, Gunn thought. Stenseth's preference for battling the elements at sea was clearly the mark of a lifelong sailor, one who never felt comfortable with his feet on the shore.

Gunn shared no similar propensity. Though he was an Annapolis graduate who had spent several years at sea, he now spent more time sailing a desk. The Deputy Director for the National Underwater and Marine Agency, Gunn was usually found in the headquarters building in Washington, D.C. With a short, wiry build and horn-rimmed glasses on his nose, he was the physical opposite of Stenseth. Yet he shared the same adventurous pursuit of oceanographic challenges and was often on hand when a new vessel or piece of underwater technology was sea-tested for the first time.

"I'd have more pity for the polar bears," Gunn said. "How long before the storm front arrives?"

Stenseth eyed a growing number of white-caps cresting off the ship's bow. "About an hour. No more than two. I would suggest re-trieving and securing the *Bloodhound* within the next thirty minutes."

"They won't like returning to the kennel so soon. I'll head down to the operations room and pass the word. Captain, please let me know if the weather deteriorates any sooner than predicted."

Stenseth nodded as Gunn left the bridge and made his way aft. The two-hundred-foot research ship was rolling steadily through a building sea, and Gunn had to grasp a hand-rail several times to steady himself. Nearing the stern, he looked down at a large moon pool cut through the vessel's hull. Surface water was already sloshing back and forth, spilling onto the surrounding deck. Stepping down a companionway, he entered a door marked LAB, which opened up into a large bay. At the far end was a sectioned area with numerous video monitors mounted on the bulkhead. Two technicians sat tracking and recording a data feed from underwater.

"Are they on the bottom?" Gunn asked one of the technicians.

"Yes," the man replied. "They're about two miles east of us. Actually crossed the border into Canadian waters, as a matter of fact."

"Do you have a live transmission?"

The man nodded and passed his communication headset to Gunn.

"*Bloodhound,* this is *Narwhal.* We're seeing a rapid deterioration in the weather conditions up here. Request you break off survey and return to the surface."

A long pause followed Gunn's transmission, and then a static-filled reply was heard.

"Roger, *Narwhal,*" came a gruff voice with a Texas accent. "Breaking off survey in thirty minutes. *Bloodhound,* over and out."

Gunn started to reply, then thought better of it. It was pointless to argue with the pair of hardheads at the other end, he thought. Yanking off the headset, he silently shook his head, then sank into a high-back chair and waited for the half hour to pass.

24

Like the canine it was named for, the *Blood-hound* scoured the earth with its nose to the ground, only the ground was two thousand feet beneath the surface of the Beaufort Sea and its nose was a rigid electronic sensor pod. A titanium-hulled two-man submersible, the *Bloodhound* was purpose-built to investigate deepwater hydrothermal vents. The submerged geysers, which spewed superheated water from the earth's crust, often spawned a treasure trove of unusual plant and sea life. Of greater interest to the men in the NUMA submersible were the potential mineral deposits associated with many hydrothermal vents. Discharged from deep under the seabed, the vents often spewed a mineral-rich concoction of small nodules containing manganese, iron, and even gold. Advances in underwater mining technology made the thermal vent fields potentially significant resources.

"Water temperature is up another degree. That ole smokestack has got to be down here somewhere," drawled the deep voice of Jack Dahlgren.

Sitting in the submersible's copilot seat, the muscular marine engineer studied a computer monitor through steely blue eyes. Scratching his thick cowboy mustache, he gazed out the Plexiglas view port at a drab, featureless bottom starkly illuminated by a half dozen high-intensity lights. There was nothing in the subsea physical landscape to indicate that a hydrothermal vent was anywhere nearby.

"We might just be chasing a few hiccups from down under," replied the pilot. Turning a sharp eye toward Dahlgren, he added, "A bum steer, you might say."

Al Giordino grinned at the jest of the much younger Texan, nearly losing an unlit cigar that dangled from his mouth. A short, burly Italian with arms the size of tree trunks, Giordino was most at home riding a pilot's seat. After spending years in NUMA's Special Projects group, where he had piloted everything from blimps to bathyscaphes, he now headed the agency's underwater technology division. For Giordino, building and testing prototype vessels such as the *Bloodhound* was more of a passion than a job.

He and Dahlgren had already spent two weeks scouring the Arctic seabed in search of thermal vents. Utilizing prior bathymetric surveys, they targeted areas of subsurface rifts and uplifts that were outgrowths of volcanic activity and potential home ground for active thermal vents. The search had been fruitless so far, discouraging the engineers, who were anxious to test the submersible's capabilities.

Dahlgren ignored Giordino's remark and looked at his watch.

"It's been twenty minutes since Rudi gave us the callback. He's probably a sack of nerves by now. We probably ought to think about punching the UP button or else there will be two storms facing us topside."

"Rudi's not happy unless he has something to fret about," Giordino replied, "but I guess there's no upside in tempting the weather gods." He turned the pilot's yoke left, angling the submersible to the west while keeping it hovering just above the seafloor. They had traveled several hundred yards when the bottom became flecked with a succession of small boulders. The rocks grew larger as Giordino noted that the seafloor was gradually rising. Dahlgren picked up a bathymetric chart and tried to pinpoint their position.

"There looks to be a small seamount in the neighborhood. Didn't look too promising to the seismic boys for some reason."

"Probably because they've been sitting inside a climate-controlled office for too many years."

Dahlgren set aside the chart and gazed at the computer monitor, suddenly jumping up in his seat.

"Hot damn! The water temperature just spiked ten degrees."

A slight grin spread across Giordino's face as he noted the cluster of rocks on the seabed growing in size and mass.

"The seafloor geology is changing as well," he said. "The profile looks good for a vent. Let's see if we can trace the water temperature to its core."

He adjusted the submersible's path as Dahlgren read out the water temperature readings. The higher temperatures led them up a sharp rise in the seafloor. A high mound of boulders blocked their path, and Giordino drove the submersible upward like an airplane, ascending nose first until they cleared the summit. As they descended down the opposite side, the scene before them suddenly changed dramatically. The gray, drab moonscape transformed into an iridescent underwater oasis. Yellow mollusks, red tube worms, and bright gold spider crabs littered the seafloor in a rainbow of color. A blue squid squirted past the view port, followed by a school of silver-scaled polar cod. Almost instantaneously, they had traveled from a desolate world of black-and-white to an electric-colored plantation teeming with life.

"Now I know how Dorothy felt when she landed in Oz," Dahlgren muttered.

"What's the water temperature now?"

"We've jetted to seventy-two degrees Fahrenheit and rising. Congratulations, boss, you've just bought yourself a thermal vent."

Giordino nodded with satisfaction. "Mark our position. Then let's exercise the mineral sniffer before . . ."

The radio suddenly crackled with a transmission sent via a pair of underwater transponders. "*Narwhal* to *Bloodhound . . . Narwhal* to *Bloodhound,*" interrupted a tense voice over the radio. "Please ascend immediately. Seas are running at ten feet and building rapidly. I repeat, you are directed to ascend immediately."

". . . before Rudi calls us home," Dahlgren said, finishing Giordino's sentence.

Giordino grinned. "Ever notice how Rudi's voice goes up a couple of octaves when he's nervous?"

"Last time I looked, he was still signing my paycheck," Dahlgren cautioned.

"I suppose we don't want to scratch the paint on our new baby here. Let's grab a few quick rock samples first, then we can head topside."

Dahlgren radioed a reply to Gunn, then reached over and grabbed the controls to an articulated arm that rested upright on the submersible's exterior hull. Giordino guided the *Bloodhound* to a patch of grapefruit-sized nodules, hovering the sensor pod over the rocks. Using the stainless steel arm as a broom, Dahlgren swept several of the rocks into a basket beneath the sensor head. On-board computers quickly assayed the density and magnetic properties of the rock samples.

"Composition is igneous, appears consistent with pyroxene. I'm seeing concentrations of manganese and iron. Also reading elements of nickel, platinum, and copper sulfides," Dahlgren reported, eyeing a computer readout.

"That's a pretty high-octane start. Save the assessment. We'll have the lab boys crack open the samples and see how accurate the sensor readings are. Once the storm passes, we can give the site a thorough inspection."

"She looks like a sweet one."

"I am still a bit disappointed, my west Texas friend," Giordino replied with a shake of his head.

"No gold?"

"No gold. I guess the closest I can get is just riding to the surface with a goldbricker."

To Dahlgren's chagrin, Giordino's laughter echoed off the interior walls of the submersible for the better part of their ascent.

25

The Beaufort Sea was boiling with twelve-foot waves and near-gale-force winds when the *Bloodhound* burst through the surface of the *Narwhal*'s moon pool. Water inside the pool sloshed onto the deck as the research ship pitched and rolled in the mounting seas. Twice the steel flanks of the submersible slapped against the cushioned rim of the moon pool before hoisting lines could be attached and the vessel yanked out of the water. Giordino and Dahlgren quickly climbed out of the *Bloodhound* and collected their rock samples before fleeing the elements into the adjacent operations center. Gunn stood waiting for them with a look of displeasure on his face.

"That's a ten-million-dollar submersible that you nearly crushed like a beer can," he said, glaring at Giordino. "You know we're not allowed to launch and recover in these kinds of weather conditions."

As if to emphasize his point, the ship's

driveshaft suddenly shuddered beneath their feet as the vessel wallowed heavily through a deep trough.

"Relax, Rudi." Giordino beamed, then tossed one of the dripping rocks over to Gunn. NUMA's Deputy Director fumbled to catch it, smearing his shirt with mud and seawater in the process.

"You're on the trail?" he asked, his brows arching as he examined the rock.

"Better than that," Dahlgren piped in. "We sniffed out some thermal deviations, and Al drove us right to the heart of the vent. A sweet mile-long rift pouring out hot soup with plenty of dumplings."

Gunn's face softened. "You'd better have found something for surfacing so late." His gaze became like that of a kid in a candy store. "Did you see indications of a mineral field?"

"A large one, by the looks of it," Giordino replied, nodding. "We only saw a section of it, but it appears widely dispersed."

"And the electronic sensors? How did the *Bloodhound* perform?"

"She was barking like a coyote under a full moon," Dahlgren replied. "The sensors diagnosed over thirteen different elements."

"We'll have to leave it for the lab analysis to determine the *Bloodhound*'s accuracy," Giordino added. "According to the sensors, that soggy rock you're holding is chock-full of manganese and iron."

"There's probably enough of that stuff littering the bottom to buy you a thousand *Bloodhound*s, Rudi," Dahlgren said.

"Did the sensors indicate any gold content?" Gunn asked.

Giordino's eyes rolled skyward, then he turned to leave the ops center.

"Everybody thinks I'm Midas," he grumbled before disappearing out the door.

26

The spring storm was not widespread but packed the concentrated punch of a heavyweight boxer as it rolled southeast across the Beaufort Sea. Pummeling wind gusts of over sixty miles per hour blew the falling snow in horizontal sheets, turning the flakes to hardened particles of ice. Gusting swirls spread thick curtains over the white ice, often plunging visibility down to zero. The already hostile environment of the Arctic north became a place of brutal savagery.

Kevin Bue listened to the frames of the mess hall creak and shudder under the bristling gale and idly contemplated the structure's strength rating. Draining the remains of a cup of coffee, he tried to concentrate on a scientific journal spread open on the table. Though he had experienced a dozen storms during his tenure in the Arctic, he still found their ferocity unnerving. While the rest of the crew went about their jobs, Bue found it hard to focus when the entire camp sounded like it was about to blow away.

A heavyset cook and part-time carpenter named Benson sat down at the table across from Bue and sipped at his own steaming mug of coffee.

"Pretty good blow, eh?" he said, grinning through a thick black beard.

"Sounds like it's about to take us along with it," Bue replied, watching the roof overhead swaying back and forth.

"Well, if it does, I sure hope it deposits us somewhere where the weather is warm and the drinks taste better cold," he replied, sipping at his coffee. Eyeing Bue's empty cup, he reached over and grabbed the handle, then stood up.

"Here, let me get you a refill."

Benson walked across the mess to a large silver urn and refilled the cup. He started back toward Bue, then suddenly froze with a quizzical look on his face. Above the din of the buffeting wind, he detected a low-pitched mechanical churn. That wasn't what bothered him, though. It was the sharp crackling sound accompanying it that struck a nerve deep in his gut.

Bue glanced up at Benson, then picked up on the sound as well. The noise was drawing upon them rapidly, and Bue thought he heard a shout somewhere off in the compound before his whole world collapsed around him.

With a crunching jar, the back wall of the

mess hall completely disintegrated, replaced by a massive gray wedge. The towering object quickly surged through the room, leaving behind a thirty-foot swath of destruction. Torn free from its supports, the hut's roof flew off in a gust, while a blast of cold air flooded the interior. Bue looked on in horror as the gray mass devoured Benson in a spray of ice and froth. For one moment, the chef was standing there holding a mug of coffee. In the next instant, he was gone.

The floor buckled up beneath Bue, throwing him and the table toward the entry door. Struggling to his feet, he stood and stared at the gray behemoth that materialized before him. It was a ship, his jumbled mind finally fathomed, storming through the center of the camp and the thin ice beneath it.

The swirling, snowy winds gave the vessel a ghostly appearance, but he was able to make out a large number 54 painted in white on the bow. As the bow burst past with a deep rumble, Bue caught a glimpse of a large American flag rippling from the ship's masthead before the vessel disappeared into a cloud of white. He instinctively staggered back toward it, calling out for Benson, until nearly stepping into a black river of water that now trailed the ship.

Dazedly shaking off his state of shock, Bue pulled on his parka, which lay crumpled on the ground, and stepped past the remains of the entryway. Fighting his way against the winds, he tried to assess the condition of the camp while noting that the ground beneath his feet seemed to sway in an odd manner. Circling a few dozen feet to his right, he stopped at a ledge where the ice dropped away to open water. Just beyond him was where all three bunkhouses had stood. Now they were all gone, replaced by scattered chunks of ice floating in the dark water.

Bue's heart sank, knowing that one of his men had been off duty and asleep in his bunk just a short time before. That still left two men unaccounted for — Case the radio operator and Quinlon the maintenance man.

Bue turned his attention toward the lab building, catching sight of the structure's blue walls still standing in the distance. Struggling to move closer, he nearly fell into the water again, finding a lead in the ice that separated him from the lab. Against his better judgment, he took a running leap and hopped over the three-foot chasm, falling hard to the ice on the opposite side. Willing himself forward, he staggered into the wind until reaching the threshold. Resting briefly, he burst through the door, then froze.

The interior of the lab, like the mess hall, had been obliterated by the passing ship. Little remained standing beyond the doorway, just some scattered remains floating in the water a few feet away. Miraculously, the radio shack had somehow survived the blow, severed from the main building but still standing upright. Through the whistling wind, Bue could hear Case's voice calling out a plea for help.

Stepping closer, Bue found Case seated at his desk talking into a dead radio set. The ice camp's power generators, stowed in the storage building, had been one of the first things to sink when the ship charged through. There was no power left in the camp, nor had there been any for several minutes.

Bue put his hand on Case's shoulder and the radioman slowly set down the transmitter, his eyes glazed with fear. Suddenly a crackling sound erupted beneath them and the ground began to shudder.

"It's the ice!" Bue shouted. "Get out of here now."

He pulled Case to his feet, and the two men scrambled out of the shack and across the ice as the crackling sound seemed to chase them. They hopped over a low rise and turned to see the ice beneath the lab and radio hut shatter like a cracked mirror. The surface splintered into a dozen chunks of loose ice that quickly fell apart, causing the remains of the structure to dissolve into the water below. In less than two minutes, the entire camp had disappeared before Bue's eyes.

As the two men stared blankly at the destruction, Bue thought he heard the shout of a man above the wind. Peering through

206

the blowing maelstrom, he strained to hear it again. But first his eyes caught sight of a figure flailing in the water, near the site of the radio shack.

"It's Quinlon," Case yelled, also spotting the man. Regaining his composure, Case bolted toward the struggling maintenance man.

Quinlon was rapidly losing a fight against shock from immersion into the icy water. Laden by his parka and boots, he would have quickly sunk had he not been able to grab hold of a floating chunk of ice. He quickly lost the energy to pull himself out of the water but propelled himself toward Bue and Case with his last ounce of effort.

The two men ran to the edge of the ice and reached out for Quinlon, desperately grasping a flailing arm. Pulling him closer, they tried to yank him from the water but could only get him a few inches out of the water before he fell back in. With his saturated boots and clothing, the average-built Quinlon now weighed over three hundred pounds. Realizing their error, Bue and Case lunged at the human load again, dragging and rolling him horizontally until finally coercing his entire body out of the water.

"We've got to get him out of the wind," Bue said, looking around for shelter. All of the man-made remnants of the camp were gone, save for a small section of the crumpled storage shed now floating away on a car-sized chunk of ice.

"The snowbank by the runway," Case replied, pointing through the swirling snow.

Quinlon's efforts to keep the airfield clear had resulted in several deep snowbanks built up from his plowing. Though most of the airfield had now vanished, Case was right. There was a high mound of snow less than fifty yards away.

Each man grabbed one of Quinlon's arms and began dragging him across the ice like a bag of potatoes. They knew the maintenance man was near death, and if he was to have any chance of survival, they would have to move him clear of the minus-twenty-degrees windchill. Panting and perspiring despite the bitter cold, they hauled Quinlon to the back side of the ten-foot snowbank, which blocked the worst of the westerly gale.

They quickly stripped off Quinlon's wet clothes, which had already frozen stiff, then they briefly rubbed snow on his body to absorb the remaining moisture. Brushing the snow aside, they then wrapped his head and body in their own dry parkas. Quinlon was blue and shaking uncontrollably, but he was still conscious, which meant he had a chance at survival. Following Case's lead, Bue helped dig a small hole in the side of the snowbank. Sliding Quinlon in first, the other two men crawled alongside, hoping to share body heat while cowering from the slashing winds.

Peering out of their meager cave, Bue could see a watery passage expanding between their shelter and the unbroken ice sheet. They were part of a separate ice floe now, drifting slowly into the Beaufort Sea. Every few minutes, the scientist would hear a deep thunderous crack as their floating ice shelf ruptured into smaller and smaller pieces. Propelled into the storm-driven waters, he knew it would be only a matter of time before their own frozen refuge would be battered to bits and all three men tossed into the sea.

With no one else even aware of their predicament, they had no hope for survival. Shivering in the frightful cold, Bue contemplated the merciless gray ship that had decimated the camp so unexpectedly and without reason. Try as it might, his frozen mind could make no sense of the brutal act. Shaking his head to clear away the marauding vessel's ghostlike image, he peered at his comrades with sad compassion, then quietly awaited death to visit them all.

27

The radio call had arrived faintly and in a single transmission. Repeated efforts by the *Narwhal*'s radio operator to verify the message were met with complete silence.

Captain Stenseth read the hand-scribbled message transcribed by his radioman, shook his head, and then read the message once more.

"Mayday, Mayday. This is Ice Lab 7. The camp is breaking up . . ." he recited aloud. "That's all you got?" he asked, his eyes glaring.

The radioman nodded silently. Stenseth turned and stepped to the helmsman.

"All ahead flank speed," he barked. "Come left, steer course zero-one-five." He turned to the executive officer. "I want a plot to the ice lab's reported position. And call three additional lookouts to the bridge."

In an instant, he was towering over the radio operator's shoulder.

"Notify the regional U.S. and Canadian

Coast Guards of the distress call and tell them that we are responding. Alert any local traffic, if there is any. Then get Gunn and Giordino to the bridge."

"Sir, the nearest Coast Guard station is Canadian, at Tuktoyaktuk. That's over two hundred miles away."

Stenseth gazed at the blowing snow buffeting the bridge's windscreens, his mind conjuring an image of the ice camp inhabitants. Softening his tone, he replied quietly, "Then I guess that means their only saving angel is wearing turquoise wings."

The *Narwhal* was rated at twenty-three knots, but even running flat out the research ship could barely muster a dozen knots lunging through the storm-whipped seas. The storm had reached its peak, with winds gusting over seventy miles per hour. The sea was a violent turmoil of thirty-foot waves that pitched and rolled the ship like it was made of cork. The helmsman nervously monitored the ship's autopilot, waiting for the mechanism to go tilt from the constant course corrections necessary to keep the vessel on a fixed northeast heading.

Gunn and Giordino soon joined Stenseth on the bridge, studying the ice camp's Mayday message.

"It is a little early in the season for the ice to be breaking up in a cataclysmic fashion," Gunn said, rubbing his chin. "Though the moving ice sheet can certainly fracture on short notice. Typically, you would have a little bit of a warning."

"Perhaps they were surprised by a small fracture that struck a portion of the camp, such as their radio facility or even their power generators," Stenseth suggested.

"Let's hope it's nothing worse than that," Gunn agreed, gazing at the maelstrom outside. "As long as they have some degree of shelter from the storm, they should be all right for a while."

"There is another possibility," Giordino added quietly. "The ice camp may have been situated too close to the sea. The storm surge could have broken up the leading edge of the ice field, taking the camp apart in the process."

The other two men nodded grimly, knowing that the odds of survival were severely diminished if that was the case.

"What's the outlook on the storm?" Gunn asked.

"Another six to eight hours before it abates. We'll have to wait it out before we can drop a search team on the ice, I'm afraid," Stenseth replied.

"Sir," the helmsman interrupted, "we're seeing large ice in the water."

Stenseth looked up to see a house-sized iceberg slip past the port bow.

"All engines back a third. What's our distance to the ice camp?"

"Just under eighteen miles, sir."

Stenseth stepped over to a large radar screen and adjusted the range to a twenty-mile diameter. A thin, jagged green line crossed the screen near the top edge, which remained fixed in place. The captain pointed to a spot just below the line, where a concentric ring on the scope indicated a distance of twenty miles.

"Here's the reported position of the camp," he said somberly.

"If it wasn't oceanfront property before, it is now," Giordino observed.

Gunn squinted at the radarscope, then pointed a finger at a fuzzy dot at the edge of the screen.

"There's a ship nearby," he said.

Stenseth took a look, noting that the ship was headed to the southeast. He ordered the radio operator to hail the ship, but they failed to receive a response.

"Maybe an illegal whaler," the captain suggested. "The Japanese occasionally slip into the Beaufort to hunt beluga whales."

"In these seas, they're probably too busy hanging on to their shorts to pick up the radio," Giordino said.

The unknown vessel was quickly forgotten as they closed in on the ice shelf and the reported position of the ice camp. As the *Narwhal* crept closer to the site, larger and larger slabs of broken ice began clogging up the sea in front of them. By now, the entire ship's complement had been alerted to the rescue mission. More than a dozen research scientists braved the harsh weather and joined the crew on deck. Dressed in full foul-weather gear, they lined the rails of the ominously rolling ship, scanning the seas for their fellow Arctic scientists.

The *Narwhal* arrived at the ice camp's reported position, and Stenseth brought the *Narwhal* to within a hundred feet of the ice sheet. The research ship cruised slowly along the jagged border, dodging around numerous icebergs that had recently severed from the ice field. The captain ordered every light on board illuminated and repeatedly let loose a blast from the ship's deafening Kahlenberg air horns as a possible rescue beacon. The powering winds began to abate slightly, allowing brief glimpses through the swirling snow. All eyes scanned the thick shelf of the sea ice as well as the frozen waters for signs of the ice camp or its inhabitants. Drifting over the camp's reported position, not a sign was detected. If anything or anybody was left at the scene, they were now residing two thousand feet beneath the dark gray waters.

28

Kevin Bue had watched their perch on the ice dissolve from a battleship-sized sheet of ice to that of a small house. The battering sea waves would rip and shove at the iceberg, splintering it into smaller fragments that would be subject to the same dissecting forces. While their refuge grew smaller, the ride grew rougher as they drifted farther into the Beaufort Sea. The shrinking berg wallowed and dipped in the churning seas, while surging waves repeatedly swept over the lower reaches. Shivering in the bitter cold, Bue found himself suffering the added discomfort of seasickness.

Looking at the two men beside him, he could hardly complain. Quinlon was close to slipping into a hypothermia-induced unconsciousness, while Case seemed to be headed down the same path. The radio operator sat curled in a ball, his glazed eyes staring blankly ahead. Bue's efforts at conversation were met with nothing more than a blink of the eyes.

Bue considered stripping the parkas off

Quinlon so that he and Case might regain some warmth but thought better of it. Although Quinlon was as good as dead, their own outlook for survival was no better. Bue stared at the turbulent gray water surrounding their frozen raft and contemplated diving into the sea. At least it would end things quickly. The idea passed when he decided it would take too much energy to walk the dozen paces to the water's edge.

A large swell rocked the ice platform, and he heard a sharp thump beneath his feet. A crack suddenly materialized beneath his snow-carved seat, extending rapidly across the berg. With a jolt from the next oncoming wave, the entire section of ice beneath him abruptly fell away, dissolving into the dark sea. Bue instinctively grabbed on to the sharp face of the snowbank, lodging a foot on the small ledge that held Quinlon. Case, sitting on the opposite side, never moved a muscle as Bue desperately clung to a vertical cleft of the ice, dangling just a few feet above the stinging waves.

Bue felt his heart pounding wildly, and with a desperate lunge he jabbed his fingers into the ice and pulled himself up and on top of the remaining snow mound. Their haven had shrunk to the size of a minivan and now rocked violently in the rough seas. Bue teetered on the top, waiting for the whole mound to turn turtle and send the three men on an icy plunge to their deaths. It would be a matter of minutes now, he knew, before their ride would come to an end.

Then through the windswept snow he saw a bright light, beaming like the sun behind a rainsquall. It blinded his eyes, and he shut his lids tightly to escape the searing beam. When he opened them a few seconds later, the light had vanished. All he could see was the white of the dry ice that peppered his face in the fierce wind. He strained to detect the light again, but there was nothing to see but the storm. Slowly, he closed his eyes in defeat, sagging as the strength ebbed from his pores.

29

Jack Dahlgren already had a fueled Zodiac winched above the gunwale when the call came from the bridge to launch. Dressed in a bright yellow Mustang survival suit, he climbed aboard and checked that a portable GPS unit and a two-way radio were stowed in a watertight bin. He started the outboard engine, then waited as a squat figure came charging across the deck.

Al Giordino didn't have time to put on an exposure suit; he simply grabbed a parka on the bridge and hustled down to the Zodiac. As Giordino leaped in, Dahlgren gave a thumbs-up sign to a waiting crewman, who quickly lowered the inflatable boat into the sea. Dahlgren waited until Giordino released the drop hook, then gunned the motor. The small inflatable burst over and through a high-rolling wave, sending plumes of icy spray skyward. Giordino ducked from the spray, then pointed an arm ahead of the *Narwhal*.

"We're after a small berg about two hundred

yards off the port bow," he yelled. "There's an ice sheet dead ahead, so you'll have to go hard around," he added, waving to the left.

Though the blinding snow, Dahlgren could just make out a fuzzy mass of white on the surface directly ahead. Taking a quick compass bearing, he eased the Zodiac to port until the ice sheet loomed up a few yards in front of him. Turning sharply, he sped along the perimeter, slowing slightly when he figured that he had reached the opposite side.

The *Narwhal* was no longer in view behind them, while the ice sheet had given way to dozens of small icebergs rolling in the heavy seas. The pounding winds blew snow particles off the nearby ice sheet, reducing visibility to less than fifty feet. Giordino sat perched on the prow scanning the seas like an eagle in search of prey, motioning Dahlgren to turn this way, then that. They motored through trunk-sized chunks of ice mixed with larger bergs, all swaying and smashing into one another. Giordino had them circle several small bergs before frantically pointing at a tall, swaying spire of ice.

"That's the one," he yelled.

Dahlgren hit the throttle, racing over to the floating wedge of ice that looked to him like all the others. Only this one had a patch of darkness on the crest. As the Zodiac drew near, Dahlgren saw that it was a human body sprawled across the top. He quickly circled the berg, looking for a place to land the boat, but the ice showed only steep vertical slopes on all sides. Reaching the opposite end, he noticed two other men wedged into a crude dugout cut a few feet above the water.

"Ram it beneath that ledge," Giordino yelled.

Dahlgren nodded, then replied, "Hang on."

He circled the Zodiac around to garner momentum, then gunned the throttle while aiming straight for the berg. The inflatable boat's prow skidded over a slight lip of ice before plunging hard into the snowbank just beneath the two hypothermic men. Both Dahlgren and Giordino barely kept from flying out of the boat as it jarred to an immediate halt.

Giordino quickly stood up, brushed some snow off his head and shoulders, then smiled at Case, who stared back through listless eyes.

"Just five minutes to some hot chicken soup, my friends," Giordino said, grabbing Quinlon like a rag doll and laying him between two bench seats. He then took Case's arm and helped the lethargic man crawl into the Zodiac. Dahlgren retrieved a pair of dry blankets from a storage locker and quickly covered both men.

"Can you reach the other one?" Dahlgren asked.

Giordino gazed at the rocking mound of

snow that rose six feet over his head.

"Yes, but keep the engine running. I think this ice cube is on its last legs."

Stepping off the inflatable, he kicked a toehold into the hardened snow and began to climb. With each step, he'd punch his fist into the crust for a handgrip and then foothold as he climbed higher. The iceberg rocked and swayed in the rolling swells, and several times he thought he might go flying off into the water. Ascending as quickly as he could, he popped his head over the top of the ridge, finding Bue spread out on the crest with his face down. Yanking Bue's torso, Giordino pulled the limp body closer until he could slide him over his shoulder. Clamping an arm around the frozen man's legs, he began the unsteady descent down the face of the berg.

Yet for all Bue's deadweight, Giordino might have been carrying a sack of potatoes. The powerful Italian wasted no time, quickly descending several steps, then kicking off the snow wall and dropping the last several feet into the Zodiac's rubber hull. Laying Bue down beside the other men, Giordino jumped back out and heaved his body against the bow of the Zodiac. Digging his short, powerful legs into the snow, he shoved the boat off the iceberg, hopping aboard as Dahlgren goosed the outboard motor into reverse.

Dahlgren had barely turned and made headway when a huge swell rolled up in front of them. Giordino reached over and pinned the prone men to the deck as the wave crashed into the bow. Icy foam sprayed everywhere as the Zodiac's bow shot skyward until the small boat stood nearly vertical. Then the big wave rolled through and away, sending the inflatable crashing into the following trough. Dahlgren steered directly into a second large wave, riding it through with slightly less violence.

As the Zodiac shook off the effects of the second swell, Dahlgren and Giordino glanced back as the two waves pummeled the iceberg. Watching with morbid fascination, they saw the first wave pitch the towering chunk of ice nearly onto its side. Before the berg could right itself, the second wave struck, completely obliterating the iceberg. As the wave rolled past, a few large chunks of ice slowly popped to the surface.

Had they not arrived when they did, Bue, Case, and Quinlon would have been washed into the frigid sea by the twin waves and perished within minutes.

30

The three Canadians, all suffering from various degrees of hypothermia, were able to cling to life until the wave-tossed Zodiac was clutched from the sea and dropped onto the deck of the *Narwhal*. Dahlgren had been fortunate enough to locate the research ship in just a few minutes. The storm had obliterated any satellite signals, rendering the GPS unit useless. He instead took a reverse compass heading and motored toward the general position of the ship. The large intervening ice floe had drifted past, allowing an unencumbered route through the high seas. Giordino detected the wail of the ship's air horn firing a stout blast, and the brightly lit *Narwhal* appeared through the swirling winds a short time later.

A heavily bundled Rudi Gunn was standing by when the Zodiac hit the deck, and he promptly directed the transfer of the injured men to the medical bay. Bue and Case were revived before long, but Quinlon remained unconscious for several hours as the ship's doctor worked feverishly to raise the man's core body temperature. Twice Quinlon's heart stopped beating and twice he was frantically resuscitated, until his body temperature gradually approached ninety-eight degrees and his blood pressure stabilized.

After shaking the ice off their garments, Giordino and Dahlgren changed into dry clothes and met Gunn on the bridge.

"Do we know if there are any other potential survivors out there?" Gunn asked the two weary men.

Dahlgren shook his head. "I asked the conscious fellow the same question. He told me there were two other men in the ice camp with them but that he is certain they were both killed when the ship tore through the camp."

"A ship?"

"Not just any ship," Dahlgren nodded grimly. "An American Navy warship. Came blasting through the ice and obliterated the entire facility."

"That's impossible," Gunn replied.

"I'm just telling you what the man said."

Gunn fell silent, his eyes bulging in disbelief. "We'll search some more, all the same," he finally said in a low voice. Then, turning a sympathetic eye toward both men, he added, "That was a heroic rescue effort under terrible conditions."

"I wouldn't have wanted to trade places with those guys," Giordino remarked. "But Dahlgren a hero? That will be the day," he added with a laugh.

"I've a good mind not to share my bottle of Jack Daniel's with you for that remark," Dahlgren retorted.

Giordino put an arm around the Texan and escorted him off the bridge.

"Just one shot, my friend, and I'll see that the Yukon is yours for the taking."

The *Narwhal* searched the surrounding seas for the next two hours, finding only the battered remnants of a blue awning among the ice-infested waters. Gunn reluctantly called off the search when most of the broken floe fragments finally drifted clear of the ice shelf.

"Prudhoe Bay would have better facilities, but Tuktoyaktuk is the closer port by about fifty miles. They do have an airfield," Stenseth said, eyeing a chart of the North American coastline.

"We'll have more of a following sea-sailing to the latter," Gunn replied, looking over the captain's shoulder. "It would probably be best to get them ashore as soon as possible. Tuktoyaktuk it is."

The town was along a sparse stretch of northern Canadian shoreline, just east of the Alaskan border. The area was well north of the Arctic Circle and beyond the northern tree line as well, a rolling, rocky land covered in snow most of the year.

The *Narwhal* plowed through rough waters for fourteen hours as the spring storm finally blew itself out. The Beaufort Sea still heaved with high breakers when the NUMA ship edged into the protected waters of Kugmallit Bay beside the town of Tuktoyaktuk. A Canadian Mountie patrol boat guided the ship to the city's industrial pier, where an empty dockside berth awaited. Within minutes, the injured scientists were loaded into a pair of vans and whisked to the local medical center. A thorough checkup deemed the men stable enough for further travel, after which they were loaded onto a plane to Yellowknife.

It wasn't until the next day, when the trio arrived in Calgary on a government jet, that their ordeal became headline news. A media circus ensued, as every major newspaper and television network jumped on the story. Bue's eyewitness account of an American warship battering the ice camp and leaving its inhabitants to die struck an angry chord with many Canadians weary of their southern neighbor's worldly might.

Fervor within the Canadian government ascended to an even higher pitch. Already stung by the embarrassing incident involving the mystery ship *Atlanta,* Coast Guard and military officials within the government showed particular wrath. The nationalistic Prime Minister, his popularity waning, quickly pounced on the incident for political gain. The rescued scientists Bue, Case, and Quinlon were feted as guests at the Prime Minister's residence on Sussex Drive in Ottawa, then trotted before the television cameras to once more describe the destruction of the ice camp at the hands of the Americans. With a calculated show of anger, the Prime Minister went so far as to denounce the incident as a barbaric act of war.

"Canadian sovereignty will no longer be violated by foreign transgressions," he shrieked to the cameras. With an angry Parliament buttressing his rhetoric, he ordered additional naval forces to the Arctic, while threatening to close the border and shut off oil and gas exports. "The great nation of Canada shall not be bullied. If protection of our sovereignty entails war, then so be it," he cried, his face turning beet red.

Overnight, the Prime Minister's popularity soared in the polls. Witnessing the public reaction, his fellow politicians clamored before the media to strike an anti-American pose. The story of the ice camp survivors took on a life of its own, propelled by a manipulated media and a self-serving national leader. It became a glory-filled tale of victimization and heroic survival. Yet somehow lost in every retelling of the tragedy was the role of the NUMA research crew and the daring rescue effort that had saved the three survivors.

31

"Jim, do you have a moment?"

Walking down a corridor of the White House West Wing, Vice President James Sandecker turned to find the Canadian Ambassador calling him from behind. A distinguished-looking man with bushy silver eyebrows, Ambassador John Davis approached with a taciturn look on his face.

"Good morning, John," Sandecker greeted. "What brings you to this neck of the woods so early in the day?"

"Good to see you, Jim," Davis replied, his face brightening a bit. "I'm afraid I was sent to hammer on your good President over my country's agitation with this business in the Northwest Passage."

"I'm headed to a meeting with the President on that very topic. A sad tragedy about the ice camp, but I've been told we had no warships anywhere near there."

"A sticky matter nevertheless. The hardliners in our government are blowing it full out of proportion." He lowered his tone to a whisper. "Even the Prime Minister is rattling his saber over the matter, though I know he's doing it strictly for political gain. I just fear a foolish escalation of some sort that will lead to further tragedy." A somber look in the Ambassador's gray eyes told Sandecker that his fear was deep-rooted.

"Don't worry, John, cooler heads will prevail. We've got too much at stake to let something like this degenerate."

Davis nodded his head weakly. "I sure hope you are right. Say, Jim, I'd like to express our thanks to your NUMA ship and crew. It has been overlooked in the press, but they made a remarkable rescue."

"I'll pass that along. Give my best to Maggie, and let's plan on going sailing again soon."

"I'd like that. Take care, Jim."

A White House aide pressed Sandecker on to the Oval Office, guiding him through the northwest entrance. Seated around a coffee table, Sandecker recognized the President's chief of staff, his National Security Advisor, and the Secretary of Defense. The President stood at a side cubby, pouring himself a cup of coffee from an antique silver pot.

"Can I get you a cup, Jim?" Ward asked. The President still had dark circles under his eyes but appeared more energized than during Sandecker's last visit.

"Sure, Garner. Make it black."

The other administration officials looked aghast at Sandecker for calling the President by his first name, but he didn't care. And neither did Ward. The President handed Sandecker his coffee, then sat down in a gold wingback chair.

"You missed all the fireworks, Jim," the President said. "The Canadian Ambassador just gave me holy blazes about those two incidents in the Arctic."

Sandecker nodded. "I just passed him in the hall. They seem to be taking it quite seriously."

"The Canadians are upset about our proposed plan to divert freshwater from the Great Lakes to replenish the Midwest farming aquifers," said Chief of Staff Meade. "Plus it is no secret that the Prime Minister's poll numbers are way down ahead of a call for parliamentary elections this fall."

"We have reason to believe there is also an effort to keep our petroleum companies out of the Canadian Arctic," added the National Security Advisor, a short-haired blond woman named Moss. "The Canadians have been very protective about their Arctic oil and gas resources, which continue to grow in significance."

"Given our current situation, it is hardly an opportune time for them to turn their backs on us," said Meade.

"You mean it's not an opportune time for

us," noted Sandecker.

"You have a point, Jim," the President replied. "The Canadians certainly have a few strong cards in their hand at the moment."

"Which they are already starting to play," said Moss. "The Ambassador gave notice that Prime Minister Barrett intends to announce a full prohibition on U.S.-flagged vessels crossing into Canadian Arctic seaways. Any violation will be deemed a trespass on territorial waters and subject to military reprisal."

"The Prime Minister is not one for subtlety," the President remarked.

"He went so far as to have the Ambassador drop the hint that reductions in oil, natural gas, and hydroelectric power exports to the U.S. are on the table," Meade said, speaking to Sandecker.

"That is playing hardball," Sandecker said. "We currently obtain ninety percent of our natural gas imports from Canada alone. And I know you are counting on the new infusion from Melville Sound to solve our immediate energy problems," he added, addressing the President.

"We can't afford to jeopardize those gas imports," the President said. "They are critical to overcoming this oil crisis and stabilizing the economy."

"The Prime Minister's actions boost the Canadian sovereignty rhetoric he has been touting recently to reverse his waning popularity," noted Moss. "He seized on the commercial possibilities of an ice-free Northwest Passage some years ago and has strongly argued Canada's ownership claims. It fits in nicely with his newfound appeal to the country's traditionalists."

"There's a good deal of power to be had in those Arctic resources," Meade noted.

"The Russians are clamoring over the same thing," Sandecker said. "The U.N. Law of the Sea Treaty opened the door for additional Arctic empire building based on the undersea extensions of existing territorial claims. We in fact have joined the same subsurface land rush as the Canadians, Russians, Danes, and Norwegians."

"That is true," Moss replied. "But our potential claims don't really impose much into Canadian waters. It's the passage that is creating all the hysteria. Perhaps because it is the key to accessing and transporting all those Arctic resources."

"It seems to me that the Canadians have a pretty sound legal basis for calling the passage part of their internal waters," the President said.

The Secretary of Defense bristled. An ex-Navy man like Sandecker, he had managed one of the major oil companies before returning to public service.

"Mr. President," he said in a deep voice, "it has always been the position of the U.S. that the Northwest Passage constitutes an international strait. The Law of the Sea Convention, I might add, also calls for the right of transit passage through waterways deemed international straits."

"Assuming we are on friendly terms with Canada, why do we care if they claim the strait as territorial waters?" asked the President.

"Doing so would undermine the precedents already set in the Strait of Malacca, Gibraltar, and Bab el-Mandeb in the Red Sea," Moss recited. "Those waterways are open to commercial ships of all nations, not to mention free passage by our own Navy ships."

"Not to mention the Bosporus and Dardanelles," Sandecker added.

"Indeed," replied Moss. "If we were to treat the Northwest Passage in a different light, that could offer legal encouragement for the Malaysians to direct traffic through the Malacca, for example. It's just too risky a proposition."

"Don't forget our submarine fleet," Sandecker added. "We can't very well walk away from the Arctic area of operations."

"Jim's absolutely right," said the Secretary of Defense. "We're still playing tag with the occasional Russian Delta up there, and now we have the Chinese fleet to worry about. They've just tested a new class of sub-launched ballistic missile with a range of five thousand miles.

It only makes sense that they'll follow the tack of the Russians by hiding their subs under the ice, in order to preserve a first-launch capability. Mr. President, the Arctic will remain a critical mission area for purposes of our national defense. We can't afford to be shut out of the seaways that are within spitting distance of our own borders."

The President quietly strolled over to the east window and gazed out at the Rose Garden. "I suppose there is no walking away. But there is also no need to fan the flames of distrust. Let's voluntarily abide by the ban for ninety days. I want no American-flagged vessels, including submarines, even to encroach on Canadian Arctic waters during that period. That should give everyone time to cool their heels. Then I'll have State work up a meeting with Prime Minister Barrett, and we'll try to reintroduce some sanity back into the equation."

"An excellent suggestion," Meade demurred. "I'll put a call in to the Secretary of State right away."

"Mr. President, there is one other thing," the Secretary of Defense stated. "I'd like to war-plan a few counterstrike scenarios, should events dictate."

"Good God," the President thundered. "We're talking about Canada here."

The room fell silent while Garner glared at the Secretary of Defense. "Do what you have to do. If I know you, you probably already have a full-blown invasion plan all worked out."

The Secretary of Defense sat stone-faced, unwilling to deny the President's accusation.

"Seems to me we should be focusing our resources on investigating who's roughing up the Canadians and why," injected Sandecker. "What exactly do we know about the two incidents in question?"

"Very little, I'm afraid, since they both occurred in remote areas," replied Moss. "The first incident involved a commercial vessel flying the American flag that rammed a Canadian Coast Guard cutter. All we know from the Canadians is that the vessel was a small containership carrying the name *Atlanta*. The Canadians thought they would nab her farther into the passage, near Somerset Island, but the ship never materialized. They believe she may have sunk, but our analysts believe it is possible she could have backtracked to the Atlantic without being seen. The marine registries show a dozen ships named *Atlanta,* although only one is of comparable size and configuration. It is sitting in a dry dock in Mobile, Alabama, where it has been parked for the last three weeks."

"Perhaps the Canadians were right, and she sank from her own damage caused by the ramming incident," the President said. "Otherwise, we have to assume it's a case of mistaken identity."

"Odd that they would aim to run the passage and then disappear," Sandecker noted. "What about the Beaufort Sea ice camp? I've been told that we had no vessels anywhere near the area."

"That is correct," Moss replied. "All three of the ice camp survivors claim they saw a gray warship flying American colors burst through the camp. One of the men identified the ship as carrying the number 54. As it happens, FFG-54 is currently on station in the Beaufort Sea."

"One of our frigates?"

"Yes, the *Ford,* out of Everett, Washington. She was supporting a submarine exercise off Point Barrow at the time of the incident, but that was over three hundred miles away. Aside from that, the *Ford* is not ice-rated, so she would have had no business plowing through the thick sea ice that supported the camp."

"Another case of mistaken identity?" the President asked.

"Nobody knows for sure. There's just not much in the way of traffic in that area, and there was a heavy storm at the time that obscured things."

"What about satellite imagery?" Sandecker asked.

Moss flipped through a folder, then pulled out a report.

"Satellite coverage in that region is pretty

sporadic, for obvious reasons. Unfortunately, we don't have any imagery available within twelve hours of the incident."

"Do we know for sure it wasn't the *Ford*? Could they have made a mistake?" the President probed.

"No, sir," the Secretary of Defense replied. "I had Pacific Command review their navigation records. The *Ford* never traveled anywhere near the position of the ice camp."

"And we've shared that information with the Canadians?"

"The Chief of the Defence Staff has seen the data and concurs off the record that the *Ford* was likely not responsible," replied the Secretary of Defense. "But the politicians don't trust what we are giving them, quite frankly. Given the mileage they have gotten out of the incident, they have no reason to backtrack now."

"Find those ships and we find our way out of this mess," the President stated.

His advisers fell silent, knowing that the window of opportunity had likely already passed. Without direct access to the Canadian Arctic, there was little they could even hope to do.

"We'll do what we can," the Secretary of Defense promised.

The chief of staff noted the time, then ushered everyone out of the Oval Office in preparation for the President's next meeting. After the others had left the room, Ward stood at the window and gazed out at the Rose Garden.

"War with Canada," he muttered to himself. "Now, there's a real legacy."

32

Mitchell Goyette peered out of the glass-walled office on the top deck of his yacht and idly watched a silver seaplane taxiing across the harbor. The small plane quickly hopped off the water and circled south, bypassing the tall buildings lining Vancouver Harbor. The magnate took a sip from a martini glass, then turned his gaze to a thick contract sitting on the desk.

"The terms and conditions are acceptable?" he asked.

A small man with black hair and thick glasses seated opposite Goyette nodded his head.

"The legal department has reviewed it and found no issues with the changes. The Chinese were quite pleased with the initial test shipment and are anxious to receive an ongoing supply stream."

"With no change in price or limits on quantity?"

"No, sir. They agreed to accept up to five

million tons a year of unrefined Athabasca crude bitumen and all the Melville Sound natural gas we can deliver, both at prices ten percent above the spot market, provided that we agree to extended terms."

Goyette leaned back in his chair and smiled. "Our oceangoing barges have proven their worth at transporting both cargoes in bulk. We've got our fifth string of LNG barges coming on line next week. The potential revenue stream from the Chinese is shaping up quite nicely."

"The gas strike at Melville Sound promises to be quite a windfall. Our projections show a net profit of nearly five million dollars is possible with each shipment to China. Provided that the government doesn't initiate restrictions on natural resource sales to China, you are well positioned to capitalize on their growing appetite for energy."

"The unfortunate death of MP Finlay seems to have alleviated that concern," Goyette replied with a knowing grin.

"With the reduction of Athabasca refining due to the restrictive carbon dioxide mandate, the Chinese deal is lucrative for your Alberta holdings as well. You will of course be defaulting on the agreements just signed with the Americans to provide them the Melville natural gas."

"The Chinese are paying me ten percent more."

"The President was relying on an influx of natural gas to halt their energy crisis," the attorney said with a cautionary tone.

"Yes, and they've called on me and my Melville Sound reserves to save them," Goyette said with a laugh. "Only we're going to turn up the heat a bit." A fire suddenly burned in his eyes. "Let them stew in their own juices until they reach a state of true desperation. Then they'll play it my way and pay my prices in order to survive. We'll have our tankers carry gas to them and haul away their liquid carbon wastes on the return trip, and we'll charge a premium for both. Of course, that will be after they finance a major expansion of our barge fleet. They'll have no choice but to accept." A grin slowly crossed his lips.

"I still worry about the political trouble. There's talk of anti-American legislation that could spill over and impact our business with China. Some of the more rabid members of Parliament are practically ready to declare war."

"I can't control the idiocy of politicians. The important point was to remove the Americans from the Arctic while we expand our acquisition of gas, oil, and mineral rights. We happened to get lucky with the Melville strike, but the strategy is clearly working quite nicely so far."

"The geophysics team is close to identifying the necessary tracts to encompass the Melville gas field, as well as some other promising locations. I just hope that the natural resources minister continues to accommodate our requirements."

"Don't you worry about Minister Jameson, he will do anything I ask. By the way, what is the latest from the *Alberta*?"

"She arrived in New York without incident, took on a commercial shipment, and is presently eastbound to India. There appear to be no suspicions raised."

"Good. Have her sent on to Indonesia for a repaint in new colors before she returns to Vancouver."

"It will be done," the attorney replied.

Goyette sat back in his chair and took a sip of his drink. "Have you seen Marcy about?"

One of a handful of ex-strippers Goyette kept on the payroll, Marcy usually wandered the boat in revealing attire. The aide shook his head firmly, taking the cue that it was time to leave.

"I'll inform the Chinese that we have a deal," he said, taking the signed contract from Goyette and quickly exiting the office.

Goyette drained his glass, then reached for a shipboard phone to call the master stateroom, when a familiar voice froze his movements.

"Another drink, Mitchell?"

Goyette turned to the far side of the office, where Clay Zak stood with a couple of martinis in one hand. He was dressed in dark slacks and a taupe turtleneck sweater, nearly blending in with the room's earth-toned walls. Casually walking closer, he set one glass down in front of Goyette, then took a seat opposite him.

"Mitchell Goyette, King of the Arctic, eh? I must say, I have seen photographs of your oceangoing barges and am quite awed. A stirring display of naval architecture."

"They were specifically designed for the task," Goyette said, finally finding his voice. A look of annoyance remained etched on his face, and he made a mental note to have a word with his security detail. "Fully loaded, they can sail through a Category 2 hurricane without risk."

"Impressive," Zak replied, between sips of his martini. "Though I suspect your environmental worshippers would be disappointed to know that you are raping the country's pristine landscape of natural resources strictly to make a buck off the Chinese."

"I didn't expect to see you back so soon," Goyette replied, ignoring the remark. "Your project to the States was accomplished with success?"

"Indeed. You were correct in taking an interest in the lab's work. I had a remarkable conversation about artificial photosynthesis with your research mole."

Zak proceeded to describe the details of Lisa Lane's work and her recent discovery. Goyette felt his anger at Zak diminish as the magnitude of Lane's scientific breakthrough sank in. He peered out the window once more.

"Sounds like they could build an industrial carbon dioxide conversion facility that could be easily replicated," he said. "Still, they've got to be talking years or decades in the future."

Zak shook his head. "I'm no scientist, but according to your boy on the inside that is not the case. He claims the actual working process requires little in the way of capital resources. He suggested that within five years, you might have hundreds of these facilities built around major cities and key industrial emission sites."

"But you put an end to such possibilities?" Goyette asked, his eyes boring into Zak.

The assassin smiled. "No bodies, remember? The lab and all their research materials are history, as you requested. But the chief researcher is still alive and she knows the formula. I'd venture there's a good chance plenty more people know the recipe by now."

Goyette stared at Zak without blinking, wondering if it had been a mistake to rein in the assassin this one time.

"Your own mole is probably off selling the results to a competitor as we speak," Zak continued.

"He won't live long if he does," Goyette replied. His nostrils flared as he shook his head.

"This could kill my carbon sequestration plant expansion. Worse still, it would permit the Athabasca refineries to come back on line, even expand. That'd drive down the price of Athabasca bitumen, it'd ruin my contract with the Chinese! I won't have it!"

Zak laughed at Goyette's greed-induced anger, which drove the mogul to more fury. Reaching into his pocket, he pulled out a small gray pebble and bounced it across the desk. Goyette instinctively caught it against his chest.

"Mitchell, Mitchell, Mitchell . . . You are missing the big picture. Where's the grand environmentalist, the King of Green, the tree hugger's best friend?"

"What are you babbling about?" Goyette sneered.

"You're holding it in your hand. A mineral called ruthenium. Otherwise known as the catalyst to artificial photosynthesis. It is the key to the whole thing."

Goyette studied the stone with quiet regard.

"Go on," he replied curtly.

"It is rarer than gold. There are only a few places on earth where the stuff has ever been mined and every one of those mines has gone kaput. This sample came from a geology warehouse in Ontario, and they might well be the last source of the stuff. Without ruthenium, there can be no artificial photosynthesis, and your problem is solved. I'm not saying it can be done, but whoever owns the supply of the mineral will own the solution to global warming. Think how your green friends would worship you then?"

It was the perfect tonic of greed and power that made Goyette tick. Zak could almost see the dollar signs light up in his eyes as he digested the possibilities.

"Yes," Goyette nodded hungrily. "Yes, we'll have to explore the market. I'll get some people on it at once."

Staring back at Zak, he asked, "You seem to have a bit of the bloodhound in you. How would you like to visit this warehouse in Ontario and find out where this ruthenium came from and how much of a supply is left?"

"Providing Terra Green Air is operating a scheduled flight," Zak replied with a smile.

"You can use the jet," Goyette grumbled. "But there's another matter of minor importance that requires your attention beforehand. It seems I have a small annoyance in Kitimat."

"Kitimat. Isn't that near Prince Rupert?"

Goyette nodded and handed Zak the fax he had received from the natural resources minister. Reading the document, Zak nodded, then gulped down his martini.

"I'll take care of it on the way to Ontario," he said, stuffing the fax into his pocket and rising from the chair. He moved toward the door, then turned back toward Goyette.

"You know, that research mole of yours, Bob Hamilton? You might consider posting him a nice bonus for the information he provided. Might make you a bit of money down the road."

"I suppose," Goyette grunted, then he closed his eyes and grimaced. "Just knock next time, will you please?" he said.

But when he opened his eyes, Zak was already gone.

33

The true die-hard members of the Potomac Yacht Club had already capitalized on the sparkling Sunday-morning weather and taken to the river in their sailboats by the time Pitt stepped onto the main dock at nine o'clock. An overweight man toting an empty gas can trudged toward Pitt, sweating profusely in the muggy morning air.

"Excuse me," Pitt asked, "can you tell me where the *Roberta Ann* is berthed?"

The fat man's face brightened at the name. "That's Dan Martin's boat. He's on the far dock, the third or fourth berth down. Tell him Tony wants his electric drill back."

Pitt thanked the man and made his way to the last dock, quickly spotting the *Roberta Ann* as he stepped down a ramp from the quay. She was a gleaming wood sailboat of just under forty feet. Built in Hong Kong in the 1930s, she was all varnished teak and mahogany, accented by loads of brass fittings that sparkled in the sunlight. In impeccable condition, she was a boat that oozed the romance of another era. Admiring the sleek lines, Pitt could practically envision Clark Gable and Carole Lombard sailing her under the stars to Catalina with a case of champagne aboard. The image was shattered by a string of four-letter words that suddenly wafted from the stern. Pitt walked closer, to find a man hunched down in a bay that housed the sailboat's small inboard motor.

"Permission to come aboard?" Pitt called out.

The man popped upright, a frustrated snarl on his face softening at the sight of Pitt.

"Dirk Pitt. What a pleasant surprise. Come to mock my seafaring ways?"

"On the contrary. You have the *Roberta Ann* looking shipshape and Bristol fashion," Pitt said, stepping aboard and shaking hands with Dan Martin. A tough Bostonian with thick brown hair, Martin gazed at Pitt through a pair of elfin blue eyes that seemed to dance with mirth.

"Trying to get her prepped for the President's Cup Regatta next weekend, but the inboard motor is giving me fits. New carburetor, wiring, and fuel pump, yet she still doesn't want to fire up."

Pitt leaned over the hatch and studied the four-cylinder engine.

"That looks like the motor from an old American Austin," he said, recalling a minuscule car built in the twenties and thirties.

"Good guess. It's actually an American Bantam motor. The second owner had an American Bantam dealership and apparently tore out the original engine and inserted the Bantam. She ran fine until I decided to overhaul her."

"Always the case."

"Can I get you a beer?" Martin offered, rubbing his oil-stained hands on a rag.

"A little early for me," Pitt replied, shaking his head.

Martin kicked open a nearby ice chest and rummaged around until he located a bottle of Sam Adams. Popping the cap, he leaned on a rail and inhaled a large swig.

"I take it you didn't come down here strictly to talk boats," he said.

"No, that's simply a bonus," Pitt said with a grin. "Actually, Dan, I was wondering what you know about the explosion at the George Washington University research lab last week."

"Since the Director of NUMA isn't calling at my office, I presume this is an unofficial inquiry?"

"Entirely off-the-record," Pitt replied with a nod.

"What's your interest?" Martin turned his gaze to the beer bottle, studying its label.

"Lisa Lane, the scientist whose lab exploded, is a close friend of my wife's. I had just walked into the building to give her a report when the place detonated."

"Amazing nobody was killed," Martin replied. "But it does appear to have been a measured blast."

"You have people working on it?"

Martin nodded. "When the D.C. police couldn't identify a cause, they flagged it as a potential terrorist act and called us in. We sent three agents over a few days ago."

Dan Martin was the director of the FBI's Domestic Terrorism Operations Unit within the agency's Counterterrorism Division. Like Pitt, Martin had an affinity for old cars as well as boats, and had become friends with the NUMA Director after competing against him at a vintage auto concours some years earlier.

"So nobody believes the explosion was an accident?" Pitt asked.

"We can't say definitively just yet, but things are looking in that direction. A ruptured gas line was the first thing police investigators looked at, but the epicenter of the explosion was well away from the nearest gas line. The building's gas line didn't in fact rupture from the explosion, which could have caused much more damage."

"That would seem to suggest that the source was a planted device, if not something in the lab itself."

Martin nodded. "I've been told that there

were canisters of oxygen and carbon dioxide in there, so that's one suspicion. But my agents have performed a full residue sampling test, so that ought to tell us if there was any foreign material involved that can't be placed in the lab. I'm expecting the results on my desk tomorrow."

"Miss Lane didn't seem to believe it was caused by anything that she brought into the lab. Are you familiar with her area of research?"

"Some sort of biochemistry related to greenhouse gases, is what I was told."

Pitt explained Lisa's attempt to create artificial photosynthesis and her breakthrough discovery right before the explosion.

"You think there might be a connection with her research work?" Martin asked, draining his beer and tossing the empty back into the cooler.

"I have no evidence, just a suspicion. You'll know as much when you determine if there was a planted explosive."

"Any likely culprits?"

Pitt shook his head. "Lane had no conceivable suspects when I asked her directly."

"If we rule out an accidental explosion, then we'll start the background investigations and see if there were any personal motivations lurking about. But I'll add potential industrial sabotage to the list. There might be some outstanding lawsuits against GWU that will give us a direction to look."

"There's one other avenue you might examine. Lane's assistant, a fellow named Bob Hamilton. Again, I've got no evidence, but something struck me as odd regarding his absence from the area when the lab went up."

Martin looked at Pitt, reading a disquieting sign in his eyes. He knew Pitt well enough to realize he wasn't engaging in baseless hunches or abject paranoia. If Pitt had an instinct, it was probably as good as money in the bank.

"I'll have him checked out," Martin promised. "Anything else on your mind?"

Pitt nodded with a sly smile. "A case of misalignment," he said, then climbed into the small engine bay. He reached over the engine and unclipped a high-mounted distributor cap. Rotating it one hundred and eighty degrees, he set it back on the distributor housing and replaced the clip.

"Try her now," he told Martin.

The FBI man stepped over to the sailboat's cockpit and hit the starter button. The little engine turned over twice, then fired to life, idling like a sewing machine on steroids. Martin let the engine warm up for a few minutes, then shut it off, a look of embarrassment on his face.

"By the way, Tony is looking for his drill," Pitt said, rising to leave.

Martin smiled. "Good of you to stop by, Dirk. I'll let you know what we come up with in the lab."

"I'd appreciate it. Good luck in the regatta."

As Pitt climbed onto the dock, Martin remembered something and yelled over.

"I heard you finished the restoration on your Auburn and have been seen racing around town in her. I'd love to see her run."

Pitt shook his head with a pained look. "A nasty rumor, I'm afraid," he said, then turned and walked away.

34

The forensic analysis of residue found in the GWU lab reached Martin's desk at ten the next morning. After consulting with the lead investigative agent, Martin picked up the phone and called Pitt.

"Dirk, I've got our first look at the lab site-residue analysis. Afraid I can't release a copy of the report to you, however."

"I understand," Pitt replied. "Can you give me the thirty-thousand-foot view of the findings?"

"You were right on the money. Our lab analysts are nearly certain it was a planted explosive. They found trace samples of nitroglycerin all over the room."

"Isn't that the explosive element of dynamite?"

"Yes, that's how it is packaged, in the familiar dynamite sticks. Not high-tech, but it is a powerful explosive that carries a wicked punch."

"I didn't realize they still made the stuff."

"It's been around for years, but there is still a heavy industrial demand for it, primarily in underground mining."

"Any chance of tracing its origin?"

"There are only a handful of manufacturers, and each uses a slightly different formula, so there is in fact an identifying signature in the compound. The lab has already matched the samples up with an explosives manufacturer in Canada."

"That narrows things down a bit."

"True, but chances are it will be the end of the line. We'll send some agents up to talk to the company and check their sales records, but I wouldn't be too hopeful. The odds are that the explosives were stolen from a mining customer who doesn't even know the stuff is missing. I just hope this isn't the start of some serial bombing campaign."

"I'd bet against it," Pitt said. "I think Lane's research was specifically targeted."

"You're probably right. There was an additional finding that would support that theory. Our bomb analysts determined that the explosives were packed in a cardboard container. Unlike a pipe bomb, where the shrapnel from the pipe is intended to maim or kill, our bomber used a relatively benign approach. It does appear as if the explosion wasn't meant to kill, or certainly kill in numbers."

"A saving grace," Pitt replied, "but I take it your work is just beginning."

"Yes, the test results will blow the investigation wide open. We will be talking to everyone in the building. That will be our next hope, that someone saw something or somebody out of place that will give us our next lead." Martin knew that random explosions were one of the worst crimes to investigate and often the most difficult to solve.

"Thanks for the update, Dan, and good luck. If anything comes to me, I'll let you know."

Pitt hung up and walked down the hall to a briefing on NUMA's hurricane-warning buoys in the Gulf of Mexico. He then cleared his afternoon calendar and made his way out of the headquarters building. The explosion at the GWU lab gnawed at his consciousness, and, try as he might, he couldn't shake the feeling that there were serious consequences at play.

He drove to the Georgetown University Hospital, hoping that Lisa had not yet been released. She was still in her room on the second floor, along with a squat man in a three-piece suit. The man rose from a corner chair and glared at Pitt as he entered.

"It's all right, Agent Bishop," Lisa said from her bed. "This is Dirk Pitt, a friend of mine."

The FBI agent nodded without emotion, then left the room to stand in the hallway.

"Do you believe that?" Lisa said, greeting

Pitt. "The FBI has been questioning me all day, and now they won't leave me alone."

"They must have a soft spot for pretty research biochemists," Pitt replied with a warm grin. He was secretly thankful for the guard, knowing that Martin was taking the matter seriously.

Lane blushed at the comment. "Loren phoned a short time ago but didn't mention that you would be coming by."

"I became a little concerned after hearing of the FBI's investigation," he said.

He noted that Lisa looked vastly improved since his last visit. Her color had returned, her eyes were clear, and her voice was strong. But a leg cast and a shoulder sling indicated that she was still far removed from participating in a game of Twister.

"What's going on? They haven't told me anything," she said, giving him a pleading look.

"They think it may have been a planted bomb that blew up."

"I figured that's what they were driving at," she said in a whisper. "I just can't believe that would be true."

"They apparently found residue of an explosive material in your lab. I know that it is hard to figure. Do you have any enemies, personal or professional, that might have a grudge?"

"I went all through that with the FBI agents this morning," she said, shaking her head.

"There's not a soul I know who could even conceive of doing such an act. And I know the same goes for Bob."

"It's possible the explosives were placed in your lab at random, perhaps by some crazy who had a beef with the university."

"That is the only rationale I can think of. Though Bob and I always lock the lab when nobody is there."

"There is another possibility," Pitt offered. "Do you think a competitor might be threatened by the results of your research?"

Lisa contemplated the question for a moment. "I suppose it is possible. I have published papers related to my general research, and there are far-reaching effects. But the fact is, only you, Loren, and Bob were aware of my catalyst breakthrough. Nobody else even knew. It seems hard to believe someone could react so quickly, if they were indeed aware of the discovery."

Pitt remained silent as Lisa looked out the window for a moment.

"It seems to me that a working means of artificial photosynthesis would have only a positive benefit. I mean, who could possibly be hurt by a reduction in greenhouse gases?"

"Answer that and we have a potential suspect," Pitt said. He eyed a wheelchair parked along the opposite side of the bed. "When are they going to cut you loose from here?"

"The doctor said tomorrow afternoon, most

likely. Not soon enough for me. I'd like to get back to work and write up my findings."

"You can resurrect the test results?" Pitt asked.

"Conceptually, it's all still up here," she said, tapping a finger to her head. "I'll have to borrow a bit of lab equipment to redocument things, however. That's providing the Ontario Miners Co-op can come up with another sample of ruthenium."

"Your source of the mineral?"

"Yes. It's very costly. The stuff may end up being my downfall."

"You should be able to obtain more grant money now, I would think."

"It's not just the cost of the ruthenium, it's the actual availability. Bob says it is almost impossible to find."

Pitt thought a moment, then smiled at Lisa.

"Don't worry, things will work out. I better not interrupt your convalescence any more. If you need someone to push your wheelchair, don't hesitate to call."

"Thanks, Dirk. You and Loren have been too kind. As soon as I'm mobile, you two are invited for dinner."

"I can't wait."

Pitt made his way back to his car, noting that the time was nearly five-thirty. Following a hunch, he called Loren and told her he would be late, then drove back to the NUMA build-

261

ing. Riding the elevator to the tenth floor, he exited into the heart of the agency's computer operations. An imposing array of the latest information processors and storage devices held an unequaled repository of data on the world's oceans. Up-to-the-second current, tide, and weather conditions from satellite-fed sea buoys gave an instant snapshot of every major body of water around the globe. The computer system also housed a mountain of oceanographic research materials, allowing instant access to the latest findings in marine science.

Pitt found a man in a ponytail seated at a large console, arguing with an attractive woman standing a few feet in front of him. Hiram Yaeger was the architect of the NUMA computer center and an expert in database management. Though dressed eclectically in a tie-dyed T-shirt and cowboy boots, Yaeger was a devoted family man who doted on his two teenage daughters. Pitt knew Yaeger always made breakfast for his wife and daughters and often sneaked away to soccer games and concert recitals in the afternoon, making up the lost time during the evening hours.

As Pitt walked near, he marveled, as he always did, that the woman arguing with Yaeger was not real but rather a hologram that looked remarkably three-dimensional. Designed by Yaeger himself as a computer interface to the vast network system, the holographic woman

262

was modeled after his wife and affectionately named Max.

"Mr. Pitt, can you please straighten out Hiram," Max said, turning toward Pitt. "He doesn't want to believe me when I tell him a woman's handbag should match her shoes."

"I always trust what you have to say," Pitt replied with a nod.

"Thank you. There you have it," she turned, lecturing Yaeger.

"Fine, fine," Yaeger replied, throwing up his hands. "Some help you are in picking out a birthday present for my wife."

Yaeger turned toward Pitt. "I should never have programmed her to argue like my wife," he said, shaking his head.

Pitt took a seat next to him. "You wanted her to be as lifelike as possible," he countered with a laugh.

"Tell me you have something to talk about besides ladies' fashions," he pleaded.

"As a matter of fact, I'd like Max to help me with a few mineralogy questions."

"A welcome change of topics," Max replied, peering down her nose at Yaeger. "I'm delighted to help you, Director. What is it that you would like to know?"

"For starters, what can you tell me about the mineral ruthenium?"

Max closed her eyes for a second, then spoke rapidly. "Ruthenium is a transition metal of the platinum group, known for its hardness.

Silvery white in color, it is the forty-fourth element, also known by its symbol Ru. The name derives from the Latin word *rus,* from which Russia originates. A Russian geologist, Karl Klaus, made its discovery in 1844."

"Are there any unique demands for or uses of the mineral?" Pitt asked.

"Its qualities as a hardener, especially when combined with other elements such as titanium, were highly valued in industry. Supply irregularities have produced a sharp rise in prices recently, forcing manufacturers to turn to other compounds."

"How expensive can it be?" asked Yaeger.

"It is one of the rarest minerals found on earth. Recent spot market prices have exceeded twelve thousand dollars an ounce."

"Wow," Yaeger replied. "That's ten times the price of gold. Wish I owned a ruthenium mine."

"Hiram raises a good question," Pitt said. "Where is the stuff mined?"

Max frowned for a moment as her computer processors sifted through the databases.

"The supplies are rather unsettled at the moment. South Africa and the Ural Mountains of Russia have been the historical sources for mined ruthenium in the last century. Approximately ten metric tons a year was mined in South Africa from a single mine in Bushveld, but their output peaked in the 1970s and fell to nearly zero by 2000. Even with the run-up in price, they've had no new production."

"In other words, their mines have played out," Pitt suggested.

"Yes, that is correct. There have been no significant discoveries made in the region in over forty years."

"That still leaves the Russians," Yaeger said.

Max shook her head. "The Russian ruthenium came from just two small mines adjacent to each other in the Vissim Valley. Their production had actually peaked back in the 1950s. A severe landslide destroyed and buried both mining operations several years ago. The Russians have abandoned both sites, stating it would take many years to return either mine to operation."

"No wonder the price is so steep," Yaeger said. "What's your interest in the mineral, Dirk?"

Pitt described Lisa Lane's artificial photosynthesis discovery and the role of ruthenium as a catalyst, along with the explosion in the lab. Yaeger let out a low whistle after digesting the implications.

"That's going to make an unsuspecting mine owner a rich man," he said.

"Only if the stuff can be found," Pitt replied. "Which makes me wonder, Max, where would I go to purchase a bulk quantity of ruthenium?"

Max looked up toward the ceiling. "Let's

see . . . there are one or two Wall Street precious-commodities brokers that would be able to sell you some for investment purposes, but the quantities available are quite small. I'm only finding a small platinum mine in South America that has trace by-product quantities for sale, which would require further processing. The present known stocks of the mineral appear to be quite meager. The only other publicized source is the Ontario Miners Co-op, which lists a limited quantity of high-grade ruthenium available by the troy ounce."

"The Co-op is where Lisa obtained her sample," Pitt stated. "What more can you tell me about it?"

"The Miners Co-op represents independently owned mines across Canada, acting as wholesale outlet for mined ore. Their headquarters is in the town of Blind River, Ontario."

"Thank you, Max. You've been a great help, as always," Pitt said. He had long ago transcended his uneasiness at speaking to the computerized image and, like Yaeger, almost felt like Max was a real person.

"A pleasure anytime," Max replied with a nod. Turning to Yaeger, she admonished, "Now, don't you forget about my advice for your wife."

"Good-bye, Max," Yaeger replied, tapping at a keyboard. In an instant, Max disappeared from view. Yaeger turned to Pitt.

"A shame your friend's discovery may be for naught if there's no ruthenium around to power the process."

"As important as the ramifications are, a source will be found," Pitt said confidently.

"If your hunch about the lab explosion is correct, then somebody else already knows about the scarcity of the mineral."

Pitt nodded. "My fear as well. If they are willing to kill to halt the research, then they are probably willing to try and monopolize the remaining supplies."

"So where do you go from here?"

"There's only one place to go," he said. "The Ontario Miners Co-op, to see how much ruthenium really is left on the planet."

■ ■ ■ ■

PART II
BLACK KOBLUNA

■ ■ ■ ■

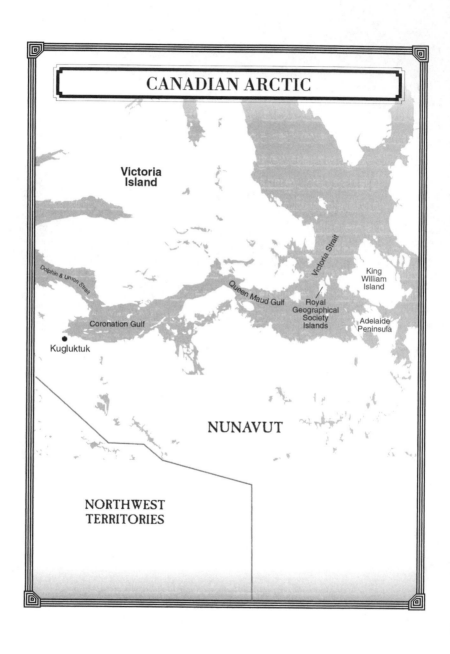

CANADIAN ARCTIC

Victoria Island

Dolphin & Union Strait

Victoria Strait

Queen Maud Gulf

King William Island

Royal Geographical Society Islands

Coronation Gulf

Adelaide Peninsula

Kugluktuk

NUNAVUT

NORTHWEST TERRITORIES

35

Summer was waiting at the dock when she spotted Trevor's boat motoring across the harbor. She wore a tight-fitting saffron-colored sweater, which accentuated the radiant red hair that dangled loose beneath her shoulders. Her gray eyes softened as the boat approached the dock and Trevor leaned out of the wheelhouse and waved.

"Going my way, sailor?" she asked with a grin.

"If I wasn't before, I am now," he replied with an approving look. He reached up and gave Summer a hand as she climbed onto the boat.

"Where's Dirk?" he asked.

"His head was still pounding this morning, so he took some aspirin and went back to bed."

Trevor shoved the boat away from the pier and motored past the municipal dock before turning into the harbor. Had he glanced at the dock's small dirt parking lot, he might have noticed a sharp-dressed man sitting in a brown Jeep observing their departure.

"Did you finish your inspection this morning?" Summer asked, as they cruised past a heavily loaded lumber ship.

"Yes. The aluminum smelter is just looking at a minor expansion of their receiving yard. Mandatory environmental impact statement sort of stuff." He looked at Summer with a twisted grin. "I was relieved not to find the police waiting for me at the boat this morning."

"I doubt anybody saw you at the Terra Green facility. It's Dirk and me who are most likely to end up on a WANTED poster at the Kitimat post office," she replied with an uneasy laugh.

"I'm sure the plant security is not going to file a report with the police. After all, as far as they know, they're responsible for Dirk's murder."

"Unless a surveillance camera caught you fishing him out alive."

"In which case, we're all in a bit of trouble." He turned and gave Summer a concerned look. "Maybe it would be a good idea if you and Dirk kept a low profile around town. A tall, gorgeous redhead tends to stand out in Kitimat."

Rather than blush, Summer moved closer to Trevor and looked deep into his eyes. He let go of the boat's wheel and slipped his arms around her waist, drawing her tight. Returning her gaze, he kissed her once, long and passionately.

"I don't want anything to happen to you," he whispered.

The pilot of a small freighter passing the other way happened to witness the embrace and blew his horn at the two. Trevor casually released one hand and waved at the freighter, then retook the wheel. Sailing briskly down Douglas Channel, he kept his other arm locked tightly around Summer's thin waist.

The turquoise NUMA boat was moored as they had left it, and Summer quickly had the vessel under way. The two boats playfully raced each other back to Kitimat, passing far around the Terra Green facility without incident. They had just tied up at the municipal pier when Dirk came rambling down the dock. His gait was slow, and he wore a baseball cap to cover the bandage across his skull.

"How's the head?" Trevor inquired.

"Better," Dirk replied. "The pounding has gone down from dynamite to sledgehammer strength. The Bells of St. Mary's are still ringing loud and clear, though."

Summer finished tying up the NUMA boat and walked over to the two men with a thick case in her hand.

"You ready to get to work?" she asked.

"The water samples," Trevor said.

"Yes, the water samples," she replied, holding

up the Kitimat municipal pool water-analyzing kit.

She stepped onto Trevor's boat and helped gather up the water samples taken the night before. Dirk and Trevor took a seat on the gunwale as Summer opened the test kit and began checking the acidity of the water samples.

"I'm showing a pH of 8.1," she said after testing the first sample. "The acidity is just a hair above the levels in the surrounding waters but not significant."

She proceeded to test all of her water samples and then the vials collected by Trevor. The results were nearly uniform for each vial tested. As she checked the results of the last sample, a defeated look crossed her face.

"Again, the pH level is reading about 8.1. Remarkably, the water around the Terra Green facility shows no abnormal levels of acidity."

"That seems to blow our theory that the plant is dumping carbon dioxide," Trevor said.

"A gold star for Mitchell Goyette," Dirk said sarcastically.

"I can't help but wonder about the tanker ship," Summer said.

Trevor gave her a quizzical look.

"We got sidetracked and couldn't prove it, but Dirk and I both thought the tanker might be taking on CO_2 rather than unloading it."

"Doesn't make much sense, unless they are transporting it to another sequestration facility. Or are dumping it at sea."

"Before trailing a tanker halfway around the world, I think we need to take another look at the site where we measured the extreme water acidity," Summer said, "and that's Hecate Strait. We've got the gear to investigate," she added, motioning toward the NUMA boat.

"Right," Dirk agreed. "We need to look at the seabed off Gil Island. The answer has to lie there."

"Can you stay and conduct a survey?" Trevor asked with a hopeful tone.

Dirk looked at Summer. "I received a call from the Seattle office. They need the boat back by the end of the week for some work in Puget Sound. We can stay two more days, then we'll have to hit the road."

"That will allow us time to examine a good chunk of territory off Gil Island," Summer said. "Let's plan for an early start tomorrow. Will you be able to join us, Trevor?" It was her turn to give a hopeful look.

"I wouldn't miss it," he replied happily.

As they were leaving the dock together, the brown Jeep with a rental-agency sticker on its bumper cruised slowly along the adjacent roadway. The driver stopped briefly at a clearing, which gave an unobstructed view of the municipal dock and harbor. Behind the wheel, Clay Zak gazed out the windshield,

275

studying the two boats at the end of the dock tied up one behind the other. He nodded to himself, then continued driving slowly down the road.

36

When Trevor arrived at the dock around seven the next morning, Dirk and Summer were already laying out their sonar equipment on the stern deck. He gave Summer a quick peck while Dirk was occupied coiling a tow cable, then he pulled a small cooler onto the boat.

"Hope everyone can stomach some fresh smoked salmon for lunch," he said.

"I'd say that's a vast improvement over Dirk's stockpile of peanut butter and dill pickles," Summer replied.

"Never have to worry about it going bad," Dirk defended. He walked into the wheelhouse and started the boat's motor, then returned to the stern deck.

"I'll need to refuel before we head out," he announced.

"There's a fuel dock just around the bend," Trevor replied. "It's a little cheaper than the gas at the city marina." He thought for a moment. "I'm a little low myself. Why don't you follow me over, and we can drop off my boat on the way out of the channel."

Dirk nodded in agreement, and Trevor hopped onto the deck and strolled down to his boat moored just behind the NUMA vessel. He unlocked the door to the wheelhouse, then fired up the inboard diesel, listening to its deep throaty idle. Checking his fuel gauge, he noted a pair of sunglasses on the dashboard that Summer had left behind. Looking up, he saw her untying the dock lines to the NUMA boat. Grabbing the glasses, he hopped off the boat and jogged down the dock.

"Some protection for those pretty gray eyes?" he asked.

Summer tossed the bow line aboard, then looked up to see Trevor standing with her sunglasses in an outstretched hand. She gazed skyward for a moment, taking in a thick layer of rain clouds overhead, before locking eyes with him.

"A tad overkill for today, but thanks for proving you are not a thief."

She reached over and grabbed the sunglasses as a sharp crack suddenly erupted behind them. The report was followed by a thunderous blast that flung them to the dock, a shower of splinters tearing over their heads. Trevor fell forward and onto Summer, protecting her from the debris, as several small chunks of wood and fiberglass struck him in the back.

A simple five-minute timed safety fuse, attached to four cartridges of nitroglycerin dynamite and wired to the ignition switch of Trevor's boat, had initiated the inferno. The blast nearly ripped the entire stern section off the Canadian boat, while flattening most of the wheelhouse. The stern quickly sank from sight while the mangled bow clung stubbornly to the surface, dangling at a grotesque angle by the attached dock line.

Dirk was standing in the cabin of his own vessel when the blast struck and was unscathed by any flying debris. He immediately scrambled onto the dock and found Summer, being helped to her feet by Trevor. Like Dirk, she was unhurt by the blast. Trevor was less fortunate. His back was soaked with blood from a large splinter embedded in his shoulder, and he limped from a timber that had slammed into his leg. He ignored the injuries and hobbled over to the smoldering remains of his boat. Summer and Dirk checked each other to ensure they were uninjured, then Dirk jumped back aboard and grabbed a fire extinguisher, dousing several smoldering piles of debris that threatened to start a larger fire.

Summer found a towel and hurried over to Trevor, who was compressing the cut on his shoulder as he stared blankly at the ruins of his boat. As a police siren wailed its imminent approach, Trevor turned and gazed at Summer with a look of hurt and anger.

"It has to be Terra Green," he muttered quietly. "I wonder if they killed my brother, too?"

At a harborside coffee shop two miles away, Clay Zak stared out the window, admiring the plume of smoke and flame that rose above the water in the distance. Finishing an espresso and Danish, he left a large tip on the table, then walked to his brown rented Jeep parked up the street.

"Smoke on the water," he muttered aloud, humming the Deep Purple rock tune before climbing into the car. Without the least concern, he drove to the airport outside of town, where Mitchell Goyette's private jet waited for him on the tarmac.

37

The business jet circled the airfield once, waiting for a small plane to take off and clear the field, before the control tower gave approval to land. Painted in the same shade of turquoise as its fellow sea vessels, the NUMA Hawker 750 touched down lightly on the runway. The small jet taxied to a redbrick building before pulling to a halt alongside a much larger Gulfstream G650. The fuselage door opened and Pitt quickly stepped out, slipping on a jacket to ward off a brisk chill in the air. He walked into the terminal building, where he was greeted by a rotund man standing behind a counter.

"Welcome to Elliot Lake. It's not often we have two jets in on the same day," he said in a friendly rural voice.

"A little short for the carriers?" Pitt asked.

"Our runway is only forty-five hundred feet, but we hope to expand it next year. Can I fix you up with a rental car?"

Pitt nodded, and soon left the terminal with

a set of keys to a blue Ford SUV. Spreading a map on the hood of the car, he studied his new surroundings. Elliot Lake was a small town near the northeast shores of Lake Huron. Situated some two hundred and seventy-five miles due north of Detroit, the town lay in the Algoma District of Ontario Province. Surrounded by Canadian wilderness, the landscape was a lush mix of rugged mountains, winding rivers, and deep lakes. Pitt found the airport on his map, carved out of the dense forest a few miles south of the town. He traced a lone highway that traveled south through the mountains, culminating on the shores of Lake Huron and the Trans-Canada Highway. About fifteen miles to the west was Pitt's destination, an old logging and mining town called Blind River.

The drive was scenic, the road winding past several mountain lakes and a surging river that dropped over a steep waterfall. The terrain flattened as he reached the shores of Lake Huron and the town of Blind River. He drove slowly through the small hamlet, admiring the quaint wooden homes, which were mostly built in the 1930s. Pitt continued past the city limits until he spotted a large steel warehouse adjacent to a field littered with high mounds of rock and ore. A large maple leaf flag flew above a weathered sign that read ONTARIO MINERS CO-OP AND REPOSITORY. Pitt turned in and parked near the entrance as a broad-shouldered man in a brown suit walked down the steps and climbed into a late-model white sedan. Pitt noticed the man staring at him through a pair of dark sunglasses as he climbed out of his own rental car and entered the building.

The dusty interior resembled a mining museum. Rusty ore carts and pickaxes jammed the corners, alongside high shelves that overflowed with mining journals and old photographs. Behind a long wooden counter sat a massive antique banker's safe that Pitt guessed held the more valuable mineral samples.

Seated behind the counter was an older man who appeared almost as dusty as the room's interior. He had a bulb-shaped head, and his gray hair, eyes, and mustache matched the faded flannel shirt he wore beneath a pair of striped suspenders. He peered at Pitt through a pair of Ben Franklin glasses perched low on his nose.

"Good morning," Pitt said, introducing himself. Gazing up at a polished tin container that resembled a large liquor flask, he remarked, "Beautiful old oil cadger you have there."

The old man's eyes lit up as he realized Pitt wasn't a lost tourist looking for directions.

"Yep, used to refill the early miners' oil lamps. Came from the nearby Bruce Mines. My grandpappy worked the copper mines there till they shut down in 1921," he said in a wheezy voice.

"A lot of copper in these hills?" Pitt asked.

"Not enough to last long. Most of the copper and gold mines shut down decades ago. Attracted a lot of dirt diggers in their day, but not too many folks got rich from it," he replied, shaking his head. Looking Pitt in the eye, he asked, "What can I do for you today?"

"I'd like to know about your stock of ruthenium."

"Ruthenium?" he asked, looking at Pitt queerly. "You with that big fellow that was just in here?"

"No," Pitt replied. He recalled the odd behavior of the man in the brown suit and tried to shake off a nagging sense of familiarity.

"That's peculiar," the man said, eyeing Pitt with suspicion. "That other fellow was from the Natural Resources Ministry in Ottawa. Here checking our supply and sources of ruthenium. Odd that it was the only mineral he was interested in and you come walking in asking about the same thing."

"Did he tell you his name?"

"John Booth, I believe he said. A bit of an odd bird, I thought. Now, what's your interest, Mr. Pitt?"

Pitt generally explained Lisa Lane's research at George Washington University and ruthenium's role in her scientific work. He neglected to disclose the magnitude of her recent discovery or the recent explosion at the lab.

"Yes, I recall sending a sample to that lab a week or two ago. We don't get too many requests for ruthenium, just a few public research labs and the occasional high-tech company. With the price going so crazy, not too many folks can afford to dabble with it anymore. Of course, that price spike has made us a nice profit when we do get an order," he smiled with a wink. "I just wish we had a source to replenish our inventory."

"You don't have an ongoing supplier?"

"Oh heavens no, not in years. I reckon my stock will be depleted before long. We used to get some from a platinum mine in eastern Ontario, but the ore they are pulling out now isn't showing any meaningful content. No, as I was telling Mr. Booth, most of our ruthenium stocks came from the Inuit."

"They mined it up north?" Pitt asked.

"Apparently so. I pulled the acquisition records for Mr. Booth," he said, pointing to an ancient leather-bound journal sitting at the other end of the counter. "The stuff was acquired over a hundred years ago. There's a detailed accounting in the logbook. The Inuit referred to it as the 'Black Kobluna' or some such. We always called it the Adelaide sample, as the Inuit were from a camp on the Adelaide Peninsula in the Arctic."

"So that's the extent of the Canadian supply of ruthenium?"

"As far as I know. But nobody knows if there

is more to the Inuit source. It all surfaced so long ago. The story was that the Inuit were afraid to return to the island where they obtained it because of a dark curse. Something about bad spirits and the source being tainted by death and insanity, or similar mumbo jumbo. A tall tale of the north, I guess."

"I've found that local legends often have some basis in fact," Pitt replied. "Do you mind if I take a look at the journal?"

"Not at all." The old geologist ambled down to the end of the counter and returned with the book, flipping through its pages as he walked. A scowl suddenly crossed his face as his skin turned beet red.

"Santa María!" he hissed. "He tore out the record, right in front of me. There was a hand-drawn map of the mine location right there. Now it's gone."

The old man slammed the book to the counter while turning an angry eye toward the door. Pitt could see where two pages had been neatly torn from the journal.

"I'd venture to say that your Mr. Booth isn't who he said he was," Pitt said.

"I should have suspected something when he didn't know what a sluice box was," the man grumbled. "I don't know why he had to deface our records. He could have just asked for a copy."

Pitt knew the reason why. Mr. Booth didn't want anyone else to know the source of the

286

Inuit ruthenium. He slid the journal around and read a partial entry ahead of the missing pages.

> *October 22, 1917. Horace Tucker of the Churchill Trading Company consigned following unrefined ore quantities:*
>   *5 tons of copper ore*
>   *12 tons of lead ore*
>   *2 tons of zinc*
>   *1/4 ton of ruthenium (Adelaide "Black Kobluna")*
> *Source and assayer comments to follow.*

"That was the only Inuit shipment you have received?" Pitt asked.

The old man nodded. "That was it. The missing pages indicated that the mineral had actually been obtained decades earlier. That trading post in Churchill couldn't find a market for the stuff until Tucker brought a sample in with some minerals from a mine in Manitoba."

"Any chance the Churchill Trading Company records still exist?"

"Pretty doubtful. They went out of business back around 1960. I met Tucker a few years later in Winnipeg shortly before he died. I remember him telling me how the old log trading post in Churchill had burned to the ground. I would imagine their trading records were destroyed in the fire."

"I guess that's the end of the line, then. I'm sorry about the theft of your data, but thank you for sharing what you know."

"Hold on a second," the man replied. He stepped over and opened the thick door to the ancient safe. He rummaged around a wooden bin inside, then turned and tossed something to Pitt. It was a tiny smooth stone, silvery white in color.

"Black Kobluna?" he asked.

"A sample on the house, so that you know what we've been talking about."

Pitt reached across the counter and shook hands with the geologist, thanking him for his time.

"One more thing," the old man said, as Pitt strolled toward the door. "You run into that Booth fellow, you be sure and tell him I'm coming after him with a pickax if I ever see him again."

The afternoon had turned colder under the cast of an approaching front, and Pitt waited anxiously for the car heater to warm up as he exited the Co-op's parking lot. Grabbing a quick lunch at a café in Blind River, he drove back through the winding mountain road toward the airport, contemplating the Inuit ruthenium tale. The ore had to have come from the Arctic, presumably near the Inuit camp at Adelaide. How had the Inuit, with primitive technology, mined the ruthenium? Were there still significant reserves in place?

And who was John Booth and why was he interested in the Inuit ore?

The questions brought no answers as he wound through the scenic hills, braking as he pulled up behind a slower-moving RV. Reaching a straight stretch in the road, the RV driver pulled to the shoulder and waved for Pitt to pass. Pitt stomped on the accelerator and sped past the motor home, which he noted had a Colorado license plate.

The road snaked sharply ahead of him, the two lanes carving into the edge of a rocky mountainside that tumbled down to a river below. Twisting through a tight bend, Pitt could see the roadway a mile ahead, where the highway nearly doubled back on a parallel facing. He caught a glimpse of a white sedan parked in a turnout. It was the same vehicle that John Booth had climbed into at the Co-op. Pitt lost sight of the car as the roadway bent and twisted once more.

Rounding through a tight S curve, the road straightened again for a short stretch. To Pitt's left, the hillside plunged in a steep drop-off, falling several hundred feet to the river below. As his rental car gained speed on the straightaway, Pitt heard a faint pop, like the burst of a distant Fourth of July firework. He glanced ahead but noticed nothing, as a deep rumble followed the initial noise. A movement caught his eye, and he looked up to see a house-sized boulder sliding down the mountainside above him. The huge rock was falling in a perfect trajectory to intersect with Pitt's car two hundred feet down the road.

Pitt instantly stomped on the brakes, mashing the pedal to the floorboard. The tires chirped and shimmied in protest, but the car's antilock braking system kept the vehicle from skidding uncontrollably. In the brief seconds Pitt waited for the car to stop, he observed that a full landslide was now under way. In addition to the huge rock, a whole wall of rocks and gravel was chasing the boulder down the mountainside. With seemingly half of the mountain barreling toward him, he knew he would have only one chance to escape.

His quick braking slowed the car just enough to prevent him from being flattened by the first mammoth boulder. The huge rock hit the asphalt just twenty feet in front of him, splintering into several smaller sections. Most of the rock pieces continued their downhill slide, smashing through the guardrail and tumbling down the steep precipice toward the river. A few large chunks died on the road, soon to be buried by the impeding landslide that followed.

Pitt's car skidded into one of the chunks, a flattened slab of granite that instantly stopped his momentum. Though it mashed the bumper and grille, the car's mechanics were undamaged. Inside, Pitt felt only a strong jolt, but it was enough to inflate the air bag, which ballooned in front of his chest as the vehicle bounced backward. Pitt's quick senses had beaten the air bag, though. He had already jammed the automatic transmission in to reverse and stomped on the accelerator at the moment of impact.

The rear tires smoked as they spun wildly before gripping the pavement and propelling the car backward. Pitt gripped the steering wheel and held it steady as the car tried to fishtail from the sudden rearward torque before settling on a stable line. The transmission screamed beneath Pitt's feet as the low-ratio reverse gear fought to maintain revolutions with the floored engine. Pitt glanced up the hill to see the sliding mass of rocks and gravel already descending upon him. The landslide had spread across a wide line, extending well to his rear. He quickly realized there was no way he could outrun it.

Like a slate-colored tidal wave, the sliding wall of rock cascaded onto the roadway, spilling first a few yards in front of him. For an instant, it appeared as if the speeding car might slip past the deluge, but then a separate cluster of boulders broke free and crashed to the road behind him. Pitt could do nothing but hold on as the car barreled into the moving layer of rocks with a screeching peal of twisted metal.

The car scraped over a large boulder, snapping off the rear axle and sending one of the drive wheels careening down the hill. Pitt was thrown back into his seat as a secondary wall of falling rocks smashed into the passenger side, lifting the car up and over onto its roof. Pitt was flung to his left, his head striking a side air bag as it inflated. Seconds later, he was jarred again to the side again, his head banging through the deflating air bag until striking the driver's-side window. A great battering roar filled his ears as the car was pummeled across the road, slamming hard to a sudden stop. Inside, Pitt teetered on the brink of consciousness as the sound of rushing gravel surrounded him. His vision went blurry as he was buffeted in his seat, he vaguely felt a warm wetness on his face, and then all feeling vanished as he dropped into a silent void of blackness.

38

Pitt knew that he was alive from the jackhammer-like pounding that wracked his skull. His auditory senses kicked in next, detecting a rhythmic scraping sound nearby. He wriggled his fingers, finding a heavy resistance but confirming that they were still wrapped around the steering wheel of the rental car. Though his legs moved freely, his head, chest, and arms felt completely restricted. The realization that he couldn't breathe suddenly struck his foggy mind and he struggled to free himself, but he felt like a bound mummy. He slowly pried open the lids of his eyes, which felt as if they had been glued shut, but all he saw was black.

The grip on his lungs grew tighter and he thrashed harder, finally freeing a hand and forearm from their mysterious hold. He heard a voice and a frantic scuffling sound, then a scraping sensation skinned his face as a burst of light blinded his eyes. He sucked in a breath of dusty air, then squinted through a thick surrounding haze. Staring back at him was a pair of affectionate brown eyes, affixed to the tiny head of a black-and-tan dachshund. Most confusing to Pitt, the dog appeared to be standing upside down. The dog inched closer, sniffing Pitt's exposed face before licking him on the nose.

"Out of the way, Mauser, he's still alive," came a man's voice from nearby.

A pair of thick hands appeared and scooped away more of the dirt and gravel that had buried Pitt's head and torso. Pitt's arms finally broke free, and he helped push the small mountain of dirt away from his body. Reaching up with his sleeve, he wiped away the matted blood and dust from his eyes and finally took a look at his surroundings. With the seat belt tugging uncomfortably across his chest, he finally realized that he was the one upside down, not the dachshund. The helping pair of hands reached in and found the release button on the seat belt, dropping Pitt to the ceiling of the car. Pitt shuffled toward the driver's-side window, but the hands yanked him toward the open passenger door.

"You don't want to go that way, mister. The first step is a doozy."

Pitt heeded the voice and crawled toward the passenger door, where he was helped out and onto his feet. The pounding in his head eased as he stood upright, but a light trickle of blood still rolled down his cheek. Looking at the damaged car, he shook his head at the good fortune that had saved him.

The sliding mass of rock and gravel that had battered the car and flipped it on its roof had also pushed it across the road, to the very edge of the steep chasm that fell to the river below. The car would have easily gone over the edge, taking Pitt to his death, but for a firmly cemented mileage signpost. The slim metal post caught the car just behind the front fender, pinning it to the edge of the road, as tons of loose rock plunged down the hill around both ends of the car. The road itself was buried under a mound of dirt and rocks for a stretch of fifty yards.

"Must be some clean living that kept you from going over the edge," Pitt heard his rescuer say.

He turned to face a robust older man with white hair and beard who stood gazing at Pitt through a pair of jovial gray eyes.

"It wasn't clean living that saved me, I can assure you," Pitt replied. "Thank you for pulling me out. I would have suffocated in there if you hadn't dug your way in."

"Don't mention it. Why don't you come on back to the RV and let me patch you up," the man said, pointing to a motor home parked on unblemished asphalt a few yards away. It was the same motor home that Pitt had passed earlier on the road.

Pitt nodded and followed the man and the

little black-and-tan dachshund as they climbed into an open side door of the RV. Pitt was surprised to find the interior finished in teak and polished brass, which gave the look of a luxury cabin on a sailing ship. On one wall he curiously noticed a bookcase filled with reference guides on mining and geology.

"Why don't you get yourself cleaned up while I find my medical kit?" the man said.

Pitt washed his hands and face in a porcelain sink as a Royal Canadian Mounted Police car raced up with its lights flashing. The old man stepped out and spoke to the police, then returned a few minutes later and helped Pitt apply a bandage to a thin gash that zigzagged across the left side of his scalp.

"The Mounties said there's a highway construction crew working just a few miles away. They can get a front-end loader over here pretty quick, and should have a lane cleared through the rocks in just an hour or two. They'll want to take a report from you when you feel up to it."

"Thanks for putting them off. I'm just starting to get my bearings back."

"Forgive me for not asking earlier, you must surely need a drink. What can I get you?"

"I'd kill for a tequila, if you have any," Pitt replied, sagging into a small leather-upholstered chair. The dachshund immediately jumped into his lap and coaxed Pitt to pet him behind the ears.

"You are in luck," the man replied, pulling a stubby bottle of Don Julio tequila out of a cabinet. Swirling the bottle around, he said, "Still a few shots left."

"I'm lucky twice today. That's a fine brand of tequila," Pitt remarked, recognizing the expensive label of blue agave cactus juice.

"Mauser and I like to travel well," the man said with a grin as he poured two healthy shots for Pitt and himself.

Pitt let the warm liquid trickle down his throat, admiring its complex flavor. He felt his head clear almost immediately.

"That was quite a slide," the man said. "Good thing you weren't a few yards farther down the road."

"I saw it coming and tried to back away from it but came up a little short."

"I don't know what kind of fool would be blasting above an open highway," he said, "but I sure hope they catch the bugger."

"Blasting?" Pitt asked, suddenly recalling the white sedan he saw parked up the road.

"I heard the pop and noticed a puff of white smoke up the hill right before those boulders started dancing. I told the Mounties about it, but they said there are no blasting crews working anywhere around here."

"You don't think it was just a large boulder that let go and kicked up the rest?"

The man knelt down and opened a wide drawer beneath the bookshelf. Digging beneath a thick blanket, he exposed a small wooden box marked DYNO NOBEL. Pitt recognized the manufacturer's name as the offshoot of Alfred Nobel, inventor of dynamite. Opening the lid, the man showed Pitt a number of eight-inch-long yellow cartridges packed inside.

"I do a little blasting myself now and then, when investigating a potential mineral vein."

"You're a prospector?" Pitt asked, nodding toward the shelf of geology books.

"More of a hobby than a profession," the man replied. "I just like searching for things of value. I would never be blasting near civilization, but that's probably what happened here. Some fool found something shiny up the hill and decided he had to have a closer look. I wouldn't want to foot his cleanup bill if he gets caught."

Pitt nodded silently, suspecting that the blast hadn't originated from an innocent miner.

"What brings you to this area?" Pitt asked.

"Silver," the prospector replied, holding up the tequila bottle and pouring Pitt a second shot. "There used to be a working silver mine up near Algoma Mills, before everyone went crazy around here for uranium. I figure if they had one big strike in the area, there's bound to be a few scraps around for a small-timer like me." He shook his head, then grinned. "So far, my theory hasn't panned out."

Pitt smiled, then downed the glass of tequila. He turned to the prospector and asked, "What do you know about the mineral ruthenium?"

The prospector rubbed his chin for a moment. "Well, it's a relative of platinum, though not associated with deposits in these parts. I know the price has skyrocketed, so there's probably a lot more folks out searching for the stuff, but I've never run across any. Can't say that I know anybody else who has either. As I recall, there are only a few places in the world where they mine it. My only other recollection about ruthenium is that some folks thought it had something to do with the old Pretoria Lunatic Mill."

"I'm not familiar with the story," Pitt replied.

"An old miners' tale out of South Africa. I read about it while doing some research on diamonds. Apparently, there was a small weaving mill built near the turn of the century near Pretoria, South Africa. After operating for about a year, they started finding the mill workers going batty. It got so bad they had to close down the factory. The lunacy probably had something to do with the chemicals they used, but it never was clearly identified. It was later noted that the plant was built next to a platinum mine rich with ruthenium, and that ruthenium ore, which had little value back then, was stockpiled in great mounds next to the mill. At least one historian thought that the unusual mineral had something to do with the crazy behavior."

"It's an interesting story," Pitt replied, recalling his discussion at the Co-op. "Have you by chance heard of any mining done by the Inuit up north in the old days?"

"Can't say that I have. Of course, the Arctic is considered a mining candy land these days. Diamonds in the Northwest Territories, coal on Ellesmere Island, and of course oil and natural gas prospects all over the place."

They were interrupted by a granite-faced Mountie, who poked his head in the door and asked Pitt to fill out a police report on his damaged rental car. The road construction crew arrived shortly after and went to work clearing a path through the debris. The loose rock and gravel was quickly pushed aside, and it was only a short while before a single lane of traffic was opened through the landslide area.

"Any chance I could bum a ride with you to the Elliot Lake airport?" Pitt asked the old prospector.

"I'm headed to the Sudbury region, so you're pretty much on my way. Grab a seat up front," he replied, taking a seat behind the wheel.

The big RV barely squeezed through the debris before finding open road on the far side of the landslide. The two men chatted about history and mining until the motor home pulled to a stop outside the tiny airport terminal.

"There you go, mister, ah . . ."

"Pitt. Dirk Pitt."

"My name's Clive Cussler. Happy trails to you, Mr. Pitt."

Pitt shook the old prospector's hand, then gave the dachshund a pat on the head, before climbing out of the RV.

"I'm obliged to you for your help," Pitt said, looking at the prospector with a familiar sense of kinship. "Good luck in finding that beckoning mother lode."

Pitt walked into the building and approached the terminal manager, whose mouth gaped when he turned his way. Pitt looked like he had just been run over by a Greyhound bus. His hair and clothes were caked in dust, while a bloodied bandage crossed his scalp. When Pitt relayed how the rental car was sitting on the highway upside down and filled with rocks, the manager nearly went into convulsions.

While filling out an endless stack of insurance papers, Pitt glanced out the window and noticed that the Gulfstream jet was no longer parked on the tarmac.

"How long ago did our fellow jet depart?" he asked the manager.

"Oh, about an hour or two ago. His stay wasn't much longer than yours."

"I think I saw him in town. Kind of a burly guy in a brown suit?"

"Yes, that was the customer."

"Mind if I ask where he was headed?"

"You two are both nosy. He asked who you were," he said, picking up a clipboard and running his finger down a short list of aircraft arrivals and departures. Pitt casually leaned over the manager's shoulder, catching the plane's tail number, C-FTGI, which he committed to memory.

"While I can't tell you who is aboard, I can tell you that the plane is bound for Vancouver, with a scheduled fuel stop in Regina, Saskatchewan."

"They visit Elliot Lake often?"

"No, I can't say I've seen that plane here before." The manager tilted his head toward a small room in the corner of the terminal. "Why don't you grab a cup of coffee in the lounge, and I'll notify your flight crew that you are here."

Pitt agreed and made his way to the lounge, where he poured a cup of coffee from a stained glass pot. A corner-mounted television was tuned to a Calgary rodeo, but Pitt stared past the bronco riders, toying with the scattered puzzle pieces of the last few days. His trip to the Miners Co-op had been made on a lark, yet his hunch had been right. Sourcing a supply of ruthenium was of global importance, and somebody else was in on the hunt. He thought back to the well-dressed man in the white sedan, John Booth. There was something familiar about the man, but Pitt knew no one in Vancouver who had the means to fly in a corporate jet.

The terminal manager popped into the lounge, refilling a large coffee cup as he spoke to Pitt.

"Your flight crew is on their way to your aircraft. I told them you would be right out."

As he spoke, he ripped open a packet of sugar to pour into his coffee. The bag ripped completely in half, though, showering the carpeted floor in white granules.

"Jeez," he groaned, tossing the empty packet aside. "Well, that will give the night janitor something to do," he muttered, staring at the mess.

Pitt was likewise staring at the mess but with a different reaction. His eyes suddenly turned bright, and a sly grin spread across his lips.

"A fortuitous disaster," he said to the manager, who looked back at him blankly. "Thanks for your assistance. I need to make a couple of phone calls, then I'll be right aboard."

When he crossed the tarmac a few minutes later, Pitt had a spry step to his aching bones and the gash to his head had ceased hurting. Across his face, the sly grin was still firmly embedded in place.

39

"Minister Jameson, I have Mitchell Goyette on line one," the gray-haired secretary said, poking her head into Jameson's office like a gopher.

Jameson nodded from his desk, then waited until his secretary closed the door on her way out before hesitantly picking up the phone.

"Arthur, how are things in our lovely capital city?" Goyette greeted with mock friendship.

"Ottawa is enjoying a warm spring, to accompany the hot jingoistic climate in Parliament."

"It's high time we retained Canada's resources for Canadians," Goyette snorted.

"Yes, so that we can sell them to the Chinese," the minister replied drily.

Goyette promptly turned serious. "There's a small pile of rocks in the Arctic southeast of Victoria Island called the Royal Geographical Society Islands. I'll be needing the mineral rights to the entire landmass," he said, as if asking for a cup of coffee.

"Let me take a look," Jameson replied, pulling a bundle of maps from his desk drawer. Finding a map marked Victoria Strait, which was overlaid with numbered grid lines, he moved to a desktop computer. Inputting the grid numbers, he accessed the ministry's records of exploration and extraction licenses issued by the government. Within a few minutes, he had an answer for Goyette.

"I'm afraid we already have a production license in place, which covers about thirty percent of the islands, primarily the southern portion of West Island. It's a ten-year license, but they are only entering their second year of operations. The license is held by Kingfisher Holdings, a subsidiary of the Mid-America Mining Company out of Butte, Montana. They have built a small mining facility and are currently extracting small quantities of zinc, apparently just in the summer months."

"An American firm holds the license?"

"Yes, but through a Canadian shell company. There's technically no law against it, providing they post the required security bond and meet the other provisions of the license agreement."

"I want the license rescinded and reissued to one of my entities," Goyette said matter-of-factly.

Jameson shook his head at Goyette's presumption. "There would have to be a violation of the license, such as environmental polluting or shortchanging the royalty payments. It can't be done unilaterally, Mitchell, without setting the government up for a major lawsuit."

"Then how do I obtain the rights?" he huffed.

"Mid-America is currently in compliance, according to the latest inspection report, so your only option would be to try and purchase the rights directly from them. They would no doubt gouge you for the pleasure." He thought for a moment. "There may in fact be another possibility."

"Go ahead," Goyette urged impatiently.

"There is a national defense clause in the license. Should this brouhaha with the United States continue to escalate, there is a possibility of using it for grounds to terminate the license. The clause allows for the termination of foreign-held licenses in the event of war, conflict, or dissolution of state relations. A long shot, of course, but one never knows. What exactly is your interest in the islands?"

"Something that is as good as gold," Goyette replied quietly. Regaining his brashness, he barked, "Prepare the necessary details for me to bid on a new license. I'll figure out a way to have this Mid-America Corporation cough it up."

"Very well," Jameson replied, his teeth gritted. "I will await your results."

"That's not all. As you know, the Melville

Sound site is showing extraordinarily rich reserves of natural gas, yet I only own rights to a tiny fraction of the fields. I will be needing to obtain the extraction rights to the entire region."

The line fell silent for several seconds before Jameson finally muttered, "I'm not sure that will be possible."

"Nothing is impossible, for the right price," Goyette laughed. "You'll find that most of the tracts are previously ice-covered regions that nobody was interested in. Until now."

"That is the problem. Word is out that major shipments are already being made from Melville. We're receiving dozens of exploration requests for the area."

"Well, don't bother responding to them. The Melville gas fields will be worth billions, and I'm not going to let them slip through my fingers," he snapped. "I will be sending you several maps shortly. They delineate my desired exploration zones, which encompass large sections of Melville Sound and some other Arctic regions. I intend to dramatically expand my exploration business in the Arctic and want wholesale exploration licenses for the entire lot. There are incredible profits available there, and you'll be aptly rewarded, so don't blow it. Good-bye, Arthur."

Jameson heard a click as the line went dead. The resources minister sat frozen for a moment until a seething anger welled up from within, then he slammed the phone down with a whack.

Two thousand miles to the west, Goyette punched off his speakerphone and leaned back in his chair. Gazing across his office desk, he stared into the cool eyes of Clay Zak.

"Nothing ever comes easy," he griped. "Now, tell me again why this ruthenium is so bloody important."

"It's quite simple," Zak replied. "If you can monopolize the supply of ruthenium, then you can control a primary solution to global warming. What you elect to do with the mineral is a matter of money . . . and ego, I suppose."

"I'm listening," Goyette grunted.

"Assuming that you control the principal supply, then you have a choice to make. Mitchell Goyette, the environmentalist, can become the savior of the planet and pocket a few bucks along the way, fueling the expansion of artificial photosynthesis factories around the world."

"But there is a risk on the demand side," Goyette argued. "We really don't know how much ruthenium will ultimately be needed, so the profits could be enormous or they could be squat. I've staked most of my worth in developing control of the Northwest Passage. I have invested heavily in natural gas and oil sands infrastructure to be able to ship through the passage, supported by my fleet of Arctic vessels. I have long-term export agreements in place with the Chinese and will soon have the Americans pleading on their knees. And I've got a potential booming business in carbon dioxide sequestration. If global warming is reversed, or even halted, I could face extended ice issues that run counter to my entire business strategy."

"In that case, I suppose we can turn to Mitchell Goyette the unrepentant capitalist, who can recognize a profit opportunity blindfolded and will stop at nothing to keep his financial empire expanding."

"You flatter me," Goyette replied sarcastically. "But you have made the decision easy. I can't afford to have the Northwest Passage revert to a solid chunk of ice. The recent melting is what has allowed me to gain control of the Melville Sound gas fields and monopolize transportation in the region. Maybe ten or fifteen years from now, when the oil sands and gas reserves are nearing depletion, I can go save the planet. By then, the ruthenium may even be exponentially more valuable."

"Spoken like a true capitalist."

Goyette reached over and picked up two thin pages of paper lying on his desk. They were the journal entries Zak had stolen from the Miners Co-op.

"The basis for this whole ruthenium claim still seems rather flimsy," he said, examining the pages. "A trader purchased the ore in 1917 from an Inuit whose grandfather acquired the stuff some seventy years earlier. The grandfather was from Adelaide but claimed the ruthenium came from the Royal Geographical Society Islands. On top of that, he called it Black Kobluna and said the source was cursed with dark spirits. Hardly the basis of a scientific mining claim." He peered at Zak, unsure whether the whole thing might be a ruse on the part of the paid assassin.

Zak stared back without blinking. "It may be a long shot. But the Inuit ruthenium had to come from somewhere, and we're talking one hundred and sixty years ago in the middle of the Arctic. The journal has a map of the island, showing exactly where it was mined. The Inuit didn't have front-end loaders and dump trucks back then, so they would have had to pretty much find the stuff lying on the ground. There has to be more there. While this Mid-America Company has appeared in the area, they're looking for zinc, and on the opposite side of the island. Yes, Mitchell, it may well be a long shot. But there could be an enormous payoff if it's there, and an enormous cost to you if someone else gets to it first."

"Aren't we the only ones who know about the Inuit deposits?"

Zak squinted slightly, his lips pressed in a tight grimace.

"There is the possibility that Dirk Pitt is

aware of the trail," he said.

"Pitt?" Goyette asked, shaking his head in nonrecognition.

"He's the Director of the National Underwater and Marine Agency in the United States. I ran into him at the research lab in Washington and noticed him giving aid to the lab manager after the explosion. He appeared again in Ontario, at the Miners Co-op, just after I took these journal entries. I tried to arrange an accident on the road out of town, but some old man helped him escape. He's obviously aware of the importance of ruthenium in triggering the artificial-photosynthesis process."

"He might be on to you as well," Goyette said, a crease crossing his troubled brow.

"I can take care of that easily enough," Zak said.

"It's not a good idea to be blowing up high-visibility government officials. He can't do anything from the States. I'll have him tailed just to make sure he stays there. Besides, I'll need you to go to the Arctic and investigate the Royal Geographical Society Islands. Take a security team with you, and I'll send along some of my top geologists. Then figure out a way to put Mid-America out of business. I want you to find the ruthenium. Obtain it at any cost. All of it."

"That's the Mitchell Goyette I know and love," Zak said with a twisted smile. "We

311

haven't talked about my share."

"It's a pipe dream at the moment. Ten percent of the royalties is more than generous."

"I was thinking of fifty percent."

"That's absurd. I'll be incurring all of the capital costs. Fifteen percent."

"It's going to take twenty."

Goyette clenched his teeth. "Get off my boat. And enjoy the cold."

40

Despite Loren's pleas for him to stay in bed and rest, Pitt rose early the next morning and dressed for work. His body ached worse than it had the day before, and he moved slowly until his joints gradually limbered up. He contemplated drinking a tequila with orange juice to deaden the pain but ultimately thought better of it. The aches of injury took longer to vanquish, he thought, cursing the mark of time and its toll on his body.

Loren summoned him to the bathroom, where she cleaned the scrape on his head and applied a fresh bandage.

"At least your hair will cover that one up," she said, scraping her finger across several scars on Pitt's chest and back. Numerous bouts with death in the past had left their share of physical marks, as well as a few mental ones.

"A lucky blow to the head," he quipped.

"Maybe it will knock some sense into you," she replied, wrapping her arms around his torso. While Pitt had told Loren of the events in Ontario, he had neglected to mention that the landslide had not occurred by accident. She reached up and lightly kissed his scalp, then reminded him that he had promised to take her to lunch later in the day.

"I'll pick you up at noon," he promised.

He reached his office by eight o'clock and sat through a pair of research briefings before phoning Dan Martin later in the morning. The FBI director sounded excited to hear from Pitt.

"Dirk, your tip yesterday was a good one. You were correct, the janitorial service at the George Washington University lab works in the evenings. We reviewed the lab's security video and found a clean shot of your wayward morning janitor. He fit your description to a tee."

Sitting in the airport lounge in Elliot Lake, Pitt had finally made the connection between the man at the Co-op and the janitor he had bumped into at the lab just prior to the explosion.

"Have you been able to identify him?" Pitt asked.

"After confirming that he was not part of the building maintenance and janitorial staff, we ran his photo through the Homeland Security identification database. Not an exact science, mind you, but we came up with a potential hit list and one pretty good match in particular. On this side of the border, he goes by Robert Ford of Buffalo, New York. We've already confirmed that the registered address is a fake, as well as the name."

Pitt repeated the name Robert Ford, then thought of the alias he had used in Blind River, John Booth. Too coincidental, Pitt thought. John Wilkes Booth was the man who had shot Lincoln, while Robert Ford had killed Jesse James.

"He has an admiration for historical assassins," Pitt offered.

"Might be his line of work. We crossed our records with the Canadian authorities, and they think they have him pegged as a fellow named Clay Zak."

"Are they going to pick him up?"

"They would if they knew where to find him. He's a suspect in a twenty-year-old murder at a Canadian nickel mine. His whereabouts have been unknown ever since."

"A nickel mine? Might be a tie to his use of dynamite."

"We're following up on that now. The Canadians might not find him, but if he sets foot in the country again we'll have a good chance at picking him up."

"Nice work, Dan. You've accomplished a lot in short order."

"A lucky break that you recalled your encounter. There's one more thing that you might be interested in knowing. Lisa Lane's lab assistant, Bob Hamilton. We were able to obtain a search warrant on the guy's financial records. It seems that he just had fifty thousand dollars wired into his bank account from an offshore entity."

"I suspected something was amiss with that one."

"We will do a little more digging, then bring him in for questioning at the end of the week. We'll see if there is a connection, but I have to say, things look promising at the moment."

"I'm glad the investigation has legs. Thanks for your efforts."

"Thank you, Dirk. You've given us a nice jump on the case."

Pitt wondered how his own research was going and took the stairwell down to the tenth-floor computer operations center. He found Yaeger seated at his console conversing again with Max, who stood before a large projection screen. A flattened map of the globe was displayed, with dozens of pinpoint lights flashing from scattered points across the oceans. Each light represented a buoy that relayed sea and weather info via satellite link to the headquarters building.

"Problem with the sea buoy system?" Pitt asked, taking a seat beside Yaeger.

"We've had an uplink problem with a number of segments," Yaeger replied. "I'm having Max run some software tests to try and isolate the problem."

"If the latest software release had been properly tested before going operational, we wouldn't be incurring this problem," Max injected. Turning to Pitt, she said good morning, then eyed Pitt's bandage. "What happened to your head?"

"I got in a slight fender bender on a rocky road," he replied.

"We've tracked the information on the jet tail number that you phoned in about," Yaeger said.

"It can wait. Fixing the sea buoy data is more important."

"I can multitask with the best of them," Max offered with a touch of indignation.

"She's running a test that will take twenty minutes," Yaeger explained. "We can exercise her until the results come back."

Turning to the holograph image, he said, "Max, bring up the data on the Canadian Gulfstream jet."

"The aircraft is a brand-new Gulfstream G650 eighteen-passenger jet, manufactured in 2009. According to Canadian aeronautical records, the tail number C-FTGI is registered to Terra Green Industries, of Vancouver, British Columbia. Terra Green is a privately held company, chaired by a man named Mitchell Goyette."

"Hence the TGI in the tail number," Yaeger said. "At least he didn't flaunt his personal initials, like most filthy rich jet owners."

"Goyette," Pitt mused. "Isn't he big into green energy?"

"His holdings include wind farms, geothermal and hydroelectric power plants, and a small number of solar panel fields," Max recited.

"Being privately held tends to obscure things," Yaeger said, "so we did a little digging. Found over two dozen other entities that trace their ownership to Terra Green. Turns out, a number of the holdings were related to gas, oil, and mining exploration activities, particularly in the Athabasca region of Alberta."

"So Terra Green is apparently not all that green," Pitt quipped.

"It's worse than that. Another Terra Green subsidiary apparently controls a recently discovered natural gas field in the Melville Sound. Its value could conceivably outweigh his other holdings combined. We also found an interesting nautical link to NUMA. It seems that over the past few years, Terra Green has contracted for the construction of several big icebreakers from a Mississippi Gulf shipyard, along with a number of very large LNG and bulk-carrier barges. It was the same yard that built our last research ship, which was delayed in launching due in part to their work for Terra Green."

"Yes, the Lowden Shipyard in New Orleans," Pitt recalled. "I saw one of those barges in dry dock. It was a massive thing. I wonder what they're transporting?"

"I have not attempted to locate the vessels, but I can try if you like," Max said.

Pitt shook his head. "Probably not important. Max, can you determine if Terra Green is conducting any research related to artificial photosynthesis or other countermeasures to greenhouse gas emissions?"

Max stood motionless as she scanned her databases for published research reports and news releases.

"I find no references to Terra Green and artificial photosynthesis. They operate a small research facility devoted to solar research and have published work in carbon sequestration. The company has in fact just opened a carbon sequestration facility in Kitimat, British Columbia. The company is known to be in discussions with the Canadian government to build an unknown number of additional sequestration facilities across the country."

"Kitimat? I just received an e-mail from Summer, who was writing from there," Yaeger said.

"Yes, the kids apparently stopped there for a few days on their way down the Inside Passage testing the local sea alkalinity," Pitt said.

"Do you think the carbon sequestration plants figure in as a motive to halt Lisa Lane's research?" Yaeger asked.

"I can't say, but it could be a possibility. It's

clear that Goyette is after the ruthenium." He explained his visit to the Miners Co-op and the chance encounter with the man he'd seen at the GWU lab. He recited the portion of the journal entry he had read, and pulled out his notes for Yaeger.

"Max, last time we talked, you indicated that there was little, if any, mining of ruthenium taking place," he said.

"That's correct, just a small quantity of low-grade ore being produced from a mine in Bolivia."

"The mining Co-op has a finite inventory left. Do you have any data on potential deposits in the Arctic?"

Max stood motionless for a moment, then shook her head. "No, sir. I find no mention in any recorded surveys or mining claims that I have access to, which mostly date from the 1960s."

Pitt eyed his journal notes, then said, "I have a record from 1917 that a quantity of ruthenium called Black Kobluna was obtained some sixty-eight years earlier by a number of Adelaide Peninsula Inuit. Does that mean anything to you, Max?"

"I'm sorry, sir, I still don't find any relevant mining references," she replied, a hurt look in her transparent eyes.

"She never calls me sir," Yaeger muttered quietly.

Max ignored Yaeger as she tried to generate

an added response to Pitt.

"The Adelaide Peninsula is located on the north coast of Nunavut, just to the south of King William Island. The peninsula is considered an essentially uninhabited landmass, historically occupied at certain seasons by small groups of migrating Inuit."

"Max, what is meant by the term 'Black Kobluna'?" Yaeger asked.

Max hesitated while accessing a linguistics database at Stanford University. She then tipped her head at Yaeger and Pitt with a confused look on her face.

"It is a contradictory phrase," she said.

"Please explain," requested Yaeger.

"*Kobluna* is an Inuit term for 'white man.' Hence it is a mixed translation of 'black white man.'"

"Contradictory, indeed," Yaeger said. "Perhaps it means a white man dressed in black or vice versa."

"Possibly," Pitt said. "But that was a remote section of the Arctic. I'm not sure a white or black man had even set foot there by that point in time. Isn't that true, Max?"

"You are nearly correct. Initial exploration and mapping of the Canadian Arctic came in a British-inspired quest for a northwest passage to the Pacific Ocean. A large portion of the western and eastern regions of the Canadian Arctic had been well charted by the mid-nineteenth century. The middle regions, including a number of passages around Adelaide Peninsula, were in fact some of the last areas charted."

Pitt glanced at his notes from the Miners Co-op. "The record indicates that the Inuit recovered the ruthenium in or around 1849."

"The historical record shows that an expedition under the guise of the Hudson's Bay Company surveyed a region of North American coastline in the vicinity between 1837 and 1839."

"That's a little too early," Yaeger remarked.

"The next known forays were made by John Rae in 1851, during his search for survivors of the Franklin Expedition. He was known to have traveled along the southeast coast of Victoria Island, which is still approximately a hundred miles from the Adelaide Peninsula. It was not until 1859 that the area was reached again, this time by Francis McClintock, who visited nearby King William Island, just north of Adelaide, during another search for Franklin."

"That's a little late in the game," said Yaeger.

"But there's Franklin," Pitt said, searching his memory. "When did he sail into those waters and where was he lost?"

"The Franklin Expedition sailed from England in 1845. They wintered the first year at Beechey Island, then traveled south until becoming trapped in the ice off King William

Island. The expedition ships were abandoned in the spring of 1848, with the entire crew later dying onshore sometime later."

Pitt mulled the dates in his head, then thanked Max for the information. The holographic woman nodded and turned aside, resuming her software test calculations.

"If Franklin's men left their ships in 1848 well north of the peninsula, it doesn't figure they would be lugging some minerals around with them," remarked Yaeger.

"It's possible that the Inuit erred in the date," Pitt replied. "The other point to consider is Max's comment about the Adelaide Peninsula being an Inuit migration stop. Just because the Inuit were known to camp on the peninsula doesn't mean that it's where they acquired the mineral."

"Good point. Do you think there's a connection with the Franklin Expedition?"

Pitt nodded slowly. "Might be our only real link," he said.

"But you heard what Max said. The entire crew perished. That would seem to eliminate any hope of finding an answer there."

"There's always hope," Pitt said, with a glint to his eye. He looked at his watch, then rose to leave. "As a matter of fact, Hiram, I fully expect to be on the right path just this afternoon."

41

Pitt borrowed an agency Jeep and picked up Loren on Capitol Hill, then drove across downtown D.C.

"You have time for a long lunch?" he asked, sitting at a stoplight.

"You're in luck, I have no hearings scheduled for today. I'm just reviewing some draft legislation. What did you have in mind?"

"A side trip to Georgetown."

"To my condo, for a little afternoon delight?" she asked coyly.

"A tempting proposition," he replied, squeezing her hand, "but I'm afraid we have a lunch reservation that can't be canceled."

The noontime traffic clogged the streets until Pitt maneuvered onto M Street, which led to the heart of Georgetown.

"How's Lisa coming along?" he asked.

"She's being released from the hospital today and is anxious to get back to work. I'm arranging a briefing with the White House Office on Science and Technology once she has the chance to document and summarize her findings. That might take a few weeks, though. Lisa called me this morning a little upset — her lab assistant has apparently taken another position out of state, just quit on her without notice."

"Bob Hamilton?"

"Yes, that's his name. The one you don't trust."

"He's supposed to talk to the FBI later this week. Something tells me he won't be leaving for that new job anytime soon."

"It started out as such a promising breakthrough, but it's certainly turned into a mess. I saw a private report from the Department of Energy which forecasts a much bleaker environmental and economic impact from global warming than anybody else is letting on. The latest studies indicate the atmospheric greenhouse gases are growing at an alarming rate. Do you think a source of ruthenium can be found quickly enough to make the artificial-photosynthesis system a reality?"

"All we've got is a tenuous historical account of a long forgotten source. It might turn up empty, but the best we can do is track it down."

Pitt turned down a quaint residential street lined with historic mansions that dated to the 1840s. He found a parking spot beneath a towering oak tree, and they made their way to a smaller residence constructed from the carriage house of an adjacent manor. Pitt rapped a heavy brass knocker, and the front door flew open a moment later, revealing a colossal man clad in a red satin smoking jacket.

"Dirk! Loren! There you are," St. Julien Perlmutter boomed in a hearty voice. The bearded behemoth, who tipped the scales at nearly four hundred pounds, gave them each a spine-crushing hug as he welcomed them into his house.

"Julien, you are looking fit. Have you lost some weight?" Loren said, patting his ample belly.

"Heavens, no," he roared. "The day I stop eating is the day I die. You, on the other hand, look more ravishing than ever."

"You'd best keep that appetite of yours focused on food," Pitt threatened with a grin.

Perlmutter leaned down to Loren's ear. "If you ever get tired of living with this adventuresome old cuss, you just let me know," he said, loud enough for Pitt to hear. Then rising like a bear, he pounded across the room.

"Come, to the dining room," he beckoned.

Loren and Pitt followed him past the entryway, through a living room, and down a hallway, all of which were filled to the ceiling with shelved books. The entire house was similarly cluttered, resembling a stately library more than a personal residence. Within its walls was the largest single collection of historic maritime books and journals in the world. An insatiable collector of nautical archives, Perlmutter himself stood as a preeminent expert on maritime history.

Perlmutter led them to a small but ornate dining room, where only a few piles of books were discreetly stacked against one wall. They took their seats at a thick mahogany table that featured legs carved in the shape of lion paws. The table had come from the captain's cabin of an ancient sailing ship, one of many nautical antiques tucked among the legion of books.

Perlmutter opened a bottle of Pouilly-Fumé, then poured each of them a glass of the dry white wine.

"I'm afraid I already finished off that bottle of *airag* that you sent me from Mongolia," he said to Pitt. "Marvelous stuff."

"I had plenty while I was there. The locals consume it like water," he replied, recalling the slightly bitter taste of the alcoholic drink made from mare's milk.

Perlmutter tasted the wine, then set down his glass and clapped his hands.

"Marie," he called loudly. "You may serve the soup."

An apron-clad woman appeared from the kitchen carrying a tray of bowls. The physical opposite of Perlmutter, she was lithe and petite, with short dark hair and coffee-colored eyes. She silently placed a bowl of soup in front of each diner with a smile, then disappeared into the kitchen. Pitt took a taste and nodded.

"Vichyssoise. Very flavorful."

Perlmutter leaned forward and spoke in a whisper. "Marie is an assistant chef at Citronelle here in Georgetown. She is a graduate of one of the top culinary schools in Paris. Better than that, her father was a chef at Maxim's," he added, kissing his fingertips in delight. "She agreed to come cook for me three times a week. Life is good," he declared in a deep bellow, the folds of fat around his chin rolling as he laughed.

The trio dined on sautéed sweetbreads with risotto and leeks, followed by a chocolate mousse. Pitt pushed his empty dessert plate away with a sigh of satisfaction. Loren threw in the towel before finishing hers.

"Outstanding, Julien, from start to finish. If you ever grow tired of maritime history, I do believe you'd have a fantastic future as a restaurateur," Loren said.

"Perhaps, but I believe there would be too much work involved," Perlmutter said with a laugh. "Besides, as you surely have learned from your husband, one's love for the sea never wanes."

"True. I don't know what you two would do with yourselves if man had never sailed the seas."

"Blasphemous thought," Perlmutter boomed. "Which reminds me, Dirk, you said your calling involved something more than just fine dining with a dear friend . . ."

"That's right, Julien. I'm on the hunt for a scarce mineral that made an appearance in the Arctic around 1849."

"Sounds intriguing. What's your interest?"

Pitt summarized the importance of ruthenium and the tale of the Inuit ore from the Miners Co-op.

"Adelaide Peninsula, you say? If my memory serves, that's just below King William Island, dead center in the Northwest Passage," Perlmutter said, stroking this thick gray beard. "And in 1849, the only explorers in that region would have been Franklin's party."

"Who was Franklin?" Loren asked.

"Sir John Franklin. British naval officer and renowned Arctic explorer. Fought at Trafalgar on the *Bellerophon* as a young lad, if I recall. Though a little past his prime at age fifty-nine, he sailed with two stoutly built ships in an attempt to find and navigate the fabled Northwest Passage. He came within a hair of pulling it off, but his ships became trapped in the ice. The surviving men were forced to abandon the ships and attempt to reach a fur-trading camp hundreds of miles to the south. Franklin and all one hundred and thirty-four men of his expedition party ultimately died, making it by far the worst tragedy in Arctic exploration."

Perlmutter excused himself to visit one of

his reading rooms, returning with several old books and a crudely bound manuscript. Flipping through one of the books, he stopped at a page and read aloud.

"Here we are. Franklin sailed from the Thames in May of 1845 with two ships, the *Erebus* and the *Terror*. They were last seen entering Baffin Bay, off Greenland, later that summer. With provisions to last the crew three years, they were expected to winter at least one year in the ice before attempting a path to the Pacific, or else return to England with proof that a passage did not exist. Franklin and his crew instead perished in the Arctic, and his ships were never seen again."

"Didn't anyone go looking for them when they failed to appear after three years?" Loren asked.

"Oh my dear, did they! Concern grew by the end of 1847 when no word had been heard, and relief efforts commenced the next year. Literally dozens of relief expeditions were sent in search of Franklin, with vessels prodding both ends of the passage. Franklin's wife, Lady Jane Franklin, famously financed numerous expeditions single-handedly to locate her husband. Remarkably, it wouldn't be until 1854, nine years after they departed England, that the remains of some of the crewmen were found on King William Island, confirming the worst."

"Did they leave any logbooks or records behind?" Pitt asked.

"Just one. A chilling note that was placed in a rock cairn on the island and discovered in 1859." Perlmutter found a photocopy of the note in one of his books and slid it over for Loren and Pitt to read.

"There's a notation that Franklin died in 1847, but it doesn't say why," Loren read.

"The note raises more questions than answers. They were tantalizingly close to transiting the worst section of the passage but may have been caught by an exceedingly short summer, and the ships probably broke up in the ice."

Pitt found a map in the book, which showed the area of Franklin's demise. The point where his ships were presumed abandoned was less than a hundred miles from Adelaide Peninsula.

"The ruthenium found in the region was referred to as Black Kobluna," Pitt said, searching for a potential geographic clue on the chart.

"Kobluna. That's an Inuit word," Perlmutter said, pulling out the crudely bound manuscript. Opening the ancient parched papers, Loren saw that the entire document was handwritten.

"Yes," Pitt answered. "It is an Inuit term for 'white man.'"

Perlmutter rapped a knuckle on the open document. "In 1860, a New York journalist named Stuart Leuthner sought to unravel the mystery of the Franklin Expedition. He traveled to the Arctic and lived in an Inuit settlement for seven years, learning their language and customs. He scoured the region around King William Island, interviewing every inhabitant he could find who had possibly interacted with Franklin or his crew. But the clues were few, and he returned to New York disillusioned, never finding the definitive answers he was looking for. For some reason he decided against publishing his findings and left his writings behind, to return to the Arctic. He took a young Inuit wife, then ventured into the wild to live off the land and was never heard from again."

"Is that his journal from his time among the Inuit?" Pitt asked.

Perlmutter nodded. "I was able to acquire it at auction a few years back, picking it up at a reasonable price."

"I'm amazed it was never published," Loren said.

"You wouldn't be if you read it. Ninety percent of it is a discourse on catching and butchering seals, building igloos, and surviving the boredom of the dark winter months."

"And the other ten percent?" Pitt asked.

"Let us see," Perlmutter smiled.

For the next hour, Perlmutter skimmed through the journal, sharing occasional passages where an Inuit described witnessing a sledge party on the distant shores of King William Island or noted the two large ships trapped in the ice. Near the very end of the journal, Leuthner interviewed a young man whose story put Loren and Pitt on the edge of their seats.

The account was from Koo-nik, a thirteen-year-old boy in 1849 when he went on a seal-hunting excursion with his uncle west of King William Island. He and his uncle had climbed a large hummock and found a massive boat wedged in a large ice floe.

"Kobluna," the uncle had said, as they made their way to the vessel.

As they moved closer, they heard much yelling and screaming coming from the depths of the ship. A wild-eyed man with long hair waved for them to come alongside. With a freshly caught seal for barter, they were quickly invited onto the deck. Several more men appeared, dirty and emaciated, with dried blood covering their clothes. One of the men stared at Koo-nik, babbling incoherently, as two other men danced around the deck. The crew sang an odd chant, calling themselves the "men of blackness." They all seemed possessed by evil spirits, Koo-nik thought. Frightened by the specter, Koo-nik clung to his uncle as the elder man traded the seal meat for two knives and some shiny silver stones that the Koblunas said had unique warming powers. The Koblunas promised more cutting tools and silver stones if the Inuit returned with more seal meat. Koo-nik left with his uncle but never saw the boat again. He reported that his uncle and some other men took a large number of seals to the boat a few weeks later and returned with many knives and a kayak filled with the Black Kobluna."

"It had to have been the ruthenium," Loren said excitedly.

"Yes, the Black Kobluna," Pitt agreed. "But where did Franklin's crew acquire it?"

"It might possibly have been discovered on one of the neighboring islands during a sledging excursion, while the ships were locked in the ice," Perlmutter ventured. "Of course a mine could have been discovered much earlier in the expedition, anywhere from Greenland to Victoria Island, covering a distance of thousands of miles. Not much to go on, I'm afraid."

"What I find strange is the behavior of the crew," Loren noted.

"I heard a similar tale of some mill workers in South Africa going loony, which was blamed on possible exposure to ruthenium," Pitt replied. "None of it makes sense, though, as there is nothing inherently dangerous about the mineral."

"Perhaps it was just the horrible conditions they endured. Starving and freezing all those winters, trapped in a dark, cramped ship," Loren said. "That would be enough to drive me crazy."

"Throw in scurvy and frostbite, not to mention botulism brought on from a shoddy supply of tinned foods sealed with lead, and you would have plenty to test a man's wits," Perlmutter agreed.

"Just one of several unanswered questions associated with the expedition," Pitt said.

"The account seems to confirm your trader's story from the Miners Co-op," Perlmutter noted.

"Maybe the answer to where the mineral came from still lies on the ship," Loren suggested.

Pitt was already mulling the same thought. He knew that the frigid waters of the Arctic allowed for remarkable preservation of antiquities. The *Breadalbane,* an 1843 wooden ship sent on one of the Franklin rescue expeditions and crushed in the ice near Beechey Island, had recently been discovered fully intact, its masts still rising over the deck. That a clue to the source of the ruthenium might still exist on the ship was entirely possible. But which ship was it, and where was it located?

"There was no mention of a second ship?" he asked.

"No," Perlmutter replied. "And the approximate location they provide is quite a bit farther south than where the Franklin ships were recorded to have been abandoned."

"Maybe the ice drifted, moving them apart," Loren suggested.

"Entirely plausible," Perlmutter replied. "Leuthner has an interesting tidbit later in the journal," he said, flipping a few pages forward. "A third-party Inuit claims to have seen one of the ships sink while the other one disappeared. Leuthner could never quite decipher the distinction from the Inuit."

"Assuming it is one of the Franklin ships, it might well be critical to identify the vessel, in case the mineral was not brought aboard both *Erebus* and *Terror*," Pitt noted.

"I'm afraid Koo-nik never identified the ship. And both vessels were nearly identical in appearance," Perlmutter said.

"But he said the crew had a name for themselves," Loren said. "What did he call them, the 'black men'?"

"The 'men of blackness' is how they were described," Perlmutter replied. "Somewhat odd. I suppose they called themselves that for having survived so many dark winters."

"Or there might be another reason," Pitt said, a wide grin slowly spreading across his face. "If they were indeed the men of blackness, then they just told us which ship they served."

Loren looked at him with a quizzical gaze, but the light went on for Perlmutter.

"But of course!" the big man roared. "It must be the *Erebus*. Well done, my boy."

Loren looked at her husband. "What did I miss?"

"Erebus," Pitt replied. "In Greek mythology, it is an underworld stopping place on the road to Hades. It is a place of perpetual darkness, or blackness, if you will."

"Fair to say that's where the ship and crew ended up," Perlmutter said. He gave Pitt a studious look. "Do you think you can find her?"

"It will be a sizable search area, but it's worth the gamble. The only thing that can prevent us from succeeding is the same peril that doomed Franklin: the ice."

"We're nearing the summer season, where the melting sea ice is navigable in the region. Can you get a vessel there in time to conduct a search?"

"And don't forget the Canadians," Loren cautioned. "They might not let you in the door."

Pitt's eyes sparkled with optimism. "It just so happens that I have a vessel in the neighborhood and the man in place to find the way," he said with a confident grin.

Perlmutter located a dusty bottle of vintage port wine and poured small glasses all around.

"Godspeed to you, my boy," he toasted. "May you shed some light on the darkened *Erebus*."

After thanking Perlmutter for the meal and

337

receiving a promise from the marine historian that he would provide copies of any materials he had on the ship's likely position, Loren and Pitt stepped out of the carriage house and returned to the car. Climbing into the car, Loren was unusually quiet. Her sixth sense had kicked in, warning of an unseen danger. She knew she couldn't stand in the way of Pitt pursuing a lost mystery, but it was always hard for her to let him go.

"The Arctic is a dangerous place," she finally said in a low voice. "I'll worry about you up there."

"I'll be sure to pack my long underwear and stay well clear of icebergs," he said with cheery comfort.

"I know this is important, but, still, I wish you didn't have to go."

Pitt smiled in reassurance, but in his eye there was a distant and determined look. Loren took one look at her husband and knew that he was already there.

42

Mitchell Goyette was sitting on the fantail of his yacht reviewing an earnings report when his private secretary appeared with a secure portable phone.

"Natural Resources Minister Jameson is on the line," the winsome brunette said as she handed him the phone.

Goyette gave her a smug leer, then picked up the receiver.

"Arthur, good of you to call. Tell me, how are you coming along with my Arctic exploration licenses?"

"It is the purpose of my call. I received the maps of your desired Arctic resource exploration zones. The requested regions encompass over twelve million acres, I was rather shocked to find. Quite unprecedented, I must say."

"Yes, well, there are riches to be had. First things first, however. Where are we on those mining claims for the Royal Geographical Society Islands?"

"As you know, a portion of the islands' exploration and production rights are held by the Mid-America Mining Company. My office has drafted up a revocation of their license for due cause. If they fail to meet production output quotas in the next three months, then we can rescind their license. If this political crisis with the U.S. heats up, then we may be able to act sooner."

"I think we can be assured that they won't meet their summer quota," Goyette said slyly.

"The rescission can be accelerated if signed by the Prime Minister. Is that a course you wish to pursue?"

"Prime Minister Barrett will be no impediment," Goyette laughed. "You might say he is something of a silent partner in the venture."

"He's publicly promoted a policy of Arctic wilderness protectionism," Jameson reminded him.

"He will sign anything I want him to. Now, what about my other license request?"

"My staff has found just a small portion of the Melville Sound area currently under license. Apparently, you've beaten most everyone to the mark."

"Yes, because a large part of the area has been inaccessible. With the warming temperatures and my fleet of icebreakers and barges, I'll be able to exploit those regions before anyone else can get their foot in the door. With your aid, of course," he added acidly.

"I'll be able to assist with your Arctic marine exploration licenses, but a portion of the terrestrial areas will have to be approved by the Indian and Native Affairs Division."

"Is the head of the division appointed by the Prime Minister?"

"Yes, I believe so."

Goyette laughed again. "Then there will be no problem. How long before I can lock up the marine sites?"

"It is a significant amount of territory to review and approve," Jameson said with hesitation.

"Don't you worry, Minister. A fat wire transfer will be headed your way shortly, and another one once the licenses are issued. I never forget to pay those who assist me in my business ventures."

"Very well. I'll try to have the documents completed within the next few weeks."

"That's my boy. You know where to find me," Goyette said, then hung up the phone.

In his office in Ottawa, Jameson hung up the phone and looked across his desk. The commissioner of the Royal Canadian Mounted Police turned off a recording device, then hung up the second handset on which he had been listening in.

"My God, he has indicted the Prime Minister as well," the commissioner muttered, shaking his head.

"Deep pockets easily corrupt," Jameson

said. "You will have my immunity agreement by tomorrow?"

"Yes," the commissioner replied, visibly shaken. "You agree to turn state's evidence and there will be no criminal charges filed against you. You will, of course, be expected to resign your post immediately. I'm afraid your career in public service will effectively be over."

"I can accept that fate," Jameson replied with a sullen look. "It will be preferable to continuing as an indentured servant to that greedy swine."

"Can you live with taking down the Prime Minister as well?"

"If Prime Minister Barrett is in Goyette's pocket, then he deserves no less."

The commissioner rose from his chair and packed the listening device and a notepad into an attaché case.

"Don't look so distraught, Commissioner," Jameson said, observing his troubled expression. "Once the truth about Goyette is revealed, you'll be a national hero for putting him away. In fact, you would make a good law-and-order candidate for the Prime Minister's replacement."

"My aspirations don't run that high. I'm just dreading the havoc a billionaire will wreak on the criminal justice system."

As he stepped toward the door, Jameson called out to him once more.

"Right will win out eventually."

The commissioner kept on walking, knowing it wasn't always the case.

43

The exposed portion of Trevor's boat was still smoldering when a lift barge borrowed from the aluminum smelter moored alongside and hoisted the wrecked vessel aboard. Chugging to a nearby boatyard, the barge deposited the waterlogged hulk onto a cement pad, where it would await investigation by the police and an insurance claims adjuster. His cuts bandaged and his report to the police completed, Trevor poked through the charred hull, then made his way back over to the NUMA research boat. Dirk waved him aboard, inquiring about the police response.

"The chief isn't ready to concede that it was a planted explosion until his arson investigator can have a look," Trevor said.

"Boats just don't blow up, certainly not in that fashion," Dirk replied.

"He asked if I had any suspicions, but I told him no."

"You don't think he can help?" Summer asked.

"Not yet. There's just not enough evidence to be able to point fingers."

"We all know someone from the sequestration plant is behind it."

"Then we need to find out what the mystery is all about," Trevor replied. He looked at Dirk and Summer steadfastly. "I know you're short on time, but can you still oblige me with a search off Gil Island before you have to leave?"

"Our boat is loaded, and we're more than ready," Dirk replied. "Man the lines and we'll be on our way."

The ride down Douglas Channel was made in relative silence, with each wondering what sort of danger they had stumbled into. As they passed the sequestration facility, Dirk took note that the LNG tanker had departed the covered dock. He nudged the throttle to its stops, anxious to get on-site and see what lay beneath the waters off Gil Island.

They were nearly to the sound when Summer stood and pointed out the windshield. The black LNG tanker loomed up around the next bend, steaming slowly down the channel.

"Look how low she's sitting," Dirk said, noting that the tanker rode near her waterline.

"You were right, Summer," Trevor said. "She was in fact taking on liquid CO_2 at the plant. It doesn't make any sense."

The NUMA vessel charged past the tanker,

quickly reaching the open strait. Dirk steered to the southern end of the strait, stopping the boat when he was even with the tip of Gil Island. He moved to the stern and lowered a sonar fish over the rail while Summer programmed a search grid into the navigation system. Within a few minutes they were under way again, moving back and forth across the strait, with the sonar fish tailing behind.

The sonar images revealed a steep and rocky bottom, which dropped from a fifty-foot depth near the shoreline to over two hundred feet in the center of the strait. Dirk had to play yo-yo with the sonar cable, raising and lowering the fish to match the changing depths.

Their first hour of searching revealed little of interest, simply a uniform sea bottom littered with rocks and an occasional sunken log. Trevor quickly grew bored watching the repetitive sonar image and turned his attention to the LNG tanker. The big ship had finally lumbered into the strait, cruising to the north of them at a snail's pace. It eventually inched around the northern tip of Gil Island and disappeared from sight.

"I'd love to know where she's headed," Trevor said.

"When we get back to Seattle, I'll see if our agency resources can find out," Summer said.

"I'd hate to think she's dumping that CO_2 at sea."

"I can't imagine that would be the case," she replied. "It would be too dangerous for the crew if the winds shifted."

"I suppose you're right. Still, something just doesn't add up."

They were interrupted by Dirk's voice from the cabin.

"Got something."

Summer and Trevor poked their heads in and gazed at the sonar monitor. The screen showed a thin spindly line on the seafloor that ran off to the side.

"Might be a pipe," Dirk said. "Definitely appears man-made. We should pick up more on the next lane."

They had to wait ten minutes, turning in front of the island and heading back into the strait on the next lane before they spotted it again. The thin line angled across the monitor, running in a northwesterly direction.

"Looks too big to be a communications line," Summer said, studying the monitor.

"Hard to figure what would be out here," Trevor remarked. "Outside of a few primitive hunting-and-fishing cabins, Gil Island is uninhabited."

"Has to lead somewhere," Dirk said. "As long as it's not buried, we'll be able to find out where."

They continued sweeping through the grid, but rather than solve the underwater mystery they only added to it. A second line soon appeared, and then a third, all aligned in a converging angle to the north. Working their way through several more search lanes, they reached the conjunction. Like a giant seven-fingered hand lying on the bottom, the sonar revealed four additional lines that joined the others in a mass convergence. Piecing the images together, they could see that the lines all fanned out for approximately fifty yards, then ended abruptly. A single, heavier line extended north from the conjunction, running parallel to the shoreline. The sonar was able to track it for a short distance before it suddenly disappeared into the sediment close to shore. When they reached the end of the search grid, Dirk stopped the motor, then pulled in the sonar fish with Trevor's assistance.

"It's nearly seven," Summer said. "We need to head back within the hour if we want to avoid running up the channel in the dark."

"Plenty of time for a quick dive," Dirk replied. "Might be our only chance."

There was no argument from the others. Dirk slipped into a dry suit as Summer repositioned the boat over a marked spot where the seven lines had converged.

"Depth is ninety-five feet," she said. "Be aware there is a large vessel on the radar headed our way, about fifteen miles to the north." She turned to Trevor and asked, "I thought you said there's no midweek cruise line traffic through here?"

Trevor gave her a confused look. "That has been my experience. They follow the schedules pretty tight. Must be a wayward freighter."

Dirk poked his head in and eyed the radar screen. "I'll have time for a good look before she gets too close."

Summer turned the boat into the current while Trevor tossed an anchor off the bow and secured their position. Dirk adjusted his tank and weight belt, then stepped over the side.

He hit the water at nearly slack tide and was relieved to find the current minimal. Swimming toward the boat's bow, he wrapped his fingers around the anchor line, then kicked to the bottom.

The cold green water gradually swallowed the surface light, forcing him to flick on a small headlamp strapped over his hood. A brown stony bottom dotted with urchins and starfish materialized out of the gloom, and he confirmed the depth at ninety-three feet as he adjusted his buoyancy. He let go of the anchor line and swam a wide circle around it until he found the object observed by the sonar.

It was a dark metal pipe that stretched across the seafloor, running beyond his field of vision. The pipe was about six inches in diameter, and Dirk could tell it had been placed on the bottom recently, as there was no growth or encrustation evident on its smooth surface.

He kicked back to the anchor and dragged it over the pipe, resetting it in some adjacent rocks. He then followed the pipe down a gradual slope into deeper water until he found its open end twenty yards later. A small crater had been blasted into the seafloor around the opening, and Dirk noted a complete absence of marine life in the surrounding area.

He followed the pipe in the other direction, swimming into shallower water, until meeting the conjunction. It was actually three joints welded in tandem that fed six lines fanning to either side, plus one line out the end. A thicker, ten-inch pipe fed into the conjunction, trailing back toward Gil Island. Dirk followed the main pipe for several hundred feet until a ninety-degree joint sent it running north at a depth of thirty feet. Tracking it farther, he found it partially buried in a slit trench that had obscured its view from the sonar. He followed the pipe for several more minutes before deciding to give up the chase and turn back, his air supply starting to dwindle. He'd just reversed course when he suddenly detected a rumble under the surface. It was a deep sound, but in the water he could not tell which direction it came from. Following along the pipe, he noticed that sand started to fall away from its sides. He placed a gloved hand on the pipe and felt a strong vibration rattling down its length. With a sudden apprehension, he began kicking urgently toward the junction.

On the deck of the boat, Summer looked at her watch, noting that Dirk had been underwater nearly thirty minutes. She turned to Trevor, who sat on the rail watching her with an admiring gaze.

"I wish we could stay here longer," she said, reading his mind.

"Me, too. I've been thinking. I'll have to travel to Vancouver to file my report on the boat and see about getting a replacement. It might take me a few days, longer if I can milk it," he added with a grin. "Any chance I can come see you in Seattle?"

"I'll be angry if you don't," she replied with a smile. "It's only a three-hour train ride away."

Trevor started to reply when he noticed something in the water over Summer's shoulder. It was a rising surge of bubbles about twenty yards from the boat. He stood to take a better look when Summer pointed to another mass of bubbles a short distance off the bow. In unison, they scanned the surrounding water, spotting a half dozen eruptions at various spots around the boat.

The rising bubbles expanded into a boiling tempest that began emitting white puffs of vapor. The vapor built rapidly, as billowing clouds of white mist emerged from the depths and expanded across the surface. Within seconds, the growing clouds had formed a circular wall around the boat, trapping Summer and Trevor in its center. As the vapor drew closer, Trevor said with alarm:

"It's the Devil's Breath."

44

Thrusting his legs in a powerful scissors kick, Dirk skimmed rapidly along the main pipe. Though the visibility was too poor to see it, he could sense a nearby turbulence in the water and knew there something dangerous about the pipe's emissions. The image of the *Ventura* and its dead crew flashed though his mind. Thinking of Summer and Trevor on the surface, he kicked his fins harder, ignoring the growing protest from his lungs.

He reached the pipe junction and immediately veered to his left, following the smaller pipe where he had first dropped down. He could now hear the turbulent rush of bubbles in the water from the high-pressure discharge. Chasing down the pipe, he finally caught sight of the anchor line ahead of him. He immediately shot toward the surface, angling toward the anchor line until joining it just below the boat's bow.

When his head broke the surface, he felt like he was in a London fog. A thick white mist billowed low over the water. Keeping his face down, he swam along the hull to the stern, then stepped up a dive ladder Summer had dropped over the rail. He rose up on the lower rung just enough to peer over the transom. The white clouds of vapor floated across the deck, nearly obscuring the pilothouse just a few feet away.

Dirk pulled his regulator out of his mouth long enough to yell for Summer. An acrid taste immediately filled his mouth and he shoved the regulator back in and took a breath from his air tank. He stood and listened for several seconds, then stepped off the ladder and dropped into the water, his heart skipping a beat.

There had been no reply, he realized, because the boat was empty.

Two hundred yards to the west and ten feet under the water, Trevor thought he was going to die. He couldn't believe how quickly the frigid water had sapped his strength and energy, and nearly his will to live. If not for the radiant pearl gray eyes of Summer visibly imploring him on, he might have given up altogether.

They were breathtaking eyes, he had to admit, as she shoved the regulator into his mouth for a breath of air. Those eyes, they almost provided warmth by themselves. He took a deep breath of air and passed the regulator back, realizing his mind was slipping. He tried to refocus on his tiring legs and kicked harder, reminding himself that they had to make it to shore.

It had been a snap decision, and the only one that would save their lives. With the expanding cloud of carbon dioxide gas completely surrounding them, they had to turn to the water. Summer considered cutting the anchor and making a frantic run through the vapor, but if there was any delay in starting the engine and fleeing they would die. Plus, there was Dirk's life to consider. If he happened to surface under the stern as they got under way, he could be cut to ribbons. He might have little chance of surviving as it was, but there was always hope he could outswim the gas with his remaining air.

"We've got to get into the water," she yelled as the gas erupted. Trevor saw her step toward a fully rigged dive tank on the side rail.

"Get into your dry suit. I'll grab the tank," he directed.

With less than a minute before the boat was engulfed by vapor, Summer jumped into her dry suit and grabbed a mask while Trevor hastily buckled on the tank. She barely had time to slip her arms through his buoyancy vest straps when the carbon dioxide wafted over the boat. They fell more than jumped over the side, splashing loudly into the cold water and submerging beneath the lethal cloud.

Unprotected from the cold, Trevor felt the immersion like an electric shock. But his adrenaline was pumping so hard that he didn't freeze up. Clinging together face-to-face, they kicked awkwardly through the water, passing the regulator back and forth for shared air. They eventually worked into something of a rhythm and soon made good headway toward the island.

But the cold quickly caught up with Trevor. The effects were imperceptible at first, but then Summer noticed his kicking slow. His lips and ears showed a tinge of blue, and she knew he was drifting toward hypothermia. She increased her kicking pace, not wanting to lose their momentum. She struggled another hundred feet, realizing that he was slowly becoming a deadweight. She looked down, hoping to find the seafloor rising up beneath them, but all she could see was a few feet of murky water. She had no clue as to how far they were from the island or whether they had in fact been swimming around in circles. The time had come to risk surfacing.

Taking a deep breath from the regulator before forcing it back into Trevor's mouth, she kicked to the surface, yanking him with her. Breaking the calm surface, she quickly spun her head in all directions, trying to get her bearings. Her worst fear proved to be unfounded. They had escaped, at least temporarily, the thick clouds of carbon dioxide, which still billowed into the sky a short distance away. In the opposite direction, the green hills of Gil Island beckoned less than a quarter mile away. Although they had not swum in a direct line, their course had been true enough to approach the shoreline.

Summer sampled a few breaths of air without consequence, then reached under Trevor's arm and pressed the INFLATE button on his buoyancy compensator. The vest quickly inflated, raising Trevor's torso from beneath the water. She looked at his face and he winked in reply, but his eyes were dull and listless. Grabbing the back of the BC, she kicked toward shore, towing him behind her while he loosely flopped his feet.

The island seemed to keep its distance as fatigue caught up with Summer, who was already burdened by a sense of desperation to get Trevor ashore. She tried to keep her eyes off the shoreline and just focus on kicking, but that only made her realize how leaden her legs felt. She was struggling to keep her pace when Trevor's BC suddenly jerked out of her hands and his body moved ahead of hers. Startled by his movements, she let go in surprise, observing that his limbs still hung limp. Then a head emerged from the water alongside Trevor's chest.

Dirk turned and gazed at Summer, then spat out his regulator.

"He must be frozen. Did he inhale the gas?" he asked.

"No, it's just the cold. We've got to get him to shore. How did you find us?"

"I saw a dive tank was missing from the boat and figured you were making for shore. I surfaced a little to the south and spotted you."

Without another word, they made for the island as quickly as they could. Dirk's appearance served as a morale boost to Summer and she suddenly swam with renewed vigor. Together they moved briskly through the water with Trevor in tow and soon yanked him up onto a thin band of rocky beachfront. Shivering uncontrollably, Trevor sat up on his own but stared off into space.

"We've got to get his wet clothes off. I'll give him my dry suit to wear," Dirk said.

Summer nodded in agreement, then pointed down the beach. A small wooden structure sat perched over the water a hundred yards down the shoreline.

"Looks like a fishing hut. Why don't you check it out, and I'll get his clothes off?"

"Okay," Dirk said, slipping off his tank and weight belt. "Don't enjoy yourself too much," he chided, then turned and headed down the beach.

He wasted no time, realizing Trevor was in real danger. Jogging in his dry suit, he crossed the distance to the structure in short order. Summer was right, it was a small fishing hut, used for overnight excursions by members of a local fishing club. A simple log structure, it was smaller than a one-car garage. Dirk noted a fifty-five-gallon drum and a cord of chopped wood stacked along an exterior wall. He approached the front door and promptly kicked it open, finding a single cot, a wood-burning stove, and a fish smoker. Spotting a box of matches and a small stack of dry wood, he promptly ignited a small fire in the stove, then hustled back down the beach.

Trevor was sitting on a log shirtless as Summer removed his soaking pants. Dirk helped him to his feet, and with Summer on the other side, they half dragged him toward the cabin. As they moved, Dirk and Summer both gazed out at the strait. The white clouds of CO_2 were still surging from the water like a volcanic eruption. The vapor had swelled into a towering mass that stretched across the strait, rising over fifty feet into the air. They noted a reddish tinge in the water and saw dozens of dead fish bobbing on the surface.

"It must be the LNG tanker," Dirk said. "They're probably pumping it from a terminal on the other side of the island."

"But why do it in broad daylight?"

"Because they know we're here," he said quietly, a touch of anger in his voice.

They reached the cabin and lay Trevor down on the cot. Summer covered him with an old wool blanket while Dirk brought in some of the cut wood from outside. The stove had already started warming the small hut, and Dirk fed more wood on the fire until a small blaze was roaring. He stood to fetch some more wood, when a deep bellow echoed in the distance, reverberating off the island hillsides.

Dirk and Summer rushed outside and looked up the strait in horror. Two miles to the north, a large Alaskan cruise liner was making its way down the passage, heading directly toward the lethal bank of carbon dioxide gas.

45

The French cruise liner *Dauphine* was scheduled for a weeklong voyage up the Alaskan coast before returning to its home port of Vancouver. But a major outbreak of gastrointestinal illness had sickened nearly three hundred passengers, forcing the captain to shorten the trip in fear that a large number would require hospitalization.

At just over nine hundred and fifty feet, the *Dauphine* was one of the largest, as well as newest, cruise ships plying the Inside Passage. With three heated swimming pools, eight restaurants, and an enormous glass-walled observation lounge above the bridge, she carried twenty-one hundred passengers in high comfort and luxury.

Standing on the Gil Island shoreline, Dirk and Summer gazed at the gleaming white liner on approach and saw only a ship of death. The toxic carbon dioxide gas still erupted from the seven pipe outlets, expanding the vapor cloud for over a half mile in every direction. A slight westerly breeze kept the gas away from Gil Island but pushed it farther across the strait. The *Dauphine* would take nearly five minutes to pass through the cloud, ample time for the heavy carbon dioxide to infiltrate the ducts and air-conditioning systems throughout the vessel. Displacing the oxygen in the air, the gas would bring quick death to every portion of the ship.

"There must be thousands of people aboard," Summer observed soberly. "We've got to warn them."

"Maybe there's a radio in the hut," Dirk said.

They bolted into the fishing hut, ignoring the mumblings from Trevor as they tore the small shack apart. But there was no radio. Stepping outside, Dirk looked into the billow of white gas, trying to spot the research boat. It was hopelessly concealed inside the vapor cloud.

"How much air do you have left in your tank?" he asked Summer hurriedly. "I can try to get back to the boat and call them on the marine radio, but I sucked my tank dry."

"No, you can't," Summer said, shaking her head. "My tank is almost empty as well, because we had to share air. You'd never make it back to the boat alive. I won't let you go."

Dirk accepted his sister's plea, knowing it would likely be a fatal attempt. He desperately searched around, looking for some way to alert the ship. Then he spotted the large barrel next to the hut. Rushing over to the grime-covered drum, he placed his hands against the top lip and shoved. The barrel resisted, then lifted with a slight sloshing sound, telling him it was nearly full. He unscrewed a cap on the top and stuck a finger in, then sniffed the liquid inside.

"Gasoline," he said as Summer approached. "An extra supply for the fishermen to refuel their boats."

"We can light a bonfire," Summer suggested excitedly.

"Yes," Dirk said with a slow nod. "Or perhaps something a little more conspicuous."

The *Dauphine*'s captain happened to be on the bridge checking the weather forecast when the executive officer called to him.

"Captain, there appears to be an obstruction in the water directly ahead."

The captain finished reading the weather report, then casually stepped over to the exec, who held a pair of high-powered binoculars to his eyes. With the whales, dolphins, and stray logs from the lumber boats, there always appeared to be floating obstructions in the passage. None of it was ever cause for concern to the big ship, which just plowed through any debris like so many toothpicks.

"Half a mile ahead, sir," the exec said, passing over the binoculars.

The captain raised the glasses, viewing a billowing white cloud of fog in their path. Just ahead of the fog was a low-lying object in the water that sprouted a black hump and a smaller adjacent blue hump. The captain studied the object for nearly a minute, adjusting the focus on the binoculars.

"There's a man in the water," he suddenly blurted. "Looks to be a diver. Helm, decrease speed to five knots and prepare for a course adjustment."

He handed the binoculars back to the exec, then stepped over to a color monitor, which displayed their position against a nautical chart of the passage. He studied the immediate water depths, finding with satisfaction that there was plenty of water on the eastern side of the strait to sail through. He was about to give the helmsman a course adjustment to veer around the diver when the exec called out again.

"Sir, I think you better take another look. There's someone on the shore who appears to be signaling us."

The captain grabbed the binoculars a second time and looked ahead. The ship had advanced enough that he could now clearly see Dirk in his blue dry suit swimming along a floating Y-shaped log. Wedged into the log's joint was a fifty-five-gallon drum. He watched as Dirk waved to the shore, then pushed away from the log and disappeared under the water.

The captain swung his gaze toward the shore, where he spotted Summer wading up to her chest in the water. She held a shard of wood over her head that appeared to be burning. He watched in disbelief as she flung the burning stick out into the channel toward the floating log. When the burning embers hit the water, the surface immediately ignited in a thin burst of flames. A narrow trail of fire slowly snaked to the floating log, engulfing the driftwood in a flickering blaze. It took just a few additional seconds for the gasoline vapors inside the barrel to ignite, erupting in a small explosion that sent the shattering drum careening across the water. The captain stared bewildered at the fiery scene, then finally came to his senses.

"Full astern! Full astern!" he shouted, waving his arms in excitement. "Then someone get me the Coast Guard."

46

Dirk surfaced twenty yards from the burning gasoline and lazily swam in the direction of the cruise ship, occasionally raising one arm and slapping it down to the surface in the diver's signal for distress. He cautiously eyed the carbon dioxide cloud, which was still burgeoning a few dozen yards behind the burning log. He could hear shouts from the shore and glanced over to see Summer yelling and waving at the ship to halt.

He looked north to see the massive ship still bearing down on him. He began to wonder if anyone was awake on the bridge and had even seen his pyrotechnic display. Questioning his own safety in the path of the ship, he turned and swam a few strokes toward the shore. Then he heard the distant wail of an alarm sounding on board. The water near the vessel's stern caught his eye as it churned into a turbulent boil. Dirk realized the fiery signal had in fact been seen and that the captain had reversed engines. But he began to wonder if it was too late.

The *Dauphine* continued gliding toward the toxic cloud without any appearance of slowing. Dirk swam harder to avoid the oncoming bow of the ship as it bore down on him. Its towering presence drew over him, the bow cutting the water just yards away. All but giving up hope that the ship would stop, he suddenly detected the liner shudder and falter. The ship's bow eased up to the dying line of flames, then ground to a halt. With a pained slowness, the *Dauphine* began backing up the strait, moving a hundred yards to the north, before drifting to a stationary position.

A small orange launch had already been lowered over the side and quickly raced toward Dirk. As it pulled alongside, two crewmen reached over and roughly yanked him aboard. An austere-faced man seated at the stern growled at him.

"What kind of fool are you? Greenpeace?" he asked in a French accent.

Dirk pointed to the billowing white vapor to the south of them.

"Sail into that and you'll be a dead man. You be the fool and ignore my warning."

He paused, staring the crewman in the eye. Flustered and suddenly unsure of himself, the Frenchman remained quiet.

"I have an injured man ashore who requires immediate medical attention," Dirk continued, pointing to the fishing hut.

Without another word, they raced the launch to shore. Dirk jumped off the boat and ran to the hut, which was now blazing hot from the stove fire. Summer was seated with her arm around Trevor, talking to him on the cot. His eyes looked brighter, but he still mumbled in a state of grogginess. The launch crewmen helped carry him to the boat, and they all returned to the *Dauphine*.

After Trevor was hoisted aboard in the launch, Summer accompanied him to the ship's medical station while Dirk was escorted to the bridge. The ship's captain, a short man with thinning hair, looked Dirk up and down with an air of disdain.

"Who are you and why did you set fire in our path?" he asked pointedly.

"My name is Pitt, from the National Underwater and Marine Agency. You can't proceed down the strait or you'll kill everyone aboard. That white mist ahead of you is a lethal cloud of carbon dioxide gas being discharged by a tanker ship. We had to abandon our boat and swim to shore, and my sister and another man barely escaped death."

The executive officer stood nearby, listening. He shook his head and snickered.

"What an absurd tale," he said to another crewman loud enough for Dirk to hear.

Dirk ignored him, standing toe-to-toe with the captain.

"What I have said is true. If you want to risk killing the thousands of passengers aboard, then go right ahead. Just put us ashore before you proceed."

The captain studied Dirk's face, searching for signs of lunacy but finding only stone-cold reserve. A crewman at the radar station broke the tension.

"Sir, we're showing a stationary vessel in the fogbank, approximately one-half mile off our starboard bow."

The captain digested the information without comment, then looked again at Dirk.

"Very well, we shall alter course and avoid further progress through the strait. Incidentally, the Coast Guard is on their way. If you are mistaken, Mr. Pitt, then you will be subject to their prosecution."

A minute later, a thumping noise approached, and an orange-and-white U.S. Coast Guard helicopter from Prince Rupert appeared out the port window.

"Captain, if you would, please advise the pilot to avoid flying into or above the white cloud. It might prove enlightening if he also did a flyby around the northwest coast of Gil Island," Dirk requested.

The captain obliged, advising the Coast Guard pilot of the situation. The helicopter disappeared for twenty minutes, then reappeared above the cruise ship and called on the radio.

"*Dauphine,* we have confirmed the presence of an LNG tanker at a floating terminal on the north coast of Gil Island. It appears you may be correct about an unlawful discharge of gas. We are issuing marine hazard warnings through the Canadian Coast Guard and Royal Canadian Mounted Police. Advise you to alter course to the channel west of Gil Island."

The captain thanked the Coast Guard pilot, then configured an alternate route around Gil Island. A few minutes later, he approached Dirk.

"It would seem that you have saved my ship from an immeasurable tragedy, Mr. Pitt. I apologize for our skepticism and thank you for the warning. If there is anything at all I can do to repay you, please let me know."

Dirk thought for a minute, then said, "Well, Captain, at some point I would like to have my boat back."

Dirk and Summer had little choice but to remain aboard the *Dauphine* until she docked in Vancouver late the following evening. Trevor was back on his feet by the time they reached port but was sent to the hospital for overnight observation. Dirk and Summer stopped for a visit before catching a train to Seattle.

"Are you finally thawed out?" Summer asked, finding Trevor under a mountain of blankets in the hospital room.

"Yes, and now they are trying to cook me alive," he replied, happy to see her so soon. "Next time, I get the dry suit."

"Deal," she said with a laugh.

"Have they nailed the LNG tanker?" he asked, turning serious.

"The *Dauphine* saw her headed to sea as we skirted around Gil Island, so they must have cut and run once they saw the helicopter. Fortunately, the Coast Guard chopper had their video camera rolling and so captured them at the floating terminal."

"No doubt they'll be able to trace the ship back to one of Goyette's holdings," Dirk added. "Though he'll find a way to palm off the blame."

"That's what killed my brother," Trevor said solemnly. "They almost got us, too."

"Did Summer tell you that she deciphered your brother's message on the *Ventura*?" Dirk said.

"No," he said, suddenly sitting up in bed and staring at Summer.

"I've been thinking about it ever since we found the *Ventura*," she said. "It came to me on the ship last night. His message wasn't that they choked. It was that they suffered from choke damp."

"I'm not familiar with the term," Trevor said.

"It comes from the old mining days, when

underground miners carried canaries with them to warn of asphyxiation. I had run across the term while investigating an old flooded quarry in Ohio that was rumored to contain pre-Columbian artifacts. Your brother was a doctor, so he would have been familiar with it. I believe he tried to write the message as a warning to others."

"Have you told anyone else?" Trevor asked.

"No," Summer replied. "I figured you'll want to have another chat with the chief of police in Kitimat when you return."

Trevor nodded but turned away from Summer with a faraway look in his eyes.

"We've got a train to catch," Dirk said, eyeing the clock. "Let's try a warm-water dive together real soon," he said to Trevor, shaking his hand.

Summer moved in and gave him a passionate kiss. "Now, remember, Seattle is only a hundred miles away."

"Yes," Trevor smiled. "And there's no telling how long I'll have to stay in Vancouver arranging a new boat."

"He'll probably be behind the wheel before we see ours again," Dirk lamented as they walked out.

But he would be proven wrong. Two days after they returned to the NUMA regional office in Seattle, a flatbed truck showed up carrying their research boat left behind off

Gil Island. It had a full tank of gas, and on the pilot's seat was an expensive bottle of French burgundy.

47

By presidential directive, the U.S. Coast
Guard cutter *Polar Dawn* steamed stridently
across the maritime boundary with Canada
just north of the Yukon. As it moved east
across the corrugated gray waters of the Beaufort Sea, Captain Edwin Murdock stared out
the bridge window in silent relief. There was
no armed Canadian flotilla there to challenge
him, as a few aboard the ship had feared.

Their mission had begun innocuously
enough several months earlier with a proposal
to seismically map the periphery sea ice along
the Northwest Passage. However, this was
well before the *Atlanta* and Ice Research Lab
7 incidents. The President, concerned about
fanning the flames of Canadian indignation,
had initially canceled the voyage, but the
Secretary of Defense had finally convinced
him to proceed with the mission, successfully
arguing that the Canadians had previously
given implicit approval. It might be years,
he asserted, before the U.S. could challenge

Canada's internal waters claim without overt provocation.

"Skies clear, radar screen empty, and seas at three-to-four," said the *Polar Dawn*'s executive officer, a rail-thin African-American named Wilkes. "Perfect conditions in which to run the passage."

"Let's hope they continue for the next six days," Murdock replied. He noticed a glint in the sky out the starboard bridge window. "Our upstairs escort is still holding the trail?" he asked.

"I believe they are going to keep an eye on us for the first fifty miles into Canadian waters," Wilkes replied, referring to a Navy P-3 Orion reconnaissance plane that lazily circled overhead. "After that, we're on our own."

Nobody really expected the Canadians to oppose them, but the ship's officers and crew were well aware of the heated rhetoric that had been erupting from Ottawa the past two weeks. Most recognized it for what it was, empty posturing by some politicians attempting to capture a few votes. Or so they hoped.

The *Polar Dawn* moved east through the Beaufort Sea, skirting along the jagged edge of the sea ice that occasionally crumbled into a mass of irregular-shaped floes. The Coast Guard vessel towed a sled-shaped seismic sensor off the stern, which mapped the depth and density of the ice sheet as they steamed by.

The waters held clear of traffic, save for the occasional fishing boat or oil exploration vessel. Sailing through the first brief Arctic night without incident, Murdock slowly began to relax. The crew settled into their varied work schedules, which would serve them for the nearly three-week voyage to New York Harbor.

The sea ice had encroached closer to the mainland as they sailed east, gradually constricting the open waterway to less than thirty miles as they approached the Amundsen Gulf, south of Banks Island. Passing the five-hundred-mile mark from Alaska, Murdock was surprised that they still hadn't encountered any Canadian picket vessels. He had been briefed that two Canadian Coast Guard vessels regularly patrolled the Amundsen Gulf, picking up any eastbound freighters that hadn't paid their passage fees.

"Victoria Island coming into view," Wilkes announced.

All eyes on the bridge strained to make out the tundra-covered island through a damp gray haze. Larger than the state of Kansas, the huge island pressed a four-hundred-mile-long coastline opposite the North American mainland. The waterway ahead of the *Polar Dawn* constricted again as they entered the Dolphin and Union Strait, named for two small boats used by Franklin on an earlier Arctic expedition. The ice shelf crept off both shorelines, narrowing the open seaway through the strait to less than ten miles. The *Polar Dawn* could easily shove through the adjacent meter-thick ice if necessary, but the ship kept to the ice-free path melted by the warm spring weather.

The *Polar Dawn* forged another hundred miles through the narrowing strait as its second Arctic night in Canadian waters approached. Murdock had just returned to the bridge after a late dinner when the radar operator announced first one and then another surface contact.

"They're both stationary at the moment," the operator said. "One's to the north, the other almost directly south. We'll run right between them on our current heading."

"Our picket has finally appeared," Murdock said quietly.

As they approached the two vessels, a larger ship appeared on the radar some ten miles ahead. The sentry vessels remained silent as the *Polar Dawn* cruised past, one on either flank. As the Coast Guard ship moved on unchallenged, Murdock stepped over to the radar station and peered over the operator's shoulder. With a measure of chagrin, he watched as the two vessels slowly departed their stations and gradually fell in line behind his own ship.

"It appears we may have trouble passing Go and collecting our two hundred dollars," he said to Wilkes.

"The radio is still silent," the exec observed. "Maybe they're just bored."

A hazy dusk had settled over the strait, painting the distant shoreline of Victoria Island a deep purple. Murdock tried to observe the ship ahead through a pair of binoculars but could only make out a dark gray mass from the bow profile. The captain adjusted course slightly, so as to pass the ship on his port side with plenty of leeway. But he would never get the chance.

In the fading daylight, they closed within two miles of the larger ship when a sudden spray of orange light burst from its gray shadow. The *Polar Dawn*'s bridge crew heard a faint whistling, then saw an explosion in the water a quarter mile off their starboard bow. The startled crew watched as the spray of water from the blast rose forty feet into the air.

"They fired a shell at us," Wilkes blurted in a shocked voice.

A second later, the long silent radio finally crackled.

"*Polar Dawn, Polar Dawn,* this is the Canadian warship *Manitoba.* You are trespassing in a sovereign waterway. Please heave to and prepare for boarding."

Murdock reached for a radio transmitter. "*Manitoba,* this is the captain of the *Polar Dawn.* Our transit route has been filed with the Foreign Affairs Ministry in Ottawa. Request you let us proceed."

Murdock gritted his teeth as he waited for a response. He had been given strict orders not to provoke a confrontation at any cost. But he had also been given assurances that the *Polar Dawn*'s passage would be uncontested. Now he was getting shot at by the *Manitoba,* a brand-new Canadian cruiser built expressly for Arctic duty. Though technically a military vessel, the *Polar Dawn* had no armament with which to fight. And it wasn't a particularly fast ship; certainly it was incapable of outrunning a modern cruiser. With the two smaller Canadian vessels blocking the rear, there was no place to run anyway.

There was no immediate answer to Murdock's radio call. Only a silent pause, and then another orange flash from the deck of the *Manitoba*. This time the shell from the warship's five-inch gun landed a scant fifty yards from the Coast Guard ship, its underwater blast sending a concussion that could be felt throughout the vessel. On the bridge, the radio crackled once more.

"*Polar Dawn,* this is *Manitoba,*" spoke a voice with a kindly charm that was incongruous to the situation at hand. "I must insist that you heave to for boarding. I'm afraid I have orders to sink you if you don't comply. Over."

Murdock didn't wait for another orange flash from the *Manitoba*.

"All stop," he ordered the helmsman.

In a heavy voice, he radioed the *Manitoba* his concession. He quickly had the radioman send a coded message to the Coast Guard sector headquarters in Juneau, explaining their predicament. Then he quietly waited for the Canadian boarders, wondering if his career was all but over.

A heavily armed team of Canadian Special Forces pulled alongside the *Polar Dawn* within minutes and quickly boarded the ship. Executive Officer Wilkes met the boarders and escorted them to the bridge. The leader of the Special Forces team, a short man with a lantern jaw, saluted Murdock.

"Lieutenant Carpenter, Joint Task Force 2 Special Forces," he said. "I have orders to take command of your vessel and bring her to port at Kugluktuk."

"And what of the crew?" Murdock asked.

"That's for the higher-ups to decide."

Murdock stepped nearer, looking down on the shorter lieutenant. "An Army soldier who knows how to pilot a three-hundred-foot ship?" he asked skeptically.

"Ex–Merchant Marine." Carpenter smiled. "Helped push coal barges up the Saint Lawrence in my daddy's tug since I was twelve."

Murdock could do nothing but grimace. "The helm is yours," he said finally, standing aside.

True to his claim, Carpenter expertly guided

the *Polar Dawn* through the strait and across the western reaches of Coronation Gulf, nosing into the small port of Kugluktuk eight hours later. A small contingent of Royal Canadian Mounted Police lined the dock as the ship tied up at a large industrial wharf. The *Manitoba,* which had shadowed the *Polar Dawn* all the way to port, tooted its horn from out in the bay, then turned and headed back into the gulf.

The *Polar Dawn*'s crew was rounded up and marched off the cutter to a white dockside building that had formerly been a fish house, its weathered exterior peeling and blistered. Inside, several rows of makeshift bunks had been hastily set up to accommodate the imprisoned crew. The men were confined in relative comfort, however, their captors providing warm food, cold beer, and books and videos for entertainment. Murdock approached the Mountie in charge, a towering man with ice blue eyes.

"How long are we to be confined here?" the captain asked.

"I don't really know myself. All I can tell you is that our government is demanding an apology and reparations for the destruction of the Beaufort Sea ice camp and an acknowledgment that the Northwest Passage is rightly part of Canada's internal waters. It's up to your government leaders to respond. Your men will be treated with all consideration, but I must warn you not to attempt an escape. We have been authorized to use force as necessary."

Murdock nodded, suppressing a smile. The request, he knew, would go over in Washington like a lead balloon.

48

Pitt had just stepped off a commercial airline flight to Calgary when news of the *Polar Dawn*'s seizure hit the newswires. Mobs of passengers were crowded around airport televisions, trying to digest the impact of the event. Pitt stopped and watched briefly as a Canadian political commentator called for a shutdown of all oil, gas, and hydroelectric power exports to the U.S. until they agreed to Canada's ownership of the Northwest Passage. Pitt stepped to a quiet corner by an empty gate and dialed a direct number to the Vice President's office. A secretary immediately put the call through, and the businesslike voice of James Sandecker burst through the phone in an irritated tone.

"Make it quick, Dirk. I've got my hands full with this Canada situation," he barked without preamble.

"I just caught the news here in Calgary," Pitt replied.

"That's a long ways from Washington. What are you doing in Calgary?"

"Waiting for a flight to Yellowknife and then a puddle jumper to Tuktoyaktuk. The *Narwhal* has been sitting in port there since picking up the survivors of the Canadian Ice Lab."

"That's what started this whole mess. I'd like to get my hands on the real joker who smashed up that camp. In the meantime, you better get that vessel out of Canadian waters pronto, then return to Washington."

"Rudi's on his way back to D.C. with a directive to suspend all NUMA research projects around Canada and immediately move our vessels to neutral waters. I've just got a special job up here to close down personally."

"This have anything to do with that pet science project your pretty wife keeps haranguing me about?"

Bless Loren's heart, Pitt thought. She had already gone after the old man.

"Yes, it does. We need to find the source of the ore, Admiral."

The line went silent, but Pitt could hear some papers being shuffled at the other end.

"Loren writes a bang-up policy paper," Sandecker finally grunted. "Like to have her on my staff if she ever gets tired of serving in Congress."

"I'm afraid her constituents wouldn't let her."

"This ruthenium . . . it's the real deal?"

"Yes, conclusively proven. And there's somebody else in the hunt for it, which confirms its worth."

"If it can make this artificial photosynthesis fly, then it would be invaluable. I can't begin to tell you how bad things are economically because of the energy crunch. The President's carbon mandate puts us on even more of a tightrope. If we don't find a way out, then we're headed for a full-blown meltdown."

"Finding the mineral might be our only chance," Pitt replied.

"Loren's cover letter says there may be a source linked to the lost Franklin Expedition?"

"There are some compelling clues in that direction. It seems to be the only real lead to a near-term supply of the mineral."

"And you want to conduct a search?"

"Yes."

"This is some poor timing on your part, Dirk."

"Can't be helped. It's too important not to try. And it's too important to come up second. I'd just like to know where things are headed with the *Polar Dawn*."

"Are you on a secure line?"

"No."

Sandecker hesitated. "The chickens want to lay some eggs, but the rooster is still pacing the henhouse."

"How soon before breakfast?"

"Soon. Very soon."

Pitt knew that Sandecker often referred to the Pentagon generals as chickens, due to the eagle insignias on their caps. The message was clear. The Secretary of Defense was pushing for a military response, but the President had not made up his mind yet. A decision would be forthcoming shortly.

"The Canadian demand is being treated seriously," Sandecker continued. "You need to collect your vessel and get on over to Alaska, assuming the Canadians will let you leave port. Don't mess around, Dirk. I can't give you any support in Canadian waters. This thing will likely blow over in a few weeks and you can resume your search then."

A few weeks could easily turn into months, and the summer season in the Arctic would be lost. Add an early cold snap and they would be shut out from searching around King William Island until the following spring thaw.

"You're right, Admiral. I'll take the *Narwhal* and sail her to calmer waters."

"Do it, Dirk. And don't delay."

Pitt hung up the phone with no intention of sailing the *Narwhal* to Alaska. If his phone conversation was being monitored, he could say nothing different. And he had not lied to Sandecker. Taking the *Narwhal* farther along the passage would indeed be sailing into much calmer waters than the Beaufort Sea.

At the other end of the line, Sandecker hung up the phone and shook his head. He knew

Pitt almost like a son. And he knew full well that he wasn't about to sail the *Narwhal* to Alaska.

49

The white flecks floated lazily in the dark sky, growing larger to the eye as they approached the earth. It was only when they reached an altitude of a hundred feet or so that their rapid speed of descent became apparent. A few seconds later, they struck the ice-covered ground, landing with a crackling thud. First to touch down was a trio of large wooden boxes, painted flat white to blend with the surroundings. Then human forms followed, ten in all, each recoiling into a ball as their feet touched the ground. Instantly, each man stripped off his harness and rolled his parachute into a ball, then quickly buried the entirety beneath a foot of ice.

A moderate breeze had scattered the men over a half-mile swath, but within minutes they had assembled near one of the crates. Though it was a moonless night, visibility was better than a hundred yards because of the stars that twinkled brightly overhead. The men quickly lined up in front of their commander, a tall, deeply tanned man named Rick Roman. Like the men under him, Roman was dressed in a white camouflage snowsuit with matching helmet and drop-down night vision goggles. On his hip, he carried a holstered Colt .45 automatic pistol.

"Quality drop, men. We've only got an hour of darkness ahead of us, so let's get to work. Green Squad has runway detail, and Blue Squad has Zodiac and base assembly. Let's move."

The men, members of the Army's elite Delta Force, quickly attacked the large crates, spilling their contents. Two of the boxes each contained a Zodiac inflatable boat along with some cold-weather bivouac gear. The third crate contained two Bobcat compact track loaders, converted to run on electric batteries. A smaller container inside held additional weapons, ammunition, meals, and medical kits.

"Sergeant Bojorquez, would you accompany me, please?" Roman called out.

A bull-shaped man with black eyes and prematurely gray hair threw down the side of a crate, then walked over and joined Roman. The Army captain strode off toward an elevated ridge that ran along one side of the landing zone.

"Nice clear night, sir," Bojorquez said.

"Clear and cold as a penguin's butt," Roman replied, grimacing in the ten-degree temperature. He had spent his youth in Hawaii and still hadn't adjusted to cold weather despite years of Arctic training.

"Could be worse," Bojorquez said, flashing a set of bright white teeth. "At least it ain't snowing."

They hiked up the ridge, stepping over and through rough sections of ice that crunched drily under their boots. Reaching the crest, they peered across a gentle slope of uneven ice that stretched down the opposite side. The inky black waters of Coronation Gulf rippled a mile away, while two miles beyond twinkled the lights of Kugluktuk. Dropped from a low-flying C-130 out of Eielson Air Force Base in Fairbanks, Roman and his team had been sent in to seize and extract the crew of the *Polar Dawn* on a mission authorized by the President.

"What's your assessment?" Roman asked, staring at the small town's lights.

The sergeant was a twenty-year man, having served in Somalia and Iraq before being recruited into the elite Delta Forces. Like most of the members of the Arctic unit, he had served multiple tours in the rugged mountains of Afghanistan.

"Satellite recon looks pretty accurate. That plateau's not too chewed up," he said, motioning behind them toward the drop zone. "We'll get a decent runway cleared, no problem."

He gazed down toward the gulf waters and

raised an arm. "That stretch to the drink is a little longer than I'd like to see."

"My concern as well," Roman replied. "We've got such short nightfall, I hate to think of the darkness we'll lose just getting the boats into the water."

"No reason we can't get a head start tonight, Captain."

Roman looked at his watch, then nodded. "Get the Zodiacs down as far as you can before daybreak and cover them up. We might as well burn some energy tonight, since we have a long day of rest tomorrow."

Under the remaining cover of darkness, the small commando team hustled across the ice like rabbits on adrenaline. The men of Green Squad quickly took up the task of carving out an ice runway capable of supporting a pair of CV-22 Ospreys, which would be their ticket out. The drop zone had been selected for just that reason, offering a flat plateau hidden from view yet within striking distance of Kugluktuk. Though the tilt-rotor Ospreys were capable of a vertical landing and takeoff, safety concerns with the fickle Arctic weather prompted orders that they be deployed conventionally. The soldiers measured and marked a narrow, five-hundred-foot path across the ice, then put the minibulldozers to work. Powered for silent running, the tiny machines furiously scraped and shoved the ice until a crude landing strip began to take shape.

At the edge of the runway, the Blue Squad hacked a small enclosure into the ice, which partially concealed a half dozen white bivouac tents that served as shelter. Once the camp was complete, the soldiers set about inflating the rubber Zodiacs, each boat large enough to carry twenty men, then the boats were placed on aluminum sled runners for transport over the ice.

Roman and Bojorquez lent a hand to the four men of Blue Squad as they pushed the two boats across the ice. The southern sky was already beginning to lighten when they reached the crest of the ridge. Roman stopped and rested for a moment, eyeing the distant light of a ship crossing the gulf toward Kugluktuk. Urging the men to keep moving, they started down the slope. Despite the declining grade, they found the ice more jagged and coarse, making the going arduous. The forward runners often jammed into small crevices, requiring added exertion to pull free.

The inflatable boats had been pushed a half mile when the golden flames of the sun arced over the southeast horizon. The men fought to push the boats faster, knowing that premature exposure was the greatest risk to their mission. Yet Roman abandoned his plan to ditch the boats at first light and pushed the team forward.

It took a full hour before the exhausted men finally reached the shores of Coronation Gulf.

Roman had the boats flipped upside down and concealed in a blanket of snow and ice. Hastily making their way back to camp, they found the landing strip completed by their cohorts. Roman made a quick inspection, then retired to his tent with a feeling of satisfaction. The mission preparations had gone without a hitch. When the long Arctic day passed, they would be ready to go.

50

The De Havilland Otter touched down harshly on the flat ice runway, then taxied to a small block building with TUKTOYAKTUK painted in faded lettering on it. As the plane's twin propellers ground to a halt, an airport worker in a thick orange jumpsuit jogged up and opened the side door, letting a blast of frigid air into the interior. Pitt waited at the back of the plane as the other passengers, mostly oil company employees, donned heavy jackets before exiting down the stairs. Eventually making his way off the plane, he was welcomed by a numbing gust that knocked the temperature several degrees below zero on the windchill factor.

Hustling toward the small terminal, he was nearly sideswiped by a rusty pickup truck that had crossed the runway and rattled to a stop in front of the door. A squat man hopped out, covered from head to foot in multiple layers of cold-weather gear. The bulky clothing gave him the effect of a giant walking pincushion.

"Would that be King Tut's mummy or my Director of Underwater Technology buried under there?" Pitt asked as the man blocked his path.

The man yanked a scarf away from his jaw, revealing the staunch face of Al Giordino.

"It is I, your tropics-loving Director of Technology," he replied. "Hop into my heated chariot before we both turn into Popsicles."

Pitt grabbed his luggage off a cart headed toward the terminal and threw it into the open truck bed. Inside the terminal, a plain-looking woman with short hair stood by the window staring out at the two men. As they climbed into the truck, she walked to a pay phone in the terminal and promptly made a collect call to Vancouver.

Giordino shoved the truck into gear, then held his gloved hands in front of the heater vent as he stepped on the gas.

"The ship's crew took a vote," he said. "You owe us a cold-weather pay bonus plus a week's vacation in Bora-Bora at the end of this job."

"I don't understand," Pitt smiled. "The long summer days in the Arctic are renowned for their balmy weather."

"It ain't summer yet. The high was twelve degrees yesterday, and there's another cold front moving our way. Which reminds me, did Rudi escape our winter wonderland successfully?"

"Yes. We missed each other in transit, but he

phoned to tell me he was warmly ensconced back at NUMA headquarters."

"He's probably sipping mai tais along the banks of the Potomac this very moment just to spite me."

The airfield was adjacent to the small town, and Giordino had only a few blocks to drive until reaching the waterfront docks. Located on the barren coast of the Northwest Territories, Tuktoyaktuk was a tiny Inuvialuit settlement that had grown into a small hub for regional oil and gas exploration.

The turquoise hull of the *Narwhal* came into view, and Giordino drove slightly past the vessel, parking the truck next to a building marked HARBORMASTER'S OFFICE. He returned the keys to the borrowed truck inside, then helped Pitt with his bags. Captain Stenseth and Jack Dahlgren were quick to greet Pitt as he boarded the NUMA ship.

"Did Loren finally take a rolling pin to your noggin?" Dahlgren asked, spotting the bandage on Pitt's head.

"Not yet. Just a result of some poor driving on my part," he answered, brushing aside the concern.

The men sat down in a small lounge near the galley as cups of hot coffee were distributed to all. Dahlgren proceeded to brief Pitt on the abbreviated discovery of the thermal vent while Stenseth discussed the rescue of the Canadian Ice Lab survivors.

"What's the local speculation on who could have been responsible?" Pitt asked.

"Since the survivor's description perfectly matches that of our frigate the *Ford*, everyone thinks it was the Navy. We've been told, of course, that she was three hundred miles away at the time," Giordino said.

"What no one seems to consider is that there are very few active icebreakers up here," Stenseth said. "Unless it was a rogue freighter risking its own skin or foolishly off course, the potential culprits are relatively small in number."

"The only known American icebreaker in these waters is the *Polar Dawn*," Giordino said.

"Make that a Canadian icebreaker now," Dahlgren said, shaking his head.

"She doesn't match the description anyway," Stenseth said. "Which leaves a handful of Canadian military vessels, the Athabasca escort ships, or a foreign icebreaker, possibly Danish or even Russian."

"Do you think it was a Canadian warship that struck the camp by accident and they are trying to cover it up?" Pitt asked.

"One of the scientists, Bue was his name, swears he saw an American flag, in addition to the hull number that matches the *Ford*," Dahlgren said.

"It doesn't figure," Giordino said. "The Canadian military wouldn't try to instigate a conflict by masquerading as an American warship."

"What about these Athabasca escort ships?" Pitt asked.

"By Canadian law, all commercial traffic through ice-clogged sections of the Northwest Passage requires an icebreaker escort," Stenseth said. "A private firm, Athabasca Shipping, handles the escort duty. They operate a number of large icebreaker tugs, which are also used to haul their fleet of oceangoing barges. We saw one towing a string of enormous liquid-natural-gas barges passing through the Bering Strait a few weeks ago."

Pitt's eyes lit up. He opened a briefcase and pulled out a photograph of a massive barge under construction in New Orleans. He handed the picture to Stenseth.

"Any resemblance to this one?" Pitt asked.

Stenseth looked at the photo and nodded. "Yes, it's positively the same type. You don't see barges of that size very often. What's the significance?"

Pitt briefed the men on his hunt for the ruthenium, its trail to the Arctic, and Mitchell Goyette's possible involvement. He checked some additional papers that Yaeger had provided, which confirmed that the Athabasca Shipping Company was owned by one of Goyette's holding companies.

"If Goyette is shipping gas and oil from the Arctic, his environmental posturing is certainly fraudulent," Giordino noted.

"A dockworker I met at a bar told me someone was shipping the Chinese massive quantities of oil sands, or bitumen, out of Kugluktuk," Dahlgren said. "He said they were bypassing the government's shutdown of refineries in Alberta due to greenhouse gas emissions."

"A good bet it's on Goyette's barges," Pitt said. "Maybe it's even his oil sands."

"It would seem that this Goyette might have a powerful incentive to obtain the ruthenium source," Stenseth said. "How do you propose beating him to it?"

"By finding a one-hundred-and-eighty-five-year-old ship," Pitt replied. He then shared Perlmutter's findings and the clues linking the mineral to Franklin's expedition ship *Erebus*.

"We know the ships were initially abandoned northwest of King William Island. The Inuit account places the *Erebus* farther south, so it is possible that a shifting ice sheet drove the ships in that direction before they sank."

Stenseth excused himself to run to the bridge, while Dahlgren asked Pitt what he hoped to find.

"Providing that the ice didn't completely crush the ships, there's a good chance the vessels are intact and in an excellent state of preservation due to the frigid water."

Stenseth returned to the lounge with an armful of maps and photographs. He opened a nautical chart that showed the area around King William Island, then produced a high-altitude photo of the same region.

"Satellite photo of Victoria Strait. We've got updates for the entire passage. Some areas north of here are still encased in sea ice, but the waters around King William have already broken up due to an early melt off this year." He laid the photograph on the table for all to see. "The seas are essentially clear in the area where Franklin became icebound one hundred and sixty-five years ago. A bit of drift ice still remains, but nothing that should impede a search effort."

While Pitt nodded with satisfaction, Dahlgren was shaking his head.

"Aren't we forgetting one mighty important tidbit?" he asked. "The Canadians have expelled us from their waters. The only reason we have been able to remain in Tuktoyaktuk so long is because we feigned problems with our rudder."

"With your arrival, those problems have now been rectified," Stenseth said to Pitt with a wily smile.

Pitt turned to Giordino. "Al, I believe you were tasked with proposing a strategy to address Jack's concern."

"Well, as Jack can attest, we have taken the opportunity to befriend the small Canadian Coast Guard contingent stationed here in

Tuk," Giordino said, using the local's abbreviation for the town's Inuit name. "And while this has personally cost me a number of high bar tabs, in addition to a hangover or two for Jack, I believe I have made commendable progress."

He opened one of the captain's charts that showed the western portion of the passage, then searched the coastline with his finger.

"Cape Bathurst, here, is about two hundred miles to the east of us. The Canadians have a radar station on the point, which they use to pick up all eastbound traffic through the passage. They can radio ahead to Kugluktuk, where a pair of vessels are stationed, or call back here to Tuk, where a small cutter is berthed. Fortunately for us, the Canadians have posted most of their intercept vessels on the other end of the passage, snaring the bulk of the traffic entering via Baffin Bay."

"Last time I checked, we didn't have stealth capabilities on our research ships," Pitt said.

"We don't necessarily need it," Giordino continued. "As luck would have it, there's a Korean freighter here in port that struggled in with engine problems. The harbormaster told me the repairs have been completed and that they'll be departing later today. The ship is only going as far as Kugluktuk with a load of oil drilling repair parts, so it'll be sailing without an icebreaker escort."

"You're suggesting that we shadow her?"

Pitt asked.

"Precisely. If we can hold tight to her port flank while we pass Bathurst, they might not pick us up."

"What about the Canadian picket vessels?" Dahlgren asked.

"The Tuk cutter just came into port this morning, so she likely won't put to sea again right away," Giordino said. "That leaves the two vessels in Kugluktuk. I'd bet one of them is probably hanging around the *Polar Dawn,* which was taken there. So that likely leaves just one vessel that we'd have to slide past."

"I'd say those are odds worth taking," Pitt stated.

"What about air surveillance? Can't we count on the Canadian Air Force to do an occasional flyby?" Dahlgren asked.

Stenseth pulled out another sheet from his pile. "Mother Nature will lend us a hand there. The weather forecast for the next week is pretty dismal. If we set sail today, we'll probably accompany a slow-moving low-pressure front that's forecast to roll through the archipelago."

"Stormy weather," Giordino said. "We'll know why there's no plane up in the sky."

Pitt looked around the table, eyeing the others with confidence. They were men of unquestioned loyalty that he could trust in difficult times.

"It's settled, then," he said. "We'll give the

freighter a couple of hours head start, then shove off ourselves. Make it look like we are headed back to Alaska. Once safely offshore, we'll circle back and catch the freighter well before Bathurst."

"Won't be a problem," Stenseth said. "We've got at least eight or ten knots on her."

"One more thing," Pitt said. "Until the politicians resolve the *Polar Dawn* situation, we are on our own. And there's a reasonable chance we could end up with the same fate. I want only a skeleton crew of volunteers aboard. Every scientist and nonessential crew member is to disembark here as quietly as possible. Do what you can to book them rooms and flights out of here. If anyone asks, tell them they are oil company employees who have been reassigned."

"It will be taken care of," Stenseth promised.

Pitt set down his coffee and stared across the table with sudden unease. A painting hung on the opposite bulkhead, depicting a nineteenth-century sailing ship caught in a harrowing gale, its sails shredded and masts falling. A jagged cluster of rocks rose in its path, ready to bash the ship to bits.

Stormy weather indeed, he thought.

51

A thick plume of black smoke sifted out the funnel of the freighter as its lines were cast and the blue-hulled ship churned slowly away from the dock. Standing on the *Narwhal*'s bridge, Bill Stenseth watched as the Korean ship steamed out of Tuktoyaktuk's small harbor and entered the Beaufort Sea. Picking up a shipboard phone, Stenseth dialed the number to a cabin belowdecks.

"Pitt here," came the response after a single ring.

"The Korean freighter is on her way."

"What's our crew status?"

"All nonessential personnel are off the ship. I think we filled up every hotel in town. Of course, there are only two hotels in town. Flights to Whitehorse have been arranged for everyone. They'll have an easy time getting to Alaska from there, or even Vancouver. We're left with a total of fourteen men aboard."

"That's a slim contingent. When can we leave?"

"I was preparing to cast off in another two hours so as not to raise suspicion."

"Then I guess we just need to notify our hosts that we are headed home," Pitt said.

"My next order of business," Stenseth reported.

The captain hung up, then collected Giordino for good measure and walked down to the Canadian Coast Guard station. The Canadian commander seemed less interested in Stenseth's imminent departure than the loss of Giordino's charity at the local seamen's bar. With little to fear from the research ship, the Coast Guard commander said farewell, neglecting to provide an escort out of Canadian waters.

"With that kind of international goodwill, perhaps there's a future for you in the diplomatic corps," Stenseth joked to Giordino.

"My liver would lodge a protest," Giordino replied.

The men stopped at the harbormaster's office, where Stenseth paid the docking fees. Leaving the office, they bumped into Pitt stepping out of a small hardware store with a triangular package under one arm.

"Were we missing something aboard?" Stenseth asked,

"No," Pitt replied with a tight grin. "Just an added insurance policy for when we get to sea."

The sky overhead had grown dark and

threatening when the *Narwhal* slipped its lines two hours later and slowly cruised out of the harbor. A small fishing boat passed in the opposite direction, seeking refuge in port from the pending rough weather. Pitt waved out the bridge, admiring the black-painted boat and its hearty breed of fishermen who braved the Beaufort Sea for a living.

The waves began rolling in six-foot swells when the Northwest Territories coastline fell from view behind them. Light snow flurries filled the air, cutting visibility to less than a mile. The foul weather aided the *Narwhal*'s stealth voyage, and the ship quickly altered course to the east. The Korean freighter had built a twenty-five-mile lead, but the faster research ship quickly began closing the gap. Within hours, the oblong image of the freighter appeared on the fringe of the *Narwhal*'s radar screen. Captain Stenseth brought the NUMA ship within three miles of the freighter, then slowed until he had matched speed with the larger ship. Like a coal tender behind a locomotive, the research ship tailed the freighter's every turn as it steamed along the uneven coastline.

Sixty-five miles ahead, Cape Bathurst jutted into the Beaufort Sea like a bent thumb. It was an ideal location to monitor the marine traffic entering the western approach to Amundsen Gulf. Though the nearest northerly landmass, Banks Island, was still a hundred miles away, the sea ice encroached to within thirty miles of the cape. With radar coverage extending more than fifty miles, the small Coast Guard station could easily track all vessels sailing through open water.

As Pitt and Stenseth studied a chart of the approaching cape, Dahlgren entered the bridge lugging a laptop computer and a string of cables. He tripped over a canvas bag near the bulkhead, dropping his cables but hanging on to the computer.

"Who left their laundry lying around?" he cursed.

He realized the bag contained a sample of rocks and picked up a small stone that had skittered out of the bag.

"That happens to be *your* laundry," Stenseth said. "Those are the rock samples that you and Al brought back from the thermal vent. Rudi was supposed to take them to Washington for analysis, but he left them on the bridge."

"Good old Rudi," Dahlgren lauded. "He could make an atom bomb out of a can of dog food, but he can't remember to tie his shoes in the morning."

Dahlgren slipped the stone into his pocket while he picked up the cables, then stepped over to the helm. Without further comment, he opened a panel beneath the ship's console and began connecting the cables.

"Not an opportune time to be reformatting our nav system, Jack," Stenseth admonished.

"I'm just borrowing a bit of data for a computer game," he replied, standing up and turning on his computer.

"I really don't think we have the need for any games on the bridge," Stenseth said, his agitation growing.

"Oh, I think y'all will like this one," he replied, quickly typing in a number of commands. "I call it Shadow Driver."

The screen on his laptop suddenly illuminated with the image of two boats sailing in tandem from bottom to top. An angular beam of gray spread from a point at the top corner of the monitor, illuminating the majority of the screen, save for a moving shadow behind the upper boat.

"A little software program I just put together, with some help from the ship's GPS and radar systems. This shaft of gray light is targeted from Bathurst, mimicking the station's radar coverage."

"Which will allow us to stay out of the eye of the ground radar system?" Pitt asked.

"You nailed her. Because of our changing angle to the radar station, we'll have to constantly adjust our position behind the freighter in order to duck the signal. We just can't chug right alongside her or else we'd be detected at the fringe angles. If the helmsman keeps us locked in the indicated shadow, then we have a darn good chance of sailing past Bathurst like the Invisible Man."

Stenseth studied the computer, then turned to the helmsman. "Let's put it to the test before we get in range. Engines ahead one-third. Take us five hundred yards off her port beam, then match speed."

"And play Shadow Driver?" the helmsman asked with a grin.

"If this works, you've got a six-pack on me, Jack," the captain said.

"Make it a six of Lone Star and you're on," he replied with a wink.

The *Narwhal* kicked it with an extra burst of speed until the running lights of the freighter flickered off the bow. The helmsman nudged the NUMA ship to port and continued drawing closer.

"One thing worries me," Stenseth said, eyeing the rust-streaked freighter. "Hanging closer to her side for any length of time is liable to generate a radio call from her captain. And I'm sure our Canadian friends at Bathurst have ears as well as eyes."

"My insurance policy," Pitt muttered. "I nearly forgot."

He stepped down to his cabin, then returned a few minutes later with the triangular package he had purchased in Tuktoyaktuk.

"Try running this up," he said, handing the package to Stenseth. The captain ripped open the package, unfurling the Canadian maple leaf flag that was folded inside.

"You really want to sail in harm's way,"

Stenseth said, displaying the flag with uncertainty.

"It's only for the freighter's benefit. Let them think we're part of Canada's Arctic ice patrol. They'll be less likely to question us hanging on their flank for a few hours."

Stenseth looked from Pitt to Dahlgren, then shook his head. "Remind me never to get on the wrong side of a shooting war with you guys."

Then he promptly ordered the flag run up the mast.

With the maple leaf rippling overhead in a stiff westerly breeze, the *Narwhal* drew alongside the Korean freighter and matched lurches in the wallowing sea. Together they sailed through the short night and into a bleak gray dawn. On the bridge, Pitt kept a tense vigil with Stenseth, spelling the helmsman while Giordino appeared every hour with mugs of strong coffee. Holding the research ship in the freighter's shadow through the turbulent waters proved to be a taxing job. Though the freighter was a hundred feet longer than the *Narwhal,* the distance between the two vessels made for a narrower shadow path. Dahlgren's computer program proved to be a godsend, and Stenseth happily agreed to increase his beer debt with each hour they advanced undetected.

When the vessels reached due north of Bathurst, the men on the bridge froze when a call suddenly came over the radio.

"All stations, this is Coast Guard Bathurst calling vessel at position 70.8590 North, 128.4082 West. Please identify yourself and your destination."

Nobody breathed until the Korean ship responded with its name and destination, Kugluktuk. After the Coast Guard acknowledged the freighter, the men fell silent again, praying there would be no second radio call. Five minutes passed, then ten, and still the radio remained silent. When twenty minutes slipped by without a call, the crew began to relax. They sailed for three more hours glued to the side of the freighter before passing well clear of the radar station without detection. When the *Narwhal* reached a bend in the Amundsen Gulf that put Bathurst out of the line of sight, the captain increased speed to twenty knots and zipped past the lumbering freighter.

The Korean ship's captain studied the turquoise ship with the maple leaf flag fluttering overhead as it steamed by. Training his binoculars on the *Narwhal*'s bridge, he was surprised to see the crew laughing and waving in his direction. The captain simply shrugged his shoulders in confusion. "Too long in the Arctic," he muttered to himself, then resumed plotting his course to Kugluktuk.

"Well done, Captain," Pitt said.

"I guess there's no turning back now,"

Stenseth replied.

"What's our ETA to King William Island?" Giordino asked.

"We've just over four hundred miles to go, or about twenty-two hours through these seas, assuming the lousy weather hangs with us. And we don't encounter any picketboats."

"That's the least of your problems, Captain," Pitt said.

Stenseth gave him a questioned look. "It is?" he asked.

"Yes," Pitt replied with a grin, "for I would like to know where in the Arctic you plan on locating two cases of Lone Star beer."

52

Kugluktuk, formerly called Coppermine after an adjacent river, is a small trading town built on the banks of Coronation Gulf. Situated on the northern coast of Canada's Nunavut province, it is one of just a handful of populated havens lying north of the Arctic Circle.

It was the deepwater port offerings that attracted Mitchell Goyette to Kugluktuk. Kugluktuk represented the closest port facility to the Athabasca oil sand fields in Alberta, and Goyette invested heavily in order to stage a terminus for exporting his unrefined bitumen. Cheaply acquiring a little-used rail line from Athabasca to Yellowknife, he financed the expansion of the line north to Kugluktuk. With special snow-clearing locomotives leading the way, a long string of tank cars transported twenty-five thousand barrels of bitumen on every trip. The valuable heavy oil was then off-loaded onto Goyette's mammoth barges and sent across the Pacific to China, where a tidy profit awaited.

With the next railroad shipment several days away, Goyette's Athabasca Shipping Company rail terminus sat ghostly quiet. The icebreaker *Otok* sat at the dock, an empty barge tied to its stern. Two more of the massive barges were moored out in the bay, riding high above their waterlines. Only the rhythmic pumping of a fuel line filling the icebreaker's tanks with diesel fuel gave an indication that the boat and dock were not completely deserted.

No such illusions were evident inside the ship, where an engaged crew made advance preparations for departing port. Seated inside the ship's wardroom, Clay Zak twirled a glass of bourbon over crushed ice as he examined a large chart of the Royal Geographical Society Islands. Sitting across from Zak was the *Otok*'s captain, a puffy-faced man with gray hair cut close to the scalp.

"We'll be refueled shortly," the captain said in a heavy voice.

"I have no desire to spend any more of my life in Kugluktuk than necessary," Zak replied. "We leave at daybreak. It looks to be about six hundred kilometers to the Royal Geographical Society Islands," he said, looking up from the chart.

The skipper nodded. "Ice reports are clear all the way to King William Island and beyond, and this is a fast ship. We'll be there easily in about a day's sail."

Zak took a sip of his bourbon. His hastily

arranged trip to the Arctic had been undertaken without a detailed plan, which made him uncomfortable. But there was little to go wrong. He would drop a team of Goyette's geologists on the north coast of the main island to search for the ruthenium mine, while he examined the Mid-America mining operations in the south. If necessary, he would put Mid-America out of business with the aid of an armed team of security specialists he had brought aboard, along with enough explosives to detonate half the island.

A door to the wardroom suddenly burst open, and a man in black fatigues and parka walked hurriedly over to Zak. He had an assault rifle strapped to his shoulder and carried a bulky pair of night vision binoculars in one hand.

"Sir, two rubber boats approached from the bay and tied up at the dock just astern of the barge. I counted seven men in total," he said, slightly out of breath.

Zak glanced from the man's binoculars to a bulkhead clock, which read half past midnight.

"Were they armed?" he asked.

"Yes, sir. They moved past the loading facility and onto the adjacent public dock before I lost sight of them."

"They're after the *Polar Dawn*," the captain said excitedly. "They must be Americans."

The *Polar Dawn* was docked only a few hundred feet away. Zak had noticed a throng of locals crowding around the American cutter when he had first arrived in Kugluktuk. He walked down and had a look for himself at the captured vessel. It was teeming with Mounties and Navy guards. There was no way that seven men would be able to retake the ship.

"No, they're here for the crew," Zak said, not knowing the ship's crew was being held in the old fish house just a stone's throw away. A devious smile crept slowly across his face. "Very kind of them to drop by. I think they will be a fine aid in ridding us of the Mid-America Mining Company."

"I don't understand," the captain said.

"Understand this," Zak said, rising to his feet. "There's been a change in plans. We depart within the hour."

With the mercenary in tow, he abruptly marched out of the room.

53

Rick Roman ducked behind a pair of empty fuel drums and looked at his watch. The luminescent dial read 12:45. They were twenty minutes ahead of schedule. Humping the Zodiacs down to the water's edge the night before was going to pay dividends now, he thought. They'd be able to make a clean evacuation without fear of losing the cover of darkness.

So far, the mission had gone flawlessly. With a six-man team, he had set off in the Zodiacs just before midnight, right after the sun had finally made its brief retreat beneath the horizon. Powered by electric motors, the inflatable boats had silently crossed the gulf into the mouth of the Coppermine River and quietly tied up at the Athabasca Shipping Company's marine dock. The satellite photos Roman carried with him had showed that the dock was empty seventy-two hours earlier. A large tug cabled to an even-larger barge now occupied the waterfront, but both vessels appeared empty and the dock deserted. Farther down the quay, he could see the *Polar Dawn*, brightly illuminated by the dock lights. Even at the late hour, he could see guards pacing her deck, moving ceaselessly in an effort to keep warm.

Roman turned his attention to a faded white building barely thirty yards in front of him. Intelligence reports had indicated it was the holding cell for the Coast Guard ship's crew. Judging by the lone Mountie standing in the doorway, the prospects still looked good. Roman had assumed that the men would be lightly guarded and he was right. The harsh surrounding environment was enough of a deterrent for escape, let alone the six-hundred-and-fifty-mile distance to the Alaskan border.

A low voice suddenly whispered through his communications headset.

"Guppies are in the pond. I repeat, guppies are in the pond."

It was Bojorquez, confirming that he had viewed the captives through a small window at the side of the dilapidated building.

"Teams in position?" Roman whispered into his mouthpiece.

"Mutt is in position," replied Bojorquez.

"Jeff is in position," came a second voice.

Roman glanced at his watch again. The rescue planes would touch down on the ice runway in ninety minutes. It was plenty of time to get the *Polar Dawn*'s crew across the bay and up to the airfield. Maybe even too much time.

He took a final look up and down the dock, finding no signs of life in either direction. Taking a deep breath, he radioed his orders.

"Commence go in ninety seconds."

Then he sat back and prayed that their luck would hold.

Captain Murdock was sitting on a concrete block smoking a cigarette when he heard a loud thump at the rear of the building. Most of his crewmen were asleep in their cots, taking advantage of the few hours of darkness. A handful of men, also finding sleep difficult, were crowded into a corner watching a movie on a small television set. One of the men, a Canadian Mountie who oversaw the captives inside the building armed with nothing but a radio, stood up and walked over to the captain.

"You hear something?" he asked.

Murdock nodded. "Sounded to me like a chunk of ice falling off the roof."

The Mountie turned to walk toward a storeroom at the back of the building when two men stepped quietly out of the shadows. The two Delta Force commandos had traded their Arctic white apparel for black jacket, fatigues, and armored vests. They each wore a Kevlar helmet with a drop-down display over one eye and a foldaway communications headset. One of the men carried an M4 carbine, which he pointed at Murdock and the Mountie, while the second man fielded a boxy-looking pistol.

The Mountie immediately reached for his radio, but before he could bring it to his lips the man with the pistol fired his weapon. Murdock noted that the gun didn't fire with a bang but emitted just a quiet pop. Instead of firing a bullet, the electroshock stun gun fired a pair of small barbs, each tailed by a thin wire. As the barbs struck the Mountie, the weapon delivered a fifty-thousand-volt charge to the man, instantly incapacitating his muscular control.

The Mountie stiffened, then fell to the ground, dropping his radio as the surge of electricity jolted through his body. He had barely hit the floor when the firing soldier was at his side, locking his wrists and ankles in plastic cuffs and slapping a piece of tape over his mouth.

"Nice shot, Mike," the other commando said, stepping forward while his eyes searched the room. "You Murdock?" he asked, turning back toward the captain.

"Yes," Murdock stammered, still shocked by the sudden intrusion.

"I'm Sergeant Bojorquez. We're going to take you and your crew on a little boat ride. Please wake your men and get them dressed quickly and quietly."

"Yes, certainly. Thank you, Sergeant."

Murdock found his executive officer, and together they quietly roused the other men. The front door of the building suddenly burst open, and two more Delta Force soldiers burst in, dragging the limp body of another Mountie guard. Stun gun barbs protruded from his legs, where the soldiers had been forced to aim in order to bypass the man's heavy parka. Like his partner, the Mountie was quickly gagged and handcuffed.

It took less than five minutes for Murdock to wake and assemble his startled crew. A few men joked about trading Moosehead for Budweiser and the *Red Green Show* for *American Idol,* but most remained quiet, sensing the danger of trying to escape without incident.

Outside the building, Roman held his observation post, eyeing the dock for a possible Canadian reaction. But the stealth assault had succeeded without alarm, and the Canadian militia aboard the *Polar Dawn* remained unaware of the pending escape.

Once he received a ready signal from Bojorquez, Roman wasted no time in getting the men moving. Slipping out the back of the building in groups of three and four, they were led through the shadows to the front of the dock and the moored Zodiacs. The two boats filled quickly, but Roman remained on edge as Bojorquez radioed that he was escorting the final group.

Roman waited until he spotted Bojorquez

making his way across the Athabasca Shipping property before taking a final look down the dock. The waterfront was still deserted on the bitter-cold night, the only sound that of some distant pumps and generators. Roman rose and shuffled quietly toward the boats, feeling confident that the mission would succeed. Extracting the *Polar Dawn*'s crew without alerting the Canadian forces was the touchy part of the operation, and they had apparently pulled it off. Now it was a simple matter of making their way back to the airfield and waiting for the rescue planes to arrive.

He moved past the dark barge to find Bojorquez climbing into one of the boats with the last of the Coast Guard crewmen. There were thirty-six men serving aboard the *Polar Dawn,* and they had all been accounted for. As the Zodiacs were untied, Roman quickly scampered off the dock and into one of the boats.

"Get us out of here," he whispered to a soldier manning the electric motor.

"I'd suggest staying right where you are," thundered a loud voice from up high.

As the words echoed across the water, a bank of halogen lights suddenly flashed on overhead. The intense lights temporarily blinded Roman as he realized that the beams originated from the stern of the barge. He instinctively raised his weapon to shoot but refrained when he heard Bojorquez suddenly barking, "Don't fire, don't fire."

His eyes adjusting to the bright lights, Roman looked up and counted no fewer than six men leaning over the rail of the barge with automatic weapons leveled at the two boats. With his own men following suit, Roman reluctantly lowered his rifle. He peered up at a large man who smiled at him from the barge.

"That's the smart move," Clay Zak said. "Now, why don't you men step back onto the dock and we'll get acquainted?"

Roman looked from Zak to the automatic weapons pointed at his men and nodded. The surprise ambush just as they were about to escape made Roman as mad as a pit bull. Rising to climb off the boat, he gazed angrily at his captors, then dejectedly spit into the wind.

54

Gunnery Sergeant Mike Tipton stared intently through the night vision binoculars, scanning the jagged ice ridge that descended to Coronation Gulf. Though the frozen eyepiece numbed his brow, he held his gaze, hoping for some sign of movement. He finally lowered the glasses when another man crawled up the ice ridge beside him.

"Any sign of the captain?" the soldier asked, a young corporal whose face was hidden behind a cold-weather mask.

Tipton shook his head, then looked at his watch. "They're late, and our aircraft are due in twenty minutes."

"Do you want me to break radio silence and issue a call?"

"Go ahead. Find out what's going on and when they'll be here. We can't keep those birds on the ground for long."

He rose to his feet and turned toward the makeshift airfield. "I'm going to activate the beacons."

Tipton walked quietly away. He didn't want to hear the radio call. Instinctively, he knew that something had gone wrong. Roman had made an early start. He should have been back with the *Polar Dawn*'s crew nearly an hour ago. They certainly should have been within sight by now. Roman was too good a commander, the team too well trained for something not to have gone dramatically wrong.

Tipton reached one end of the airfield and turned on a pair of battery-operated blue lights. He then paced to the opposite end of the coarsely graded runway and activated a second pair of lights. Returning to the base camp, he found the corporal vainly calling the assault team over a portable radio, as one other soldier stood lookout nearby.

"I'm not getting any response," the corporal reported.

"Keep trying until the planes have landed." Tipton faced both men. "We have our orders. We'll evacuate whether the rest of the team is here or not."

Tipton stepped closer to the soldier on lookout, who was barely distinguishable from the corporal in his heavy white parka.

"Johnson, instruct the pilots to hold for five minutes. I'll be on the ridge keeping lookout for the captain. Just don't leave without me," he glowered.

"Yes, Sergeant."

A minute later, a faint buzz split the frozen

night air. The sound grew louder until evolving into the recognizable whine of an aircraft, followed by another. The two Ospreys flew without navigation lights and were invisible against the black sky. Specially modified for expanded range, the two aircraft had flown nearly seven hundred miles from an airstrip in Eagle, Alaska, just over the Yukon border. Skimming low over the tundra, they had easily evaded detection flying over one of Canada's most remote regions.

Tipton reached the top of the ridge and looked back toward the runway as the first plane made its approach. Waiting until it was just fifty feet off the ground before hitting its landing lights, the Osprey came in low and slow, jostling to a quick stop on the uneven surface well short of the perimeter blue lights. The pilot quickly gunned the plane to the end of the runway and whipped it around in a tight arc. An instant later, the second Osprey touched down, bouncing roughly over the ice, before taking its place in line for takeoff behind the first Osprey.

Tipton turned his attention to the gulf, scanning the shoreline again with his binoculars.

"Roman, where are you?" he hissed aloud, angry at the team's disappearance.

But there was no sign of the rubber boats or the men who had sailed off in them. Only an empty expanse of sea and ice filled the lenses. He patiently waited five minutes and then five more, but it was a futile gesture. The assault team was not coming back.

He heard one of the idling aircraft rev its engines and he pulled himself away from the frozen vigil. Running clumsily in his heavy cold-weather gear, he made for the open side door of the first airplane. Jumping in, he caught a dirty look from the pilot, who immediately jammed the throttle forward. Tipton staggered to an empty seat next to the corporal as the Osprey bounced down the runway and lunged into the air.

"No sign?" the corporal yelled over the plane's noisy motors.

Tipton shook his head, painfully reciting the mantra "no man left behind" in his head. Turning away from the corporal, he sought solace by staring out a small side window.

The Osprey, with its sister ship following close behind, flew over Coronation Gulf to gain altitude, then slowly banked around to the west in the direction of Alaska. Tipton absently stared down at the lights of a ship steaming to the east. In the first rays of dawn, he could see it was an icebreaker towing a large barge in its wake.

"Where are they?" Tipton murmured to himself, then closed his eyes and forced himself to sleep.

55

Tipton never knew that he had gazed down upon his Delta Force comrades. What he also didn't know was that the men were suffering all the creature comforts of a medieval dungeon.

Zak's security team had carefully stripped the commandos of their weapons and communication gear before marching them onto the deck of the barge, along with the *Polar Dawn*'s crew. The Americans were then unceremoniously forced at gunpoint into a small storage hold at the bow of the barge. As the last captive was forced down the hold's steel steps, Roman glanced back to see two men hoisting the Zodiac inflatables aboard and securing them along the stern rail.

In the only sign of pity shown the captives, two cases of bottled water, frozen solid in the cold, were tossed into the hold before its heavy steel door was slammed shut. The door's locking turn lever was flung over, then the rattling of a chain could be heard securing the lever in place. Standing silently inside the freezing black bay, the men felt an impending sense of doom hanging over them.

Then a penlight popped on, and soon another. Roman found his in a chest pocket and twisted it on, thankful that he had something of use that hadn't been confiscated.

The multiple beams scanned the bay, taking in the scared faces of the forty-five other men. Roman noticed that the hold was not large. There was an open hatchway on the stern bulkhead in addition to the locked hatch through which they had entered. Two high coils of thick mooring line were stacked in one corner, while a small mountain of tires lined one bulkhead. The grimy, worn tires were extra hull bumpers, used to line the barge when at dock. As he took inventory, Roman heard the powerful diesel engines of the adjacent icebreaker fire up and then idle with a deep rumble.

Roman turned his light toward the crew of the *Polar Dawn*. "Is the captain amongst you?" he asked.

A distinguished-looking man with a gray Vandyke beard stepped forward.

"I'm Murdock, ex-captain of the *Polar Dawn*."

Roman introduced himself and recited his mission orders. Murdock cut him off.

"Captain, it was an admirable effort to rescue us. But pardon me if I don't thank you for freeing us from the hands of the Canadian Mounties," he said drily, waving an arm around the dank confinement.

"We were obviously not anticipating outside interference," Roman replied. "Do you know who these people are?"

"I might well ask you the same question," Murdock replied. "I know that a private firm runs these icebreakers as commercial escort ships under license from the Canadian government. They evidently own the barges, too. Why they would have armed security and an interest in taking us hostage, I have no clue."

Roman was equally stumped. His pre-mission intelligence outlined no threats besides the Canadian Navy and the Mounted Police. It just didn't make sense.

The men heard the icebreaker's engines throttle higher, then felt a slight jar as the lead ship pulled away from the dock, towing the barge with it. After clearing the port waters, the engine revolutions increased again, and the confined men could begin to feel the barge pitch and roll as they entered the choppy waters of Coronation Gulf.

"Captain, any speculation as to where they might be taking us?" Roman asked.

Murdock shrugged. "We are a considerable distance from any significant points of civilization. I wouldn't think that they would leave Canadian waters, but that could still leave us in for a long, cold ride."

Roman heard some grunting and kicking across the hold and shined his light up the entry steps. On the landing, Sergeant Bojorquez was wrestling with the door, slamming his weight against the hatch lever, before releasing a string of profanities. Noting the beam of light on him, he straightened up and faced Roman.

"No-go on the door, sir. The outside lever is chained tight. We'd need a blowtorch to get this thing off."

"Thanks, Sergeant." Roman turned to Murdock. "Is there another way out of here?"

Murdock pointed to the open hatchway facing the stern.

"I'm sure that leads down a ladder into the number 1 hold. This tub has four holds, each big enough to park a skyscraper in. There should be an interior passageway from one hold to the next, accessible by climbing down that ladder and up another on the opposite side."

"What about the main hatch covers? Any chance of prying them off?"

"No way, not without a crane. Each one probably weighs three tons. I would think our only chance is out the stern. There's probably a similar hold or separate access way to the main deck." He stared at Roman with resolve. "It will take some time to search with just a penlight."

"Bojorquez," Roman called. The sergeant

quickly materialized alongside.

"Accompany the captain aft," Roman ordered. "Find us a way out of this rat hole."

"Yes, sir," Bojorquez replied smartly. Then with a wink to his superior, he added, "Worth a stripe?"

Roman smirked. "At least one. Now, get moving."

A glimmer of hope seemed to inspire all of the men, Roman included. But then he remembered Murdock's comment about a long voyage and realized the Arctic environment was still going to offer them a fight for survival. Walking about the hold once more, he began plotting how to keep everyone from freezing to death.

56

In the warm confines of the *Otok*'s bridge, Clay Zak sat comfortably in a high-back chair watching the ice-studded waters slip by. It had been an impulsive and dangerous act to capture the Americans, he knew, and equally impulsive to toss them into the barge and tow them along. He still wasn't quite sure what he was going to do with the captives, but he praised his own good luck. The *Polar Dawn*'s crew had fallen right into his lap and, with them, the opportunity to ignite the flames of contention between Canada and the U.S. The Canadian government would be seething in the belief that the *Polar Dawn*'s crew had escaped via an American military operation that had crossed its territorial borders. Zak laughed at the prospect, knowing that Canada's contemptuous Prime Minister wouldn't be letting the Americans set foot in the Canadian Arctic for quite some time to come.

It was more than Goyette could have hoped for. The industrialist had told him of the riches in the Arctic that were there for the taking, as global warming continued to melt the barriers of access. Goyette had already struck it rich with the Melville Sound natural gas field, but there was also oil to be had. By some estimates, potentially twenty-five percent of the planet's total oil reserves were trapped under the Arctic. The rapid melt off in Arctic ice was making it all accessible now to those with foresight.

The first to grab the rights and lock up the resources would be the one to prosper, Goyette had said. The big American oil companies and mining conglomerates had already been expanding their influence in the region. Goyette could never hope to compete head-to-head. But if they were removed from the playing field, it was a different picture. Goyette could monopolize vast chunks of Arctic resources, setting himself up for billions in profits.

That would be a bigger payoff than the ruthenium, Zak thought. But he might well score on both fronts. Finding the mineral without interference was almost assured. Eliminating the American competition from future exploration was well within reach. Goyette would owe him and owe him big.

With a contented look on his face, Zak stared back at the passing ice and casually waited for the Royal Geographical Society Islands to draw closer.

PART III
NORTHERN PURSUIT

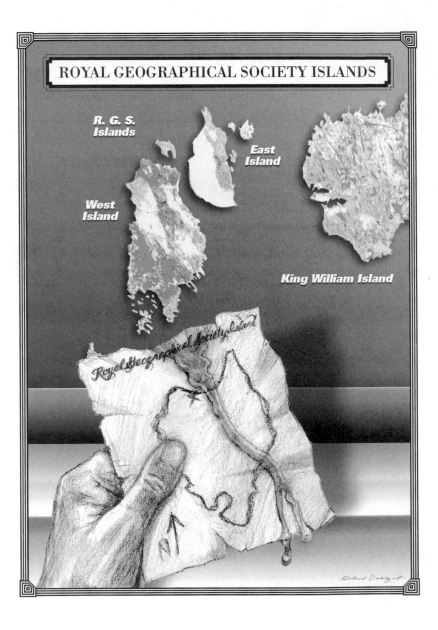

57

For a few brief weeks in late summer, Canada's Arctic archipelago resembles the painted desert. Receding snow and ice lay bare a desolate beauty hidden beneath the frozen landscape. The rocky, treeless terrain is frequently laden with startling streaks of gold, red, and purple. Lichens, ferns, and a surprising diversity of flowers, fighting to absorb the waning summer sunlight, bloom with added bouquets of color. Hare, musk oxen, and birds are found in great numbers, softening the cold aura of morbidity. A richly diverse wildlife, in fact, thrives in the intense summer months, only to vanish during the long, dark days of winter.

For the rest of the year, the islands are a forbidding collection of ice-covered hills edged by rock-strewn shorelines — an empty, barren landscape that for centuries has drawn men like a magnet, some in search of destiny, others in search of themselves. Staring out the bridge at a ribbon of sea ice clinging to the tumbled shoreline of Victoria Island, Pitt could not help but think it was one of the loneliest places he had ever seen.

Pitt stepped to the chart table, where Giordino was studying a large map of Victoria Strait. The stocky Italian pointed to an empty patch of water east of Victoria Island.

"We're less than fifty miles from King William Island," he said. "What are your thoughts on a search grid?"

Pitt pulled up a stool, then sat down and studied the chart. The pear-shaped landmass of King William Island appeared due east of them. Pitt took a pencil and marked an "X" at a point fifteen miles northwest of the island's upper tip.

"This is where the *Erebus* and *Terror* were officially abandoned," he said.

Giordino noted a sense of disinterest in Pitt's voice.

"But that's not where you think they sank?" he asked.

"No," Pitt replied. "The Inuit account, though vague, seemed to indicate that the *Erebus* was farther south. Before I left Washington, I had some folks in the climatology department do some modeling for me. They attempted to re-create the weather conditions in April 1848, when the ships were abandoned, and predict the potential behavior of the sea ice."

"So the ice didn't just melt and the ships

dropped to the bottom where X marks the spot?"

"It's possible but not likely." Pitt pointed to a large body of water north of King William called Larsen Strait.

"The winter freeze propels the pack ice in a moving train from the northeast, down Larsen Strait. If the sea ice off King William didn't melt in the summer of 1848, which the climatologists suggest, then the ships would have been pushed south during the winter freeze of 1849. They might have been reboarded by a small party of survivors, we just don't know. But it is consistent with the Inuit record."

"Swell, a moving target," Giordino said. "Doesn't make for a compact search zone."

Pitt drew his finger down the western shore of King William Island, stopping at a conglomeration of islands located twenty miles off the southwest coast.

"My theory is that these islands here, the Royal Geographical Society Islands, acted as a rampart against the southerly moving ice pack. That rock pile probably diverted some of the ice floe, while breaking up a good deal more piling up on its northern shore."

"That is a pretty direct path from your X," Giordino noted.

"That's the presumption. No telling how far the ships actually moved before falling through the ice. But I'd like to start with a ten-mile grid just above these islands and then move north if we come up empty."

"Sounds like a good bet," Giordino agreed. "Let's just hope they dropped to the bottom in one piece so they'll give us a nice, clean sonar image." He looked at his watch. "I better rouse Jack and get the AUV prepped before we get on-site. We've got two aboard, so we can lay out two separate grids and search them simultaneously."

While Pitt laid out the coordinates for a pair of adjoining search grids, Giordino and Dahlgren prepared the AUVs for launching. The acronym stood for autonomous underwater vehicles. Self-propelled devices that were shaped like torpedoes, the AUVs contained sonar and other sensing devices that allowed them to electronically map the seafloor. Preprogrammed to systematically scan a designated search grid, they would cruise a few meters above the seabed at nearly ten knots, adjusting to the changing contours as they ran.

As he passed just north of the Royal Geographical Society Islands, Captain Stenseth slowed the *Narwhal* as they entered the first of Pitt's search grids. A floating transponder was dropped off the stern, then the ship raced to the opposite corner of the grid where a second buoy was released. Keyed to the orbiting GPS satellites, the transponders provided underwater navigation reference points for the roving AUVs to keep on course.

On the stern of the ship, Pitt helped Giordino and Dahlgren download the search plan into the first AUV's processor, then watched as a crane hoisted the large yellow fish over the side. With its small propeller spinning, the AUV was released from its cradle. The device shot forward and quickly dived beneath the dark, rolling waters. Guided by the bobbing transponders, the AUV scooted to its starting point, then began weaving back and forth, scanning the bottom with its electronic eyes.

With the first vehicle safely released, Stenseth piloted the ship north to the second grid area and repeated the process. A biting wind cut through the men on the deck as they released the second AUV, and they hurried to the warmth of the nearby operations center. A seated technician already had both search grids displayed on an overhead screen, with visual representations of both AUVs and the transponders. Pitt slipped out of his parka as he eyed several columns of numbers quickly being updated on the side of the screen.

"Both AUVs are at depth and running true," he said. "Nice work, gentlemen."

"They're out of our hands now," Giordino replied. "Looks like it will take about twelve hours for the fish to run their course before surfacing."

"Once we get them back aboard, it won't take long to download the data and swap batteries, then we can set 'em loose again on the

441

next two grids," Dahlgren noted.

Giordino raised his brows while Pitt shot him a withering look.

"What did I say?" he asked in a bewildered tone.

"On this ship," Pitt replied, a razor-sharp grin crossing his face, "the first time's the charm."

58

Sixty miles to the west, the *Otok* churned through the wind-whipped waters on a direct path to the Royal Geographical Society Islands. In the wheelhouse, Zak studied a satellite image of the islands through a magnifying glass. Two large islands dominated the chain, West Island separated by a thin channel from the smaller East Island. The Mid-America mining operation was located on the southern coast of the West Island, facing Queen Maud Gulf. Zak could make out two buildings and a long pier in the photograph, as well as evidence of an open-pit mine nearby.

"A message came in for you."

The *Otok*'s unshaven captain approached and handed Zak a slip of paper. Opening it up, Zak read the contents:

Pitt arrived Tuktoyaktuk from D.C. early Saturday. Boarded NUMA research vessel Narwhal. Departed 1600, presumed destination Alaska. M.G.

"Alaska," he said aloud. "They can't very well go anywhere else now, can they?" he added with a smile.

"Everything all right?"

"Yes, just a tardy effort by the competition."

"What's our approach to the islands?" the captain asked, peering over Zak's shoulder.

"The south coast of West Island. We'll make for the mining operation first. Let's run right up to the pier and see if anyone is home. It's early in the season, so they may not have opened up summer operations yet."

"Might be a good place to dump our captives."

Zak gazed out the aft window, watching the barge that was tailing behind wallow in the turbulent seas.

"No," he replied after contemplation. "They should be quite comfortable where they are."

Comfortable was hardly the sentiment that came to Rick Roman's mind. But under the circumstances, he had to admit they had made the best of things.

The cold steel deck and bulkheads of their floating prison quickly sapped their efforts to keep warm, but a solution lie in the debris left behind. Roman organized the men under penlight and had them attack the mound of tires. First, a layer of the old rubber was laid on the deck, then a series of walls were built up, creating a smaller den where all the men could still fit. The mooring ropes were then unwound and draped over the tire walls and floor, creating an extra layer of insulation, as well as padding for the men to lie on. Huddled into the tight enclave, the men had a combined body heat that gradually forced a rise in the temperature. After several hours, Roman flashed his light on a bottle of water at his feet and noted an inch or two of liquid sloshed atop the frozen contents. The insulated den had warmed above freezing, he noted with some satisfaction.

It was the only satisfaction he had received in some time. When Murdock and Bojorquez returned after a two-hour inspection of the barge's interior, the news was all bleak. Murdock had found no other potential exit points astern of their storage hold, save for the cavernous holds themselves. The mammoth overhead hatch covers might as well have been welded shut for the chance they had at moving them.

"I did find this," Bojorquez said, holding up a small wood-handled claw hammer. "Somebody must have dropped it in the hold and didn't bother to retrieve it."

"Even a sledgehammer wouldn't do us a lot of good on that hatch," Roman replied.

Undeterred, Bojorquez began attacking the locked hatch lever with the small tool. Soon the *tap-tap-tap* of the pounding hammer became a constant accompaniment to the creaking sounds of the moving barge. Men lined up to have a go at the hammer, mostly out of boredom, or in an attempt to warm themselves from the exertion. Against the incessant rapping, Murdock's voice suddenly raised over the din.

"The tow ship is slowing."

"Cease the hammering," Roman ordered.

Ahead of them, they could hear the engines of the icebreaker slow their deep-throated drone. A few minutes later, the engines dropped to an idle, then the barge bumped against a stationary object. Listening in silence, the men anxiously hoped that their frozen imprisonment was over.

59

The Royal Geographical Society Islands appeared as a mass of buff-colored hills rising above the choppy slate waters. The islands were christened by the explorer Roald Amundsen in 1905, during his epic voyage on the *Gjoa,* when he became the first man to successfully navigate the length of the Northwest Passage. Remote and forgotten for over a century, the islands remained a footnote until a freelance exploration company found an exposed deposit of zinc on West Island and sold its claims to Mid-America.

The Mid-America mining camp was built on a wide cove along the island's rugged southern coast, which zigzagged with numerous inlets and lagoons. A naturally formed deepwater channel allowed large ships to access the cove, providing that the sea ice had vanished for the season. The company had built a three-hundred-foot semifloating dock that stretched from the cove, sitting empty and alone amid the chunks of ice bobbing in the surrounding waters.

Zak had the captain pull to the dock while he scanned the shoreline through a pair of binoculars. He viewed a pair of prefabricated buildings perched beneath a small bluff alongside a gravel road that ran inland a short distance. The windows of the buildings were dark, and piles of drifting snow could be seen accumulated in the doorways. Satisfied that the facility was still abandoned from the winter shutdown, he had the *Otok* tie up to the dock.

"Have the team of geologists assembled and put ashore," Zak instructed the captain. "I want to know the mineral content of the ore they are extracting here, as well as the geology of the general area."

"I believe the team is anxious to get ashore," the captain quipped, having seen a number of the geologists suffering from seasickness in the galley.

"Captain, I had a large package sent to the ship before I arrived. Did you receive a delivery in Tuktoyaktuk?"

"Yes, a crate was taken aboard there. I had it placed in the forward hold."

"Please have it delivered to my cabin. It contains some materials that I'll need on shore," he said.

"I'll have it taken care of right away. What about our captives on the barge? They're probably near death," he said, eyeing a digital thermometer on the console that indicated the outside temperature was five degrees.

"Ah yes, our frozen Americans. I'm sure their disappearance has a few people excited by now," Zak said with an arrogant tone. "Toss them some food and blankets, I suppose. It may still do for us to keep them alive."

While the geologists made their way ashore accompanied by an armed security team, Zak stepped down to his cabin. His package, a metal-skinned trunk toting a heavy padlock, sat waiting for him on the carpeted floor. Inside was a carefully organized array of fuses and detonators, along with enough dynamite to flatten a city block. Zak selected a few of the items and placed them in a small satchel, then relocked the trunk. Slipping into a heavy parka, he made his way to the main deck and was about to step off the ship when a crewman stopped him.

"You have a call on the bridge. The captain asks that you come right away."

Zak took a companionway to the bridge, where he found the captain talking on a secure satellite telephone.

"Yes, he's right here," the captain said, then turned and handed the phone to Zak.

The testy voice of Mitchell Goyette blared through the earpiece.

"Zak, the captain tells me that you are tied up at the Mid-America facility."

"That's right. They haven't initiated their

summer operations yet, so the place is empty. I was just on my way to make sure they stay out of commission for the season."

"Excellent. The way things are heating up in Ottawa, I doubt an American would even be able to set foot up there." Goyette's greed began to chime in. "Try not to destroy any infrastructure that might be useful for me when I purchase the lot at a fire-sale price," he said with a snort.

"I'll keep that in mind," Zak replied.

"Tell me, what have you learned about the ruthenium?"

"The geologists are just now making an initial survey around the mining camp. But we're presently on the south side of the island, and the trader's map indicated that the Inuit mine was located on the north coast. We'll reposition there in a few hours."

"Very well. Keep me apprised."

"There is something you should be aware of," Zak replied, dropping the bombshell. "We have the American crew of the *Polar Dawn* in our captivity."

"You what?" Goyette howled, forcing Zak to pull the receiver away from his ear. The industrialist's temper burned white-hot, even after Zak described the circumstances of the abduction.

"No wonder the politicians are going ballistic," he hissed. "You're about to set off World War Three."

"It makes it a sure thing that the Americans won't have access to this region for a long time," Zak argued.

"That may be true, but I won't enjoy profiting from their absence if I'm sitting in a jail cell. Dispose of the matter, and without incident," he barked. "Whatever you do, there had better be no link to me."

Zak hung up the phone as the line went dead. Just another unimaginative thug who had bullied his way to billions, Zak thought. Then he slipped his parka back on and went ashore.

A brown ring of rock and gravel encircled the island's cove, melding into a white sheet of ice as one moved inland. The exception was a large rectangular rut that ran several hundred feet into the hillside, ending in a flat, vertical wall clearly cut by machine. The zinc-mining operation was simply cutting straight into the landscape, where the mineral-rich ore was readily accessible. In the distance, Zak noticed a few of the geologists poking around the tailings of the most recent diggings.

The interior of the cove was protected from the worst of the westerly winds, but Zak still moved quickly down the dock, not wishing to prolong his exposure to the cold. He quickly sized up the mining operation before him, which was simple and low-tech. The larger of two buildings was a warehouse that housed the mining equipment — bulldozers, back-hoes, and a dump truck — which dug up the island soil and transferred it onto a small conveyor system for shipboard loading. A smaller building next door would be the crew's bunkhouse and administrative office.

Zak made his way to the smaller building first, curiously finding that the door had been locked. Pulling a Glock automatic from his pocket, he fired twice at the deadbolt, then kicked the door open. The interior was like an expansive house, with two large bedrooms filled with bunk beds, plus an oversize kitchen, a dining room, and a living area. Zak walked directly to the kitchen and looked at the stove, which trailed a gas line to a storage closet containing a large tank of propane. Digging into his satchel, he removed a charge of dynamite and placed it beneath the tank, then affixed a blasting cap with a timed fuse. Checking his watch, he set the fuse to ignite in ninety minutes, then exited the building.

He walked to the equipment-storage building, studying its exterior for some time before hiking around to the back side. Towering over the building was a small bluff, which was strewn with ice-covered rocks and boulders. He struggled up the steep slope to a slight ledge that ran horizontally across the upper face of the hill. Kicking a divot in the frozen ground beneath a car-sized boulder, he removed his gloves and placed another charge of dynamite under the rock. With his fingers freezing, he quickly set the fuse to the blasting cap. Moving a few yards away, he set a second charge beneath a similar clump of large boulders.

Scampering down the hillside, he returned to the front of the building and set one more charge by the hinge of a large swinging door. After setting the fuse, he quickly stepped back to the dock and headed for the icebreaker. As he approached the ship, he could see the captain peering down at him from the bridge. Zak pumped his arm, motioning for him to blow the ship's horn. A second later, two deafening blasts echoed off the hills, signaling the geologists to return to the ship.

Zak turned to see that the geologists took note of the message, then he walked to the barge at the end of the pier. The dock just reached to the bow of the barge, and Zak waited until the current nudged the vessel against the pylons before jumping onto an embedded steel ladder that rose to the vessel's deck. Climbing up, he made his way astern, passing the number 4 hold on the way to an indented well on the aft side. Kneeling against an exterior bulkhead, he packed his remaining explosives, this time affixing a radio-controlled detonator. It wasn't positioned beneath the waterline as he would have liked, but he knew it would do the job in the rolling seas that they had been encountering. Ignoring the lives of the men huddled a few feet away, Zak stepped off the barge with a wry sense of satisfaction. Goyette wasn't going to be happy losing a newly built barge, but what could he say? Zak's instructions were to leave no evidence, and disposing of the barge where nobody could find it was the perfect solution.

The last of the geologists and security guards were climbing aboard the icebreaker when Zak reached the gangplank. He headed straight to the bridge, thankful to enter its warm interior.

"Everyone is back aboard," the captain reported. "Are you ready to leave or did you wish to speak to the geologists first?"

"They can brief me on the way. I'm anxious to investigate the north shore." He looked at his watch. "Though we might want to enjoy the show before shoving off."

Two minutes later, the bunkhouse kitchen blew up, leveling the walls of the entire structure. The propane tank, which was nearly full of gas, exploded in a massive fireball that sent waves of orange flame skyward, its concussion rattling the windows on the ship. A few seconds later, the storage-building charge went off, blowing off the front door and crumbling the roof. The hillside charges were next, creating a tumbling landslide of rocks and boulders that poured onto the mangled roof. When a thick cloud of airborne dust finally settled, Zak could see that the entire building was pulverized under a layer of rock and rubble.

"Very effective," mumbled the captain. "I guess we don't need to worry about an American presence in the vicinity now."

"Quite," Zak replied in a tone of arrogant certainty.

60

The westerly winds whipped across Victoria Strait, kicking up whitecaps that washed over the sporadic chunks of floating ice. Forging through the dark waters, the bright turquoise NUMA ship appeared like a beacon in a colorless world. With the Royal Geographical Society Islands visible off its bow, the ship steamed slowly south into the first of Pitt's search grids.

"Looks to be a vessel rounding the northwest coast," the helmsman reported, eyeing the radarscope.

Captain Stenseth picked up a pair of binoculars and viewed a tandem pair of dots on the horizon.

"Probably an Asian freighter making an escorted attempt through the passage," he said. He turned to Pitt, who was seated at the chart table studying a blueprint of the Franklin ships. "We'll be approaching the finish line shortly. Any idea when your torpedo will pop up?"

Pitt glanced at his orange-faced Doxa dive watch. "She ought to surface within the next half hour."

It proved to be twenty minutes later when one of the crewmen spotted the yellow AUV bobbing to the surface. Stenseth maneuvered the ship alongside, and the AUV was quickly hoisted aboard. Giordino removed its one-terabyte hard drive and hustled the data to a small viewing room, where a computer and projection system awaited.

"You headed to the movies?" Stenseth asked as Pitt stood up and stretched.

"Yes, the first of two rather long double features. You have a fix on the transponders?"

Stenseth nodded. "We'll go grab them next. They've actually been pushed quite far along, due to the strong southerly current here. We will have to make a bit of a dash for them before they pile up on the island rocks."

"I'll tell Dahlgren to be standing by," Pitt replied. "Then we can go grab fish number 2."

Pitt made his way down to the darkened viewing room, where Giordino already had the sonar's collected data displayed on the screen. A gold-colored image of the seafloor was scrolling by, revealing a largely flat but rocky bottom.

"A nice crisp image," Pitt said, taking a seat next to Giordino.

"We boosted the frequency for a higher

resolution," Giordino explained. He handed Pitt a bowl of microwave popcorn. "But it still ain't *Casablanca,* I'm afraid."

"That's okay. As long as we find something worth playing again, Sam."

The two men sat back and stared at the screen as an endless swath of sea bottom began scrolling by.

61

The Zodiac pounded over the choppy swells, careening off small chunks of ice as a freezing mist sprayed into the air. The pilot kept the throttle open until approaching a wide expanse of unbroken ice that stretched from the shoreline. Finding a section with a sloping front edge, he drove the inflatable boat up and onto the sea ice. The hardened hull of the Zodiac slid several feet before mashing to a halt against a low knoll. Seated near the stern, Zak waited for the geology team to exit the boat before he stepped out, following a guard carrying a hunting rifle whose sole job was to ward off any inquisitive bears.

"Pick us up a mile down the coast in exactly two hours," Zak ordered the pilot, waving an arm to the west. Then he helped shove the Zodiac back into the water and watched as the rubber boat sped to the *Otok,* idling a half mile away.

Zak could have stayed in the warmth of his cabin, reading a biography of Wild Bill

Hickok that he had brought along, but he feared the geologists would dawdle in the cold. What actually drove him ashore, he didn't want to admit, was the disappointment he felt with their geological assessment of the Mid-America mining camp.

While it was hardly a surprise when they confirmed the rich ground content of zinc and iron on the south side of the island, he had expected that some trace elements of ruthenium might be present. But none were found. The geologists in fact found no evidence of any platinum-related elements in the exposed stratum.

It meant nothing, he assured himself, since he knew exactly where the ruthenium would be found. Digging into the pocket of his parka, he pulled out the journal pages that he had stolen from the Miners Co-op. In heavy charcoal was a hand-drawn circular diagram that clearly resembled West Island. A small X was marked on the northern shore of the island. At the top of the page, a different hand had written "Royal Geographical Society Islands" with a quill pen in a Victorian script. It was, according to an earlier page in the journal, the copied diagram of an Inuit map where the Adelaide seal hunters had obtained the ruthenium they oddly called Black Kobluna.

Zak matched the contours with a modern map of the islands and identified the targeted spot slightly west of their landing site.

"The mine should be a half mile or so down the coastline," he announced after the group had hiked over the ice to a rock-covered beachfront. "Keep your eyes open."

Zak marched off down the beach ahead of the geologists, anxious to make the discovery himself. The cold seemed to fade away as he envisioned the potential riches that waited just down the coast. Goyette would already owe him for ridding the Canadian Arctic of American investors. Finding the ruthenium would be frosting on the cake.

The rugged shoreline was fronted by an undulating series of gullies and bluffs that climbed toward the island's interior. The ravines were filled with hard-packed ice, while the hilltops were bare, creating a mottled pattern like the dappled coat of a gray mare. Trudging well behind Zak, the geologists moved tentatively in the cold weather, stopping frequently to examine exposed sections of the hillsides and collect samples of rock. Reaching his target area without finding physical evidence of a mine, Zak anxiously paced back and forth until the geologists drew near.

"The mine should be in this vicinity," he shouted. "Search the area thoroughly."

As the geologists fanned out, the security guard waved Zak over to the edge of the sea ice. Splayed at the man's feet, he found the mutilated carcass of a ringed seal. The mammal's flesh had been torn from its skin in large, jagged chunks. The guard pointed to the animal's skull, where a wide set of claw marks had scratched through the skin.

"Only a bear would have left a mark like that," the guard said.

"By the look of the decay, it was a fairly recent meal," Zak replied. "Keep a sharp lookout, but don't mention this to our scientific friends. They're already distracted enough by the cold."

The polar bear never materialized, and, to Zak's dismay, neither did the ruthenium. After an hour of diligent searching, the frozen geologists staggered to Zak with confused looks on their faces.

"The visual results are on par with the south side of the island," said one of the geologists, a bearded man with droopy hazel eyes. "We see some outcrop mineralization with signs of iron, zinc, and a bit of lead content. There's no obvious evidence of platinum-group ores, including ruthenium. However, we'll have to assay our samples back on the ship to definitely rule out its presence."

"What about indications of a mine?" Zak asked.

The geologists all looked at each other and shook their heads.

"Any mining performed by the Inuit one hundred and sixty years ago would be by primitive means at best," the lead geologist said. "There would have been evidence of surface disruptions. Unless it is under one of these ice sheets, we didn't see any such indications."

"I see," Zak said in a pallid tone. "All right, back to the ship, then. I want to see your assay results as soon as possible."

As they marched across the sea ice to their pickup site, Zak's mind churned in bewilderment. It didn't make sense. The journal was clear that the ruthenium had come from the island. Was it possible that the ore had all been played out in a small quantity? Was there a mistake in the journal or was it all a ruse? As he stood waiting for the Zodiac to arrive, he stared offshore, suddenly spotting a turquoise research ship bearing down on the island.

His bewilderment quickly turned to rage.

62

Pitt and Giordino were three hours into their review of the sonar data when the shipwreck appeared. Giordino had set the viewing speed at double the capture rate, so they were nearly complete with the first grid's results. The rapidly scrolling seabed images had turned the men glassy-eyed, but they both popped out of their seats when the wreck appeared. Giordino immediately hit a keyboard command that froze the image.

It was a distinct shadow image of a large wreck sitting upright on the bottom, tilted at just a slight angle. The perimeter of the wreck appeared fully intact, except for a mangled crevice running horizontally across the bow.

"She's a wooden ship," Pitt remarked, pointing to a trio of long, tapering masts that stretched across the deck and onto the adjacent seafloor. "Looks to have a blunt-shaped bow, characteristic of the bomb ships that the *Erebus* and *Terror* were originally built to be."

Giordino used the computer's cursor to measure the wreck's dimensions.

"How does thirty-two meters in length fit?" he asked.

"Like a glove," Pitt replied, flashing a tired smile. "That's got to be one of the Franklin ships."

The door to the viewing room burst open and Dahlgren strode in, carrying a hard drive under his arm.

"Second AUV is back on board, and here's what she's got to say," he declared, handing Giordino the device. He glanced at the screen, then stared with bulging eyes.

"Shoot, you already found her. Mighty fine-looking wreck," he added, nodding at the clear image.

"Half of the pair," Pitt said.

"I'll start getting the submersible prepped. That will make for a sweet dive to the bottom."

Pitt and Giordino finished reviewing the first AUV's imagery, then tore through the data from the second vehicle. The remaining data came up empty. The sister shipwreck was somewhere outside the two initial search grids. Pitt decided against expanding the grids until they determined which wreck they had found.

He made his way to the bridge with the wreck coordinates, where he found Captain Stenseth gazing out the starboard wing. Less than two miles away, the icebreaker *Otok* came steaming north with its empty barge in tow.

"Lo and behold, a match for one of your friend Goyette's barges," Stenseth remarked.

"A coincidence?" Pitt asked.

"Probably," Stenseth replied. "The barge is riding high, so she's empty. Likely headed for Ellesmere Island for a load of coal, then back through the passage to China."

Pitt studied the vessels as they moved closer, marveling at the massive size of the barge. He stepped over to the chart table and retrieved the photograph Yaeger had provided of the Goyette barge under construction in New Orleans. He looked at the picture and saw it was an exact duplicate of the vessel approaching off the starboard beam.

"We have a match," Pitt remarked.

"You think they'll report our position to the Canadian authorities?"

"I doubt it. But there's a chance they're here for the same reason we are."

Pitt kept a wary eye on the icebreaker as it steamed past a quarter mile away. There was no friendly chitchat over the radio, just the silent rocking from the barge's wake as the vessels passed by. Pitt continued to watch as the icebreaker held a steady northbound course.

Stenseth must be right, he thought. It only made sense that an empty barge in these parts was headed to pick up a shipment, and Ellesmere Island was well to the north of them. Still, there was something uncomfortable about the appearance of the two vessels. Somehow, he knew, their appearance was no simple coincidence.

63

"Her name's the *Narwhal*. She's Canadian."

Zak reached over and snatched the binoculars out of the captain's hands and looked for himself. Studying the research ship, he read her name in white letters across the transom. Peering astern, he found a yellow submersible on the rear deck with NUMA painted on the side. He noted with chagrin a maple leaf flag flying atop the bridge.

"A bold move, Mr. Pitt," he muttered. "That's no Canadian ship, Captain. That is an American research ship operated by NUMA."

"How could an American research ship make its way here?"

Zak shook his head. "With some measure of deception, apparently. I have no doubt that they are here after the ruthenium. The fools must think that it is underwater."

He watched the NUMA ship fade from view as they continued steaming north.

"Hold our course until we are clear of radar

coverage. Stay out of range for an hour or two, then creep back just to the point where you can detect them. If they move, then tail them." He glanced at the bridge clock. "I'll return shortly before nightfall with our next move."

Zak climbed down a companionway to his cabin, intending to take a nap. Failure was making him irritable, however. The mineral assays for the rocks collected on the north shore had come back negative for ruthenium, and now there was the presence of the NUMA ship. Reaching for a bottle of bourbon, he poured himself a glass but spilled a shot when the ship took a sudden roll. A few drops landed on the Inuit map, which he had set on his nightstand. He grabbed the map, holding it up as a trail of bourbon ran down the page. The liquid bisected the island like a brown river, making it appear to be two separate islands. Zak stared at the map a long while, then hurriedly yanked out a satellite image of the island grouping. Comparing the images of West Island, he matched the south and west coastlines exactly but not the eastern shoreline. Sliding the Inuit map over, he then compared its shape to the satellite image of East Island. The eastern coastlines matched perfectly, but there the similarities ended.

"You idiot," he muttered to himself. "You're looking in the wrong spot."

The answer was right in front of him. The

narrow waterway that had split the West and East islands had obviously been frozen solid one hundred and fifty years ago. The Inuit map had actually represented both islands, drawn as one landmass. The difference shifted the position of the ruthenium source nearly two miles farther east than he had estimated.

Climbing into his bunk, he swallowed the glass of bourbon, then lay down with a renewed sense of hope. All was not lost, for the ruthenium mine must still be there. It had to be. Content in the knowledge, he turned his thoughts to more immediate issues. First, he reasoned, he had to figure out what to do with Pitt and the NUMA ship.

64

The strong westerly winds finally began to abate, reducing the seas to a moderate chop. The settling winds brought with it a wispy gray fog that was common to the region during the spring and summer months. The thermometer finally climbed into double digits, prompting shipboard jokes about the balmy weather.

Pitt was just thankful that the weather had calmed enough to launch the submersible without risk. Climbing through the hatch of the *Bloodhound,* he settled into the pilot's seat and began checking a bank of power gauges. Beside him in the copilot's seat, Giordino reviewed a predive checklist. Both men wore just light sweaters, shivering in the cold cabin they knew would soon turn toasty from the electrical equipment aboard.

Pitt looked up as Jack Dahlgren stuck his poker face into the hatch.

"You boys remember, those batteries don't hold their charge so well in this cold weather.

Now, you go bring me back the ship's bell and I might just leave the lights on for you."

"You leave the lights on and I just might let you keep you job," Giordino uttered back.

Dahlgren smiled and started humming the Merle Haggard standard "Okie from Muskogee," then closed and sealed the hatch. A few minutes later, he worked the controls of a small crane, lifting the submersible off the deck and depositing it in the center of the ship's brightly illuminated moon pool. Inside, Pitt signaled for its release, and the yellow cigar-shaped submersible began its descent.

The seafloor was just over a thousand feet deep, and it took the slowly drifting *Bloodhound* almost fifteen minutes to reach the bottom. The gray-green waters quickly melded to black outside the submersible's large viewing port, but Pitt waited until they passed the eight-hundred-foot mark before powering up the bright bank of exterior high-intensity lights.

Rubbing his hands together in the slowly warming cabin, Giordino looked at Pitt with mock suffering.

"Did I ever tell you that I'm allergic to the cold?" he asked.

"At least a thousand times."

"My mama's thick Italian blood just doesn't flow right in these icebox conditions."

"I'd say the flow of your blood has more to

do with your affinity for cigars and pepperoni pizzas than with your mother."

Giordino gave him a thankful look for the reminder and pulled the stubby remains of an unlit cigar out of his pocket and slid it between his teeth. Then he retrieved a copy of the shipwreck's sonar image and spread it across his lap.

"What's our plan of attack once we reach the wreck site?"

"I figure we have three objectives," Pitt replied, having earlier planned the dive. "First, and most obvious, is to try and identify the wreck. We know that the *Erebus* had a role in the ruthenium that was obtained by the Inuit. We don't know if the same holds true for the *Terror*. If the wreck is the *Terror*, there may well be no clues whatsoever aboard. The second objective is to penetrate the hold and determine if there are any significant quantities of the mineral still there. The third objective is the most tenuous. That would be to search the Great Cabin and the captain's cabin to determine if the ship's log still exists."

"You're right," Giordino agreed. "The log of the *Erebus* would be the holy grail. It surely would tell us where the ruthenium was found. Sounds like a long shot to hope that it survived intact, though."

"Admittedly, but far from impossible. The log was probably a heavy leather-bound book stored in a chest or locker. In these cold waters, there's at least a chance that it's still in one piece. Then it would be up to the preservationists to determine if it could be conserved and ultimately deciphered."

Giordino eyed the depth gauge. "We're coming up on nine hundred and fifty feet."

"Adjusting for neutral buoyancy," Pitt replied, regulating the submersible's variable ballast tank. Their descent slowed to a crawl as they passed the thousand-foot mark, and, minutes later, a flat, rocky seafloor appeared beneath them. Pitt engaged the propulsion controls and drove the vessel forward, skimming a few feet off the bottom.

The craggy brown seafloor was mostly devoid of life, a cold and empty world not far removed from the frozen lands protruding above the surface. Pitt turned the submersible into the current, guiding the vessel in a sweeping series of S turns. Though the *Narwhal* had been stationed directly above the wreck, Pitt knew that they had drifted considerably south during their descent.

Giordino was the first to spot the wreck, pointing out a dark shadow on their starboard flank. Pitt steered the *Bloodhound* hard to the right until the stately wreck materialized under their spotlights.

Before them sat a nineteenth-century wooden sailing ship. It was one of the most remarkable shipwrecks Pitt had ever seen.

The frigid Arctic waters had retained the ship's condition in a near-perfect state of preservation. Covered in a fine layer of silt, the ship appeared fully intact, from its bowsprit to its rudder. Only the masts, which had slipped from the deck during the long plunge to the bottom, lay out of place, dangling over the side railing.

Mired in its desolate eternal mooring, the ancient ship exuded a forlorn aura. To Pitt, the ship appeared like a tomb in an empty graveyard. He felt an odd chill thinking about the men who had sailed her, then been forced to abandon their home of three years under desperate conditions.

Slowly engaging the submersible, Pitt cruised in a tight arc around the vessel while Giordino activated a forward-mounted video camera. The hull timbers still appeared thick and sound, and in places where the silt was thin they could see a coat of black paint still adhering to the wood. As they rounded the stern, Giordino was startled to see the tips of a propeller protruding from the sand.

"They had steam power?" he asked.

"A supplement to sail, once they reached the ice pack," Pitt confirmed. "Both ships were equipped with coal-fired locomotive engines installed for added propulsion through the thinner sea ice. The steam engines were also used to provide heat for the ship's interior."

"No wonder Franklin had the confidence to try to plow through Victoria Strait in late summer."

"What he may not have had enough of by that point in the expedition was coal. Some figure they ran short of their coal supplies, and that may have accounted for the ships becoming trapped in the ice."

Pitt pushed the submersible around to the ship's port side, anxious to find lettering on the bow that might reveal the ship's name. But he was disappointed to find instead the only real evidence of damage to the ship. The hull beneath the bow was blown out in a jagged mass of timbers, caused by the constricting ice. The damage had extended to the topside deck when the weakened section had struck the seafloor, causing the timbers above to buckle. A broad section of the bow on both sides of the centerline had crumpled like an accordion just a few feet astern of the vessel's blunt prow. Pitt patiently hovered off both sides of the bow as Giordino brushed aside the silt with an articulated arm, but no identifying script work could be found.

"I guess this one wants to play hard to get," Pitt muttered.

"Like too many of the women I've dated," Giordino grimaced. "I guess we'll have to take Dahlgren up on his ship's bell offer after all."

Pitt elevated the submersible above the

deck, then swept toward the stern. The deck was remarkably clear of debris, the ship obviously configured in its winter hibernation mode when it was abandoned. The only unusual item was a large canvas structure that lay across the deck amidships. Pitt knew from the historical accounts that a tentlike covered structure was set up on the deck in winter so that the crew could escape the interior confines of the ship for exercise.

Pitt continued aft, where he found the helmsman's station and the large wooden ship's wheel, still standing upright and attached to the rudder. A small bell was mounted nearby, but, after careful scrutiny, he could find no markings on it.

"I know where the ship's bell is," Pitt stated, cruising back toward the bow. Hovering over the tangled mass of timbers and debris where the bow had buckled, he pointed down.

"It's in the garbage pit here."

"Must be," Giordino agreed with a nod. "It's not our day. Or night." He checked a console of dials in front of him. "We have just under four hours of battery power remaining. Do you want to rummage around for the bell or have a look inside?"

"Let's take Rover for a walk. There's one upside to this damage, I suppose. It will allow us easier access to the interior."

Pitt edged the *Bloodhound* to a clear section of the deck, then carefully set the submersible down. When the ship's timbers gave no indication of stress, he powered off the propulsion motors.

In the copilot seat, Giordino was busy engaging another device. Tucked between the submersible's support skids was a small, tethered ROV the size of a small suitcase. Equipped with a micro-sized video camera and small array of lights, it could maneuver into the smallest corners of the shipwreck.

Jockeying a controlling joystick, Giordino guided the Rover out from its cradle and toward the open section of the deck. Pitt flipped down an overhead monitor, which displayed the live video feed from the device. Methodically weaving above and around the debris, Giordino finally found a large gap in the deck and guided the ROV into the bowels of the ship.

Pitt unrolled a cutaway diagram of the *Erebus* and tried to track the ROV's location as it moved beneath the main deck. The ship had two levels belowdecks, plus a dank hold where the engine, boiler, and coal reserves were housed below the waterline. The living and dining areas for both crew and officers were located on the lower deck, one level down from the main deck. Beneath the lower deck was the orlop deck, which was strictly a storage area for provisions, tools, and ship's spares.

"You should be dropping near the galley,"

Pitt remarked. "It's adjacent to the crew's living quarters, which is a sizable compartment."

Giordino guided the Rover down until the deck came into view, then he turned and panned the bay. The still water inside the ship was exceedingly translucent, providing perfectly clear visibility. Pitt and Giordino could see, not five feet away from the ROV, the galley's large cookstove, built up on a layer of bricks. It was a massive structure made of cast iron and crowned by six large burners on its flat cooking surface. Sitting atop it were several black iron pots of varying sizes.

"One galley, as ordered," Giordino remarked.

He then steered the ROV aft, slowly scanning back and forth. The thin bulkheads surrounding the galley had fallen to the deck, revealing the open crew's quarters. The bay was mostly empty of debris, save for a large number of planked wooden slabs that lay evenly spaced across the deck.

"Mess tables," Pitt explained as the Rover's cameras focused in on one of the tabletops. "They were stowed overhead to make way for the crew's hammocks but lowered on ropes at mealtimes. They've fallen to the deck as the ropes deteriorated."

The ROV moved aft as the compartment narrowed until fronting a wide bulkhead.

"That will be the main hatchway," Pitt explained. "Keep moving aft and we should reach a ladderway that descends to the orlop deck. They covered it with an enclosure to keep out the draft from below, but we'll have to hope it was dislodged when the ship sank."

Giordino steered the ROV around the hatchway, then brought it to a sudden halt. Tilting it toward the deck, the camera revealed a large circular hole cut through the deck.

"No door here," he said.

"Of course, we can drop through the deck collar," Pitt replied.

The deck collar held one of the ship's three masts as it ran down to the hold. When the masts pulled free during the sinking, they left an open passageway into the lowest depths of the ship.

The Rover squeezed through the opening, then sprayed its lights on the black orlop deck. For the next fifty minutes, the ROV scoured the corners of the deck, Giordino methodically searching for possible traces of the ore. But all they found was a vast supply of tools, weapons, and the ship's stowed canvas sails, which would never feel a sea breeze again. Returning to the mast stand, they delved into the lower hold, finding only a few scraps of coal near the massive steam boiler. Coming up empty on both levels, Giordino began threading the ROV back up to the lower deck, when the submersible's radio crackled.

"*Narwhal* to *Bloodhound,* have you got your ears on?" came the readily distinguishable voice of Jack Dahlgren.

"*Bloodhound* here. Go ahead, Jack," Pitt replied.

"The captain wanted me to let you know that our friend with the barge has moseyed back onto the radar screen. Appears to be sitting stationary about ten miles north of us."

"Affirmative. Please keep us advised."

"Will do. You boys having any luck down there?"

"We sure are, but it has all been bad. We've got Rover on the leash and are about to try for the captain's cabin."

"How are you doing on power?"

Pitt eyed a bank of dials and meters overhead. "We're good for another ninety minutes on the bottom, and we'll probably need it all."

"Roger. We'll look for you up top in less than two. *Narwhal* out."

Pitt stared at the dark abyss beyond the submersible, contemplating the icebreaker on the surface above. Were they in fact monitoring the *Narwhal*? His gut told him so with certainty. It wouldn't be his first encounter with the forces of Mitchell Goyette, he now knew. And what of Clay Zak? Could it be possible that Goyette's thug was aboard the icebreaker?

Giordino nudged him back to the task at hand.

"Ready to move aft."

"The clock is ticking," Pitt said quietly. "Let's get it done."

65

A dense, icy fog crept across the *Otok* as dusk settled over Victoria Strait. The *Narwhal* was long lost from physical view, and Zak searched for her on the radarscope, finding the research ship as a narrow smudge on the top of the screen. Across the bridge, the icebreaker's captain paced back and forth, having grown bored with holding his ship stationary for the past few hours.

But the captain saw no signs of boredom in Zak's face. On the contrary, there was an odd intensity about him. Like in the moment before an assassination, he was fully alert, his senses in high gear. While he had murdered many times before, he had never done so on a large scale. It was a test of cunning, he liked to think, that made his blood run fast. It gave him a sensation of invincibility, inflated by the knowledge that he had always come out on top.

"Bring us to within eight kilometers of the *Narwhal*," he finally directed the captain.

"And do so nice and easy."

The captain engaged the helm and brought the ship and attached barge around on a southerly heading. Aided by the swift-moving current, the icebreaker ran just above idle, covering the distance in less than an hour. Reaching the new position, the captain swung his bow around to the current in order to remain stationary.

"Eight kilometers and holding," he reported to Zak.

Zak eyed the gloomy darkness outside the bridge window and creased his lips in satisfaction.

"Prepare to release the barge at my command," he said.

The captain stared at him as if he were insane.

"What are you saying?" he asked.

"You heard me. We are going to release the barge."

"That's a ten-million-dollar vessel. In this fog and current, there's no way we'll be able to tie back up to her. She'll rip her hull open on some ice or run aground on the islands. Either way, Mr. Goyette will have my head."

Zak shook his head with a thin smile. "She won't be traveling very far. As for Goyette, please recall the signed letter I gave you in Kugluktuk giving me complete authority while I'm aboard this ship. Believe me, he will consider it a small price to pay to eliminate a problem that could cost him hundreds of millions of dollars. Besides," he added with a conniving grin, "isn't that what marine insurance is for?"

The captain reluctantly ordered his deckhands to the stern of the ship to man the towlines. The men waited in the cold while Zak ran down to his cabin, then returned to the bridge carrying his leather satchel. At Zak's command, the captain reversed power and backed down on the barge until the thick towlines fell slack in the water. The deckhands released a lock plate, then heaved the looped ends of the towlines up and off the stern bollards. The men watched morbidly as the lines slid down the stern and disappeared into the black water below.

When the bridge received an all-clear signal, the captain pulled the ship forward, then came around the barge's starboard flank at Zak's urging. The dark mass of the barge could barely be seen a few yards away as the fog continued to thicken. Zak reached into his satchel and pulled out a high-frequency radio transmitter, then stepped out onto the bridge wing. Extending a small antenna, he powered on the device and immediately pushed a red TRANSMIT button.

The radio signal only had to travel a short distance to trigger the detonator cap planted on the stern of the barge. Less than a second later, the dynamite charge ignited.

The explosion was neither loud nor visually impressive, just a resounding pop that reverberated within the barge, followed by a light puff of smoke that rose from the rear deck. Zak observed the scene for just a few seconds, then returned to the warmth of the bridge, putting the transmitter back into his bag.

"I don't like having the blood of those men on my hands," the captain grumbled.

"But you have it all wrong, Captain. The loss of the barge was quite accidental."

The captain simply stared at Zak with a look of dismay.

"It's very simple," Zak continued. "You shall write in your log, and report to the authorities back in port, that the American research ship inadvertently collided with our barge in the fog and both vessels sank. We, of course, were most fortunate to release the towlines in the nick of time and suffered no casualties. Regrettably, we were unable to find any survivors in the water from the NUMA ship."

"But the NUMA ship has not sunk," the captain protested.

"That," Zak replied with a snarl, "is about to change."

66

A thousand feet below the surface, the intervening hour had been one of complete frustration for Pitt and Giordino. While guiding the Rover aft along the lower deck, Giordino watched as the ROV jerked to a standstill and refused to move forward. Retracing its trail of cable, he found the power cord had become tangled in some debris at the head of the galley. Matters only got worse when the ROV's thrusters kicked up a huge cloud of silt around the snagged area. He had to wait ten minutes just for the visibility to return before he could see enough to free the cable.

The interior of the submersible had finally grown hot, and sweat dribbled down Giordino's face as he tensely guided the ROV back through the crew's quarters and down the main passageway toward the stern of the ship.

"Where's the lounge on this boat? I think Rover and I could both use a cold beer about now," he muttered.

"You would have needed to break into the Spirit Room belowdecks, where the rum was stored. Of course, if this is the *Erebus,* then you might be out of luck, as Franklin was a teetotaler."

"That seals it," Giordino said. "No further proof required. My present state of luck dictates that this has to be the *Erebus.*"

Despite the minutes ticking down on their bottom time, neither man was ready to give up. They pressed the ROV onward, striking down the single aft passageway, past the cramped officers' cabins, until finally arriving at a large compartment at the very stern of the ship. Called the Great Cabin, it stretched from beam to beam, offering the one truly comfortable haven for the men of the ship, or at least its officers. Stocked with a library, chess sets, playing cards, and other sources of entertainment, it was also a potential repository for the ship's log. But like the rest of the vessel, the Great Cabin offered no clues to the ship's identity.

Scattered across the deck and around an upturned table was a knee-deep pile of books. Lined on wide shelves across each side of the cabin, the large collection of books had smashed through the glass cases during the sinking and been strewn everywhere. Giordino slowly flew the ROV back and forth across the cabin, surveying the wall-to-wall mess.

"Looks like the San Francisco Library after the great earthquake," Giordino said.

"The ship's library contained twelve hundred volumes," Pitt replied, studying the mess with disappointment. "If the ship's log is buried in there, it will take a couple of fortnights and a good rabbit's foot to find it."

Their frustration was interrupted by another radio transmission from Dahlgren.

"Sorry to break up the fiesta, but the big hand on the clock says it's time for you to begin your ascent," he said.

"We'll be on our way shortly," Pitt replied.

"Fair enough. The captain says to tell you that our shadow has closed to within four miles and is sitting pretty again. I think the captain would feel a whole lot better if you boys got yourselves aboard pronto."

"Understood. *Bloodhound* out."

Giordino looked at Pitt and noticed a look of concern in his green eyes.

"You think that pal of yours from the Miners Co-op is aboard the icebreaker?"

"I'm beginning to wonder," Pitt replied. "Let's try the captain's cabin and then we'll skedaddle."

The captain's cabin was located off the far side of the Great Cabin and represented a faint hope for containing the ship's log. But a small sliding door to the cabin was locked and no amount of bumping or cajoling by the ROV would shake it loose. With less than an hour

489

of battery power left and a twenty-minute ride to the surface, Pitt called the survey off and told Giordino to fetch Rover back home.

Giordino steered the ROV back to the galley and toward the entry gap in the bow, as a take-up spool reeled in the power cable. Pitt powered up the submersible's thrusters, then gazed out the view port at the *Bloodhound*'s electronic pod while waiting for the ROV.

"How did the mineral sensor test out?" he asked, pointing at the pod.

"Seems to work like a champ," Giordino replied, his eyes glued to the overhead monitor as he threaded the ROV through the forward debris. "We won't be able to gauge its full accuracy until we can assay our samples back at headquarters."

Pitt reached over and powered on the sensor, watching a nearby monitor as it computed the mineral readings. Of no surprise to Pitt, the screen registered a very large iron concentration nearby, along with some trace elements of copper and zinc. The iron made perfect sense, as the ship was loaded with it, from the anchors and anchor chains directly below them to the locomotive engine in the hold. But it was one of the other trace elements that caught his eye. Waiting until the ROV snaked out of the lower deck, he engaged the thrusters and elevated the submersible. Moving slowly, he brought the craft to a hover over the damaged section of the bow while keeping one eye on the sensor's output.

"If you can find us some gold on this tub, it would redeem an otherwise forgettable dive," Giordino said.

Pitt danced the submersible over the debris area, gradually focusing on a small section near the ship's centerline. Easing to a stable section of the deck, he again set the submersible down. Giordino had pulled the ROV's cable slack and was preparing to drop it into its cradle.

"Hold on," Pitt said. "Do you see that broken timber standing upright about ten feet in front of us?"

"Got it."

"There's a covered object near its base, a little to the right. See if you can blast it off with the ROV."

Giordino had the Rover in place within seconds. He cut the power and let the ROV sink to a small pile of debris covered in silt. When the ROV made contact, he applied full power to its tiny thrusters. The little ROV shot upward, kicking up a thick cloud of silt in the process. The steady bottom current that rippled over the ship quickly cleared away the murky water. Both men could see a curved object with a gold luster lying in the debris.

"My gold bars," Giordino said facetiously.

"Something better, I think," Pitt replied. He didn't wait for Giordino to fly the ROV over the object, instead propelling the submersible over for a close-up look. Peering down through the view port, they saw the unmistakable shape of a large bell.

"Holy smokes, how did you pick that out of the muck?" Giordino asked.

"The *Bloodhound*'s sniffer did it. I noticed a small reading of copper and zinc, and remembered that they're the two components of brass. I figured it was either a cleat or the ship's bell."

They stared down at the bell, observing an engraving on the side, which they couldn't quite make out. Pitt finally backed off a few feet and let the ROV zoom in for a closer look.

The bell was still caked with silt and crustaceans, but a close-up view from the Rover's camera revealed two of the engraved letters: ER.

"Can't spell *Erebus* without it," Giordino remarked with some relief.

"Give it another blast," Pitt directed.

While Giordino maneuvered the ROV in for another go at the silt, Pitt checked their battery reserves, finding their remaining power was down to thirty minutes. There was little time left to lose.

The silt burst upward in a massive cloud of brown particulates from the Rover's second burst. It seemed to Pitt that the water took hours to clear when in fact in was just a few seconds. Giordino immediately guided the

ROV back over the bell as they waited for the murky cloud to drift away. They both stared silently at the monitor as the bell's engraved lettering slowly materialized in its entirety.

It spelled TERROR.

67

After three days of confinement in the frozen darkness, the barge captives were living a different kind of terror. Roman had ordered the fading penlights to be used sparingly, so most of the time the men spent groping around in complete blackness. Initial feelings of anger and determination to escape had waned to despair in the bleak hold, where the men huddled close together to stave off hypothermia. Hope had flourished when the barge had come to a rest at the dock and the hatch was briefly thrown open. It proved to be nothing more than an inspection from several armed guards, but at least they had provided some food and blankets before their hasty exit. Roman took it as a good sign. They wouldn't be given food if they were not intended to be kept alive, he reasoned.

But now he wasn't so sure. When Bojorquez had awakened him to report a change in the sound of the icebreaker's engines, he suspected that they had reached their destination. But then the rhythmic tugging of the towropes had suddenly ceased while the rocking motion from the choppy seas remained. He could sense that they had been cut adrift.

Second's later, Zak's explosives detonated with a jolt. The explosion reverberated through the empty holds of the barge like a thunderstorm in a bottle. Instantly, the commandos and *Polar Dawn*'s crew were on their feet, wondering what had happened.

"Captain Murdock," Roman called out, turning on his penlight.

Murdock shuffled forward, a haggard look to his eyes from a lack of sleep.

"Speculation?" Roman asked quietly.

"Sounded well aft. I suggest we go take a look."

Roman agreed. Then seeing the apprehensive look in the faces of the nearby men, he called over to Bojorquez.

"Sergeant, get back to work on that hatch. I'd like some fresh air in here before breakfast."

Moments later, the stocky sergeant was pounding away at the locked hatch again with his small hammer. The clanging racket, Roman hoped, would give the men a small lift while masking the sound of whatever was happening aft.

Roman led Murdock to the open stern hatchway and shined his light over the threshold. A steel-rung ladder led straight down into an empty black void.

"After you, Captain," Murdock said curtly.

Roman slipped the penlight between his teeth, then grabbed the top rung and slowly started climbing down. Though not afraid of heights, he found it unnerving to climb into a seemingly bottomless black hole inside a rolling ship.

The bottom rung seemed elusive, but after a forty-foot drop he reached the base of the number 1 hold. Shining his light at the foot of the ladder, Murdock appeared right behind him. A rock solid man just over sixty, the gray-bearded captain was not even breathing hard.

Murdock led the way across the hold, startling a pair of rats that somehow flourished even in the bitter cold.

"Didn't want to say it in front of the men but that sounded like an onboard explosion to me," he said.

"My thoughts as well," Roman replied. "Do you think they mean to sink us?"

"We'll know soon enough."

The two men found another steel ladder on the opposite side of the hold, which they climbed up to a short passage that led to the number 2 hold. They repeated the process twice more, crossing the next two holds. As they climbed up the far side of the third hold, they could hear a distant sound of sloshing water. Reaching the last passageway, Roman scanned the number 4 hold with his light.

On the opposite corner, they spied a small river of water streaming down the bulkhead, splashing into a growing pool below. The explosion had left no gaping hole in the side of the hull but rather created a series of buckled steel plates that let the water seep in like a broad sieve. Murdock studied the damage and shook his head.

"Nothing we can do to slow that down," he said. "Even if we had the proper materials, it's too widely dispersed."

"The water inflow doesn't look too extreme," Roman said, searching for something positive.

"It will only get worse. The damage appears to be just above the waterline, but the rough seas are spilling in. As the hold fills, the barge will begin to settle by the stern, allowing more water to rush in. The flooding will only accelerate."

"But there's a hatch on the passageway that we can lock. If the water is confined to this hold, shouldn't we be all right?" Roman asked.

Murdock pointed overhead. Ten feet above their heads, the bulkhead ended, replaced by a series of support beams that rose several more feet to the overhead deck.

"The holds are not watertight compartments," he said. "When this hold floods, it will spill over into the number 3 hold and keep moving forward."

"How much flooding can she withstand?"

"Since she's empty, she should stay afloat with two holds flooded. If the seas are calm, she might hang on with a third flooded. But once the water starts hitting that number 1 hold, it will be all over."

Dreading the answer, Roman asked how much time they had left.

"I can only guess," Murdock said, his voice turning low. "I'd say two hours, tops."

Roman aimed the dimming bulb of his penlight toward the trickle of water and slowly traced it down toward the bottom of the hold. A growing pool of black water was reflected in the distance, its shimmering surface a calling card of death.

68

At the first visible signs of a listing stern, Zak ordered the *Otok* to pull away from the barge. The sinking black hulk was quickly swallowed up by a bank of fog, its death throes proceeding without an audience. Zak himself quickly turned his back on the barge and its condemned occupants.

"Make for the NUMA ship," he ordered. "And kill the running lights."

The captain nodded, bringing the helm in line with the research ship's fixed position, then gradually building speed until the icebreaker was running at ten knots. The lights of the *Narwhal* were unseen under the blanket of fog, so its pursuit was accomplished by radar. The research ship still held to a stationary position as the icebreaker quickly closed the gap between the vessels.

"Captain, when we approach to within three kilometers, I want to accelerate under full power. We'll cross her bow about a kilometer off, to make her think we are running inland, then we will arc back as we draw near and strike her amidships."

"You want me to ram her?" the captain said incredulously. "You'll kill us all."

Zak gave him a bemused look. "Not hardly. As you well know, this vessel has a five-foot-thick steel prow fronting a highly re-inforced double hull. She could bull through the Hoover Dam without a scratch. Providing you avoid the *Narwhal*'s own heavy bow, we'll slice through her like butter."

The captain peered at Zak with grudging respect. "You've studied my vessel well," he said brusquely. "I just hope that Mr. Goyette takes the dry-dock repairs out of your salary and not mine."

Zak let out a deep chortle. "My good Captain, we play our cards right and I'll personally buy you your own fleet of icebreakers."

Though the dark night and fog masked the sea, Bill Stenseth attentively tracked every movement of the icebreaker. With his radar operator absent, one of the many crewmen sent ashore in Tuktoyaktuk, Stenseth sat down and monitored the radar set himself. He had become alerted when he noted the distant radar image slowly split in two. Correctly guessing that the barge had been separated from the tow ship, he carefully began to track both images.

He anxiously watched the icebreaker

close within three miles on an intercept course when he reached for the marine VHF radio.

"Unidentified vessel approaching south at 69.2955 North, 100.1403 West, this is the research vessel *Narwhal*. We are presently conducting an underwater marine survey. Please give clearance of two kilometers, over."

Stenseth repeated the call but received no reply.

"When's the *Bloodhound* due up?" he asked the helmsman.

"Dahlgren's last report was that they were still on the wreck site. So they are at least twenty minutes off."

Stenseth watched the radar screen closely, noticing a gradual increase in speed by the icebreaker as it approached within two miles. There looked to be a slight change in the ship's course, drifting off the *Narwhal*'s bow as if to pass on her starboard beam. Whatever their intent, Stenseth was not in a trusting mood.

"Ahead a third," he ordered the helmsman. "Bearing three hundred degrees."

Stenseth well knew that the prospect of a collision in thick fog was one of a mariner's worst nightmares. With visions of the *Stockholm* striking the *Andrea Doria* in his mind, he powered his ship to the northwest, in order to avoid a similar head-on collision.

With a minute degree of relief, he saw that the other vessel was holding to its southeast course, widening the angle between their paths. But the appearance of a safe passing was short-lived.

When the two vessels approached within a mile, the icebreaker suddenly accelerated, nearly doubling its speed in short order. Driven by a massive pair of gas turbine engines capable of towing a string of heavy barges, the icebreaker was a behemoth of torque. Freed to run unencumbered, the tow ship turned into a greyhound, capable of slicing through the water at over thirty knots. Under Zak's order, the ship found its full legs and blasted through the waves under maximum throttle.

It took only a few moments for Stenseth to detect the change in the icebreaker's speed. He held his course steady until the radar told him that the other vessel was sharply veering to the west.

"Ahead flank speed!" he ordered, his eyes glued to the radar screen

He was aghast at the track of the icebreaker as it swept in a short arc toward his own vessel. He shook off any doubts about the intent of the other vessel. It clearly intended to ram the *Narwhal*.

Stenseth's order to accelerate thwarted Zak's attempt to catch the ship and crew off guard. But the icebreaker still had a decided advantage in speed, if no longer surprise. The *Otok* had closed to within a quarter mile before the research ship could break twenty knots. Stenseth peered out the aft bridge window but could see nothing through the black fog.

"She's coming up quick," the helmsman said, watching the icebreaker's radar smudge approach the center of the radar screen. Stenseth sat down and readjusted the range to read in hundred-yard increments.

"We'll let her come in tight. But when she touches the hundred-yard mark, I want you to bring us hard to starboard, on a due east heading. There's still plenty of sea ice along the shore of King William Island. If we can get close enough, they might lose our radar signature against it."

He gazed at an open chart, noting their distance to King William Island was over fifteen miles. Much too far away, he knew, but his options were few. If they could parry a bit longer, maybe the pursuers would give up the hunt. He stood and watched the radar screen until the tailing target drew near, then he nodded at the helmsman.

The heavy research ship shook and groaned as the rudder was jammed full over, the vessel heeling onto its new course. It was a lethal game of blindman's bluff. On the radar screen, the icebreaker seemed to merge with their own position, but Stenseth still caught no sight of the icebreaker. The *Otok* continued on its westerly course for nearly a full minute before detecting the *Narwhal*'s maneuver and turning sharply to the east in pursuit.

Stenseth's action gave the ship precious seconds to build more speed while the crew was alerted and ordered topside. But it wasn't long before the icebreaker was closing in on their stern once again.

"Hard to port this time," Stenseth ordered, when the *Otok* crossed the hundred-yard mark once again.

The icebreaker anticipated the move this time but guessed wrong and veered to starboard. She quickly took up the chase again as Stenseth attempted to angle closer to King William Island. The faster ship quickly moved in and the *Narwhal* was forced to juke again, Stenseth opting to turn hard to port once more. But this time, Zak guessed correctly.

Like a hungry shark striking from the depths of a murky sea, the icebreaker suddenly burst through the fog, its lethal prow slashing into the flank of the *Narwhal*. The shattering blow struck just aft of the moon pool, the icebreaker's bow slicing fifteen feet in from the rail. The *Narwhal* nearly keeled over from the impact, shuddering sideways into the waves. A massive spray of freezing water poured over the deck as the ship struggled to regain its center of gravity.

The collision brought with it a thousand cries of mechanical agony — steel grating on steel, hydraulic lines bursting, hull plates splintering, power plants imploding. As the destruction reached its climax, there was an odd moment of silence, then the wails of violence turned to the gurgling moans of mortality.

The icebreaker slowly slid free of the gaping wound, breaking off a section of the *Narwhal*'s stern as it backed away. The vessel's sharp bow had been bludgeoned flat, but the ship was otherwise fully intact, its double hull not even compromised. The *Otok* lingered on the scene a few moments, as Zak and the crew admired their destructive handiwork. Then like a deadly wraith, the murderous ship disappeared into the night.

The *Narwhal,* meanwhile, was on its way to a quick death. The ship's engine room flooded almost instantly, tugging the stern down in an immediate list. Two of the bulkheads fronting the moon pool were crushed, sending additional floodwaters to the lower decks. Though built to plow through ice up to six feet thick, the *Narwhal* was never designed to withstand a crushing blow to its beam. Within minutes, the ship was half underwater.

On the bridge, Stenseth picked himself up off the deck to find the bridge a darkened cave. They had lost all operating power, and the emergency generator located amidships had also been disabled in the collision. The entire ship was now as black as the foggy night.

The helmsman beat Stenseth to an emergency locker at the rear of the bridge and quickly produced a flashlight.

"Captain, are you all right?" he asked, sweeping the beam across the bridge until it caught Stenseth's towering figure.

"Better than my ship," he replied, rubbing a sore arm. "Let's account for the crew. I'm afraid we're going to have to abandon ship in short order."

The two men threw on their parkas and made their way down to the main deck, which was already listing heavily toward the stern. They entered the ship's galley, finding it illuminated by a pair of battery-operated lanterns. Most of the ship's skeleton crew was already assembled with their cold-weather gear, a look of fear etched in their eyes. A short man with a bulldog-like face approached the two men.

"Captain, the engine room is completely flooded and a section of the stern has been torn away," said the man, the *Narwhal*'s chief engineer. "Water has reportedly breached the forward hold. There's no stopping it."

Stenseth nodded. "Any injuries?"

The engineer pointed to the side of the galley, where a grimacing man was having his left arm wrapped in a makeshift sling.

"The cook broke his arm in a fall when she

hit. Everyone else came through clean."

"Who are we missing?" Stenseth asked, quickly counting heads and coming up two short.

"Dahlgren, and Rogers, the ship's electrician. They're trying to get the tender launched."

Stenseth turned and faced the room. "I'm afraid we must abandon ship. Every man onto the deck — now. If we can't board the tender, then we'll use one of the port-side emergency rafts. Let's make it quick."

Stenseth led the men out the galley, stopping briefly to note that the water had already crept to the base of the superstructure. Quickening his pace, he moved onto the frozen expanse of the forward deck, fighting to keep his balance against the increasing slope underfoot. Across the deck, he saw a beam of light flash between two men cranking on a manual winch. A twelve-foot wooden skiff dangled in the air above them, but the rakish angle of the deck prevented the skiff's stern from clearing the side railing. The sound of obscenities embroidered in a Texas accent rattled through the cold night air from one of the men.

Stenseth rushed over and, with the help of several more crewmen, heaved the stern up and over the railing. Dahlgren reversed the lever on the winch and quickly lowered the skiff into the water. Grabbing its bow line, Stenseth walked the boat aft twenty feet until the water on the deck reached his boots. The crew then quickly climbed aboard by simply stepping off the *Narwhal*'s side rail.

Stenseth counted off a dozen-plus heads, then followed the injured chef as the last man aboard, stepping into the cramped wooden tender and taking a seat near the stern. A light breeze had picked up again, blowing scattered holes in the fog while casting an added chop to the seas. The tender quickly drifted a few yards away from the dying ship, staying in sight of her final moments.

They were barely away when the bow of the turquoise ship rose high into the night air, struggling against the forces of gravity. Then releasing a deep moan, the *Narwhal* plunged into the black water with a hiss of bubbles, disappearing to the depths below.

A burning anger welled within Stenseth, then he gazed upon his crew and felt relief. It was a minor miracle that no one had died in the collision and everyone had made it safely off the ship. The captain shuddered to think of the death toll had Pitt not put most of the crew and scientists ashore in Tuktoyaktuk.

"I forgot the dang rocks."

Stenseth turned to the man next to him, realizing in the dark that it was Dahlgren sitting at the tiller.

"From the thermal vent," he continued. "Rudi left them on the bridge."

"Consider yourself lucky that you escaped

with your skin," Stenseth replied. "Good work in getting the tender away."

"I didn't really want to bob around the Arctic in a rubber boat," he replied. Lowering his voice, he added, "Those guys play for keeps, don't they?"

"Fatally serious about the ruthenium, I'm afraid." He held his head to the air, trying to detect the presence of the icebreaker. A faint rumbling in the distance told him the ship wasn't lingering in the area.

"Sir, there's a small settlement called Gjoa Haven on the extreme southeast tip of King William Island," the helmsman piped in from a row up. "A little over a hundred miles from here. Nearest civilization on the charts, I'm afraid."

"We should have enough fuel to make King William Island. Then it will have to be on foot from there," Stenseth replied. Turning back to Dahlgren, he asked, "Did you get a message off to Pitt?"

"I told them we were vacating the wreck site, but we lost power before I could warn them we wouldn't be coming back." He tried to make out the dial on his watch. "They should be surfacing shortly."

"We can only guess as to where. Finding them in this fog would be a near impossibility, I'm afraid. We'll try a pass through the area, then we'll have to break for the coastline and seek help. We can't risk being offshore if the winds should stiffen."

Dahlgren nodded with a grim look on his face. Pitt and Giordino were no worse off than they were, he thought. Coaxing the tender's motor to life, he turned the boat south and disappeared into a dark bank of fog.

69

Pitt and Giordino had been hovering over the ship's bell when they received a brief transmission from Dahlgren that the *Narwhal* was moving off-site. Preoccupied with uncovering the bell's inscription, they had not followed up the call.

The discovery that the shipwreck was the *Terror* proved to be a small relief for Pitt. With no indication that there was any ruthenium aboard, there was still room for hope. The Inuit must have obtained the ore from the *Erebus,* and perhaps she alone held the secret to the coveted mineral. The question lingered as to where had the *Erebus* ended up. The two ships were known to have been abandoned together, so presumably they would have sunk close to each other. Pitt felt confident that expanding the AUV's search area would turn up the second ship.

"*Bloodhound* to *Narwhal,* we're beginning our ascent," Giordino radioed. "What's your status?"

"We're on the move at the moment. I'm trying to get an update from the bridge. Will let you know when I do. Over."

It was the last they were to hear from Dahlgren. But having extended their bottom time, they were more concerned about reaching the surface with auxiliary power to spare. Pitt shut off the external lights and sensing equipment to save power, while Giordino did the same with the nonessential interior computers. As the submersible fell dark and they began gliding upward, Giordino sat back in his chair, crossed his arms, and closed his eyes.

"Wake me when it's time to let in some fresh ten-below air," he muttered.

"I'll make sure that Jack has your slippers and newspaper waiting."

Pitt again reviewed the electrical power readings with a wary eye. There was plenty of reserve power for the life-support systems and the ballast-control pumps, but little else. He reluctantly shut down the submersible's propulsion system, knowing they would be subject to the strong currents during their ascent. Plugging the *Narwhal*'s moon pool would be out, as they would likely end up a mile or two down current when they broke the surface. And that's only if the *Narwhal* was back on-site.

Pitt shut down a few more electrical controls, then stared out at the black abyss beyond the view port. Suddenly, an urgent cry rang out on the radio.

"*Bloodhound,* we've been . . ."

The transmission was cut midsentence and was followed by complete silence. Giordino popped forward in his chair and was returning the call even before he had his eyes open. Despite repeated attempts, his transmissions to the *Narwhal* went unanswered.

"We might have lost their signal in a thermocline," Giordino offered.

"Or the transponder link was broken when they began running at speed," Pitt countered.

They were manufactured excuses to reason away the truth neither man wanted to accept, that the *Narwhal* was in real trouble. Giordino continued making radio calls every few minutes, but there was no response. And there was nothing either man could do about it.

Pitt looked at the submersible's depth gauge and wondered if they were tied to the bottom. Since receiving the interrupted call, their ascent rate had slowed to a crawl, or so it seemed to Pitt. He tried to keep his eyes away from the gauge, knowing the more he watched it, the slower it moved. Sitting back, he closed his eyes for a time, imagining the troubles the *Narwhal* might be facing, while Giordino diligently kept up his radio vigil.

He finally opened his eyes to see they were just over a hundred feet deep. A few minutes later, they rocked to the surface amid a rush of bubbles and foam. Pitt kicked on the external lights, which simply reflected back a surrounding billow of fog. The radio remained silent as they rocked back and forth in the heaving waters.

Alone in a cold and empty sea, Pitt and Giordino both knew that the worst had happened. The *Narwhal* was no more.

70

"What do you mean the rescue team disappeared?"

The President's angry voice echoed off the walls of the White House Situation Room on the lower level of the West Wing. An Army colonel, brought in by the Pentagon generals to serve as a sacrificial lamb, responded in a quiet monotone.

"Sir, the team failed to appear at the extraction site at the appointed time. The airfield support squad was not advised of any problems from the strike team and were themselves evacuated on schedule."

"I was promised a low-risk mission with a ninety percent probability of success," the President said, glaring at the Secretary of Defense.

The room fell silent, no one wishing to antagonize the man further.

Seated two seats down from the President, Vice President Sandecker found a touch of amusement to the inquisition. When called to an emergency meeting by the National Security Advisor, he was surprised to find no less than five generals seated around the Secretary of Defense in the conference room. It was not an omen of good things to come, he knew. Sandecker was no fan of the secretary, a man he found to be narrow-minded and trigger-happy. Yet he quickly put his personal feelings aside for the crisis at hand.

"Colonel, why don't you tell us exactly what you know," Sandecker said, deflecting the President's anger.

The colonel described the planned mission in detail and the intelligence that supported the rescue strike. "The befuddling aspect is that there are indications that the team was successful in freeing the captives. Radio intercepts from Canadian forces in Tuktoyaktuk report an assault on the holding complex and the subsequent escape of the *Polar Dawn*'s crew. We've detected no indications that they were recaptured."

"What if the Special Forces team was simply delayed?" Sandecker asked. "The nights are short up there right now. Perhaps they were forced into hiding somewhere for a period before making it back to the airfield."

The colonel shook his head. "We sent an aircraft back to the extraction site under darkness just hours ago. They touched down briefly, but no one was there, and additional radio calls went unanswered."

"They couldn't have just vanished," the President grumbled.

"We've analyzed satellite reconnaissance, radio traffic, and local contacts on the ground. They've all come up empty," stated Julie Moss, the President's National Security Advisor. "The only conclusion that can be made is that they were quietly recaptured and relocated to a new location. They might be back on the *Polar Dawn* or possibly flown out of the area."

"What has been the official Canadian response to our request for release of the ship and crew?" Sandecker asked.

"There has been no response," Moss said. "We've been curtly ignored through diplomatic channels, while the Prime Minister and Parliament continue to make outlandish claims of American imperialism that are straight out of a banana republic."

"They have not limited themselves to words," the Secretary of Defense interjected. "They have placed their military forces on alert status, in addition to their recent port closures."

"That's true," Moss echoed. "The Canadian Coast Guard has started turning away all American-flagged ships approaching Vancouver and Quebec, as well as Toronto-bound barge traffic. It's expected that their border crossings will be temporarily closed in a day or two."

"This is getting quite out of hand," the

President said.

"It is even worse. We've received word that our pending natural gas imports from Melville Sound have been suspended. We have reason to believe the gas has been diverted to the Chinese, although we don't know if this was directed by the government or the gas field operator."

The President slunk into his chair with a dazed look on his face. "That threatens our entire future," he said quietly.

"Sir," the Secretary of Defense declared, "with all due regard, the Canadian government has wrongfully blamed us for the loss of their Arctic ice lab and damage to one of their patrol craft. They have illegally captured a U.S. Coast Guard vessel in international waters and are treating the crew as prisoners of war. They have done the same to our Delta Forces team, or perhaps killed them and the ship's crew as well, for all we know. On top of that, they are threatening our entire nation with energy blackmail. Diplomacy has failed, sir. It is time for another option."

"We've hardly met the threshold for a military escalation," Sandecker said bitterly.

"You may be right, Jim, but those men's lives are at stake," the President said. "I want a formal demand presented to the Prime Minister for the release of the crew and rescue team within twenty-four hours. Do it privately, so that the media-happy PM can save face. We can negotiate for the ship later, but I want those men freed now. And I want a reversal on those natural gas shipments."

"What's our response if they don't comply?" Moss asked.

The Secretary of Defense piped up. "Mr. President, we've drawn up several options for a limited first-strike engagement."

"A 'limited engagement' . . . What is that supposed to mean?" the President asked.

The conference room door opened and a White House aide silently entered and handed a note to Sandecker.

"A limited engagement," the Secretary of Defense continued, "would be deployment of the minimum resources required to incapacitate a high percentage of Canada's air and naval forces through surgical strikes."

The President's face turned red. "I'm not talking about a full-blown war. Just something to get their attention."

The Secretary of Defense quickly backed down. "We have options for single-target missions as well," he said quietly.

"What do you think, Jim?" the President asked, turning to Sandecker.

A grim look spread across the Vice President's face as he finished reading the note and held it up before him.

"I've just been informed by Rudi Gunn at NUMA that their research vessel *Narwhal* has gone missing in the Northwest Passage, off

Victoria Island. The ship is presumed captured or sunk with all hands, including the Director of NUMA, Dirk Pitt."

The Secretary of Defense broke into a wolfish grin as he gazed across the table at Sandecker.

"It would seem," he said pointedly, "that we have suddenly found your threshold."

71

The United States has launched armed incursions into Canada on at least a half dozen occasions. The bloodiest invasion occurred during the Revolutionary War, when General Richard Montgomery marched north from Fort Ticonderoga and captured Montreal, then moved on Quebec City. He was joined by a secondary force that had entered Canada via Maine, led by Benedict Arnold. Attacking Quebec City on December 31, 1775, the Americans briefly captured the city before being beaten back in a fierce battle with the British. A shortage of supplies and reinforcements, as well as the loss of Montgomery during the fight, meant that the Americans had little choice but to break off the foray into Canada.

When hostilities heated up again during the War of 1812, the Americans launched repeated strikes into Canada to fight the British. Most ended in failure. The most notable success occurred in 1813, when Toronto (then

York) was sacked and its parliamentary buildings burned to the ground. The victory would prove to haunt the U.S. a year later when the British marched on Washington. Angered by the earlier destructive act, the British returned the favor by taking a torch to the public buildings of the American capital.

With colonial independence achieved in 1783, Canada and the United States quickly grew to be amicable neighbors and allies. Yet the seeds of distrust have never completely vanished. In the 1920s, the U.S. War Department developed strategic plans to invade Canada as part of a hypothetical war with the United Kingdom. "War Plan Red," as it was named, called for land invasions targeting Winnipeg and Quebec, along with a naval assault on Halifax. Not to be outdone, the Canadians developed "Defence Scheme No. 1," for a counterinvasion of the United States. Albany, Minneapolis, Seattle, and Great Falls, Montana, were targeted for surprise attacks, in hopes that the Canadians could buy time until British reinforcements arrived.

Time and technology had changed the world considerably since the 1920s. Great Britain no longer stood in Canada's defense, and America's military might made for a dominating power imbalance. Though the disappearance of the *Narwhal* angered the President, it hardly justified an invasion. At least not yet. It would take weeks to organize a ground offensive anyway, should things degrade that far, and he wanted a quick and forceful response in forty-eight hours.

The strike plan agreed to, barring the release of the captives, was simple yet pain-inducing. U.S. Navy warships would be sent in to blockade Vancouver in the west and the Saint Lawrence River in the east, effectively blocking Canada's foreign trade. Stealth bombers would strike first, targeting Canadian fighter air bases at Cold Lake, Alberta, and Bagotville, Quebec. Special Forces teams would also be on standby to secure Canada's major hydroelectric plants, in case of an attempted disruption in exported electric power. A later strike would be used to seize the Melville gas field.

There was little the Canadians could do in response, the Secretary of Defense and his generals had argued. Under threat of continued air strikes, they would have to release the captives and agree to open terms on the Northwest Passage. All were in agreement, though, that it would never come to that. The Canadians would be warned of the circumstances if they didn't comply with the twenty-four-hour deadline. They would have no choice but to acquiesce.

But there was one problem that the Pentagon hawks had failed to consider. The Canadian government had no idea what had become of the *Polar Dawn*'s crew.

72

Trapped in their sinking iron coffin, the *Polar Dawn*'s crew would have begged for another twenty-four hours. But their prospect for survival was down to minutes.

Murdock's prediction had so far held true. The barge's number 4 hold had steadily filled with water until spilling over into the number 3 compartment. As the stern sank lower under the weight, the water poured in at a faster rate. In the small forward storage compartment, the deck listed ominously beneath the men's feet as the sound of rushing water drew nearer.

A man appeared at the aft hatch, one of Roman's commandos, breathing heavily from scaling the hold's ladder.

"Captain," he gasped, waving a penlight around the bay until spotting his commander, "the water is now spilling into the number 2 hold."

"Thank you, Corporal," Roman replied. "Why don't you sit down and take a rest.

There's no need for further recon."

Roman sought out Murdock and pulled him aside. "When the barge starts to go under," he whispered, "will the hatch covers pop off the holds?"

Murdock shook his head, then gave a hesitant look.

"She'll surely go under before the number 1 hold is flooded. That means there will be an air pocket underneath, which will build in pressure as the barge sinks. There's probably a good chance it will blow the hatch cover, but we might be five hundred feet deep before that happens."

"It's still a chance," Roman said quietly.

"Then what?" Murdock replied. "A man won't last ten minutes in these waters." He shook his head with irritation, then said, "Fine. Go ahead and give the men some hope. I'll let you know when I think this tub is about to go down, and you can assemble the men on the ladder. At least they'll have something to hang on to for the ride to perdition."

At the entry hatch, Bojorquez had listened to the exchange, then resumed his hammering on the locked latch. By now, he knew it was a futile gesture. The tiny hammer was proving worthless against the hardened steel. Hours of pounding had gouged only a small notch in the lock spindle. He was many hours, if not days, away from wearing into the lock mechanism.

Between whacks, he looked over at his fellow captives. Cold, hungry, and downcast, they stood assembled, many staring at him with hopeful desperation. Surprisingly, there was little trace of panic in the air. Their emotions frozen like the cold steel of the barge, the captive men calmly accepted their pending fate.

73

The *Narwhal*'s tender was perilously over-loaded. Designed to hold twelve men, the boat easily accommodated the fourteen crewmen who had evacuated the ship. But the extra weight was just enough to alter her sailing characteristics in a rough sea. With choppy waves slapping at her sides, it was only a short time before a layer of icy water began sloshing around the footwells.

Stenseth had taken hold of the tiller after a laborious effort to start the frozen motor. With a pair of ten-gallon cans of gasoline, they had just enough fuel to reach King William Island. But Stenseth already had an uneasy feeling, realizing that they would have to march in the footsteps of Franklin's doomed crew if they were to reach safety at Gjoa Haven.

Leery of swamping the boat, the captain motored slowly through the whitecapped seas. Fog still hung heavy over the water, but he could detect a faint lightening of the billows as the brief Arctic night showed signs of passing. He refrained from turning directly east toward King William Island, holding to his word to make a brief search for Pitt and Giordino. With next to no visibility, he knew the odds of locating the submersible were long. To make matters worse, there was no GPS unit in the tender. Relying on a compass distorted by their nearness to the magnetic north pole, Stenseth dead reckoned their way back to the site of the shipwreck.

The helmsman estimated that they had collided with the icebreaker some six miles northwest of the wreck site. Guessing at the current and their own speed, Stenseth piloted the boat southeast for twenty minutes, then cut the motor. Dahlgren and the others shouted out Pitt's name through the fog, but the only sound they heard in reply was the slap of the waves against the tender's hull.

Stenseth restarted the motor and cruised to the southeast for ten minutes, then cut the motor again. Repeated shouts through the fog went unanswered. Stenseth motored on, repeating the process once more. When the last round of shouts fell empty, he addressed the crew.

"We can't afford to run out of fuel. Our best bet is to run east to King William Island and try and locate some help. Once the weather clears, the submersible can be found easily. And I can tell you that Pitt and Giordino are probably a lot more comfortable in that sub than we are."

The crew nodded in agreement. Respect ran high for Pitt and Giordino, but their own situation was far from harmless. Getting under way once more, they ran due east until the outboard motor sputtered to a halt, having sucked dry the first can of gas. Stenseth switched fuel lines to the second can and was about to restart the motor when the helmsman suddenly cried out.

"Wait!"

Stenseth turned to the man seated nearby. "I think I heard something," he said to the captain, this time in a whisper.

The entire boat fell deathly quiet, each man afraid to breathe, as all ears were trained to the night air. Several seconds passed before they heard it as one. A faint tinging sound in the distance, almost like the chime of a bell.

"That's Pitt and Giordino," Dahlgren shouted. "Has to be. They're tapping out an SOS on the *Bloodhound*'s hull."

Stenseth looked at him with skepticism. Dahlgren had to be wrong. They had moved too far from the submersible's last-known position. But what else could be signaling through the bleak Arctic night?

Stenseth engaged the outboard motor and sailed the tender in an ever-widening series of circles, cutting the throttle at periodic intervals to try to detect which direction the sound was coming from. He finally noted a rising pitch emanating from the east and turned in that direction. The captain motored slowly but anxiously, fearful that the tapping might cease before he had determined a true bearing. The fog blew in thick wisps while the morning dawn still struggled to appear. As close as they might be, he knew it would be all too easy to lose the submersible if it fell silent.

Fortunately, the clanging went on. The rapping only grew louder, audible even over the rumble of the outboard. Changing course with slight shifts to the tiller, Stenseth zeroed in on the sound until it echoed in his ears. Cruising blindly through a dark bank of fog, he suddenly cut the throttle as a huge black shape rose up in front of them.

The barge seemed to have lost its mammoth scale since Stenseth had last seen it, being towed by the icebreaker. Then he saw why. The barge was sinking by the stern, with nearly half of its length already submerged. The bow rose at a rakish angle, reminiscent of the last minutes of the *Narwhal*. Having just witnessed his own ship's demise, he knew the barge was down to its last minutes, if not seconds.

Stenseth and the crew reacted with disappointment at their discovery. Their hopes had been pinned on finding Pitt and Giordino. But their disillusionment quickly turned to horror when they realized that the barge was about to go under.

And that the tapping sound came from someone locked aboard.

74

Dahlgren played a flashlight beam across the exposed deck of the barge, searching for an entry point, but found only fixed bulkheads ahead of the forward hold.

"Take us around to the starboard side, Captain," he requested.

Stenseth motored the tender around the towering bow of the barge, slowing as he approached the forward hold. The rhythmic metallic rapping suddenly became noticeably louder.

"There," Dahlgren exclaimed, finding the side-compartment hatch with his light. A chain was visible, wrapped around the hatch door lever and secured to a rail stanchion.

Without a word, Stenseth ran the tender alongside the barge until it bumped into a metal railing that angled out of the water. Dahlgren was already on his feet and leaped onto the barge's deck, landing aside the partially flooded number 3 hold hatch cover.

"Be quick, Jack," Stenseth yelled. "She's not

long above water."

He immediately backed the tender away from the barge, not wanting to get caught in its suction should it suddenly plunge to the bottom.

Dahlgren had already sprinted across the angled deck and up a short flight of steps to the locked storage compartment. Banging a gloved hand on the hatch, he shouted, "Anybody home?"

The startled voice of Sergeant Bojorquez replied instantly.

"Yes. Can you let us out?"

"Will do," Dahlgren replied.

He quickly studied the securing length of chain, which had been crudely knotted around both the hatch lever and the deck stanchion. There had been little slack to begin with, but the twisting girders of the sinking ship had pulled the chain drum tight. Checking each end under the beam of his flashlight, he quickly realized that the stanchion knot was more accessible, and he focused his efforts there.

Yanking his gloves off, he grabbed hold of the knot's outer links and pulled with all his might. The frozen steel links dug into his flesh but refused to budge. Gathering his breath, he tugged again, putting the full power of his legs into the effort while nearly ripping his fingers from their sockets. But the chain wouldn't move.

The deck beneath his feet took a sudden lurch, and he felt the ship twist slightly from the uneven pull of the rapidly flooding holds. Releasing his mangled and frozen fingers from the links, he looked at the chain and tried another tack. Leaning over the landing in order to attack from a right angle, he began kicking at the knot with his boots. Inside the storage compartment, he could hear panicked shouts from several voices urging him to hurry. From the water nearby, a few of the *Narwhal*'s crew yelled over, echoing the sentiment. As if to add its own pressure, the barge let out a deep metallic groan from somewhere far beneath the surface.

With his heart pounding, Dahlgren kicked at the chain with his toe. Then he stomped with his heel. He kicked harder and harder, with a growing sense of anger. Furiously he kicked, as if his own life depended on it. He kept on kicking until a single link of chain finally slipped over the tightly wound coil.

It created just enough slack to allow the next link to slip through with a subsequent kick, and then one more. Dahlgren dropped to his knees, jerking the free end of the chain through the loosened knot with his numb fingers. He quickly uncoiled the chain from the stanchion, allowing the hatch lever to move free. Rising to his feet, he yanked up on the lever, then pulled the hatch open.

Dahlgren didn't know what to expect and

fumbled with his flashlight as a number of shapes moved toward the hatch. Turning the light inside, he was shocked to find forty-six gaunt, frozen men staring back at him like a savior. Bojorquez was closest to the hatch, still clutching his small hammer.

"I don't know who you are, but I'm sure glad to see you," the sergeant said with a toothy smile.

"Jack Dahlgren, of the NUMA research ship *Narwhal*. Why don't you boys come on out of there?"

The captives rushed through the hatchway, staggering out onto the listing deck. Dahlgren was surprised to see several of the men dressed in military garb, small U.S. flags on their shoulders. Roman and Murdock were the last to exit and approached Dahlgren with a relieved look on their faces.

"I'm Murdock of the *Polar Dawn*. This is Captain Roman, who tried to rescue us in Kugluktuk. Is your vessel standing by?"

Dahlgren's astonishment at the realization he had found the captured Americans was tempered by the news he had to bear.

"Our ship was rammed and sunk by your tow vessel," he said quietly.

"Then how did you get here?" Roman asked.

Dahlgren pointed to the tender just visible a few yards off the sinking barge.

"We barely escaped ourselves. Heard your

rapping on the hatch and thought it was a submersible of ours."

He looked around at the beaten men standing around him, quietly trying to fathom their ordeal. Their escape from death was temporary, and now he felt like their executioner. Turning to Roman and Murdock, he spoke a grim apology.

"I'm sorry to have to tell you, but we don't have room to take on a single man."

75

Stenseth watched the waves lap over the barge's number 2 hold, leaving just the number 1 hold and bow section still above water. Why the barge hadn't yet headed for the bottom, he couldn't say, but he knew her time was short.

He turned his gaze to the haggard men lining the rail with looks of pleading desperation in their eyes. Like Dahlgren, he was shocked to count so many men step out of the storage hold. The blatant attempt at mass murder by the crew of the icebreaker astounded him. What sort of animal was commanding the tow ship?

His fears turned toward the safety of his own men. When the barge went under, he knew it would turn into an ugly free-for-all as the castaway men tried to climb aboard the tender. He couldn't risk swamping the already overloaded boat and sending his own men to their grave. He kept the tender at a safe distance from the barge, wondering how he could get Dahlgren off without the rest of the men trying to climb aboard with him.

He spotted Dahlgren talking to two men, one of whom pointed toward the flooded stern of the barge. Dahlgren then stepped to the rail and shouted for Stenseth to approach. The captain eased the tender up the barge just beneath Dahlgren, keeping a wary eye on the other men. But none of them rushed the boat as Dahlgren climbed aboard.

"Captain, please head to the stern of the barge, about two hundred feet back. Quickly," Dahlgren urged.

Stenseth turned the tender around and cruised past its sinking hulk toward the hidden stern. He didn't notice Dahlgren pull off his boots and strip down to his underwear before pulling his parka back on.

"They had two Zodiacs stowed aft," he shouted by way of explanation.

Little good they would do now, Stenseth thought. They've either drifted off or are tied to the deck forty feet underwater. He noticed Dahlgren standing in the bow pointing his flashlight toward something bobbing in the water.

"Over there," he urged.

Stenseth guided the tender toward a number of dark objects floating on the surface. They were two pairs of conical-shaped protrusions that bobbed in unison several feet apart. Drawing closer, Stenseth recognized them as the tapered pontoon ends of a pair of Zodiac boats. The two inflatable boats were standing on end under the water, their bows affixed by a common line to the barge below.

"Anybody have a knife?" Dahlgren asked.

"Jack, you can't go in the water," Stenseth exhorted, realizing that Dahlgren had stripped off his clothes. "You'll die of exposure."

"I ain't planning a long bath," he grinned in reply.

The chief engineer had a folding knife and pulled it out of his pocket and handed it to Dahlgren.

"A little closer, please, Captain," Dahlgren asked, slipping out of his parka.

Stenseth inched the tender to within a few feet of the Zodiacs, then cut the throttle. Dahlgren stood in the bow, flipped open the knife, then without hesitation took a deep breath and dove over the side.

An expert diver, Dahlgren had dived in cold seas all over the world, but nothing had prepared him for the shock of immersion into twenty-eight-degree water. A thousand nerve endings instantly convulsed in pain. His muscles tensed and an involuntary gasp of air burst from his lungs. His entire body froze rigid from the shock, ignoring the commands from his brain to move. A panic sensation then took hold, urging him to immediately head for the surface. Dahlgren had to fight the instinct while forcing his dead limbs to move. Slowly he overcame the shock, mentally forcing his body to swim.

He had no flashlight, but he didn't need one in the black water. Brushing a hand against one of the Zodiac's hulls gave him all the guidance he needed. Kicking forcefully, he descended several feet along the hull before feeling it angle inward toward the prow. Using his fingers to see, he reached beyond the bow until grazing the threads of the taut bow line. Grasping it with his free hand, he pulled and kicked his way down the line, searching for the mooring point to both Zodiacs.

The exposure to the frigid water quickly began to slow down his motor skills and he had to will himself to keep descending. Twenty feet below the Zodiac, he reached the barge, his hand sliding against a large cleat that was securing the lines to both boats. He immediately attacked the first line with the knife, sawing furiously to break it. The blade was not sharp, however, and it took him several seconds before he cut the line free and it jerked toward the surface. Reaching for the second line, his lungs began to ache from holding his breath while the rest of his body turned numb. His body signaled him to let go of the line and kick to the surface, but his inner determination refused to listen. Shoving the knife forward until it met the line, he sawed the blade back and forth with all his remaining energy.

The line broke with a twang that was audible underwater. Mimicking the other inflatable, the second Zodiac shot to the surface like a rocket, arching completely out of the water before splashing down onto its hull. Dahlgren missed most of the ride, being jerked only a foot or two toward the surface before losing his grip on the line. The momentum propelled his ascent, though, and he broke the surface gasping for air as he flailed to stay afloat with his frozen limbs.

The tender was on him instantly as three sets of arms reached over and plucked him from the water. He was briskly rubbed dry with an old blanket, then dressed in multiple layers of shirts and long underwear contributed by his fellow crew members. Lastly wedged into his parka and boots, he stared wide-eyed at Stenseth while shivering incessantly.

"That's one cold pond," he muttered. "Don't care to try that again."

Stenseth wasted no time, whipping the tender alongside the Zodiacs until their bow lines could be grabbed, then he gunned the motor. With the Zodiacs bounding in tow, the tender shot across the open expanse of water toward the rapidly diminishing bow structure. The water level had crept partway across the number 1 hold hatch cover, yet the big vessel still refused to let go.

The captives were huddled forward of the hold, certain that the tender had left them to die. When the outboard motor suddenly grew louder, they peered into the darkness with anxious hope. Seconds later, the tender appeared out of the gloom with the two empty Zodiacs in tow. A few of the men began to cheer, and then more joined in, until the barge erupted in an emotionally charged howl of gratitude.

Stenseth drove the tender right up the face of the number 1 hold, skidding to a halt as the two Zodiacs rushed alongside. As the haggard men quickly climbed in, Murdock stepped over to the tender.

"God bless you," he said, addressing the entire crew.

"You can thank that frozen Texan up front as soon as he stops shivering," Stenseth said. "In the meantime, I suggest we both get away from this behemoth before she sucks us all under."

Murdock nodded and stepped over to one of the Zodiacs. The inflatable boats were filled in no time and quickly pushed away from the barge. With flooded motors and no paddles, they were at the mercy of the tender for propulsion. One of the *Narwhal*'s crew tossed a towline to one of the Zodiacs while the other inflatable tied on in tandem.

The three boats drifted off the sinking barge before Stenseth took up the slack and engaged the outboard motor. There was no lingering or emotional farewell to the dying barge, which had represented only misery to its men held captive. The three small boats plowed east, quickly leaving the stricken vessel behind in the fog. With nary a gurgle, the black leviathan, its holds nearly filled to the top, silently slipped under the waves a moment later.

76

"It's as black up here as the bottom is at a thousand feet."

There was little exaggeration in Giordino's assessment of the scene out of the submersible's view port. Just moments before, the *Bloodhound* had punched through the surface amid a boil of foam and bubbles. The two occupants still had hopes of finding the lights of the *Narwhal* twinkling nearby but instead found a cold, dark sea enshrouded in a heavy mist.

"Better try the radio again before we're completely out of juice," Pitt said.

The submersible's battery reserves were nearly extinguished, and Pitt wanted to conserve the remaining power for the radio. He reached down and pulled a lever that sealed the ballast tanks closed, then shut down the interior air-filtration system, which was barely functioning on low voltage. They would have to crack the top hatch for fresh but bitterly cold air.

They called on the surface, but their radio calls continued to go unanswered. Their faint signals were picked up only by the *Otok* and blithely ignored at the order of Zak. The *Narwhal,* they were now convinced, had vanished from the scene.

"Still, not a word," Giordino said dejectedly. Contemplating the radio silence, he asked, "How friendly would your pal on the icebreaker be if he had a run-in with the *Narwhal?*"

"Not very," Pitt replied. "He has a penchant for blowing things up with little regard for the consequences. He's after the ruthenium at all costs. If he's aboard the icebreaker, then he'll be after us as well."

"My money says that Stenseth and Dahlgren will be a handful."

It was little consolation to Pitt. He was the one who had brought the ship here and it was he who had placed the crew in danger. Not knowing what had happened to the ship, he assumed the worst and blamed himself. Giordino sensed the guilt in Pitt's eyes and tried to change his focus.

"Are we dead on propulsion?" he asked, already knowing the answer.

"Yes," Pitt replied. "We're at the mercy of the wind and current now."

Giordino gazed out the view port. "Wonder where the next stop will be?"

"With any luck, we'll get pushed to one of

the Royal Geographical Society Islands. But if the current throws us around them, then we could be adrift for a while."

"If I had known we were going to take a cruise, I would have brought a good book . . . and my long underwear."

Both men wore only light sweaters, not anticipating the need for anything warmer. With the submersible's electronic equipment shut down, the interior quickly turned chilly.

"I'd settle for a roast beef sandwich and a tequila myself," Pitt said.

"Don't even start with the food," Giordino lamented. He leaned back in his chair and crossed his arms, trying to maintain warmth. "You know," he said, "there are days when that cushy leather chair back in the headquarters office doesn't sound so bad."

Pitt looked at him with a raised brow. "Had your fill of days in the field?"

Giordino grunted, then shook his head. "No. I know the reality is, the second I set foot in that office, I want back on the water. What about you?"

Pitt had contemplated the question before. He'd paid a heavy price, both physically and mentally, for his adventurous scrapes over the years. But he knew he'd never have it any other way.

"Life's a quest, but I've always made the quest my life." He turned to Giordino and grinned. "I guess they'll have to pry us both off the controls."

"It's in our blood, I'm afraid."

Helpless to control their fate, Pitt sat back in his chair and closed his eyes. Thoughts of the *Narwhal* and her crew scrolled through his mind, followed by visions of Loren back in Washington. But mostly his mind kept returning to a lone portrait of a broad-shouldered man with a menacing face. It was the image of Clay Zak.

77

The submersible pitched and rolled through the choppy seas while driven south at nearly three knots. The Arctic dawn gradually emerged, lightening the thick gray fog hanging low over the water. With little to do but monitor the radio, the two men tried to rest, but the plunging interior temperature soon rendered it too uncomfortable for sleep.

Pitt was adjusting the overhead hatch when a scraping sound filled the interior and the submersible jarred to a halt.

"Land ho," Giordino mumbled, popping open his sleepy eyes.

"Almost," Pitt replied, peering out the view port. A light breeze blew a small opening in the fog, revealing a white plateau of ice in front of them. The unbroken expanse disappeared into a billow of mist a hundred feet away.

"A good bet there is land on the opposite side of this ice field," Pitt speculated.

"And that's where we'll find a hot-coffee stand?" Giordino asked, rubbing his hands together to keep warm.

"Yes . . . roughly two thousand miles south of here." He looked at Giordino. "We have two options. Stay here in the cozy confines of our titanium turret or take a crack at finding relief. The Inuit still hunt in the region, so there could be a settlement nearby. If the weather clears, there's always a sporting chance of flagging down a passing ship." He looked down at his clothes. "Unfortunately, we're not exactly dressed for a cross-country excursion."

Giordino stretched his arms and yawned. "Personally, I'm tired of sitting in this tin can. Let's go stretch our legs and see what's in the neighborhood."

"Agreed," Pitt nodded.

Giordino made one last attempt to contact the *Narwhal,* then shut down the radio equipment. The two men climbed out of the top hatch and were promptly greeted by an eight-degree chill. The bow had wedged tightly into the thick sea ice, and they were easily able to step off the submersible and onto the frozen surface. A stiffening breeze began to scatter the low-hanging mist. Nothing but ice lay in front of them, so they started trudging across the pack, the dry snow crunching under their feet.

The sea ice was mostly flat, sprinkled by

small hummocks that rose in tiny uplifts at scattered points. They had hiked only a short distance when Giordino noticed something off to his left. It appeared to be a small snow cave, crudely carved into a ridge of high ice.

"It looks man-made," Giordino said. "Maybe somebody left us a pair of earmuffs inside."

Giordino walked over to the cave's entrance, then hunched down on one knee and stuck his head in. Pitt approached, then stopped to study an imprint in the snow nearby. He stiffened when he recognized the shape.

"Al," he whispered in a cautionary tone.

Giordino had already hesitated. A few feet up the darkened passageway, he saw the cave expanded into a large den. Inside the darkened interior, he barely distinguished a large tuft of white fur rising and falling with heavy breaths. The polar bear was past hibernating but revisiting its winter haunt for a spring nap. Known for its unpredictability, a hungry polar bear could easily make a meal out of both men.

Immediately recognizing the danger, Giordino silently backed out of the cave. Mouthing the word "bear" to Pitt, they hurriedly moved away from the cave, stepping lightly on the ice. When they were well out of earshot, Giordino slowed his gait while the color returned to his pale face.

"I only hope the seals are slow and plentiful

in these parts," he said, shaking his head at the discovery.

"Yes, I'd hate to see you end up as a throw rug inside that bear's den," Pitt replied, suppressing a laugh.

The danger was all too real, they knew, and they kept a sharp lookout behind them as they moved farther from the sea.

As the bear cave vanished in the fog behind them, a dark rocky ribbon of land appeared through the mist ahead. Patches of brown and gray rose off the near horizon in a wavy pattern of ridges and ravines. They had come aground on the northern coast of the Royal Geographical Society Islands, as Pitt had predicted, landing on West Island. Heavy ice, built up from the winter floes that churned down Victoria Strait, clogged the shoreline in a wide band that stretched a half mile wide in some areas. Approached from the frozen sea, the barren island landscape nearly shrieked of cold desolation.

The two men were nearly to the shoreline when Pitt stopped in his tracks. Giordino turned and saw the look on Pitt's face, then cocked an ear to the wind. A faint crackling sound echoed in the distance, accompanied by a dull rumble. The noise continued unabated, growing louder as the source drew near.

"Definitely a ship," Giordino muttered.

"An icebreaker," Pitt said.

"*The* icebreaker?"

Giordino's question was answered a few minutes later when the hulking prow of the *Otok* emerged from the mist a hundred yards offshore. Its high bow cut through the foot-thick ice like it was pudding, spraying chunks of frozen detritus in all directions. As if detecting Pitt and Giordino's presence, the icebreaker's rumbling engines slowly quieted to a low idle, and the vessel ground to a halt against the buckling ice.

Pitt stared at the vessel, a sick feeling gripping his frozen insides. He had immediately observed that the ship's bow was mashed blunt, the obvious result of a hard collision. It was a recent blow, as evidenced by several of the steel plates being stripped of paint by the impact and yet to show any signs of oxidation. More telling were the flecks of turquoise paint, which overlaid portions of the scraped and mangled bow.

"She rammed the *Narwhal*," Pitt stated without speculation.

Giordino nodded, having come to the same conclusion. The sight numbed both men, since they knew that their worst fears had been realized. The *Narwhal* was surely at the bottom of Victoria Strait, along with her crew. Then Giordino noticed something nearly as disturbing.

"The *Narwhal* isn't the only thing that she has rammed," he said. "Look at her hull plates around the hawsehole."

Pitt studied the hull, noticing a light gouge mark incurred during the collision. The icebreaker's red hull paint had been scraped away, revealing a gray undercoating. A rectangular patch of white surfaced at the tailing edge of the gouge.

"A gray warship in a former life?" he ventured.

"How about FFG-54, to be exact. A Navy frigate of ours known as the *Ford*. We passed her in the Beaufort Sea a few weeks back. The survivors of the Canadian ice camp offered a similar description. That sure as beans looks like a number 5 painted underneath in white."

"A quick repaint in U.S. Navy gray and, next thing you know, you have an international incident."

"Zapping through the ice camp in the middle of a blizzard with the Stars and Stripes flying, it's not hard to see how the ice lab scientists could have been fooled. The question is, why go to the trouble?"

"Between the ruthenium and the oil and gas resources around here, I'd say Mitchell Goyette wants to play Arctic ice baron," Pitt said. "It's a lot easier game for him to win if the U.S. presence is cleared from the region."

"Which, at the moment, is pretty much down to you and me."

As he spoke, three men bundled in black parkas appeared on the icebreaker's deck and approached the rail. Without hesitation, they each raised a Steyr light machine gun, trained their sights on Pitt and Giordino, and opened fire.

78

Miles to the northeast, a loud sputtering and coughing sound resonated over the waves. Gasping for fuel, the tender's outboard motor wheezed through its last few drops of gasoline, then gurgled to a stop. The men aboard remained silent as they looked at one another nervously. Finally, the *Narwhal*'s helmsman raised an empty ten-gallon gas can into the air.

"She's bone-dry, sir," he said to Stenseth.

The *Narwhal*'s captain knew it was coming. They would have made it to shore had they sailed solo. But the two fully laden Zodiacs tailing behind had acted like a sea anchor, sapping their forward progress. Fighting choppy seas and a strong southerly current had not helped matters. But there was never a thought of abandoning the men in the other boats.

"Break out the oars, a man to a side," Stenseth ordered. "Let's try and hold our heading."

Leaning over toward the helmsman, who

was an expert navigator, he quietly asked, "How far to King William Island, would you estimate?"

The helmsman's face twisted.

"Difficult to gauge our progress under these conditions," he replied in a low tone. "It seems to me that we ought to be within five miles or so of the island." He shrugged his shoulders slightly, indicating his uncertainty.

"My thoughts as well," Stenseth replied, "though I hope we're a far sight closer."

The prospect of not reaching land began to gnaw at his fears. The seas had not turned, but he was certain that the breeze had stiffened slightly. Decades at sea had honed his senses to the weather. He could feel in his bones that the waters were going to roughen a bit more. In their precarious state of navigation, it would probably be enough to do them all in.

He gazed back at the black inflatable boats trailing behind in the mist. Under the faintly brightening dawn, he could begin to make out the faces of the rescued men. A number of them were in poor shape, he could tell, suffering the ill effects of prolonged exposure. But as a group, they were a model of quiet bravery, not a one lamenting their condition.

Murdock caught Stenseth's gaze and shouted out to him.

"Sir, can you tell us where we are?"

"Victoria Strait. Just west of King William

Island. Wish I could say that a passing cruise liner is on its way, but I have to tell you that we're on our own."

"We're grateful for the rescue and for keeping us afloat. Do you have an extra set of oars?"

"No, I'm afraid you are still at our mercy for propulsion. We should reach landfall before long," he called out in a falsely optimistic tone.

The *Narwhal*'s crew took turns pulling at the oars, with even Stenseth working a shift. It was a laborious effort to make headway, made frustrating by the inability to gauge their progress in the misty gloom. Stenseth occasionally strained his ears to detect the sound of waves rolling against a shoreline, but all he could hear was the sound of swells slapping against the three boats.

True to his forecast, the seas began to gradually rise with the stiffening breeze. More and more waves started splashing over the sides of the tender, and several men were soon assigned bailing detail to stem the flooding. Stenseth noted that the Zodiacs were suffering the same fate, taking on water repeatedly over the stern. The situation was rapidly becoming dire, and there was still no indication that they were anywhere near land.

It was when a change of oarsmen took place that a crewman seated in the bow suddenly yelled out.

"Sir, there's something in the water."

Stenseth and the others immediately gazed forward, spotting a dark object at the edge of the fog. Whatever it was, Stenseth thought, he knew it wasn't land.

"It's a whale," somebody shouted.

"No," Stenseth muttered quietly, noting that the object sitting low in the water was colored black and unnaturally smooth. He looked on suspiciously, observing that it didn't move or make a sound.

Then a loud voice, electronically amplified to thundering proportions, burst through the fog. Every man jumped, losing a beat of the heart at the sudden divulgence. Yet the words came forth with a puzzling sentiment, incongruous with the harsh surrounding environment.

"Ahoy," called the invisible voice. "This is the USS *Santa Fe*. There is a hot toddy and a warm bunk awaiting any among you that can whistle 'Dixie.'"

79

Clay Zak could not believe his eyes.

After disposing of the NUMA ship, he'd turned the icebreaker back toward the Royal Geographical Society Islands, then retired to his cabin. He'd tried to sleep but only rested fitfully, his mind too focused on locating the ruthenium. Returning to the bridge after just a few hours, he ordered the ship to West Island. The vessel plowed through the bordering sea ice, advancing to his revised location of the ruthenium mine.

The geologists were roused from their bunks as the ship slowly ground to a halt. A minute later, the helmsman noted a bright object at the edge of the sea ice.

"It's the submersible from the research ship," he said.

Zak jumped to the bridge window and stared in disbelief. Sure enough, the bright yellow submersible was wedged in the ice off to their starboard, just barely visible through the gray fog.

"How can they know?" he cursed, not realizing the submersible had drifted to the spot of its own accord. His heart began pounding fast in anger. He alone possessed the mining co-op's map to the Inuit ruthenium. He had just destroyed the probing NUMA ship and moved directly to the site. Yet he still found Pitt there ahead of him.

The icebreaker's captain, asleep in his bunk, detected the halting ship and staggered to the bridge with droopy eyes.

"I told you to stay out of the sea ice with that damaged bow," he grumbled. Receiving a cold glare in return, he asked, "Are you ready to deploy the geology team?"

Zak ignored him as the executive officer pointed out the port-side window.

"Sir, there's two men on the ice," he reported.

Zak studied the two figures, then noticeably relaxed.

"Forget the geologists," he said with an upturned grin. "Have my security team report to me. Now."

It was not the first time that Pitt and Giordino had been shot at, and they reacted at the sight of the first muzzle flash. Scattering as the first bullets plinked the ice just inches away, they both bolted toward the island at a sprint. The uneven surface made it difficult to run but forced them to move in a natural zigzag pattern, casting a more difficult target. Wisely splitting up, they angled away from each other, forcing the shooters to choose between them.

The trio of guns echoed a rapid *tat-tat-tat-tat* as chunks of ice danced off the ground around their feet. But Pitt and Giordino had gotten a good jump, and the accuracy of the marksmen waned as the two of them distanced themselves from the ship. Both men ran hard toward a thin bank of fog hanging over the beach. The gray mist eventually enveloped them like a cloak as they reached the shoreline, rendering them invisible to the gunmen on the ship.

Panting for air, the two men approached each other along an ice-covered stretch of beach.

"Just what we needed, another warm welcome to this frozen outpost," Giordino said, huge clouds of vapor surging from his mouth.

"Look on the bright side," Pitt gasped. "There were a couple of seconds there when I forgot how cold it is."

Without hats, gloves, and parkas, both men were certifiably frozen. The abrupt sprint had gotten their blood surging, but their faces and ears tingled in pain while their fingers had nearly turned numb. The physiological effort to keep warm was already sapping their energy reserves, and the short run left them both feeling weakened.

"Something tells me our warmly dressed new pals will be along shortly," Giordino said. "Have a preference to which way we run?"

Pitt looked up and down the coastline, his visibility limited by the slowly dissipating fog. A steep ridge appeared in front of them, which appeared to rise higher to their left. The ridge eased lower to their right, rolling into another, somewhat rounder hill.

"We need to get off the ice so we're not leaving tracks to follow. I'd feel better taking the high ground as well. Looks like our best bet to move inland will be down the coast to our right."

The two men took off at a jog as a brief gust of frozen ice particles blasted their faces. A rising wind would become their enemy now, scattering the fog that provided concealment. They hugged the face of the low cliff, approaching a steep, ice-filled ravine that bisected the ridge. Deeming it impassable, they ran on, searching for the next cut that would lead them inland. They advanced a half mile down the beach when another extended gust swirled down the shoreline.

The wind scorched their exposed skin while their lungs labored to absorb the frozen air. Just breathing became an exercise in agony, but neither man slowed his pace. Then the metallic rapping of machine-gun fire echoed again, the bullets ripping a seam across the cliff a few yards behind them.

Glancing over his shoulder, Pitt saw that the gusting wind had cleared an opening in the fog behind them. Two men were visible in the distance, advancing in their direction. Zak had split his security team into three groups, angling them ashore in different directions. The duo sent to the west had caught a break with the wind, exposing the two men on the run.

Up the coast, Pitt saw another bank of fog billowing toward them. If they could stay clear of gunfire for another minute, the moving mist would conceal them again.

"Those guys are starting to annoy me," Giordino gasped as both men stepped up their pace.

"Hopefully, that polar bear is thinking the same thing," Pitt replied.

Another burst of fire ripped into the ice well short of them. The gunmen conceded accuracy by shooting on the run but were not too far away to rip off a lucky shot. Sprinting toward the fog, Pitt studied the ridge to his left. The cliff dropped down into another gully just ahead, this one broader than the earlier ravine. It was filled with rock and ice, but it appeared that they could climb their way up it.

"Let's try to leg up this next ravine when the fog blows over," he gasped.

Giordino nodded, struggling toward the

wall of fog, which was still fifty yards away. Another burst of fire chattered into the ice, this time striking just behind their heels. The gunmen had halted their pursuit to take a clearly aimed shot.

"I don't think we're going to make it," Giordino muttered.

They were almost to the gully, but the fog still beckoned in the distance. A few yards ahead, Pitt noticed a large vertical slab of ice-covered rock jutting from the ravine. Gasping for breath, he simply pointed to it.

The hillside just above their heads suddenly erupted in debris as the gunmen found their range. Both men instinctively ducked, then stretched for the rock slab, diving behind it as a seam of bullets ripped up the ground just inches away. Sprawled on the ground, they struggled to catch their breath in the icy air, their bodies aching and nearly spent. The gunfire ceased as they lay concealed from their pursuers, while the wispy edge of the fogbank finally arrived to enshroud their location.

"I think we should climb here," Pitt said, struggling to his feet. A dark mass of icy rock filled the ravine above them, but a negotiable gulch rose to the side.

Giordino nodded, then stood up and stepped toward the slope. He started to climb, then noticed that Pitt wasn't moving. He turned to find his companion staring up at the rock slab and rubbing a hand across its surface.

"Maybe not the best time to be hanging around admiring the rocks," he admonished.

Pitt traced the slab toward the ice-covered hillside, then looked up. "It's not a rock," he said quietly. "It's a rudder."

Giordino looked at Pitt like he was crazy, then followed his gaze up the ravine. Overhead was a dark mass of rock buried beneath a thin layer of ice. Surveying the hillside, Giordino suddenly felt his jaw drop. It wasn't a mound of rock at all, he realized with astonishment.

Above them, embedded in the ice, the men found themselves staring at the wooden black hull of a nineteenth-century sailing ship.

80

The *Erebus* stood like a forgotten relic of a bygone era. Caught in an ice floe that had separated her from her damaged sister ship, the *Erebus* had been pushed onto the shore by a mammoth caravan of winter sea ice that pressed down Victoria Strait some one hundred and sixty years earlier. A shipwreck that refused to die at sea, she had been thrust into the ravine and gradually entombed in ice.

The ice had encased the hull and cemented the port side of the ship to the steep hillside. The ship's three masts still stood upright, tilted at an irregular angle and sheathed in a layer of ice that melded into the adjacent ridge. The starboard sides and deck were remarkably free of ice, however, as Pitt and Giordino found when they hiked up the gulch and climbed over the side rail. The men gazed in awe, incredulous that they were pacing the deck of Franklin's flagship.

"Melt all the ice and she looks like she could sail back to England," Giordino remarked.

"If she's carrying any ruthenium, then I might consider a side trip up the Potomac first," Pitt replied.

"I'd settle for a couple of blankets and a shot of rum."

The men were shivering nonstop with cold, their bodies fighting to keep their internal temperature from dropping. Each felt a touch of lethargy, and Pitt knew they would have to find warmth soon. He stepped over to a ladderway aft of the main hatch and pulled off a crumbling canvas cover.

"Got a light?" he asked Giordino while peering down into the darkened interior.

Giordino pulled out a Zippo lighter and tossed it to him. "I'll need that back if there should be any Cuban cigars aboard."

Pitt led the way down the steeply inclined steps, snapping on the lighter as he reached the lower deck. He spotted a pair of candle lanterns mounted to the bulkhead and ignited their blackened wicks. The ancient candles still burned strong, casting a flickering orange glow over the wood-paneled corridor. Giordino found a whale oil lamp hanging on a nail nearby, which provided them a portable light.

Stepping down the passageway, the lamp illuminated a bizarre scene of murder and mayhem aboard the ship. Unlike the *Terror,* with its spartan appearance, the *Erebus* was a mess. Crates, garbage, and debris littered the corridor. Tin cups were scattered everywhere, while the distinct smell of rum hung in the air, along with a number of other dank odors. And then there were the bodies.

Moving forward to take a quick peek in the crew's quarters, Pitt and Giordino were met by a macabre pair of shirtless frozen men sprawled on the deck. One had the side of his skull crushed, a bloodied brick lying nearby. The other had a large kitchen knife protruding from his rib cage. Frozen solid and in an eerie state of preservation, Pitt could even tell what color eyes the men had. Inside the crew's quarters, they found an additional array of bodies in a similar state. Pitt couldn't help noticing that the dead men had a tormented look about them, as if they had perished from something more terrible than just the elements.

Pitt and Giordino spent little time examining the gruesome scene, backtracking to the ladder well and descending to the orlop deck. They took a break from searching for ruthenium when they reached the Slop Room. A storeroom for the crew's outerwear, the bay contained racks of boots, jackets, caps, and thick socks. Finding a pair of heavy wool officer's coats that nearly fit their frames, the two men bundled into the clothes, adding watch caps and mittens. At last feeling a slight semblance of warmth, they quickly resumed their search of the deck.

Like the deck above, the orlop deck was a scattered mess. Empty casks and food containers were stacked in huge piles, attesting to the large amount of food stores once housed on the ship. They entered the unlocked Spirit Room, which housed the ship's supply of alcohol and weapons. Though a rack of muskets lay untouched, the rest of the bay was a mess, with splintered rum and brandy casks scattered on the deck and tin cups everywhere. They moved aft to find large bins that housed a portion of the steam engine's coal. The bins were empty, but Pitt noticed some silvery dust and nuggets lying at the base of one bin. He picked up one of the nuggets, noting it was far too heavy for coal. Giordino observed a rolled-up burlap sack nearby, kicking it over to read BUSHVELD, SOUTH AFRICA printed on the side.

"They had it here, but it was evidently all traded to the Inuit," Pitt mused, tossing the nugget back into the bin.

"Then it's down to finding the ship's log to reveal the source," Giordino said.

A faint shout was suddenly heard outside the ship.

"Sounds like our friends are drawing near," Giordino said. "We better get moving." He took a step toward the ladderway but noted Pitt didn't follow. He could see the wheels churning in Pitt's mind.

"You think it's worth staying aboard?"

Giordino asked.

"It is if we can give them the warm welcome that I think we can," Pitt replied intently.

Waving the oil lamp, he led Giordino back to the Spirit Room. Setting the lamp on a long ice-covered crate, he stepped to a rack of Brown Bess muskets he had eyed earlier. Pulling one off the rack, he held it up and examined it closely, finding the weapon to be in pristine condition.

"It's not an automatic, but it should even the odds a bit," he said.

"I guess the previous owner won't mind," Giordino replied.

Pitt turned around, puzzled at his friend's comment. He found Giordino pointing at the crate that supported the lamp. Pitt stepped closer, suddenly realizing it was no crate but a wooden coffin supported by a pair of sawhorses. The light from the whale oil lamp shimmered off a tin plate hammered to the enlarged end of the coffin. Leaning forward, Pitt brushed off a layer of loose ice, revealing a script of white lettering hand-painted on the tin. A chill ran up his spine as he read the epitaph.

SIR JOHN FRANKLIN
1786–1847
HIS SOUL BELONGS TO THE SEA

81

Zak waited until his security team had closed in on Pitt and Giordino before leaving the warm confines of the icebreaker. Though he had no way of knowing for sure whether either man was Pitt, his instincts told him it was so.

"Thompson and White trailed them trying to move inland," reported one of the mercenaries, who had returned to the ship. "There's an old boat up on shore that they apparently climbed into."

"A boat?" Zak asked.

"Yes, some old sailing ship. It's lodged in a ravine and covered with ice."

Zak glanced at the stolen co-op map, which was lying on the chart table. Had he miscalculated again? Was it no mine at all but a ship that was the source of the Inuit ruthenium?

"Take me to the ship," he barked. "I'll go sort this out."

The wind still blew in sporadic gusts, stinging his face as they trudged across the sea ice. The freshening winds began to clear the ground fog, and Zak could see down the coastline to where several of his men stood at the base of a narrow bluff. There was no sign of any ship, and he started to wonder if his security team had been out in the cold too long. But when he approached the ravine, he saw the massive black hull of the *Erebus* wedged against the ridge and he stared in wonderment. His attention was diverted by one of his approaching men.

"Their tracks lead up the gulch. We're pretty certain they climbed aboard the ship," said the man, the gap-toothed tough named White.

"Select two other men and board the ship," Zak replied, as an additional five men gathered around him. "The rest of you spread out on the beach, in case they try to backtrack."

White pulled two men aside and began climbing up the gulch with Zak trailing behind. The ice-strewn terrain rose to within a few feet of the upper deck, requiring a short climb up the hull sides and over the rail to get aboard. White was the first to climb up, slinging his gun over his shoulder as he scaled the hull and threw a leg over the railing. As his foot touched the deck, he looked straight across to find a black-haired man stepping up the ladderway with an armful of old muskets.

"Freeze!" White yelled with deafening authority.

But Pitt didn't.

It was instantly a deadly race to bring their arms to bear, neither man hesitating a second. White had the advantage of a smaller weapon, but he was caught in an awkward position with one leg still over the rail. He quickly grabbed at the gun grip and flipped the barrel forward but nervously squeezed the trigger before taking aim. A harmless seam of bullets ripped across the deck and into a mound of ice near the ladderway before a loud pop erupted from across the deck.

With nerves as cold as the ice that encompassed the ship, Pitt had calmly dropped all the weapons but one, pulling the thick stock of a loaded Brown Bess musket to his shoulder. The gunman's bullets ricocheted off the deck nearby as he quickly aimed the long barrel, then squeezed the trigger. It felt like minutes to Pitt before the external percussion cap ignited the black powder charge and sent a lead ball blasting out the muzzle.

At short range, the Brown Bess was deadly accurate, and Pitt's aim held true. The lead ball struck White just below the collarbone, the impact throwing him clear off the rail. His body cartwheeled over the side, slamming into the frozen turf at Zak's feet. With a confused look in his eye, he stared up momentarily at Zak, then died.

Zak callously stepped over the body while pulling out his Glock automatic pistol.

"Take them," he hissed at the other two men, waving his gun at the ship.

The gun battle quickly descended into a deadly game of cat and mouse. Pitt and Giordino took turns popping out of the ladder well and rapidly firing two or three of the antique weapons, ducking bursts from the incoming automatic weapons. A heavy pall of smoke from the burnt black powder soon obscured visibility on the deck, making aim difficult for the shooters on both sides.

Pitt and Giordino established an ad hoc reloading station at the base of the ladderway, allowing one man to shoot while the other reloaded additional weapons. Pitt had found a small cask in the Spirit Room containing five pounds of black powder, which he carried to the lower deck. The cask was used to fill a number of small hand flasks, which in turn were used to load black powder into the muskets, shotguns, and percussion pistols found below. In the lengthy reloading process from the days of old, the powder was poured into the barrel and compressed with a ramrod, followed by the lead shot and a layer of wadding, which was rammed yet again. Pitt was no stranger to firing antique weapons and showed Giordino the proper quantity of powder and ramming technique to speed the process. Loading a long-barreled musket took half a minute, but with repeated efforts both men were soon reloading in less than fifteen seconds. Popping out of the ladderway, they would then fire singly or in succession, trying to keep their opponents guessing.

Despite their superior firepower, Zak and his men had a tough time getting a clean shot off. Forced to climb up the hull, they had to grab the side rail and cower behind its planking while trying to bring their guns to bear. Pitt and Giordino could easily spot their movements and soon had bloodied the hands of the gunmen by splintering the rail with lead. Zak quietly moved in front of the other two gunmen, clinging deftly to the outer rail. He turned and whispered to the other men between rounds.

"Rise and fire together after the next shot."

Both men nodded, holding their heads down while waiting for the next burst of musket fire. It was Pitt's turn to fire, and he crouched atop the ladderway with a flintlock pistol on the top step and two muskets across his lap. Shouldering one of the muskets, he peered over the lip of the deck, scanning the side rail through the gun smoke left from Giordino's last shots. The top of a black parka wavered above a point on the rail, and he quickly drew a bead on the target. He waited for a head to pop up but the gunman refused to budge. Deciding to test the stopping power of the side rail, Pitt lowered his aim a foot and pulled the trigger.

The shot bore through the aged planking and into the calf muscle of the gunman crouching behind. But his body was already reacting to the sound of the musket shot, and he rose with his machine gun to fire. Ten feet down the rail, the second gunman followed suit.

Through the black haze, Pitt detected both men rising and immediately ducked into the ladderway. But as he back-stepped, his instincts took over, and he grabbed the pistol on the step. As his body ducked below the deck, his arm went up with the pistol. His hand was aligned closer to the second gunmen, and he whipped the barrel toward the man's head and quickly squeezed the trigger.

A simultaneous explosion of lead ripped across the surrounding deck, blasting a shower of splinters on top of him. His ears told him that one of the machine guns had ceased firing, while the other still peppered the ladderway. Sinking to the lower deck with a slight dizziness, he turned to Giordino, who was headed up with a pair of wood-handled pistols and a Purdey shotgun.

"I think I got one of them," he said.

Giordino stopped in midstep, noticing a pool of blood growing on the deck next to Pitt's feet.

"You've been hit."

Pitt looked down, then raised his right arm. A V-shaped hole had been ripped through the sleeve beneath his lower forearm, dripping a steady flow of blood. Pitt squeezed his hand, which still gripped his pistol.

"Missed the bone," he said.

He slipped off the wool jacket as Giordino stepped over and ripped open the sleeve on Pitt's sweater. Two ugly holes tore through the meaty part of his forearm, somehow missing nerves and bone. Giordino quickly tore strips from Pitt's sweater and wrapped them tightly around the wound, then helped Pitt back into his jacket.

"I'll reload," Pitt said, regaining some color in his pale face. Gritting his teeth, he looked Giordino in the eye with a determined plea.

"Go finish them off."

82

Zak had remained hidden behind the rail when his two gunmen rose and fired. Using their barrage as a cover, he then stood and rolled over the rail, scurrying across the deck to the ice-encased foremast. He looked aft, but there was no way he could make a clean shot on the ladder well, as a mound of ice amidships created a high barrier between the two positions.

It was an absurd situation, he thought, being held up by men armed with weapons over a century and a half old. He had to admire their cunning, which seemed noticeably absent from his own security team. He looked for another vantage point from which to fire, but, finding none, he searched for a way belowdecks. He spotted the forward hatch, but it was buried under two feet of ice, and there was no forward ladderway on the ship. Then he looked up, noticing that the foremast was tilted at an awkward angle. A cross-spar had ground onto the ridge and jammed the mast to starboard. The heavy mast had cracked the deck around its base, opening a two-foot gash that led below.

Had Zak looked back at the exchange of gunfire, he might have witnessed the death of his second gunman and reconsidered his next move. But he was already thinking three steps ahead as he tucked the Glock into his pocket, then lowered himself through the gap in the deck and dropped into the black interior below.

Giordino climbed cautiously to the head of the ladderway and quickly peered over the ledge. The deck was silent, and he caught no sight of any movement. Then he heard a cry, close by but not from aboard the ship. With the shotgun cocked and at the ready, he crept out of the ladderway and tentatively stepped to the side rail.

Aside the exterior hull, he observed two bodies lying faceup on the ice. The mercenary White, the first casualty, lay with his eyes still open, a pool of red around his torso. Beside him was a second gunman, who had a large hole through his forehead from Pitt's last pistol shot. Giordino spotted a third man down on the beach, who was shouting for help. He clutched his leg and moved with a limp, trailing a thin stain of red.

Giordino heard a noise behind him and turned to see Pitt climb uneasily out of the ladderway, a pistol in his good hand and a musket over his shoulder.

"Did we manage to scare them off?" he asked.

"Thanks to your eagle-eyed marksmanship," Giordino replied, motioning over the rail at the two dead gunmen. "I'd say you won the turkey shoot today."

Pitt eyed the bodies with little remorse. Though he felt no comfort in killing another man, he had no pity for hired murderers, especially those that had had a hand in sinking the *Narwhal*.

"Sounds like they have some companions on the beach," he said. "They'll be back in force shortly."

"My thoughts as well," Giordino replied. Looking at Pitt's bloodied sleeve, he gave his friend a concerned look. "No offense, but I don't relish making this old tub my personal Alamo."

"Better odds up the ravine?"

Giordino nodded. "I think it's time to vacate the premises. They could wait until dark and overrun us, or, worse, set fire to this matchbox. There's only so long we can hold out with these popguns. They'll come back slow and cautious, which will give us some time to get up the hill. We can carry plenty of shot and powder to discourage them from following too close. Hopefully, they'll just give up the chase and let us freeze to death on our own," he added wryly.

"There's one other thing that we'll be needing," Pitt remarked.

"I can't believe you haven't already absconded with it," Giordino replied with a grin. "The key to the whole shebang. The ship's log."

Pitt simply nodded, hoping the log could be found and that its contents would prove worthy of the sacrifices already incurred.

"Take a rest, I'll go find it," Giordino said, stepping toward the ladderway.

"No, I'll go," Pitt replied, rubbing his wounded arm. "With this maimed wing, I'll have trouble aiming the long gun if company arrives." He slipped the musket off his shoulder and passed it to Giordino, along with the pistol. "Go ahead and shoot well before you see the whites of their eyes."

Pitt climbed down the ladderway, feeling somewhat dizzy from the loss of blood. Moving aft, he made his way down the passageway toward the officers' quarters under the dim light of the bulkhead candles he had lit earlier. The passageway eventually turned black as he reached an unexplored portion of the ship. He cursed himself for forgetting to grab the whale oil lamp and was about to turn back when he noticed a faint glow ahead in the darkness. Taking a few steps forward, he saw that there was a flickering light at the end of the passage. It was a light that neither he nor

Giordino had left behind.

Stepping lightly, he approached the end of the passageway, which opened into the Great Cabin. A candle light flickered within, casting long black shadows on the bulkheads. Pitt crept to the doorway and peered in.

With his teeth glimmering under the amber light, Clay Zak looked up from a large table at the center of the room with a malicious smile.

"Come on in, Mr. Pitt," he said coldly. "I've been waiting for you."

83

A dozen yards from the edge of the sea ice, a bearded seal frolicked in the dark green water, searching for a stray Arctic cod. The gray-coated mammal caught sight of a black protrusion rising out of the water and swam over to investigate. Pressing a whiskered snout against the cold metal object, it detected no sign of potential nourishment, so turned and swam away.

Sixty feet beneath the surface, Commander Barry Campbell chuckled at the close-up image of the seal. Refocusing the viewing lens of the Type 18 search periscope at the red-hulled icebreaker a quarter mile away, he carefully examined the ship. Stepping away from the periscope, he waved over Bill Stenseth, who stood nearby in the USS *Santa Fe*'s cramped control room.

Stenseth had taken an immediate liking to the submarine's energetic captain. With sandy hair and beard, sparkling eyes, and a ready laugh, Campbell reminded Stenseth of a youthful Santa Claus, pre belly and white hair. A twenty-year Navy man, the jovial Campbell operated with a sense of purpose. There was no hesitation when Stenseth urged him to conduct an electronic search for Pitt and Giordino and the missing submersible. Campbell immediately piloted the attack sub to the south, with its full complement of sonar at play. When the icebreaker was detected lingering in the area, Campbell had ordered the sub to dive in order to maintain its stealth.

Stenseth stepped over to the periscope and peered through its dual eyepiece. A crystalline image of the red icebreaker burst through the magnified lens. Stenseth studied the flattened bow of the vessel, surprised that the damage wasn't greater from its high-speed collision with the *Narwhal*.

"Yes, sir, that's the vessel that rammed us," he said matter-of-factly. Keeping his face pressed against the eyepiece, he focused on a man in black approaching the ship on foot. Tracing his path, he observed several additional men congregated on the beach.

"There are several men on the shoreline," he said to Campbell. "They appear armed."

"Yes, I saw them, too," Campbell replied. "Swing the periscope to your right about ninety degrees," he requested.

Stenseth obliged, rotating the periscope until a bright yellow object blurred past. Moving back, he refocused the lens while a lump grew in his throat. The *Bloodhound* appeared through the lens wedged against the sea ice, its top hatch thrown open.

"That's our submersible. Our men Pitt and Giordino must have gone ashore," he said, a rising tone of urgency in his voice. He stood up and faced Campbell.

"Captain, the men on that icebreaker sank my ship and tried to murder the crew of the *Polar Dawn*. They'll kill Pitt and Giordino, too, if they haven't already. I have to ask you to intervene."

Campbell stiffened slightly. "Captain Stenseth, we sailed into Victoria Strait for the strict purposes of a search-and-rescue mission. My orders are clear. I am not to engage Canadian military forces under any circumstances. Any deviation will require a request up the chain of command, which will likely take a twenty-four-hour response."

The submarine captain exhaled deeply, then gave Stenseth a crooked smile as his eyes suddenly gleamed. "On the other hand, if you tell me that two of our own are lost in the elements, then it is within my duty to authorize a search-and-rescue mission."

"Yes, sir," Stenseth replied, reading his drift. "I believe two of the *Narwhal*'s crew are either aboard the icebreaker awaiting transfer or are ashore without proper food, clothing, or shelter, and require our assistance."

"Captain Stenseth, I don't know who these

people are, but they sure don't look or act like the Canadian military to me. We'll go get your NUMA boys. And if these jokers interfere with our rescue ops, I guarantee you they will wish they hadn't."

There was no way Rick Roman was going to be denied. Though he and his commando team were severely weakened by their ordeal on the barge, they knew there was unfinished business to take care of. When word filtered down that a SEAL team was being assembled to search for Pitt and Giordino, Roman pleaded with the *Santa Fe*'s captain to participate. Knowing that his SEAL team was undermanned, Campbell reluctantly agreed. And in a nod toward just retribution, he let Roman lead the team to board and search the icebreaker.

With a hot shower, dry clothes, and two extended trips to the officers' mess, Roman almost felt human again. Dressed in a white Arctic assault suit, he stood assembled with his team and the SEAL commandos in the enlisted mess area.

"Ever thought you'd be making an amphibious assault off a nuclear sub?" he asked Bojorquez.

"No, sir. I'm still and always will be a land-lubber. Though after tasting the chow they serve these squids, I am beginning to rethink my choice about joining the Army."

A deck above them in the control room, Commander Campbell was easing the submerged *Santa Fe* to the edge of the ice field. He had spotted a large hummock nearby that appeared to offer some measure of concealment from the distant icebreaker. Dropping the periscope, he watched as the diving officer inched the submarine under the ice, then stopped and gently rose to the surface.

With uncanny precision, the *Santa Fe*'s sail barely broke through the ice, protruding just a few feet above the surface. Roman's team and a pair of SEALs were quickly ushered out the bridge and onto the adjacent sea ice. Five minutes later, the sail and masts sank out of sight and the submarine again became a phantom of the deep.

The commandos quickly split up, the two SEALs moving to investigate the *Bloodhound,* while Roman and his men crept toward the icebreaker. The ship was a half mile away across a mostly flat sheet of ice that offered only sporadic ridges and hummocks for concealment. In their Arctic whites, however, they blended perfectly. Moving methodically, Roman approached the vessel from the sea side, then circled wide around its bow, having to avoid the watery lead that tailed the stern. Spotting a side stairwell that dropped down the ship's port hull, he moved the team within twenty yards, then ducked behind a small ridge. A few anxious seconds ticked by when a pair of men in black parkas descended the steps, but they turned toward shore without even a glance in the direction of Roman and his team.

With their position secure, Roman sat and waited as a chill wind rifled over their prone bodies.

84

A deckhand posting watch duty on the *Otok*'s bridge was the first to detect it.

"Sir," he called to the captain, "there's something breaking up the ice off our port beam."

Seated at the chart table drinking a cup of coffee, the visibly annoyed captain rose and walked slowly to the port bridge window. He arrived in time to witness a house-sized mass of ice rise up and crumble as a pair of gray-speckled tubes poked through the surface. A second later, the black teardrop-shaped sail of the *Santa Fe* burst through, scattering shards of ice in all directions.

A 688-I Los Angeles class attack submarine, the *Santa Fe* had been modified for under-the-ice operations. With strengthened hull, fairwater, and mast components, she was easily capable of penetrating ice three feet thick. Rising fifty yards off the *Otok*'s beam, the *Santa Fe*'s full hull cracked through the ice field, exposing a narrow black strip of steel three hundred feet long.

The *Otok*'s captain stared in disbelief at the sudden appearance of the nuclear warship. But his mind began to race when he saw a steady flow of white-clad men burst out of the sub's forward hatch armed with machine guns. He felt only minimal solace when he noticed that the armed men all raced toward the island rather than his ship.

"Quick, pull up the drop steps," he shouted at the deckhand. Turning to a crewman seated at the radio set, he barked, "Alert whatever security force is still aboard."

But it was too late. A second later, the bridge wing door burst open and three figures dressed in white charged in. Before the captain could react, he found the muzzle of an assault rifle jammed into his side. With a shocked sense of submission, he raised his arms, then stared into the brown eyes of the tall man wielding the weapon.

"Where . . . where did you come from?" he stammered.

Rick Roman looked the captain in the eye, then gave him a frosty grin.

"I came from that icebox of a caboose you decided to sink last night."

85

Zak sat comfortably at the head of the thick wooden table positioned in the center of the Great Cabin. A flickering candle lantern on the table illuminated a large leather-bound book pushed to one side. In front of Zak was stacked a pile of glass plates, each the size of a large postcard. Lying a few inches from his right hand was his Glock pistol.

"A rather remarkable old ship," Zak said, "with an interesting record of documentation."

"The *Erebus* came very close to being the first to navigate the Northwest Passage, Clay," Pitt replied.

Zak's brow rose a fraction at the mention of his name.

"I see you've done your homework. Not surprising, I suppose. You are quite an accomplished man, I have learned. And rather dogged in the chase."

Pitt stared at Zak, angry with himself for not bringing the percussion-cap pistol. With an injured arm and no weapon, he was nearly helpless against the assassin. Perhaps if he could stall for time, Giordino would come looking armed with his shotgun.

"I'm afraid that all I know about Clay Zak is that he is a lousy janitor and enjoys murdering innocent people," Pitt said coldly.

"Joy doesn't enter into it. A necessity of business, you might say."

"And exactly what business of yours requires ruthenium at any cost?" Pitt asked.

Zak flashed a humorless grin. "It is little more than a shiny metal to me. But it is worth much more to my employer. And it is obviously of strategic value to your country. If one were to prevent the mineral from feeding your artificial-photosynthesis factories, then my employer continues to be a very rich man. If he can control the supply of ruthenium outright, then he becomes an even richer man."

"Mitchell Goyette has more money than he could ever hope to spend. Yet his pathological greed outweighs the potential benefit to millions of people around the world."

"A sentimentalist, eh?" Zak said with a laugh. "A sure sign of weakness."

Pitt ignored the comment, still stalling for time. Zak didn't seem to notice or care that the gunfire above deck had ceased. Perhaps he assumed that Giordino had been killed.

"A pity that the ruthenium is but a myth," Pitt said. "It would appear that both of our efforts have been in vain."

"You searched the ship?"

Pitt nodded. "There's nothing here."

"A clever deduction that the Inuit ore had come off a ship. How did you rationalize that? I was searching for a mine on the island."

"The records that you neglected to steal from the Miners Co-op referred to the ore as Black Kobluna. The name and dates matched up to Franklin's ship *Erebus,* but it was a wrong assumption on my part," Pitt lied.

"Ah, yes, that decrepit Miners Co-op. Apparently, they obtained all the ruthenium that was aboard. And it *was* aboard," he added with a penetrating gaze.

Zak picked up one of the glass plates and slid it across the table. Pitt picked it up and studied it under the candlelight. It was a daguerreotype, the output of an early photographic process whereby an image was captured on a polished silver surface, then encased in glass for protection. Pitt recalled Perlmutter's having mentioned that Franklin had carried a daguerreotype camera on the expedition. The exposed plate showed a group of *Erebus* crewmen hauling a number of heavy sacks aboard that bulged as if loaded with rocks. A glimpse of the horizon behind the ship showed an ice-covered terrain, indicating that the ore had been taken on somewhere in the Arctic.

"You were quite right in your assumption," Zak said. "The ore was aboard the ship.

Which leaves the question as to where it was mined."

He reached over and patted the leather book near the center of the table.

"The captain was kind enough to leave the ship's logbook aboard," he said smugly. "The source of the ruthenium would be recorded inside. What do you think this book is worth, Mr. Pitt? A billion dollars?"

Pitt shook his head. "Not the lives that it has already cost."

"Or the lives that it is about to cost?" Zak added with a twisted grin.

Beyond the thick timbers of the ship's hull, the sound of automatic gunfire suddenly erupted. But the noise was oddly distant. It was clearly too far away to be directed at the ship, and there was no return fire from Giordino above deck. There were also two distinct tones of fire, representing different types of weaponry. Somewhere out on the ice, a pitched battle was going on between unknown parties.

Under the dim light of the cabin, Pitt could detect a subtle look of concern cross Zak's face. There was no sign of Giordino, but the wheels of determination in Pitt's head had finally devised an alternative game plan. Though he felt faint from loss of blood, he knew the time to act was now. He might not get another chance.

He stood back a bit and lowered the glass

plate, as if he was done studying it. Then he casually flipped it back toward Zak, or at least attempted to make it look casual. But instead of sliding it across the table, he flung it sharply a few inches above the surface. And rather than aiming for Zak, he whipped it toward the candle lantern in the center of the table.

The heavy glass plate easily smashed through the side of the lantern, scattering glass shards across the table. But of more importance to Pitt, the plate knocked debris across the candlewick, extinguishing the short flame that burned inside. In an instant, the Great Cabin plunged into total darkness.

As the plate struck the lantern, Pitt was already on the move. He immediately dropped to the deck, falling to one knee behind the end of the table. Zak was not a fool, however. The professional assassin had his hand on the gun even before the candle flickered out. He quickly raised the gun and fired at the opposite end of the table.

The bullet flew harmlessly over Pitt's head. Ignoring the shot, he placed his hands on the two stubby table legs beside him and started shoving the table toward Zak. The assassin fired two more shots, using the muzzle flash to try to locate Pitt in the black room. Realizing Pitt was shoving the table forward, he fired at the far tabletop while trying to rise from his seat. His aim was dead-on, but his move to stand was too slow.

A short seam of bullets struck the tabletop inches from Pitt's head, but the thick mahogany surface devoured the lead slugs. Protected by the hard wood, Pitt propelled the table with rising momentum. Driving against the wooden legs, he bulled forward with every ounce of energy he could muster, ignoring the ache in his arm and the dizziness in his head.

The far edge of the table caught Zak in his midsection, throwing him back into his chair before he could get to his feet. The pile of glass plates dumped on top of him, disrupting his attempts to keep firing. Pitt continued to drive his rectangular battering ram, which now took Zak with it, sliding him backward in his chair. Both bits of furniture slid several feet until the rear legs of the chair struck an uneven deck plank. The legs held while the table kept coming, knocking Zak over and backward, where he fell to the deck with a crash. In his hand, the Glock still barked, firing harmlessly into the tabletop even as Zak tumbled over.

Pitt heard the crash, but it was only through the brief muzzle flash that he knew Zak was knocked down. He was now exposed to Zak's fire from under the table, but he didn't hesitate, even as he heard the gun discharge again. Digging his shoulder into the underside of the table, Pitt drove his legs into the deck and pushed upright with his last burst of strength, tilting the burly table up on its end, until it landed on Zak's legs. Pitt nearly had the table turned over when he felt his left leg buckle from under him. Lying on his back, Zak had fired three blind shots under the table, then slid his legs free. Two rounds whizzed by harmlessly but the third found Pitt's leg, burying the bullet into his thigh. Losing his balance, Pitt quickly shifted his weight onto his right leg and leaned into the table.

He was a second too late. Zak had got to his knees and deflected the table to the side, shifting Pitt's momentum. As the massive table began to totter, Zak rose and used his superior strength to twist it aside.

Suddenly lacking in leverage, Pitt was thrown sideways with the table, crashing into the bookshelves in the stern. The sound of shattering glass filled the darkened bay as Pitt was flung into the paned shelf doors. He then dropped to the deck, followed by the hefty table that collapsed onto him with a dull thud. The table ripped through a half dozen bookshelves along the way, releasing a cascade of books and wooden shelves and glass that tumbled on top of the overturned table.

Zak stood nearby, breathing heavily as he caught his wind, while keeping the gun pointed at the table. But straining his ears, he heard not a sound. There were no groans, no shuffles or movements at all from Pitt's buried body. As his eyes adjusted to the darkness,

Zak could faintly detect Pitt's lifeless legs protruding from beneath the table. Scouring the floor around his own feet, he put his hands on the heavy ship's logbook. Pulling it to his chest, he stepped cautiously toward the lighted passageway, then moved slowly down the corridor without looking back.

86

Above deck, Giordino was having his own troubles. After a lengthy break in the action, he spotted three new gunmen broaching the base of the ravine undercover. While he crouched at the rail waiting to get a clear shot, additional gunfire broke out somewhere on the ice. Blocked by the ravine and misting fog, Giordino had no clue what the firing was about but noted that it had no effect on the three men advancing toward the ship. He let them draw closer before popping up with the musket and firing at the nearest gunman. The man dropped to the ground at the sight of the defender, and Giordino's shot just barely missed, the bullet ripping harmlessly through the man's parka. The gunmen learned their lesson and began to provide covering fire alternately, allowing the others to advance. Giordino moved along the ship's rail, sprouting up and firing from different locations before having to duck the return fire. He wounded one of the gunmen in the leg before the other two closed on the ship under combined fire. Emptying the last of his loaded muskets, Giordino was forced to fall back to the ladder well, wondering what was taking Pitt so long. Focused on his own firefight, he had not noticed the gunshots fired below in the Great Cabin.

"Dirk, I need a reload on the muskets," he shouted down the ladderway, but there was no answer. He aimed the shotgun at the side rail, then readied two percussion-cap pistols in his lap. Just a few more shots and he'd be helpless, unless Pitt arrived quickly.

Near the base of the ladderway, a tall figure slowly waded through a mass of antique armament lying on the deck and peered up. Giordino sat ten feet above, perched on the top two steps with his eyes fixated on the side rail. Had he looked down, he probably wouldn't have even spotted Zak staring at him from the dimly lit lower deck. Zak contemplated letting his security team finish the job but figured it would be more expedient to kill Giordino himself. Shifting the ship's logbook into his left arm, he steadied his feet and raised his automatic pistol at Giordino.

He failed to detect the sound of pained steps shuffling down the passageway somewhere behind him. But he flinched when a loud warning cry suddenly echoed down the corridor just as he was about to squeeze the trigger.

"Al!"

Zak turned and gazed down the passageway in disbelief. Standing beneath a candle lantern twenty feet away and looking like death personified was Dirk Pitt. His face was a bloody mess from a dozen glass cuts while an ugly purple knot glistened on his forehead. His right sleeve was wet with crimson, matching his left leg, and a bloody trail followed him down the corridor. He held no weapons and leaned on his good leg with a grimace of agony on his face. But battered and shot, he stared at Zak with complete defiance.

"You're next," Zak hissed, then turned his focus back up to Giordino, who had returned Pitt's call but was still unaware of the situation below. Zak aimed the Glock at Giordino a second time but was distracted by a bright blur that flashed toward him. Turning to Pitt, he saw that the wounded man had hurled the candle lantern at him. A weak throw, Zak thought to himself, as the lantern fell short of the mark. He gazed at Pitt and snickered with a shake of his head as the lantern shattered near his feet.

Only the throw wasn't weak. The lantern struck the deck exactly where Pitt had aimed it, a few inches shy of the black powder cask they were using to reload the muskets. Awash

with powder spilt from their rapid reload-
ings, the deck beneath the ladderway was an
inferno-in-waiting. The shattered lantern immediately ignited the loose powder in a flash
of smoke and sparks that flared at Zak's feet.
The assassin instinctively recoiled, backing
away from the flare-up while unknowingly
moving closer to the black powder cask. An
instant later, a trail of black powder burned
up to the cask and it detonated in a deafening
explosion.

The blast rocked the ship, shooting smoke
and flames up and out the ladder well. Pitt
was knocked to the deck and showered with
flying debris, most of which was absorbed by
his heavy wool jacket. With his ears ringing,
he waited several minutes for the smoke to
clear before limping over to the ladderway,
coughing from the acrid residue in the air.
The side bulkheads were blown out and a
large hole in the deck now opened through
to the orlop deck, but the remaining damage
was relatively limited.

Pitt saw a boot lying near the hole and realized grimly that a detached foot was still
inside. Looking up, he saw the boot's owner a
few feet away.

Clay Zak had been blown partially up the
ladder well, and his mangled body was now
embedded in the steps. He hung upside down,
his open eyes staring vacantly off into space.
Pitt stepped closer and stared at the dead as-

sassin without pity.

"I think you were due for a blast," he said to the corpse, then turned and peered up the smoky ladder well.

87

The force of the black powder explosion had launched Giordino up and off the top steps of the ladderway, throwing him onto the deck eight feet away. His clothes singed, his lungs burning, and his body nicked by a bounty of splinters and bruises, he had nonetheless survived the blast in one piece. As the explosion's thick cloud of black smoke drifted away from the ship, he struggled to shake off the daze. He fought a pounding in his head and a symphony of bells ringing in his ears as he painfully rolled to his side. Wiping some grit from his eyes, he stiffened as one of the black-clad gunmen poked his head over the rail.

Giordino had lost his weapons in the explosion and the gunman quickly realized it. Rising without fear, he stood at the rail and calmly swung his machine gun to bear on Giordino.

The burst was short, just four or five shots. Giordino could barely hear it through his ringing ears. Yet he saw the results. Not a ripping seam through his own flesh or the deck about him. Instead, it was the gunman himself who was ruptured by the shots. A mouthful of blood spilled from his lips, and then he slowly sunk beneath the rail, dropping to the ice-covered ground below.

Giordino stared blankly, hearing additional bursts of gunfire. Then another body appeared at the rail, armed like the last and pointing a gun in his direction. Only this gunman was dressed in white, with an ivory ski mask and protective goggles covering his entire face. A second armed man in white joined him, and the two scaled the rail and stepped toward Giordino, their guns trained on him.

Giordino was too focused on the approaching men to notice a third man appear at the rail. The newcomer looked across the deck at Giordino, then shouted something at the other two men. It took a second or two for Giordino's ringing ears to decipher the words.

"Hold your horses, Lieutenant," the third man yelled in a familiar Texas accent. "That man is one of ours."

The two Navy SEALs from the *Santa Fe* stopped in their tracks but held their weapons fixed until Jack Dahlgren rushed to Giordino's side. Grabbing the sleeve of Giordino's antique wool jacket and helping him to his feet, Dahlgren couldn't help but ask, "You go and join the Royal Navy?"

"We got a little chilly when you weren't

around to pick us out of the drink," Giordino managed to reply, stunned at Dahlgren's appearance.

"Where's Dirk?"

"He was below. That's where the explosion originated," he replied with a concerned look.

Wincing in pain, Giordino staggered past Dahlgren to the edge of the ladderway and peered down. A few feet below, he saw the singed and smoking body of a dark-haired man sprawled on the steps, and he shut his eyes. It was nearly a minute before he could open them again, by which time Dahlgren and the SEALs had crowded around him. When he looked down, he suddenly saw a light wavering from the deck below. A bloody and battered Pitt slowly staggered into view at the base of the steps and peered up at his friend. In his arms, he clutched a large and slightly singed leather book.

"Somebody got a light?" he asked with a pained grin.

Pitt was immediately carried back to the *Santa Fe* and ushered into the submarine's sick bay with Giordino in tow. Despite a severe loss of blood, Pitt's injuries were not life-threatening, and his wounds were quickly cleaned and bandaged. Though the ship's surgeon ordered him to remain in bed, Pitt found a cane and was hobbling around the sub an hour later, reuniting with the crew of the *Narwhal*. Limping into the officers' mess with Giordino, they found the three captains, Campbell, Murdock, and Stenseth, seated at a table discussing the icebreaker.

"Shouldn't you two be bedridden?" Stenseth asked.

"There will be plenty of time to sleep on the voyage home," Pitt replied. Stenseth helped him to a chair while Campbell grabbed coffees, and the men swapped tales of their ordeals and discoveries.

"You boys flipping a coin to see who drives the icebreaker?" Giordino asked a short while later.

"We boarded her strictly to search for you two," Campbell replied. "I had no intention of confiscating her, but these gentlemen were just telling me the details of her full role in the *Polar Dawn* crew's abduction and the sinking of the *Narwhal*."

"There's something else you need to know about her," Pitt said. "Al?"

Giordino described the underlying coat of gray paint on the icebreaker's hull and the partial appearance of the number 54 in white lettering.

"I'd bet the farm she destroyed the Canadian ice camp while masquerading as a Navy frigate," he said.

Campbell shook his head. "These people are some serious maniacs. They're on the verge of starting World War Three. I guess we've got no choice but to take her to port in U.S. waters as soon as possible."

"She's a known Canadian-flagged ship, so there shouldn't be any trouble clearing the passage," Pitt said.

"And you've got two captains ready and willing to take her back," Stenseth said, with Murdock nodding in agreement.

"Piracy it is, then," Campbell said with a smile. "We'll head for Anchorage, and I'll be your underwater tail just in case of trouble." He gazed around the small confines of the mess. "Truth be told, we're a bit overcrowded as it is."

"We'll take both our crews to man the ship," Murdock said, nodding his head toward Stenseth. "Captain Roman reported plenty of empty berths on the icebreaker."

"Al and I will be happy to accompany the icebreaker," Pitt said. "Al's claustrophobic, and I've got some reading to catch upon."

"Then we have our traveling orders," Campbell agreed. "I'll transfer half my SEAL team aboard to help with security, then we can be on our way."

The three captains excused themselves to organize the crews as Pitt and Giordino finished their coffees. Giordino leaned back in his chair and looked at the ceiling with a broad smile.

"You seem awful merry," Pitt remarked.

"You heard what the man said," Giordino replied. "We're going to Anchorage. Anchorage, Alaska," he repeated lovingly. "South of the Arctic Circle. Did ever a place sound so warm and inviting?" he asked with a contented grin.

88

The B-2 Spirit had been airborne for over five hours. Taking off from Whiteman Air Force Base in Missouri, the wedge-shaped stealth bomber had flown west on what appeared to be a normal training flight. But five hundred miles out over the Pacific, the black-and-gray aircraft, which resembled a giant manta ray in flight, turned northeast, flying toward the coast of Washington State.

"AC-016 bearing zero-seven-eight degrees," the mission commander said in a soft Carolina accent. "She's right on time."

"I've got her," replied the pilot.

Tweaking the throttles on the four turbofan jet engines, he banked the plane by thrust until matching the flight bearing, then closed in on a small white target visible out the cockpit window. Satisfied with his position, the pilot backed off on the throttles to match the speed of the leading aircraft.

Less than a quarter mile ahead and a thousand feet below was an Air Canada Boeing

777, bound for Toronto from Hong Kong. The pilots aboard the commercial airliner would have choked had they known that a billion-dollar bomber was tailing them into Canadian airspace.

With a nearly invisible radar signature, the crew of the B-2 need not have worried about hiding in the 777's shadow to complete their mission. But with heightened military alerts on both sides of the border, they were taking no chances. The bomber tailed the jetliner over Vancouver and across British Columbia into Alberta. Approximately fifty miles west of Calgary, the Canadian airliner made a slight course adjustment to the southeast. The B-2 held its position, then veered sharply to the northeast.

Its target was the Canadian Forces Base at Cold Lake, Alberta, one of two Canadian air bases that housed F-18 fighter jets. A "quarter stick" of seven five-hundred-pound laser-guided bombs was to be dropped on the airfield, with the intent to damage or destroy as many fighter jets as possible while minimizing loss of life. With no response from the Canadian government after his twenty-four-hour admonition, the President had elected to halve the first-strike recommendation from the Pentagon and proceed with an attack on a single military installation.

"Eight minutes to target," the mission commander announced. "Performing final weapons arming now."

As he cycled through a computerized weapons-control sequence, an urgent radio call suddenly transmitted over their headsets.

"Death-52, Death-52, this is Command," came the unexpected call from Whiteman. "You are ordered to abort mission. I repeat, we have a mission abort. Please stand down and acknowledge, over."

The mission commander acknowledged receipt of the last-minute command, then immediately cycled down the bomber's armaments. The pilot slowly reversed course, flying back toward the Pacific before setting a course to their home air base.

"The boss man cut it a little close there," the pilot said a short while later.

"You're telling me," the mission commander replied, a deep sense of relief in his voice. "That's one mission I'm glad was scrubbed."

Gazing out at the Canadian Rockies passing beneath their wings, he added, "I just hope nobody else finds out how close we really came."

89

Bill Stenseth listened to the deep rumble of the icebreaker's powerful gas turbine engines, then nodded at the *Narwhal*'s helmsman beside him to get the big vessel under way. As the ship slowly began to bull its way through the ice, Stenseth stepped out onto the frozen bridge wing and gave a friendly salute to the *Santa Fe,* still positioned in the ice a short distance away. Standing atop the sail, Commander Campbell returned the gesture, then prepared his own vessel to return to the depths.

The *Otok* turned and forged its way through the ice toward the NUMA submersible, easing to a halt just alongside. A pair of crewmen were let down onto the ice, where they attached a lifting cable to the *Bloodhound*. A large swing crane then lifted the submersible aboard the icebreaker, depositing it in a tight corner on the stern deck. In an adjacent unheated storage shed, the bodies of Clay Zak and his dead security team mercenaries were laid out, wrapped in makeshift canvas body bags.

A short distance across the ice, a polar bear stuck his head over a ridge and observed the operations. The same bear that Giordino had nearly awakened, it stood and stared at the icebreaker with annoyed disturbance, then turned and padded across the ice in search of a meal.

Once the *Bloodhound* was secured, the icebreaker moved on again, breaking into open water much to Stenseth's relief. The ship steamed west, on a tack through Queen Maud Gulf and on toward the Beaufort Sea. The *Santa Fe* had by now slipped under the ice and trailed the icebreaker a mile or two behind. Stenseth would have been surprised to learn that by the time they'd leave Canadian waters, there would be no fewer than three American submarines sailing a silent escort, while a bevy of long-range patrol aircraft monitored their progress high overhead.

Along with Murdock, Stenseth enjoyed the opportunity to command a new vessel. With his own crew from the *Narwhal* and most of the *Polar Dawn*'s crew aboard, he was surrounded by able assistants. The icebreaker's former crew was safely under guard below-decks, watched closely by the *Santa Fe*'s SEAL contingent and Rick Roman's commando team. Almost every man had wanted to sail home on the icebreaker, as a show of retribution for the ordeal suffered at the hands of her crew.

Once the ship was free of the sea ice, Stenseth turned toward a noisy congregation behind him. Crowded around the chart table with his bandaged leg propped up on a folding chair, Pitt sat sipping a hot coffee. Giordino and Dahlgren were wedged alongside, wagering over the contents of the thick leather logbook that sat at the table's center.

"Are you going to find out what's in the *Erebus* log or continue to torture me with suspense?" Stenseth asked the trio.

"The captain is right," said Giordino, who, like Pitt, had an assorted array of bandages taped to his face. He gingerly shoved the logbook over to Pitt.

"I believe you have the honors," he said.

Pitt looked down with expectation. The *Erebus* logbook was bound in hand-tooled leather, with an etching of a globe on the front cover. The book had received little damage from the black powder explosion, showing only a few small burn marks on the binding. Zak had held the logbook opposite the powder cask when it exploded, unwittingly protecting it with his body. Pitt had found the book wedged in a step beside his mangled corpse.

Pitt slowly opened the cover and turned to the first formal entry.

"Going to build the suspense, eh?" Stenseth asked.

"Cut to the chase, boss," Dahlgren implored.

"I knew I should have kept this in my cabin," Pitt replied.

With prying eyes and endless questions, he gave up thoughts of digesting the journal chronologically and skipped to the last entry.

"'April 21, 1848,'" he read, silencing the crowd. "'It is with regret that I must abandon the *Erebus* today. A portion of the crew remains in a maniacal state, imposing danger to the officers and other crewmen alike. It is the hard silver, I suspect, although I know not why. With eleven good men, I shall embark for the *Terror,* and therewith await the spring thaw. May the Almighty have mercy on us, and on the ill men who stay behind. Captain James Fitzjames.'"

"The hard silver," said Giordino. "That must be the ruthenium."

"Why would it cause the men to go crazy?" Dahlgren asked.

"There's no reason that it should," Pitt said, "though an old prospector told me a similar tale of lunacy that was blamed on ruthenium. The crew of the *Erebus* faced lead poisoning and botulism from their canned foods, on top of scurvy, frostbite, and the hardship of three winters bound on the ice. It might have just been an accumulation of factors."

"He seems to have made an unfortunate choice to leave the ship," Giordino noted.

616

"Yes," Pitt agreed. "The *Terror* was crushed in the ice, and they probably figured the *Erebus* would be as well, so it is easy to see their rationale for going ashore. But the *Erebus* somehow remained locked in the ice and was apparently driven ashore sometime later."

Pitt moved backward through the logbook, reading aloud the entries from the prior weeks and months. The journal told a disturbing tale that quickly silenced the anxious bridge crowd. In tragic detail, Fitzjames wrote of Franklin's ill-fated attempt to dash down Victoria Strait in the waning summer days of 1846. The weather turned rapidly, and both ships became trapped in the unprotected sea ice far from land. Their second Arctic winter set in, during which Franklin became ill and died. It was during this time that signs of madness began to afflict some of the crew members. Curiously, it was recorded that such behavior was notably absent aboard the sister ship, *Terror.* The *Erebus*'s crew's lunacy and violent behavior continued to proliferate until Fitzjames was forced to take his remaining men and withdraw to the *Terror.*

The earlier logbook entries turned routine, and Pitt began skipping pages until finding a lengthy entry that referenced the hard silver.

"I think this is it," he said in a low tone, as every man on the bridge crowded in close and stared at him silently.

"'August 27, 1845. Position 74.36.21'

617

North, 92.17.432 West. Off Devon Island. Seas slight, some pancake ice, winds westerly at five knots. Crossing Lancaster Sound ahead of *Terror* when lookout spots sail at 0900. At 1100, approached by whaler *Governess Sarah,* Capetown, South Africa, Captain Emlyn Brown commanding. Brown reports vessel was damaged by ice and forced into Sound for several weeks, but is now repaired. Crew is very low on provisions. We provide them one barrel of flour, fifty pounds of salt pork, a small quantity of tinned meats, and 1/4 cask rum. It is observed that many among G.S.'s crew exhibit odd behavior and uncouth mannerisms. In gratitude for provisions, Captain Brown provides ten bags of 'hard silver.' An unusual ore mined in South Africa, Brown claims it has excellent heat retention properties. Ship's crew has started heating buckets of ore on galley stove and placing under bunks at night, with effective results.

" 'We make for Barrow Strait tomorrow.' "

Pitt let the words settle, then slowly raised his head. A look of disappointment hung on the faces of the men around him. Giordino was the first to speak.

"South Africa," he repeated slowly. "The burlap bag we found in the hold. It was marked Bushveld, South Africa. Regrettably, it supports the account."

"Maybe they're still mining the stuff in Africa?" Dahlgren posed.

618

Pitt shook his head. "I should have remembered the name. That was one of the mines that Yaeger checked out. It essentially played out some forty years ago."

"So there's no ruthenium left in the Arctic," Stenseth said soberly.

"Nope," Pitt replied, closing the logbook with a look of defeat. "Like Franklin, we've pursued a cold and deadly passage to nowhere."

■ ■ ■ ■

EPILOGUE
THE ROCK

■ ■ ■ ■

FRANKLIN'S FINAL REST

90

Though far from a creature of habit, Mitchell Goyette did have one conspicuous ritual. While in Vancouver, he lunched every Friday afternoon at the Victoria Club. A posh private golf club in the hills north of town, the secluded enclave offered a stunning view of Vancouver Harbor from its ornate clubhouse near the eighteenth green. As a young man, Goyette had his membership application unconditionally rejected by the haughty high-society icons that controlled the club. But he had exacted revenge years later when he acquired the golf course and club in a major land deal. Promptly tossing out all of the old members, he'd repopulated the private club with bankers, politicians, and other power brokers whom he could exploit to augment his fortune. When not pressing the flesh to close a business deal, Goyette would relax over a three-martini lunch with one of his girlfriends in a corner booth overlooking the harbor.

At exactly five minutes to noon, Goyette's chauffeur-driven Maybach pulled up to the front guard gate and was promptly waved through to the clubhouse entrance. Two blocks down the road, a man in a white panel van watched the Maybach enter the grounds, then started his own car. With a magnetic sign affixed to the side reading COLUMBIA JANITORIAL SUPPLY, the van pulled up to the guard gate. The driver, wearing a work hat and sunglasses, rolled down the window and stuck out a clipboard that had a printed work order attached.

"Delivery for the Victoria Club," the driver said in a bored voice.

The guard glanced at the clipboard, then passed it back without reading it.

"Go on in," he replied. "Service entrance is to your right."

Trevor Miller smiled faintly as he tossed the clipboard with the phony work order onto the passenger seat.

"Have a good one," he told the guard, then sped on down the lane.

Trevor had never imagined that the day would come when he would be compelled to take the life of another. But the death of his brother and countless others in the wake of Goyette's industrial greed was tantamount to murder. And the murders would continue, he knew, accompanied by continued environmental devastation. There might be public retribution against Goyette's entities, but the man himself would always be protected by a veneer of corrupt politicians and high-priced attorneys. There was only one way to put an end to it and that was to put an end to Goyette. He knew the system was incapable of doing the job, so he rationalized that it was up to him. And who better to carry out the act than a nondescript state employee who aroused little suspicion and had little to lose?

Trevor pulled the van around to the back of the clubhouse kitchen, parking next to a produce truck that was delivering fresh organic vegetables. Opening the back door, he removed a dolly, then loaded four heavy boxes onto the hand truck. Wheeling it through the back door, he was apprehended by the club's head chef, a plump man with a lazy right eye.

"Restroom and cleaning supplies," Trevor stated as the chef blocked his path.

"I thought we just had a delivery last week," the chef replied with a puzzled look. Then he waved Trevor toward a set of swinging doors at the side of the kitchen.

"Restrooms are out the doors and to the left. The storage closet is right alongside," he said. "The general manager should be working the reservations desk. You can get him to sign for it."

Trevor nodded and proceeded out the kitchen and down a short hall, which ended at the men's and ladies' restrooms. He poked his head inside the windowless men's room, then stepped back out and waited until a club member in a gold polo shirt exited. He wheeled the dolly in and stacked the boxes onto the toilet seat in the last stall, then closed the door. He returned to the van and quietly wheeled in four more loads, stacking the additional boxes against the back wall. He opened one of the boxes and removed a portable space heater, which he plugged in beneath a sink but left turned off. He then slid one of the boxes across the floor to the center of the room. Using it as a step stool, he reached up with a wad of paper towels and unscrewed half of the overhead lightbulbs, casting the bathroom in a dim glow. Locating the room's single air-conditioning vent, he closed the levers, then sealed the vent with duct tape.

Satisfied with his initial work, he stepped into a stall and took off his hat and unzipped his workman's jumpsuit. Underneath, he was dressed in a silk shirt and dark slacks. Reaching into the opened box, he pulled out a blue blazer and dress shoes, which he quickly slipped on. Checking himself in a mirror, he figured he would easily pass muster as a member or guest. He had shaved his thin beard and cut his hair short, greasing it back with a temporary dye that gave it a raven sheen. He slipped on a pair of stylish-looking eyeglasses, then proceeded to the clubhouse bar.

The bar and adjacent restaurant were lightly crowded with businessmen and overdressed golfers taking a noontime lunch. Catching sight of Goyette in his corner booth, Trevor took a seat at the bar that offered an unimpeded view of the tycoon.

"What can I get you?" asked the bartender, an attractive woman with short black hair.

"A Molson, please. And I wonder if you can send one over to Mr. Goyette as well," he said, pointing to the corner.

"Certainly. Whom may I say it is from?" she asked.

"Just tell him the Royal Bank of Canada appreciates his business."

Trevor watched as the beer was delivered and was thankful when Goyette made no acknowledgment or even bothered looking toward the bar. Goyette was already on his second martini and downed the beer as his lunch was served. Trevor waited until Goyette and his girlfriend started their meal, then he returned to the restroom.

Trevor held the door open as an old man exited, grumbling about the poor lighting, then he placed a cardboard sign on the outside that read CLOSED FOR REPAIRS — PLEASE USE CLUBHOUSE RESTROOM. Returning inside, he placed a strip of yellow caution tape across the urinals, then slipped on a pair of gloves. With a utility knife in hand, he went from box to box, slicing open the seams and

627

dumping the contents upside down. Out of each box tumbled four eleven-pound blocks of commercial-grade dry ice, frozen carbon dioxide, that was wrapped in plastic. Flattening the cardboard boxes and stashing them in the end stall, he stacked the dry ice around the back of the bathroom, then methodically shredded open their plastic wrappings. Gaseous vapor began to rise immediately, but Trevor covered the blocks with the flattened boxes to limit their melting. Under the dim lighting, he was relieved to see that the vapor was barely noticeable.

Checking his watch, he hurriedly placed a small toolbox and his hat and jumpsuit near the door. With a penlight and screwdriver, he unscrewed the interior door handle until it hung just barely attached. Throwing the tools in the box, he carefully opened the door and returned to the bar.

Goyette was nearly done with his meal, but Trevor sat and casually ordered another beer, keeping a sharp eye on his intended victim. Guffawing loudly, Goyette was everything that Trevor expected the tycoon to be. Vulgar, selfish, and savagely arrogant, he was a walking psychiatric ward of deep-seated insecurities. Trevor looked at the man and fought the temptation to walk over and stick a butter knife in his ear.

Goyette finally pushed his lunch plate away from his belly and rose from the table. Trevor instantly left some bills for the barmaid and hurried down the hall. Pulling the CLOSED sign from the door, he ducked inside and slipped back into his jumpsuit, just barely affixing his hat when Goyette walked in. Eyeing Trevor in his workman's attire, the industrialist scowled.

"Why's it so dark in here?" he huffed. "And where's that steam coming from?" He pointed to a low cloud of vapor visible at the back of the restroom.

"Plumbing leak," Trevor replied. "Condensation is creating the vapor. I think the leak may have shorted out some of the lights as well."

"Well, get it fixed," Goyette barked.

"Yes, sir. Right away."

Trevor watched Goyette as he eyed the barricaded urinals then made his way to the first stall. As soon as the door clicked shut, Trevor stepped over and turned the portable heater on to HIGH. Then he stripped away the flattened cardboard boxes, exposing the stacked blocks of dry ice. He quickly spread a few of the blocks around the rapidly warming room, as the melting vapor began to quickly rise.

Moving to the doorway, Trevor opened his toolbox and retrieved his screwdriver and a triangular rubber doorstop with a string attached to the narrow end. Pulling the door open a few inches, he inserted the doorstop to hold it in place. He then finished unscrewing the interior door handle and tossed it into the toolbox.

Turning to face the interior, he could feel the temperature already rising from the space heater and, with it, the billowing clouds of carbon dioxide gas. He heard the sound of Goyette zipping his pants and called out.

"Mr. Goyette?"

"Yes?" came the reply in an annoyed voice. "What is it?"

"Steve Miller sends his regards."

Trevor stepped to the door and turned off the lights, then smashed the plastic flip lever to bits with the base of his toolbox. Slipping out the door, he knelt down and reversed the doorstop, placing it inside the restroom and sliding the string under the door. Letting the door close, he yanked the string from the outside, pulling the rubber wedge tight against the interior door.

As he placed the CLOSED sign back on the door, he could hear Goyette cursing inside. With a grin of accomplishment, Trevor picked up his toolbox and exited through the kitchen. Within minutes, he was off the club's grounds and headed toward a local rental-car company in neighboring Surrey.

With a sublimation temperature of minus one hundred and nine degrees Fahrenheit, dry ice converts directly to a gaseous state at room temperature. The six hundred pounds of dry ice in the restroom began vaporizing rapidly as the space heater warmed the confined space to over ninety degrees. Stumbling around blindly in the darkened room, Goyette could feel a cold dampness in his lungs with each breath he took. Feeling his way to the door with increasing dizziness, he fumbled for the light switch with his left hand while reaching for the door handle with his right. In a sudden moment of terrifying comprehension, he realized they were both absent. Trying without success to work the door open with his fingertips, he finally began pounding his fists against the thick wood while screaming for help. He began to cough as the air grew colder and heavier, and, with a fearful sense of panic, he realized something was dreadfully wrong.

It was several minutes before a busboy heard his cries and discovered that the door was jammed from the inside. It took another twenty minutes before a maintenance worker was summoned with some tools to take the door off its hinges. The assembled crowd was aghast when a white plume of vapor poured out of the restroom and Goyette's lifeless body was found lying in the doorway.

It was a week later when the Vancouver District Coroner's Office released its autopsy report, revealing that the billionaire had died of asphyxiation from exposure to acute levels of carbon dioxide.

"Used to call it 'chokedamp,'" the veteran

medical examiner told reporters at an assembled press briefing. "Haven't seen a case of it in years."

91

Nearly a hundred members of the media, more than half from the Canadian press, pushed and jostled on the Coast Guard pier in Anchorage as the *Otok* appeared in the harbor. The big icebreaker approached slowly, allowing the press an ample photo opportunity to capture her smashed bow and multiple paint jobs, before tying up behind a Coast Guard cutter named *Mustang*.

The White House and the Pentagon wasted no time in diffusing the hostility between Canada and the U.S., bypassing diplomatic channels by taking their case directly to the public. Press briefings had already been distributed, documenting the *Otok*'s role in destroying the Canadian ice camp under the guise of an American warship. Enlarged color photos of her hull, taken by the *Santa Fe,* revealed the gray undercoat and the *Ford*'s number 54 hidden beneath a coat of red paint. An eyewitness had even been produced, who testified about seeing a gray ship entering a

Goyette-owned dry dock near Kugluktuk in the dead of night, only to reappear a few days later painted red.

The press delighted in photographing the captain and crew of the icebreaker as they were marched off the ship under armed guard and placed in immediate custody until later extradition by the Royal Canadian Mounted Police. Word was quickly leaked of the crew's admission to destroying the ice camp, as well as their kidnapping of the *Polar Dawn*'s crew.

Captain Murdock and his crew then met with the reporters, who were stunned to learn of their abduction in Kugluktuk and their near-death ordeal in the barge. Roman and Stenseth took their turns at answering questions until the overwhelmed journalists and broadcasters began trickling off to file their stories. Within hours, a horde of investigative reporters began descending on Terra Green Industries to scrutinize Mitchell Goyette's corrupt activities in the Arctic.

The press was long gone when Pitt hobbled off the ship with a crutch under one arm. Giordino walked by his side, hefting two small duffel bags and the logbook from the *Erebus*. As they reached the end of the dock, a slate-colored Lincoln Navigator with black-tinted windows pulled up in front of them. The driver's window lowered just a crack, revealing a thickheaded man in a crew cut who gazed at them with unblinking eyes.

"The Vice President requests that you climb in back," the driver said without pleasantry.

Pitt and Giordino gave each other a look of trepidation, then Pitt opened the rear door and threw in his crutch, then climbed inside as Giordino entered from the opposite door. Sandecker eyed them from the front passenger seat, a thick cigar protruding from his lips.

"Admiral, this is a nice surprise," Giordino said with his usual sarcasm. "But we could have taken a cab to the airport."

"I was about to say that I'm glad to see you jokers alive, but I may have to rethink that," Sandecker replied.

"It's good to see you, Admiral," Pitt said. "We weren't expecting to find you here."

"I promised both Loren and the President that I'd get you two home in one piece."

He nodded to the driver, who exited the Coast Guard station and began driving across the city to the Anchorage International Airport.

"You promised the President?" Giordino asked.

"Yes. I caught hell when he found out that the *Narwhal,* with NUMA's Director aboard, was smack in the middle of the Northwest Passage."

"By the way, thanks for sending in the *Santa Fe* when you did," Pitt said. "They're the ones who saved our bacon."

"We were fortunate that they happened to

be in the northern Arctic and could reach the area quickly. But the President is well aware that the *Polar Dawn*'s crew would have been lost if you hadn't sailed into harm's way."

"Stenseth and Dahlgren are to thank for saving the *Polar Dawn*'s crew," Pitt replied.

"More important, you pegged the ruse of the icebreaker. I can't tell you how close we were to a hot fight with the Canadians. The President rightly credits you with averting a major crisis."

"Then the least he can do is fund us a replacement vessel for the *Narwhal*," Giordino said.

The Lincoln motored down the rain-slicked streets, turning past Delaney Park, a wide strip of grass and trees that had been the city's original airfield. Anchorage International Airport had been built later on a flat to the southwest of downtown.

"How did the press briefings go?" Pitt asked.

"Just as we hoped. The Canadian press is all over the story. They're already fighting to get to Ottawa to grill the Prime Minister over his mistaken claims about the Arctic incidents. He and his party will have no choice but to face the music and retract their earlier blame against us."

"I certainly hope this all catches up to Mitchell Goyette in a big way," Giordino said.

"I'm afraid it's too late for him," Sandecker replied.

"Too late?" Giordino asked.

"Goyette was found dead in Vancouver yesterday. He apparently died under mysterious circumstances."

"Justice served," Pitt said quietly.

"The CIA acted that fast?" Giordino asked.

Sandecker gave him a withering stare. "We had nothing to do with it."

The Vice President turned back to Pitt with an anxious look. "Did you find the ruthenium?"

Pitt shook his head. "Al's got the *Erebus* logbook right here. The Franklin ruthenium was real, but it was obtained in trade with a whaler from South Africa. There is no ruthenium source in the Arctic, and the South African mines played out years ago. I'm afraid we came up empty."

There was a long silence in the car.

"Well, we will just have to find another way," Sandecker finally said quietly. "At least you found Franklin," he added, "and put to bed a one-hundred-and-sixty-five-year-old mystery."

"I just hope he finally makes it home himself," Pitt said solemnly, staring at the distant peaks of the Chugach Mountains as the Lincoln pulled alongside Air Force Two.

92

Mitchell Goyette's death did little to quell
the media tempest swirling about his empire.
A number of environmental reporters had
already uncovered the carbon dioxide dumping associated with the Kitimat sequestration
plant and the near accident with the Alaskan
cruise ship. Investigators from Canada's Environment Ministry had swarmed the facility, closing it down and removing its workers
as criminal and civil charges against Terra
Green were prepared. Though it took several
weeks, the LNG tanker responsible for the carbon dioxide dumping was ultimately tracked
down to a Singapore shipyard. Local authorities promptly impounded the Goyette-owned
ship.

The mogul's illicit activities became repeated headline news across both Canada
and the U.S. It wasn't long before the police
investigation into Goyette's years of corrupt
bidding for oil, gas, and mineral rights came
to light. With an immunity deal in place for

Resources Minister Jameson, incriminating details began toppling forward like a string of dominoes. A series of high-dollar wire transfers made to the Prime Minister was exposed, bribes paid by Goyette to further the expansion of carbon sequestration plants across Canada. The money trail led to dozens of other underhanded deals between Goyette and Prime Minister Barrett to jointly exploit the country's natural resources.

Opposition leaders quickly jumped on the news accounts and investigations, inciting a full-blown witch hunt against the Prime Minister. Already beleaguered by his false accusations in the Arctic incidents, the criminal allegations fell like a ton of bricks. Abandoned of all support, Prime Minister Barrett resigned from office a few weeks later, along with most of his cabinet. Publicly despised, the ex–Prime Minister would fight criminal charges for years until finally agreeing to a nonsentencing plea bargain. His reputation shattered, Barrett quietly faded into obscurity.

Goyette's Terra Green Industries would face a similar demise. Investigators pieced together his strategy of dominating the Arctic resources by expelling the American presence, monopolizing the local transportation, and bribing his way to controlling rights. Beset by corruption fines and environmental penalties that rose into the hundreds of millions, the private company quietly fell into receivership. Some of the company's assets, including the LNG tanker, the Victoria Club, and Goyette's personal yacht, were sold at public auction. Most of the energy assets and the fleet of vessels were acquired by the government, which operated the properties at cost. One icebreaker and a fleet of barges were leased to a nonprofit food bank for a dollar a year. Relocated to Hudson Bay, the barges hauled surplus Manitoba wheat to starving regions of East Africa.

Among the Terra Green fleet holdings, analysts discovered a small containership called the *Alberta*. An astute team of Mountie investigators proved that it was the same vessel that had rammed the Coast Guard patrol boat *Harp* in Lancaster Strait, with a few letters in its name repainted to read *Atlanta*. Like the crew of the *Otok,* the men who served aboard the *Alberta* readily testified at the mercy of the court that they were acting on direct orders from Mitchell Goyette.

As moderate forces of influence regained power in the Canadian government, relations with the U.S. warmed quickly. The *Polar Dawn* was quietly returned to the Americans, along with a small remuneration for its crew. The ban on U.S.-flagged vessels sailing the Northwest Passage was lifted and a strategic security agreement signed a short time later. For purposes of a shared mutual defense, the agreement stated, Canada pledged that American military vessels would forever be granted unrestricted transit through the passage. More important to the President, the Canadian government opened up access to the Melville Sound gas field. Within months, major quantities of natural gas were flowing unabated to the United States, quickly suppressing the economic disruption caused by the spike in oil prices.

Behind the scenes, the FBI and Royal Canadian Mounted Police jointly reopened their files on Clay Zak. The bombings at the George Washington University lab and the zinc-mining camp in the Arctic were easily pinned on him, but his other crimes were not so traceable. Although suspicions were raised, he was never fully linked to Elizabeth Finlay's death in Victoria. He was, however, suspected in a dozen more unsolved deaths involving known opponents of Mitchell Goyette. Even though he was buried in a pauper's grave at the North Vancouver Cemetery, his murderous activities would keep investigators busy for years to come.

The only Goyette associate to successfully navigate the flood of judicial and media probes was the natural resources minister, Arthur Jameson. Despite his deep involvement in the corruption, Jameson survived the ordeal with an odd mark of public admiration. Contempt for Goyette was so great, even in death, that

Jameson's crimes were overlooked by his act of turning evidence and blowing open the entire case.

Resigning his minister's post, Jameson was offered a provost position at a respected private college in Ontario, where he was called upon to teach a popular course in ethics. His stature grew as his past misdeeds were eventually forgotten, and Jameson soon embraced the scholarly life and a modestly downsized lifestyle. Only his four children were starkly reminded of his past activities, when, upon reaching the age of thirty-five, they each inherited a Cayman Islands trust account worth ten million dollars.

As for Goyette himself, he gained little sympathy in death. His bribery, vice, and greed, as well as his total disregard for the environmental impact of his pursuits, created a universal spite. The attitude pervaded even the Royal Canadian Mounted Police, who assigned only a cursory investigation into his death. Officials knew his murderer would be lionized and downplayed the circumstances of his death as potentially accidental. Public interest in the crime quickly waned, while internally the police cited few clues and an endless enemies list that precluded a solution to the crime. With little fanfare, the death of Mitchell Goyette quickly became a cold case that nobody cared to solve.

93

An elite Royal Navy color guard unit carried the dark-wood casket down the steps of the neoclassic Anglican chapel and carefully placed it onto an ornate nineteenth-century gun carriage. The eulogy had been long, as was the norm for a royal ceremonial funeral, with obligatory remarks recited by the Prime Minister and the Prince of Wales, among other notables. The sentiments were blustery and patriotic but not very personal, for no one still living had even known the deceased.

The funeral of Sir John Alexander Franklin was a grand and noble affair and, at the same time, an uplifting event. The discovery of Franklin's body aboard the *Erebus* had aroused a nostalgic romance amongst the British people, rekindling the days of glory when Wellington commanded the ground and Nelson ruled the seas. Franklin's exploits in the Arctic, a largely forgotten historical footnote to modern generations, was regaled in detail to a suddenly enthralled public that clamored for more.

The public fascination had placed great pressure on the team of archaeologists and forensic specialists tasked with examining the ship and retrieving his body. Working round the clock, they solved two key mysteries, even before Franklin's body arrived in London and was placed on view in Westminster Abbey.

Though a variety of ails contributed to his death at age sixty-one, the scientists determined that a case of tuberculosis, easily contracted within the tight confines of a winter-bound ship, most likely finished him off. More intriguing was the revelation as to why a large portion of the *Erebus*'s crew had turned mad. Based on the account in the ship's log, which Pitt had sent to British authorities, the scientists tested a sample of ruthenium found in an officer's cabin. Assay testing revealed that the South African ore contained high quantities of mercury. When heated on the cookstove in buckets and bedpans, the ore released toxic fumes that accumulated in the galley and crew's quarters. As with the mad hatters of later years, mercury poisoning created neurological damage and psychotic reactions after months of exposure.

The tragic myriad events just added to the allure of the story, and the public flocked to pay their respects to Franklin. The gates of Kensal Green, an ancient, sprawling cemetery west of London akin to Forest Lawn, had to be closed on the day of his funeral after thirty thousand people congregated on its storied grounds.

It was a hot and humid summer day, far removed from the Arctic conditions in which he had died. The horse-drawn caisson pulled slowly away from the chapel, rattling over a cobblestone path, as the steel-shod hooves of the black shire mares clacked loudly with each dropped step. With a long procession following behind on foot, the caisson rolled slowly toward a secluded section of the cemetery crowned by towering chestnut trees. The driver pulled to a stop next to a family plot fronted by an open gate. A freshly dug grave lay empty alongside a tomb marked LADY JANE FRANKLIN, 1792–1875.

Franklin's beloved wife, more than anyone, had resolved the fate of the lost expedition. Through tireless appeal and expense, she had personally outfitted no fewer than five relief expeditions on her own. Scouring the Arctic in search of her husband and his ships, the early expeditions had failed, along with those sent by the British government. It was another Arctic explorer, Francis McClintock, who had ultimately discovered Franklin's fate. Sailing the steam yacht *Fox* on Lady Franklin's behalf, he'd found important relics and a note on King William Island that revealed Franklin's death in 1847 and the crew's subsequent abandonment of the ships trapped in the ice.

It had taken one hundred and sixty-eight years since kissing her good-bye on the shores of the Thames, but John Franklin was reunited with his wife once more.

His soul would have been happy for another reason, as he was laid to rest beside Jane. When a Royal Navy frigate had retrieved his coffin from the *Erebus* and transported it back to England, the ship had traveled the long route, through the Bering Strait and down the Pacific to the Panama Canal.

In death, if not in life, Sir Franklin had finally sailed the Northwest Passage.

94

Pitt stared out his office window at the Potomac River far below, his mind drifting aimlessly like the river's current.

Since returning from the Arctic, he had been out of sorts, carrying a mild angst mixed with disappointment. Part of it was his injuries, he knew. His leg and arm wounds were healing well, and the doctors said he would make a full recovery. Though the pain was mostly absent, he still hated the loss of mobility. He had long since abandoned the crutch but still required the use of a cane at times. Giordino had lightened the need by providing a walking stick that contained a hidden vial of tequila inside. Loren had stepped up as well, performing her best Florence Nightingale routine by nursing him at every opportunity. But something still held him back.

It was the failure, he knew. He just wasn't used to it. The quest for the ruthenium had momentous importance, yet he had come up dry. He felt like he had let down not only Lisa

Lane but also every person on the planet. It wasn't his fault, of course. He'd followed the clues as he found them, and would have done nothing differently. Crack geologists throughout the government were already on the hunt for new sources of ruthenium, but the near-term prospects were grim. The mineral just didn't exist in quantity, and there was nothing he could do about it.

His instincts had been wrong for a change and it gave him doubts. Maybe he'd been at the game too long. Maybe it was time for a younger generation to take the reins. Perhaps he should go back to Hawaii with Loren and spend his days spearfishing.

He tried to conceal his melancholy when a knock came to the door and he called for the visitor to enter.

The door blew open and Giordino, Gunn, and Dahlgren came marching into his office like they owned it. Each man had a suppressed grin on his face, and Pitt noticed they were all hiding something behind their backs.

"Well, if it isn't the three wise men. Or wise guys, in this case," Pitt said.

"Do you have a minute?" Gunn asked. "There's something we'd like to share with you."

"My time is yours," Pitt said, hobbling over to his desk and taking a seat. Eyeing the men suspiciously, he asked, "What is it that you are all trying to conceal?"

Dahlgren waved a short stack of plastic cups that he was carrying.

"Just thought we'd have a little drink," he explained.

Giordino pulled out a bottle of champagne that he was hiding behind his stubby arms.

"I'm a bit thirsty myself," he added.

"Hasn't anyone told you about the rules regarding alcohol in a federal building?" Pitt admonished.

"I seem to have misplaced those," Giordino replied. "Jack, do you know anything about that?"

Dahlgren attempted to look dumb and shook his head.

"All right, what is this all about?" Pitt asked, losing patience with the antics.

"It's really Jack's doing," Gunn said. "He sort of saved the day."

"You mean, he saved your rear," Giordino said, grinning at Gunn. He slipped the foil off the neck of the champagne bottle and popped the top. Grabbing Dahlgren's cups, he poured everyone a glass.

"It came down to the rock," Gunn tried to explain.

"The rock . . ." Pitt repeated with growing suspicion.

"One of the samples from the thermal vent that we located off Alaska," Giordino interjected, "just before the Canadian ice camp business. We put all of the rock samples in a bag that Rudi was supposed to bring here to headquarters for analysis. But he left the bag on the *Narwhal* when he departed Tuktoyaktuk."

"I remember that bag," Pitt replied. "Almost tripped over it every time I stepped onto the bridge."

"You and me both," Dahlgren muttered.

"Wasn't it still on the bridge?" Pitt asked.

"Was and is," Giordino said. "It's still sitting with the *Narwhal* at the bottom of Victoria Strait."

"That still doesn't explain the champagne."

"Well, it seems our good buddy Jack found a rock in his pocket when he got home," Gunn said.

"I'm really not a klepto, I swear," Dahlgren said with a grin. "I tripped over that bag, too, and happened to pick up one of the loose rocks and stick it in my pocket. Forgot all about it until I was changing clothes on the *Santa Fe* and thought I better hang on to it."

"A very wise decision," Gunn agreed.

"I took it down to the geology lab last week to have it assayed and they called this morning with the results."

Gunn produced the rock sample and slid it across the desk to Pitt. He picked it up and studied it, noting its heavy weight and dull silver color. His heart began to race as he recalled the similar characteristics of the ore

650

sample the old geologist at the Miners Co-op had given him.

"It doesn't look like gold to me," he said to the trio, eyeing their reaction.

The three men looked at one another and grinned. Giordino finally spoke.

"Would you consider ruthenium?"

Pitt's eyes twinkled as he immediately sat up in his chair. He studied the rock carefully, then looked at Gunn.

"Is it true?" he asked quietly.

Gunn nodded. "High-grade, no less."

"How do we know if it is there in any quantity?"

"We pulled the sensor records from the *Bloodhound* and took a second look. Though she is not configured to sense ruthenium, she can identify its platinum-based grouping. And according to the *Bloodhound,* the thermal vent has more platinum and platinum derivatives lying around than Fort Knox has gold. It's a sure bet that a significant quantity of that platinum-based ore around the vent is ruthenium."

Pitt couldn't believe the news. He felt like he'd been injected with a shot of adrenaline. His whole demeanor perked up, and a glisten returned to his intelligent green eyes.

"Congratulations, boss," Gunn said. "You've got your very own ruthenium mine a thousand feet under the sea."

Pitt smiled at the men, then grabbed one of

the champagnes.

"I think I will drink to that," he said, hoisting his cup up and toasting the others.

After they each took a sip, Dahlgren looked at his glass and nodded.

"You know," he said in his slow Texas drawl, "this stuff is almost as good as Lone Star."

95

TEN MONTHS LATER

It was a rare cloudless spring day in Kitimat, the kind that turned the waters cerulean blue and made the crisp air taste of pure oxygen. On the grounds of the former Terra Green sequestration plant, a small group of dignitaries and media reporters was gathered for a ribbon-cutting ceremony. A cherub-faced man in a beige suit, Canada's newly appointed minister of natural resources, bounded up to a podium placed before the seated crowd.

"Ladies and gentlemen, it is my distinct pleasure to officially declare open the Kitimat Photosynthesis Station, the first of its kind in the world. As you know, the Natural Resources Ministry inherited this facility last year, built as a carbon sequestration site, under less-than-ideal circumstances. But I am delighted to report that the facility has been successfully reengineered as the very first artificial-photosynthesis conversion plant in existence. The Kitimat Photosynthesis Station will safely and efficiently convert carbon dioxide to water and hydrogen without any risk to the environment. We are excited that the plant can use the existing pipeline to Athabasca to convert nearly ten percent of the carbon dioxide generated from the oil sands refineries. Here today we have the prototype for a new weapon against atmospheric pollutants, and ultimately global warming."

The assembled crowd, including many Kitimat residents, applauded loudly. The resources minister smiled broadly before continuing.

"Like any historic venture, this facility conversion was accomplished by the work of a great many people. It has also been one of the more fruitful collaborative efforts that I have ever witnessed. The joint venture between the Natural Resources Ministry, the United States Department of Energy, and George Washington University stands as a testament to the great things that can be accomplished in the pursuit of the common good. I would like to especially recognize the achievements of Miss Lisa Lane, for whom credit can be given for the genesis of this facility."

Seated in the first row, Lisa waved to the crowd while blushing deeply.

"I see momentous changes for all of mankind here today, and I look forward to the dawn of a new world from our humble beginnings here in Kitimat. Thank you."

The crowd applauded again, then sat through the orations of several more politicians before a large ceremonial ribbon was cut for the cameras. As the speeches ended, the resources minister stepped over to the front row where Pitt and Loren were seated next to Lisa.

"Miss Lane, it is good to see you again," he greeted warmly. "This must be a very exciting day for you."

"It certainly is. I would not have imagined that a working artificial-photosynthesis facility would come on line so rapidly," she said.

"Your President and our new Prime Minister showed great will in moving things forward."

"Minister, I would like you to meet my dear friend Congresswoman Loren Smith, and her husband, Dirk Pitt."

"A pleasure to meet you both. Mr. Pitt, it was you who recommended converting the sequestration plant, was it not?"

"It was my kids' idea, actually," he said, pointing to Dirk and Summer, who were making their way to the bar. "We all figured that a positive light might be shone on one of Mitchell Goyette's past sins."

The minister shuddered at the mention of Goyette's name but soon smiled again. "Your discovery has proved a blessing on many fronts, Miss Lane," he said to Lisa. "We'll be able to expand our oil sands operations in Athabasca now, as additional photosynthesis facilities are brought online to capture the greenhouse gas emissions. That will go a long way in abating oil shortages in both our countries. I am pushing the Prime Minister to authorize funding for twenty more plants. How are things progressing in the States?"

"Thanks to the efforts of Loren and the Vice President, thirty plants have been funded, with plans for an additional fifty facilities to be built over the next three years. We are starting with our coal-fired power plants, which emit the most pollution. There is excitement that we will finally be able to safely burn coal, fueling our utilities for decades to come."

"Perhaps as important, we have a signed agreement with the Chinese as well," Loren said. "They have promised to build seventy-five plants over the next eight years."

"My, that is good news, since the Chinese are now the largest emitters of greenhouse gases. It's a fortunate thing that the technology is easily replicated," the minister said.

"And that we have an abundant supply of the catalyst to make the process work," Lisa added. "If Mr. Pitt's NUMA organization hadn't made the discovery of ruthenium off the coast of Alaska, none of this would be possible."

"A lucky break," Pitt acknowledged. "Our undersea mining operation is now up and running, and the yield is very encouraging so far. We hope to mine enough of the mineral to supply thousands of plants like this around the world."

"Then we can look forward to a possible end to global warming in our lifetime. A remarkable accomplishment," the minister said, before being pulled aside by an aide.

"It looks like your days of scientific anonymity are over," Loren quipped to Lisa.

"It is all exciting, but the truth is I'd rather be back in the lab. There are plenty of refinements that can be made, and we still haven't perfected the efficient conversion to hydrogen yet. Thankfully, I've got a new and even better lab at the university. Now I just need to find a new lab assistant."

"Bob has been officially charged?" Loren asked.

"Yes. He had over two hundred thousand dollars in various places that were traced back to Goyette. I can't believe that my own friend sold me out."

"As Goyette proved, unmitigated greed will catch up to you in the end."

A horde of reporters suddenly appeared, surrounding Lisa and barraging her with questions about the facility and her scientific discovery. Pitt and Loren slipped off to the side, then strolled across the grounds. Pitt had recovered fully from his injuries and enjoyed stretching his legs outdoors.

"It's so beautiful here," Loren remarked. "We should stay a few extra days."

"You forget your congressional panel hearings next week. Besides, I need to get back to Washington and ride roughshod over Al and Jack. We have a new submersible to test in the Mediterranean next month that we need to prepare for."

"Already on to the next project, I see."

Pitt simply nodded, a twinkle in his green eyes. "As somebody once said, it's in my blood."

They walked past the facility until reaching the shoreline.

"You know, there is a potential downside to this technology," she noted. "If global warming can one day be reversed, the Northwest Passage is liable to permanently freeze over again."

Pitt stared out at the nearby channel.

"I think Franklin would agree with me; that's as it should be."

Across the compound, a white boat motored up to the channel front dock and tied up behind a rented press boat. Trevor Miller stepped onto the pier and studied the large crowd spread across the grounds before spotting a tall woman with flowing red hair. Snatching a beer along the way, he walked up to Dirk and Summer, who stood laughing near the former security hut.

"Mind if I steal your sister?" he said to Dirk.

Summer turned to him with a look of relief, then quickly kissed him.

"You're late," she said.

"I had to put gas in my new boat," he tried to explain.

Dirk looked at him with a grin. "Go ahead and take my sister. Keep her for as long as you like."

Trevor walked Summer back to the boat and released the dock line. Gunning the throttle, he shot off the dock and was soon racing down Douglas Channel. He ran the boat all the way to Hecate Strait before cutting the motor and letting the boat drift as the sky overhead began to darken. Slipping an arm around Summer, he moved to the stern with her at his side and looked out toward Gil Island. They stood together, staring across the calm waters for a long while.

"The best and worst things in my life seem to happen out here," he finally whispered in her ear.

She slipped an arm around his waist and held him tight as they watched the crimson sun sink slowly beneath the horizon.

ABOUT THE AUTHORS

Clive Cussler grew up in Alhambra, California. He attended Pasadena City College for two years, then enlisted in the Air Force during the Korean War and served as an aircraft mechanic and flight engineer in the Military Air Transport Service. Upon discharge he became a copywriter and later creative director at two of the nation's leading ad agencies. He wrote and produced radio and television commercials in Hollywood that won numerous international honors including an award at the prestigious Cannes Film Festival.

Cussler began writing novels in 1965 and published his first work featuring his continuous series hero, Dirk Pitt, in 1973. His first non-fiction, *The Sea Hunters,* was released in 1996. The Board of Governors of the Maritime College, State University of New York, considered *The Sea Hunters* in lieu of a Ph.D. thesis and awarded Cussler a Doctor of Letters degree in May, 1997. It was the first time since the College was founded in 1874 that such a degree was bestowed.

Cussler is an internationally recognized authority on shipwrecks and the founder of the National Underwater and Marine Agency, (NUMA) a 501C3 non-profit organization (named after the fictional Federal agency in his novels) that dedicates itself to preserving American maritime and naval history. He and his crew of marine experts and NUMA volunteers have discovered more than 60 historically significant underwater wreck sites including the first submarine to sink a ship in battle, the Confederacy's **Hunley**, and its victim, the Union's **Housatonic**.

Cussler has been married to his wife, Barbara Knight, for more than 44 years. They have three children, two grandchildren, and divide their time between the mountains of Colorado and the deserts of Arizona.

Dirk Cussler, has an MBA from Berkeley, worked many years in the financial arena and has been an active participant in the real-life NUMA® expeditions, and served as president of the NUMA® advisory board of trustees. He lives in Arizona.

We hope you have enjoyed this Large Print book. Other Thorndike, Wheeler, and Chivers Press Large Print books are available at your library or directly from the publishers.

For information about current and upcoming titles, please call or write, without obligaton, to:

Publisher
Thorndike Press
295 Kennedy Memorial Drive
Waterville, ME 04901
Tel. (800) 223-1244

or visit our Web site at:

http://gale.cengage.com/thorndike

OR

Chivers Large Print
published by BBC Audiobooks Ltd
St. James House, The Square
Lower Bristol Road
Bath BA2 3SB
England
Tel. +44(0) 800 136919
email: bbcaudiobooksbbc.co.uk
www.bbcaudiobooks.co.uk

All our Large Print titles are designed for easy reading, and all our books are made to last.